TALES OF HEROES, GODS & MONSTERS

JAPANESE

MYTHS & LEGENDS

FLAME TREE PUBLISHING
6 Melbray Mews, Fulham,
London SW6 3NS, United Kingdom
www.flametreepublishing.com

First published and copyright © 2022
Flame Tree Publishing Ltd

22 24 26 25 23
1 3 5 7 9 10 8 6 4 2

ISBN: 978-1-83964-889-2

Cover and pattern art was created by Flame Tree Studio, with elements courtesy of
Shutterstock.com/insima

Judith John (Glossary) is a writer and editor specializing in literature and history. A former
secondary school English Language and Literature teacher, she has subsequently worked
as an editor on major educational projects, including *English A: Literature* for the Pearson
International Baccalaureate series. Judith's major research interests include Romantic and
Gothic literature, and Renaissance drama.

Other contributors, authors, editors and sources for this series include:
Loren Auerbach, Norman Bancroft-Hunt, George W. Bateman, James S. de Benneville,
E.M. Berens, Katharine Berry Judson, W.H.I. Bleek and L. C. Lloyd, Laura Bulbeck, Jeremiah
Curtin, F. Hadland Davis, Elphinstone Dayrell, O.B. Duane, Dr Ray Dunning, W.W.
Gibbings, William Elliot Griffis, H. A. Guerber, Lafcadio Hearn, Stephen Hodge, James A.
Honey M.D., Jake Jackson, Joseph Jacobs, Judith John, J.W. Mackail, Donald Mackenzie,
Chris McNab, Minnie Martin, A.B. Mitford (Lord Redesdale), Yei Theodora Ozaki, Professor
James Riordan, Sara Robson, Lewis Spence, Henry M. Stanley, Capt. C.H. Stigand, Rachel
Storm, K.E. Sullivan, François-Marie Arouet a.k.a. Voltaire, E.A. Wallis Budge, Dr Roy
Willis, Epiphanius Wilson, Alice Werner, E.T.C. Werner.

A copy of the CIP data for this book is available
from the British Library.

Designed and created in the UK | Printed and bound in China

COLLECTOR'S EDITIONS

TALES OF HEROES, GODS & MONSTERS

JAPANESE

MYTHS & LEGENDS

Reading List & Glossary of Terms
with a New Introduction by
JUN'ICHI ISOMAE & HIROSHI ARAKI

FLAME TREE PUBLISHING

CONTENTS

CONTENTS

5

CONTENTS

CONTENTS

TALES OF HEROES, GODS & MONSTERS

JAPANESE MYTHS & LEGENDS

SERIES FOREWORD

Stretching back to the oral traditions of thousands of years ago, tales of heroes and disaster, creation and conquest have been told by many different civilizations in many different ways. Their impact sits deep within our culture even though the detail in the tales themselves are a loose mix of historical record, transformed narrative and the distortions of hundreds of storytellers.

Today the language of mythology lives with us: our mood is jovial, our countenance is saturnine, we are narcissistic and our modern life is hermetically sealed from others. The nuances of myths and legends form part of our daily routines and help us navigate the world around us, with its half truths and biased reported facts.

The nature of a myth is that its story is already known by most of those who hear it, or read it. Every generation brings a new emphasis, but the fundamentals remain the same: a desire to understand and describe the events and relationships of the world. Many of the great stories are archetypes that help us find our own place, equipping us with tools for self-understanding, both individually and as part of a broader culture.

For Western societies it is Greek mythology that speaks to us most clearly. It greatly influenced the mythological heritage of the ancient Roman civilization and is the lens through which we still see the Celts, the Norse and many of the other great peoples and religions. The Greeks themselves learned much from their neighbours, the Egyptians, an older culture that became weak with age and incestuous leadership.

It is important to understand that what we perceive now as mythology had its own origins in perceptions of the divine and the rituals of the sacred. The earliest civilizations, in the crucible of the Middle East, in the Sumer of the third millennium BC, are the source to which many of the mythic archetypes can be traced. As humankind collected together in cities for the first time, developed writing and industrial scale agriculture, started to irrigate the rivers and attempted to control rather than be at the mercy of its environment, humanity began to write down its tentative explanations of natural events, of floods and plagues, of disease.

Early stories tell of Gods (or god-like animals in the case of tribal societies such as African, Native American or Aboriginal cultures) who are crafty and use their wits to survive, and it is reasonable to suggest that these were the first rulers of the gathering peoples of the earth, later elevated to god-like status with the distance of time. Such tales became more political as cities vied with each other for supremacy, creating new Gods, new hierarchies for their pantheons. The older Gods took on primordial roles and became the preserve of creation and destruction, leaving the new gods to deal with more current, everyday affairs. Empires rose and fell, with Babylon assuming the mantle from Sumeria in the 1800s BC, then in turn to be swept away by the Assyrians of the 1200s BC; then the Assyrians and the Egyptians were subjugated by the Greeks, the Greeks by the Romans and so on, leading to the spread and assimilation of common themes, ideas and stories throughout the world.

The survival of history is dependent on the telling of good tales, but each one must have the 'feeling' of truth, otherwise it will be ignored. Around the firesides, or embedded in a book or a computer, the myths and legends of the past are still the living materials of retold myth, not restricted to an exploration of origins. Now we have devices and global communications that give us unparalleled access to a diversity of traditions. We can find out about Native American, Indian, Chinese and tribal African mythology in a way that was denied to our ancestors, we can find connections, match the archaeology, religion and the mythologies of the world to build a comprehensive image of the human experience that is endlessly fascinating.

The stories in this book provide an introduction to the themes and concerns of the myths and legends of their respective cultures, with a short introduction to provide a linguistic, geographic and political context. This is where the myths have arrived today, but undoubtedly over the next millennia, they will transform again whilst retaining their essential truths and signs.

Jake Jackson
General Editor

TALES OF HEROES, GODS & MONSTERS

JAPANESE

MYTHS & LEGENDS

INTRODUCTION
& FURTHER READING

INTRODUCTION TO JAPANESE MYTHOLOGY

WHAT IS MYTHOLOGY?

A 'myth' can be defined as a story of the gods. But myths rarely include the gods of what we generally call 'religion', for instance, Christianity, Islam or Buddhism. Rather, myths are divine stories that are rooted in primitive societies among the primeval people who lived before institutionalized religions were formed.

Just as the concept of 'religion' is founded on the principles of Christianity, likewise the concept of 'myth' originated from the archetypes of ancient Greek and Roman legends. In post-Christian societies, myths are juxtaposed against institutionalized religions as non-systematic legends held in the popular primordial psyche, hence labelled as folklore or folk beliefs.

WHAT IS JAPANESE MYTHOLOGY?

Naturally then, the next question would be what is the 'Japanese myth'? First, the idea of Japan in the ancient period must not be confused with the modern notion of the nation-state as we know it today. Japan in ancient times was simply a concept believed by the people living in the region that was known as Japan. The sense of common brotherhood, and viewing the society and culture through the prism of Japan, was not yet apparent in the premodern era. Therefore, Japanese myths are divine stories highly characterized by loose regional flavours, something that cannot be subsumed easily by the institutionalized religious concept of gods.

One of the most famous examples is collectively known today as the *Kiki*, or 'Chronicles', myths, including the *Kojiki*, or 'Record of Ancient Matters', and the *Nihon Shoki*, or 'Chronicles of Japan'. The Chronicles myths are believed to have originated during the Yamato Kingship – the unified kingdom of western Japan covering present-day Nara and Kyoto prefectures – in the sixth century. The Chronicles start with the myths of Izanagi and Izanami, and covers the divine creation of the Japanese nation by giving birth to Amaterasu and her descendant Jimmu. The first volume of the *Kojiki* (AD 712), which is the oldest historical text in Japan, and the first two volumes of the *Nihon Shoki* (AD 720), depict the age of the gods that thoroughly covers these divine myths. Then volume two of *Kojiki* and book three of *Nihon Shoki* include the history of Japan, describing the foundation of the Japanese nation by Jimmu and his descendants.

DIVERSITY OF JAPANESE MYTHS

It is believed that different kinds of myths existed in various parts of Japan in the ancient period. Some of them can be found in Fudoki, or the local gazetteers, of which the *Harima*

Fudoki is perhaps the most famous. These gazetteers are still extant, albeit in fragments, and record the origins of their respective regions based on the history specific to each region. Incidentally, most of the myths that can be found today were chronicled by the intelligentsia class using Chinese characters. Moreover, all the myths up to the medieval period can be found only in written forms. But from the writing styles, we can safely conclude that the texts handed down to us in written forms are only a fraction of the ancient myths. The share of unrecorded oral histories is believed to far outweigh the extant written accounts.

Sokichi Tsuda, a historian of Eastern thoughts, aptly pointed out in his *New Research on the Kojiki and Nihon Shoki* (1919) that some homogeneous spiritual entities like 'Japanese society' or 'Japanese culture', which could form the archetypes of the Japanese nation, never existed in Japan. Precisely for this reason, the editors of this book use as the title the plural form of the phrase 'Japanese Myths' instead of 'Japanese Myth'. The myths of Japan are a composite body that proliferated and dwindled over time, including not only the Yamato Kingship myths, but also the myths associated with the regional kingships, as well as the folklore and folk beliefs of ordinary people living in the countryside.

HISTORY OF MYTHOLOGICAL INTERPRETATIONS

One of the characteristic features of the Chronicles is the multiple variations of the recorded tales. There are several variations and discrepancies in appellations and legends in the descriptions of the *Kojiki* and the *Nihon Shoki*. Even within the *Nihon Shoki*, there are references like 'according to one source', which clearly suggests the plural nature of the legends. During the Heian period (AD 794–1185), in the aftermath of the removal of the capital to Heian-kyo (present-day Kyoto), lectures were instituted to form a shared understanding of the contents of the *Nihon Shoki*, followed by the production of several commentaries of the work, which made possible a variety of new interpretations. Indeed, authenticity during the medieval period was sought not from the original text but from new interpretations of the *Nihon Shoki*. At times, its accounts were falsified, and even nonexistent accounts were manufactured. They are collectively known today as *Nihongi-den*: the works that referred to the *Nihon Shoki*. Sometimes, certain legends became very authoritative and popular, which contributed to the proliferation of the mythological sphere. Today these myths are broadly known as the *Chūsei Nihongi*, or 'medieval Japanese chronicles'. Among these newly developed medieval interpretations is the iconographic representation of Amaterasu-Ōmikami, who is originally presented as a female deity in the *Nihon Shoki*, as a male figure.

ENGI SHIKI AND THE IMPERIAL FESTIVALS

In fact, we can find many more gods, in addition to those mentioned in the Chronicles, who were worshipped during the Yamato court's rituals in ancient Japan. For instance, the Jingi-shiki (Shinto regulations) section of the *Engi shiki*, or 'Procedures of the Engi Era', which was completed and came into force during the tenth century, mentions the rites of the four seasons, special rites, the Ise Grand Shrine and so forth. *Engi shiki* also provides a list of the *kampeisha*, or the ranked Shinto shrines, from all over the country, effectively establishing the basic categories of the Japanese gods. Among the festivals, the three imperial festivals were particularly important: the Kamo Festival (also known as Aoi Festival), which took place at the Kamigamo Shrine; the Iwashimizu Festival (also known as Hoseikai) at the Iwashimizu Hachimangu Shrine; and the Kasuga Festival at the Kasuga Taisha Shrine in Nara.

IWASHIMIZU HACHIMANGU SHRINE

Amongst the three shrines involved in the imperial festivals, the Iwashimizu Hachimangu Shrine is especially important for our understanding of Japanese mythology, because even though this shrine was not part of the *kampeisha* shrines, it was still deeply revered and placed among the top three imperial shrines. And the presiding deity (kami) here is famous for its Buddhist characteristic. The deity of the Usa Hachimangu Shrine in the Kyushu region of Japan is enshrined, in the attire of a Buddhist priest named Gyokyo, at the Iwashimizu Shrine located on Mount Otokoyama. With this began the worship of Sogyo Hachiman, a deity embodying the syncretism of both Shintoism and Buddhism. This particular form of the Iwashimizu Hachiman deity had a decisive influence on the concept of the Japanese kami's unique manifestation, a theory that is popularly known as *honji suijaku*. Buddhism maintained an vast, organized collection of sutras, and excelled at representing them in the forms of Buddhist iconographies, imagery and temple architecture. In Japan, especially in esoteric Buddhism, Japanese kamis were accommodated through the framework of Shinto-Buddhist syncretism: it propagated the idea that Japanese deities were originally a form of the Buddha, but that they manifested in Japan in the forms of kamis. This, in short, is the concept of *honji suijaku*.

HONJI SUIJAKU OR SHINTO-BUDDHISM SYNCRETISM

Soon, stories of numerous both original and manifested Shinto and Buddhist gods began to appear and circulate. The Shinto god Amaterasu, for instance, was claimed as the manifestations of the Buddhist gods Dainichi Nyorai (the Great Buddha) and the Eleven-Faced Kannon. Popular Buddhist deities like Kannon, Jizo, Amida and Dainichi Nyorai were all syncretized through the *honji suijaku* framework from the medieval period and received popular attention.

The *honji suijaku* doctrine also resulted in the anthropomorphic representation of the deities as the protagonists of various Japanese traditions. One of the best examples is a work called the *Shintōshō*. This work was compiled in the fourteenth century and includes a collection of legends. It is believed that it was composed by a Buddhist monk irrespective of its Shinto-like title. The story of Kumano Gongen (Kumano Incarnation) included in this work is particularly conspicuous.

THE LEGEND OF KUMANO SANSHO GONGEN

A summary offered in Watsuji Tetsuro's *Umoreta Nihon*, or 'Buried Japan', about this story goes like this: the female protagonist, a beautiful court lady, was a devout follower of Kannon. The court at that time had as many as a thousand court ladies and seven empresses in attendance to the Emperor. Nonetheless, Mikado chose the protagonist from among the thousand court ladies, and she became pregnant with Mikado's child. Due to her closeness to Mikado, she attracted a lot of jealousy from the rest of the nine hundred and ninety-nine court ladies. All sorts of antagonistic moves and curses were hurled at her, and finally, she was taken to a deep mountain and beheaded.

But just before she was beheaded, she gave birth to the crown prince. Her body and limbs remained completely unscathed even after she was beheaded, and she was able to nurse the crown prince with her breasts. The tribulations caused by the rest of the empresses and court ladies, and the headless mother's nursing of the crown prince, form the essence of this tale. When the prince turned four years old, he was placed under the care of a monk of the Gionshouja temple, who was also the elder brother of the protagonist. At the age of seven, the prince was brought before the Emperor, who in turn explained all that had happened in the past and promptly handed over the throne to the prince. But very soon, at the age of fifteen, the new emperor flew to the Kumano region of Japan on a flying chariot accompanied by the former emperor and the monk, thus evading the dreadful realm of vengeful women. This is known as the legend of Kumano Sansho Gongen (three incarnations of Kumano).

HONJIMONO AND OTOGI-ZŌSHI

The Kumano Sansho Gongen story that Watsuji referred to in his *Umoreta Nihon* differs from the *Shintōshū* in some details. Watsuji, in fact, did not refer to the *Shintōshū*. Instead, he consulted a medieval narrative work (originally a picture book or picture scroll) belonging to the literary genre called otogi-zōshi. These narrative works depict the origin of deities and the manner through which they acquired divine status. They are called *honjimono*. The circulation of *honjimono* was one of the important factors that made the *otogi-zōshi* genre extremely popular until the early modern period. What's more, the legends of Kumano, Nissho Gongen (two incarnations) and Suwa Daimyōjin that are depicted in the *Shintōshū* have their origins in India. The stories of these deities with their intertwined relationship with Buddhism are thus a critical aspect of Japanese mythology.

Likewise, Watsuji's famous statement of 'suffering deities, resurrecting deities', which is the hallmark of Japanese deities, is another critical aspect of Japanese myths that must not be forgotten. His statement is equally relevant today. The idea developed and became popular long before the Ōnin War, or perhaps even prior to the composition of the *Shintōshū*. The eleven-year Ōnin War fought in Kyoto resulted in many structures being burnt down, especially in the Kamigyō area of Kyoto, and caused large-scale destruction of many shrines and temples. Even the three imperial festivals were suspended during the war. It was a major blow to Shintoism, causing great suffering to the Shinto deities, only to be resurrected later.

THE TALE OF OTAGA NO MYOJIN

Yoshida Kanetomo (1435–1511), a late medieval thinker and witness to this tumultuous period, brought a major shift in the contemporary Japanese intellectual currents. The Yuiitsu Shintō that he founded disproved the hitherto popular *honji suijaku* doctrine. Rather his newly founded faith was a sort of synthesis religion with ideas drawn skilfully from Confucianism, Buddhism, Taoism and Onmyōdō, or 'Way of Yin and Yang'. During the following Edo period, the Yoshida family gained control of the Shinto shrines throughout Japan and exerted considerable influence as the head family of Yoshida Shinto until the end of the Edo era.

The aforementioned structure of medieval myths helped to broaden its appeal by integrating ordinary people into the origins of local deities within the formulation of *honjimono*. Following is one such example: in the province of Shinshu, there lived a dirty man, the ultimate symbol of laziness, who never worked and always lazily spent time in miserable hovels, barely surviving on food offered by others. Unexpectedly, one day he was selected to go to Kyoto to work as a long-term labourer, something that people hated very much. But this visit to the capital city completely transformed the lazy man's life. Once in Kyoto, he stalked a woman who he met at the Kiyomizu Temple, a sacred place for the Kannon, and successfully won her, presenting himself as a handsome, talented man. He became so successful that ultimately the legend appeared in an otogi-zōshi-style work called *Monokusa Taro* in which he is presented as the manifestation of the Otaga no Myojin, or the Deity of Otaga, in the Shinshu region. The first half of the story partly resembles the well-known folktale of 'Three Years' Sleeping Taro', but its representation in the *otogi-zōshi* style within the *honjimono* framework gave it an all-new divine dimension and it became very popular.

THE LEGEND OF URASHIMA TARŌ

Here goes another popular story. Long ago, a fisherman named Urashima was guided to the Dragon Palace by a turtle that he caught in the sea. Urashima, upon realizing that the turtle was actually the princess of the Dragon Palace, married her. He spent some time in the castle but soon became homesick and returned home, only to find an altogether different world, where many decades had passed. Now lonely, Urashima opened a jade box given to him by the turtle princess. A cloud of white smoke came out of the box and suddenly Urashima transformed into an old man as if all those trapped years suddenly came into effect. Later, Urashima became a crane, and together with the turtle princess, he was enshrined as a god. This, in short, is the popular Urashima Tarō legend. There are many variants of this story with different endings. In these stories, we can see a profound desire of common people from the lower classes for material success.

CHARACTERISTICS OF MODERN JAPANESE MYTHS

What, then, are the defining features of myths in modern Japan? Modernity, of course, refers to the particular historical horizon in which we, including you, the readers of this volume, currently live. Japanese myths are deeply intertwined with the origin of the imperial system, the political symbol of the modern Japanese nation-state. It is not uncommon, however, that myths concerning ancient kingship were closely linked to contemporary political conditions in ancient stories. For example, the *polis* was closely connected to ancient Greek mythologies. However, what makes Japanese mythologies different is that they are still deeply intertwined with the political authority of the modern nation-state. The following examples show it clearly.

Japanese novelist Ogai Mori's novel *Kanoyōni* (*As If*, 1912) is one of the many instances that depicts how politicized Japanese mythology was during the Meiji period. In the novel, Ogai expresses his apprehension that if he were to talk about the absurdity of the existence of the deities found in myths, it would amount to insulting the Japanese imperial system, thus violating a national taboo. Herein lies the challenge of critically examining Japanese myths in the modern era. In fact, the debate concerning the nature of Japanese myths that took place between Toshio Takagi and Masaharu Anasaki in 1899 throughout the next year is considered to be the beginning of Japanese mythology scholarship. Such a free atmosphere for debate, however, came to an abrupt end in 1910 with the High Treason Incident, which was followed by a sweeping roundup of socialist intellectuals. *Ogai's Kanoyōni* was authored under these circumstances, tackling the question of how to perform critical mythological scholarship within the prevailing Japanese societal situations.

CRITICAL SCHOLARSHIP OF JAPANESE MYTHS

Critical scholarship of Japanese mythology witnessed another revival during the subsequent Taisho era (1911–1925). This period is also known as the Taisho Democracy, because freedom of speech, at least to a certain extent, was recognized during this time. Sokichi Tsuda was instrumental in triggering the debate during this period. Tsuda was a historian of Eastern thought, and he did not confine his scholarship within the narrow framework of the Japanese nation. Instead, he sought the origins of written Japanese mythologies, namely the *Kojiki* and *Nihon Shoki*, in the Confucian cultural sphere of East Asia. He claimed that the origins of these myths can at best be traced back to the Sinitic knowledge of the Yamato court intellectuals in the sixth century, not any further, and that the Yamato court used this knowledge to gain political legitimacy for its authority over the Japanese archipelago.

THE NATURE OF JAPANESE MYTHS

Tsuda's arguments prompted a heated debate within the Japanese academia. The conservatives vehemently rejected his claims and branded them as an insult to the *kokutai*, or the 'national body'. The progressives, on the other hand, reinterpreted *Kojiki* and *Nihon Shoki* based on Tsuda's arguments and maintained that Japanese myths represent only the emperor system, not Japanese people as a whole. Ironically, Tsuda himself was a supporter of the emperor system, and all he intended was to reconstruct Japanese history through reinterpretation of the myths based on modern reasons that could be acceptable to everyone. This is precisely why he called the stories of *Kojiki* and *Nihon Shoki* the 'history of the age of the gods', distinguishing them from the myths of primitive societies from other regions. This is where the Japanese liberalism of the Taisho Democracy era and modern reasons failed.

Yet Tsuda did not just refute the existence of something called 'Japanese mythology' in ancient Japan. He also claimed that the myths of the Chronicles, which were compiled drawing knowledge from the Chinese intelligentsia, gradually spread among ordinary folks in the countryside. This resulted in a blending of the Chronicles' myths with local oral traditions, which in turn gave birth to unique medieval Japanese chronicles whose protagonists were based on the *Kojiki* and *Nihon Shoki*.

Later, when Buddhism was introduced to Japan, a variety of new artistic genres, such as the Buddhist *Setsuwa* (tales), Noh and Kyogen plays based on historical figures and *otogi-zōshi* narratives set in actual places like the Heian-kyo, emerged successively. The public imagination took free flight from the late ancient to medieval period through these plays and tales, appearing on the stage of history. In that sense, as one of Tsuda's rivals, Watsuji Tetsuro, once said, what is now collectively known as 'Japanese mythology' is not just the political memory of the elite ruling classes – comprising the aristocracy and nobility – but also the crystallization of the cumulative memories of ordinary folks from various sections of society.

PROJECTING THE PAST INTO THE FUTURE

Japanese mythology, as explained above, has a high degree of affinity with the literary genre called *monogatari* (Japanese tales), and is creative in nature. Myths, therefore, have become prototypes for further cultural productions, by mythologizing and sacralizing the motifs of present-day popular culture. On the one hand, there are works like the *Nihon Shoki* and *Kojiki*, which made full use of Chinese Taoist and Confucian texts to systematically adapt them into literary texts to maintain the authority of the Yamato Kingship. On the other hand, there are the medieval Japanese chronicles and other works that employed (and at times rejected) the *honji suijaku* notion to tell tales. Yet again there is the world of popular beliefs included in the *otogi-zōshi* narratives. The history of such a long process of putting oral narratives into written words, and of their further interpretations under Western influence in the modern age, came to be collectively called 'Japanese mythology'.

The book that you hold now in your hands is the crystallization of all those stories produced through the passage of such long and diverse periods. Naturally then, it is pointless to judge which myths are real Japanese stories and which are not. Rather, you should understand them as something accumulated over centuries and enjoy them in different ways. The reverberation of dynamic readings between the historical horizons of Japanese myths and the reader's standing in the present horizon will give birth to new Japanese myths. Undoubtedly, Japanese mythology is never a monolithic body of static narratives. It is a realm that has the immense potential to give birth to infinite diversity.

Jun'ichi Isomae & Hiroshi Araki
(Trans. by Gouranga Charan Pradhan)

FURTHER READING

ORIGINAL TEXTS OF JAPANESE MYTHS AND FOLKLORES

Aston, William George , trans., *Nihongi: Chronicles of Japan from the Earliest Times to* AD 697 (New York: Cosimo, 2008)

Aston, William George; Chamberlain, Basil Hall, trans., Translation of *"Ko-ji-ki," or Records of ancient matters.* (Tokyo: Synapse, 2000)

Hearn, Lafcadio, *KWAIDAN: Stories and Studies of Strange Things* (Rutland Vermont: Tuttle, 2014)

Heldt, Gustav, trans., *The Kojiki: An Account of Ancient Matters* (New York: Columbia University Press, 2014)

Kamens, Edward, *The Three Jewels: A Study and Translation of Minamoto Tamenori's Sanboe* (Ann Arbor: Center for Japanese Studies, University of Michigan, 1988)

Kimbrough, Keller and Shirane, Haruo, eds., Atherton, David, trans., *Monsters, Animals, and Other Worlds: A Collection of Short Medieval Japanese Tales* (New York: Columbia University Press, 2018)

Morrell, Robert E., *Sand and Pebbles (Shasekishu)* (Albany: State University of New York Press, 1984)

Nakamura, Kyoko Motomochi, trans. & ed., *Miraculous Stories from the Japanese Buddhist Tradition: The Nihon Ryoiki of the Monk Kyokai* (Cambridge, MA: Harvard University Press, 1974)

Skord, Virginia, trans., *Short Tales of Tears and Laughter, Short*

Fiction of Medieval Japan (Honolulu: University of Hawaii Press, 1993)

Watson, Burton, trans., *Record of Miraculous Events in Japan: The Nihon Ryoiki* (New York: Columbia University Press, 2013)

Watson, Burton, trans., ed., with an introduction by Haruo Shirane, *The Demon at Agi Bridge and Other Japanese Tales* (New York: Columbia University Press, 2011)

SUPPLEMENTARY READING

Ebersole, Gary L., *Ritual Poetry and the Politics of Death in Early Japan* (Princeton: Princeton University Press, 1992)

Eubanks, Charlotte, *Miracles of Book and Body: Buddhist Textual Culture and Medieval Japan* (Berkeley: University of California Press, 2011)

Foster, Michael Dylan, *The Book of Yokai: Mysterious Creatures of Japanese Folklore* (Berkeley: University of California Press, 2015)

Isomae, Jun'ichi, *Japanese Mythology: Hermeneutics on Scripture* (London: Routledge, 2009)

Kimbrough, R. Kellar, *Preachers, Poets, Women, and the Way: Izumi Shikibu and the Buddhist Literature of Medieval Japan* (Ann Arbor: Center for Japanese Studies, the University of Michigan, 2008)

Li, Michelle Osterfeld, *Ambiguous Bodies: Reading the Grotesque in Japanese Setsuwa Tales* (Stanford, CA: Stanford University Press, 2009)

MacWilliams, Mark W. and Okuyama, Michiaki, eds., *Defining Shinto: A Reader* (London and New York: Routledge, 2020)

Shirane, Haruo and Suzuki, Tomi, eds., *Inventing the Classics: Modernity, National Identity, and Japanese Literature* (Stanford, CA: Stanford University Press, 2002)

Teeuveen, Mark and Rambelli, Fabio, eds., *Buddhas and Kami in Japan: Honji Suijaku as a Combinatory Paradigm* (London & New York: Routledge Curzon, 2003)

Zhong, Yijiang, *The Origin of Modern Shinto in Japan: The Vanquished Gods of Izumo* (London: Bloomsbury Publishing, 2016)

Jun'ichi Isomae (co-author of new introduction) is a Professor at the International Research Center for Japanese Studies, Kyoto, Japan. He specializes in Religious Studies and Critical Theory, including the concept of the divine. His books include *Japanese Mythology: Hermeneutics on Scripture* (2010) and *Religious Discourse in Modern Japan: Religion, State, and Shintō* (2014). He has published many books and articles, is on the advisory board for Cromohs (Fierenze University Press, Italy) and Global Perspectives on Medieval and Early Modern Historiography (Brepols Publishers, Belgium), and is a member of the American Academy of Religion and the Association for Asian Studies.

Hiroshi Araki (co-author of new introduction) is a Professor at the International Research Center for Japanese Studies, Kyoto, Japan. He specializes in Medieval Japanese literature with a particular focus on Japanese narrative tales. He has worked extensively on Dream Culture and the projection of Classical literature on contemporary culture. His latest ongoing project is a comparative study of the notion of 'impermanence' from a multicultural and transdisciplinary perspective. His books include *Konjaku Monogatarishū: Tracing its Composition and Representation of the World*

Outside Japan (Monograph, 2021), *Kojidan, Zoku, Kojidan* (Annotation and Commentary, 2005), and *Projecting Classicism: The Futurology of Japanese Classics* (Editor, 2020). His latest essay 'Reviewing Japanese Dream Culture and Its History: Where Ancient, Medieval and Modern Times Meet' appeared in LATVIJAS UNIVERSITĀTES RAKSTI 2021, 819. sēj. ORIENTĀLISTIKA. He serves on the boards of several academic associations for premodern Japanese literature and Buddhist studies, and is a member of the European Association of Japanese Studies.

Gouranga Charan Pradhan (translator of the new introduction) is a Research Fellow at Nichibunken, Kyoto, where he researches the global circulation of Japanese classical literature and Japan's cultural-intellectual interactions abroad with a focus on the late nineteenth to the early twentieth century. His first monograph *Sekai Bungaku toshite no Hōjōki* (in Japanese) is scheduled for a February 2022 launch.

KEY THEMES & BEINGS

Japan may have absorbed the religion, art and social life of China, but it has stamped its own national seal upon what it borrowed from the Celestial Kingdom and created a genuine Japanese world view and mythology. The *Kojiki* and the *Nihon Shoki* are two primary literary texts among various literary and oral sources from which we learn the early myths and legends of Japan. In their pages we are introduced to Izanagi and Izanami, Amaterasu, Susanoo and numerous other divinities, and these august beings provide us with stories that are quaint, beautiful, quasi-humorous and sometimes a little horrible.

In studying Japanese legend one is particularly struck by its multiplicity and variations. The Japanese have described the red blossoms of azaleas as the fires of the gods, and the white snow of Fuji as the garments of divine beings. Their legend, on the one hand at any rate, is essentially poetical, and those who worshipped Mount Fuji also had ghostly tales to tell about the smallest insect. Too much stress cannot be laid upon Japan's love of nature. However, there is plenty of crude realism in Japanese legend. We are repelled by the Thunder God's favourite repast, amazed by the magical power of foxes and cats; and the story of 'Hōichi-the-Earless' and of the corpse-eating priest afford striking examples of the combination of the weird and the horrible. But first let us take a look at the origins and background of the people and their mythology.

THE CREATION

The Japanese creation myth as recounted in the *Kojiki* and *Nihon Shoki* does not tell of a creation ex nihilo but speaks of an unaabounded, amorphous, chaotic mass. This existed for many aeons until an area of light and transparency arose within it – Takama-gahara, the High Plains of Heaven. Three primordial gods materialized there, followed by a further two lesser gods who in turn engendered five generations of gods culminating in the primal couple, Izanagi and Izanami. Little is related about the divine beings who existed before Izanagi and Izanami beyond their names; these may just be remembered remnants of earlier, lost mythologies.

IZANAGI AND IZANAMI

Izanagi and Izanami were charged by the other divinities with bringing creation to completion and to this end they stood on the Floating Bridge of Heaven and together stirred the oily brine below with a jewelled spear. Drops falling from this spear fell to produce the first island where they took up residence. There they were joined together as the first couple, but their offspring was the deformed Hiruko (Leach Child), whom they abandoned in a reed boat. In consultation with the other gods, it was found that this child had been deformed since, during their courtship ritual, the goddess Izanami had spoken first to Izanagi. When they re-enacted their marriage in the correct manner with precedence being given to the god Izanagi, Izanami was able to give birth successfully to a large number of offspring. This episode, it is believed by scholars, was included through Chinese patriarchal influences.

Among Izanami's children were the other islands that make up the Japanese archipelago, as well as the gods of the mountains, the plains, wind, trees and so on. While giving birth to her last child, Kagutsuchi, the god of fire, Izanami was so badly burnt that she died. However, like the Greek Orpheus, Izanagi decided to seek out Izanami in the underworld of Yomi, the abode of darkness, and bring her back with him. Izanami said she would discuss this with the gods of the underworld, but as she disappeared into the gloom, she warned him not to look at her. Wanting to see her again, Izanagi broke off a tooth from his hair-comb and lit it as a torch. He was horrified to see that Izanami was now a maggot-infested, rotting corpse and tried to flee from her. Angered by his act, Izanami sent a horde of demon hags and warriors to pursue him. When he reached the entrance back into the realm of the living, Izanagi found three peaches, which he threw at his pursuers and managed to turn them back. At this point, Izanami, now transformed into a demon, gave chase herself. Before she could reach him, Izanagi barred her way with a great boulder with which he sealed the entrance to the underworld. Here they confronted each other a final time and dissolved their marriage vows.

FOCUS ON: EARLY LITERARY SOURCES

The first historical mention of Japan is found in AD 57 in the annals of the Chinese Han Dynasty in which Japan is described as a land divided into about a hundred tribal communities, lacking any central government. Later Chinese sources indicate that there was a degree of consolidation into larger political units in the following centuries, but the details are sparse. The Japanese themselves did not begin to keep accounts of their society until around AD 600 when a writing system was introduced, along with many other cultural innovations from China. The two main sources for Japanese mythology and early history are the *Kojiki* and the Nihon Shoki. The *Kojiki*, or Record of Ancient Matters, was compiled in Chinese in AD 712, but was based on earlier oral traditions. It relates various myths, legends and historical events concerning the imperial court from the age of the gods down to the time of the Empress Suiko (AD 593–628). The slightly later but longer *Nihon Shoki*, or Chronicles of Japan, written in AD 720, betrays a greater influence of Chinese cultural attitudes but covers broadly similar ground to the *Kojiki* although it relates events until AD 697.

AMATERASU, SUN GODDESS

The sun goddess Amaterasu is of central significance to Japanese mythology, since the imperial family claimed descent from her until Japan's defeat in the Second World

41

War. She is also unusual as a paramount female deity in a land where male pre-eminence has always been the norm. After his return from the underworld, Yomi, Izanagi bathed to purify himself ritually from the pollution (imi) of contact with the dead. He then gave birth to a further sequence of gods and goddesses, culminating in the sun goddess Amaterasu, the moon god Tsuki-yomi and the storm god Susanoo. Before withdrawing from the world, Izanagi entrusted Amaterasu with rulership of the High Plains of Heaven, Tsuki-yomi with the realm of the night and Susanoo with the ocean. Susanoo was dissatisfied with his assignment and jealous of the ascendancy of his sister Amaterasu and so was banished by Izanagi.

DIVINE CONFLICT

Before he was due to leave, Susanoo arranged to meet with Amaterasu to say farewell but suspecting that he was plotting to overthrow her, Amaterasu armed herself and confronted her brother. He then challenged her to a contest that would prove who was really the mightiest – whoever could give birth to male gods would be the winner. Amaterasu took Susanoo's sword and broke it into three pieces from which she produced three goddesses, while Susanoo took her sacred magatama beads and produced five male gods. Amaterasu claimed she had won since his gods had come from her beads but Susanoo refused to accept defeat.

Susanoo then embarked on a series of foul outrages against Amaterasu, such as destroying the heavenly rice fields, defecating in the ritual hall of offerings and casting a skinned pony through the roof of the sacred weaving hall. This last act resulted in the death of one of Amaterasu's maidens after a shuttle pierced her genitals (according to some accounts it was Amaterasu herself who was injured). Either way, she was so terrified that she hid and sealed herself inside a cave. The entire human world and the heavens were cast into darkness and misery ensued. In vain the gods tried to entice her out with various stratagems but they all failed. Then the beautiful goddess of the dawn, Ama-no-uzume, who was the archetypal miko, or shamaness, stood on an upturned rice barrel and began a sacred erotic dance baring her body. Hearing the excitement of the gods and their praises for Ama-no-uzume, Amaterasu peeped out of a crack. As she opened the crack wider and gazed out, one of the gods held up a sacred mirror and Amaterasu saw her own reflection in it. While Amaterasu was entranced with her own reflection, one of the other gods seized her by the hand and pulled her out of the cave while others barred the cave with a magic rope. Upon this Amaterasu returned to the heavens where all the deities agreed to punish Susanoo with banishment from the heavens, fined him and cut off his beard and nails. Izumo was the place where the god Susanoo lived after he was exiled from heaven.

This account of divine rivalry may preserve distant memories of ancient power struggles in Japanese society between rival patriarchal and matriarchal systems of rule, although the outcome is uncharacteristic in world mythology inasmuch as it was the female, the goddess Amaterasu, who eventually emerged the winner rather than the male.

SUSANOO AND OKUNINUSHI

One of Susanoo's descendants, possibly his grandson, the god Okuninushi, also features in many of these myths as a bringer of civilization and culture. Okuninushi had numerous older brothers who wanted to marry Ya-gami-hime of neighbouring Inaba. Going to visit her, they meet a furless rabbit, which they torment. Okuninushi kindly helps the rabbit regain its fur and in return is told that he will be the successful suitor of the princess while his brothers will become his retainers. This all comes true but his brothers soon become dissatisfied and quarrelsome. Though they manage to kill him twice, each time he comes back to life and he eventually decides to visit Yomi, the underworld, for advice about ridding himself of his troublesome brothers.

SUSERI-HIME

In the underworld, Okuninushi meets Suseri-hime, the daughter of Susanoo, and marries her without Susanoo's consent. Angered by this, Susanoo tries to kill Okuninushi three times, but on each occasion Okuninushi is saved by a magic scarf given to him by Suseri-hime. Eventually the pair decide to escape to the land of the living while stealing a bow, sword and koto that belongs to Susanoo. Although Susanoo eventually catches up with him, he forgives Okuninushi. It is at this point that Okuninushi – Great Ruler of the Land – is given his name, foretelling his conquest of the whole country.

After his return from Yomi, the underworld, Okuninushi followed Susanoo's advice and hunted down his older brothers, eventually killing them all and becoming sole ruler of Izumo. Abandoning Ya-gami-hime, his earlier wife, he then went to live with Suseri-hime in a palace he built at Uga-no-yama in Izumo. After his return to Izumo, Okuninushi takes on many of the characteristics of a cultural hero. Much of the country was still wild and unformed at that time, and there was nothing but dense forests, swamps, ferocious animals and evil spirits. Mindful of Susanoo's prediction, Okuninushi began to clear the regions near Izumo with a magical weapon called Yachihoko, 'Eight Thousand Spears'. With it he walked tirelessly around the land and killed many demons, making places safe for people to live in.

FOCUS ON: CULTIC CENTRES

The divine forces of nature (kami) are thought to reside in rivers, rocks, mountains and trees, meaning that almost any feature in the Japanese landscape may act as a cultic centre. These may be marked by a small shrine for offerings or else just a torii, a stylized gateway demarking the boundary between the profane and the sacred. Other places in Japan are home to much larger shrines, which act as national cultic centres though their importance has waned since the political demotion of Shinto in the wake of the Second World War. Most notable are the ancient great shrines at Ise and Izumo, both of which have their origins in prehistoric times. Ise in central Japan is connected with the sun goddess, Amaterasu, and Toyouke-no-okami, the god of rice and harvests. Until the fifteenth century the Ise shrine was considered to be so sacred that only members of the imperial family were allowed to visit it. The shrine at Izumo in western Japan is associated with Amaterasu's rival brother, Susanoo and his grandson, Okuninushi. A characteristic feature of all Shinto shrines is the complete absence of any form of iconographic depiction of the divinities enshrined in them. Instead, certain sacred objects are displayed on a simple altar such as a mirror, a sword or the comma-shaped magatama beads.

THE FOUNDATION OF THE YAMATO KINGSHIP

After Okuninushi and his descendants had made the land prosperous, their rule grew lax and evil gods once again made life unpleasant for the people. Amaterasu, who had wanted to extend her rule to that region for her descendants, decided to take advantage of the situation. After several failed attempts, she sent two trusted and brave gods, Futsunushi-no-mikoto and Takemikazuchi-no-mikoto, to tell Okuninushi to surrender the land to her. They sat on the tips of their upturned swords embedded in the crest of a wave in the sea off Inasa in Izumo and then delivered their ultimatum to him. Okuninushi was most impressed by this and after consulting with his son, he eventually conceded – on condition that a place should be reserved for him among the gods worshipped in Izumo.

THE ORIGINS OF THE JAPANESE STATE

After this, Okuninushi's clan was supplanted by Amaterasu's descendants. Her grandson Ninigi-no-mikoto came to earth carrying the three symbols of sovereignty: the mirror, the magatama beads and a sword. He had two sons – Hoderi (Fireshine) and Hoori (Fireshade). Hoderi, the eldest, fished using a hook, while Hoori was a hunter. Hoori was dissatisfied and suggested changing their occupations, which they did, but Hoori was unsuccessful, even losing the fishing hook. When Hoderi asked him to return it, he offered several substitutes, but Hoderi insisted on having the original. Hoori drifted far out to sea in shame and eventually reached the palace of the sea god, Watatsumi-no-kami, who not only retrieved the fish hook, but also gave Hoori his daughter in marriage. When the time came for Hoori to return home, Watatsumi-no-kami gave him two jewels, one to make the sea rise and one to make it fall. When Hoori got home, he returned the hook to Hoderi who, nevertheless, continued to complain, so Hoori then threw one jewel in the sea causing a flood. In terror, Hoderi begged for forgiveness so Hoori threw the other jewel into the sea and it receded. In gratitude, Hoderi swore that he would serve his younger brother in perpetuity. The grandson of Hoori was Jimmu, the legendary first emperor of Japan. Jimmu seems to have come from the island of Kyushu but conquered the whole of western Japan and finally reached east–central Japan, where he married a local princess and founded the Yamato State. This state formed the precursor of the historic ruling hegemony.

FOCUS ON: SHINTO

Shinto is the indigenous religion that flourished in Japan before the introduction of Buddhism in the sixth century AD and has remained a vital force in all aspects of Japanese culture up to the present day. Shinto means 'the way of the gods' and as its name suggests, its central concern is the kami, a term that includes both the gods of myth and also the numinous powers inherent in all natural things. Though lacking a sophisticated metaphysical theology or philosophy, the aim of Shinto is to regulate human activities within the natural world in a harmonious manner. Unlike in Buddhism, the concept of ritual pollution (imi) – anything that disturbed the intrinsic harmony of nature – played an important role in Shinto in the past, and various methods of ritual cleansing were prescribed. Though early Shinto sacred places are natural features such as waterfalls, tall trees or imposing rocks, shrines were also built and maintained by families of ritual specialists who emerged by the sixth century AD; to a certain extent these places are still recognized as being sacred today. Although every town and village has its own Shinto shrine, those at Ise and Izumo are of national importance.

JIZO, GOD OF CHILDREN

Jizo, the god of little children and the god who makes calm the troubled sea, is certainly the most lovable of the Buddhist divinities, though Kwannon, the Goddess of Mercy, has somewhat similar attributes. The most popular gods, be they of the east or west, are those gods with the most human qualities. Jizo, though of Buddhist origin, is essentially Japanese, and we may best describe him as being the creation of innumerable Japanese women who have longed to project into the Infinite, into the shrouded Beyond, a deity who should be a divine Father and Mother to the souls of their little ones. And this is just what Jizo is, a god essentially of the feminine heart, and not a being to be tossed about in the hair-splitting debates of hoary theologians. Jizo has all the wisdom of the Lord Buddha himself, with this important difference, namely, that Jizo has waived aside Nirvana, and does not sit upon the Golden Lotus, but has become, through an exquisitely beautiful self-sacrifice, the divine playmate and protector of Japanese children. He is the god of smiles and long sleeves, the enemy of evil spirits, and the one being who can heal the wound of a mother who has lost her child in death. We have a saying that all rivers find their way to the sea. To the Japanese woman who has laid her little one in the cemetery, all rivers wind their silver courses into the place where the ever-waiting and ever-gentle Jizo is.

'THE DRY BED OF THE RIVER OF SOULS'

Under the earth there is the Sai-no-Kawara, or 'the Dry Bed of the River of Souls'. This is the place where all children go after death, children and those who have never married. Here the little ones play with the smiling Jizo, and here it is that they build small towers of stones, for there are many in this river bed. The mothers of these children, in the world above them, also pile up stones

49

around the images of Jizo, for these little towers represent prayers; they are charms against the oni, or wicked spirits. Sometimes in the Dry Bed of the River of Souls the oni for a moment gain a temporary victory, and knock down the little towers that the ghosts of children have built with so much laughter. When such a misfortune takes place, the laughter ceases, and the little ones fly to Jizo for protection. He hides them in his long sleeves, and with his sacred staff drives away the red-eyed oni.

The place where the souls of children dwell is a shadowy and grey world of dim hills and vales through which the Sai-no-Kawara winds its way. All the children are clad in short white garments, and if occasionally the evil spirits frighten them there is always Jizo to dry their tears, always one who sends them back to their ghostly games again.

KWANNON, GODDESS OF MERCY

Kwannon, the Goddess of Mercy, resembles in many ways the no less merciful and gentle Jizo, for both renounced the bliss of Nirvana that they might bring peace and happiness to the humans. Kwannon, however, is a much more complex divinity than Jizo, and though she is most frequently portrayed as a very beautiful and saintly Japanese woman, she nevertheless assumes a multitude of forms. We are familiar with certain Indian gods and goddesses with innumerable hands, and Kwannon is sometimes depicted as Senjiu-Kwannon, or Kwannon of the Thousand Hands. Each hand holds an object of some kind, as if to suggest that here indeed was a goddess ready in her love to give and to answer prayer to the uttermost.

Then there is Jiu-ichi-men-Kwannon, the Kwannon of the Eleven Faces. The face of Kwannon is here represented as 'smiling with eternal youth and infinite tenderness', and in her glowing presence the ideal of the divine feminine is presented with infinite beauty of conception. Sometimes the tiara of Kwannon takes another form, as in Bato-Kwannon, or Kwannon with the Horse's Head. The title is a little misleading, for such a graceful creature is very far from possessing a horse's head in any of her manifestations. Images of this particular Kwannon depict a horse cut out in the tiara. Bato-Kwannon is the goddess to whom peasants pray for the safety and preservation of their horses and cattle, and Bato-Kwannon is not only said to protect dumb animals, particularly those who labour for mankind, but also she extends her power to protecting their spirits and bringing them ease and a happier life than they experienced while on earth. The gods of love and wisdom are frequently represented in conjunction with this goddess, and the 'Twenty-eight Followers' are personifications of certain constellations.

KWANNON IN CHINESE MYTHOLOGY

In China, Kwannon is known as Kwanjin, and is the spiritual son of Amitâbha, but this divinity always appears as a goddess, as her images in both China and Japan testify. The Chinese claim that Kwanjin is of native origin, and was originally the daughter of the King of the Chow dynasty. She was sentenced to death by her father because she refused to marry, but the executioner's sword broke without inflicting a wound. We are told that later on her spirit went to Hell. There was something so radiantly beautiful about the spirit of Kwanjin that her very presence turned Hell into Paradise. The King of the Infernal Regions, in order to maintain the gloomy aspect of his realm, sent Kwanjin back to earth again, and he caused her to be miraculously transported on a lotus flower to the Island of Pootoo.

BENTEN, GODDESS OF THE WATER

Benten, the Goddess of the Water, who originated from the Hindu goddess Saraswati, is also one of the Seven Divinities of Luck; and she is romantically referred to as the Goddess of Love, Beauty and Eloquence. She is represented in Japanese art as riding on a dragon or serpent, which may account for the fact that in certain localities snakes are regarded as being sacred. Images of Benten depict her as having eight arms. Six hands are extended above her head and hold a bow, arrow, wheel, sword, key and sacred jewel, while her two remaining hands are reverently crossed in prayer.

THE GODS OF LUCK

Daikoku, the God of Wealth, Ebisu, his son, the God of Labour, and Hotei, the God of Laughter and Contentment, belong to that cycle of deities known as the Gods of Luck. Daikoku is represented with a magic mallet, which bears the sign of the Jewel, embodying the male and female spirit, and signifies a creative deity. A stroke of his mallet confers wealth, and his second attribute is the Rat. Daikoku is, as we should suppose, an extremely popular deity, and he is frequently portrayed as a prosperous Chinese gentleman, richly apparelled, and is usually shown standing on bales of rice, with a bag of precious things on his shoulder.

Ebisu and his father Daikoku are usually pictured together: the God of Wealth seated upon bales of rice, pressing the Red Sun against his breast with one hand, and with the other holding the wealth-giving Mallet, while Ebisu is depicted with a fishing-rod and a great tai fish under his arm.

Hotei, the God of Laughter and Contentment, is one of the most whimsical of the Japanese gods. He is represented as extremely fat, carrying on his back a linen bag (ho-tei), from which he derives his name. In this bag he stows the Precious Things, but when in a particularly playful mood he uses it as a receptacle for merry and inquisitive children.

SUPERNATURAL BEINGS

The Kappa

The kappa is a river goblin, a hairy creature with the body of a tortoise and scaly limbs. Its head somewhat resembles that of an ape, in the top of which there is a cavity containing a mysterious fluid, said to be the source of the creatures' power. The chief delight of the kappa is to challenge human beings to single combat, and the unfortunate man who receives an invitation of this kind cannot refuse. Though the kappa is fierce and quarrelsome, it is, nevertheless, extremely polite. The wayfarer who receives its peremptory summons gives the goblin a profound bow. The courteous kappa acknowledges the obeisance, and in inclining its head the strength-giving liquid runs out from the hollow in its cranium, and becoming feeble, his warlike characteristics immediately disappear. To defeat the Kappa, however, is just as unfortunate as to receive a beating at its hands, for the momentary glory of the conquest is rapidly followed by a wasting away of the unfortunate wayfarer.

The Tengu

We will refer to the tengu in the story of Yoshitsune and Benkei. In that legend, Yoshitsune, one of the greatest warriors of Old Japan, learnt the art of swordsmanship from the king of the tengu. Professor B.H. Chamberlain (1850–1935), a leading Japanologist of his time, described the tengu as 'a class of goblins or gnomes that haunt the mountains and woodlands, and play many pranks. They have an affinity to birds; for they are winged and beaked, sometimes clawed. But often the beak becomes a large and enormously long human nose, and the whole creature is conceived as human, nothing bird-like remaining but the fan of feathers with which it fans itself.'

In brief, the tengu are minor divinities, and are supreme in the art of fencing, and, indeed, in the use of weapons generally. The ideographs with which the name is written signify 'heavenly dog', which is misleading, for the creature bears no resemblance to a dog, and is, as we have already described, partly human and partly bird-like in appearance. The tengu are still believed to inhabit certain forests and the recesses of high mountains. Generally speaking, the tengu are not malevolent beings, for they possess a keen sense of humour, and are fond of a practical joke. Sometimes, however, the tengu mysteriously hide human beings, and when finally they return to their homes they do so in a demented condition. This strange occurrence is known as tengu-kakushi, or 'hidden by a tengu', and features in a story later in this collection: 'The Adventures of Kiuchi Heizayemon'.

The Mountain Woman and the Mountain Man

The Mountain Woman's body is covered with long white hair. She is looked upon as an ogre (kijo), and, as such, figures in Japanese romance. She has cannibalistic tendencies, and is able to fly about like a moth and traverse pathless mountains with ease.

The Mountain Man is said to resemble a great, dark-haired monkey. He is extremely strong, and thinks nothing of stealing food from the villages. He is, however, always ready to assist woodcutters, and will gladly carry their timber for them in exchange for a ball of rice. It is useless to capture or kill him, for an attack of any kind upon the Mountain Man brings misfortune, and sometimes death, upon the assailants.

Sennin

The sennin are mountain recluses, and many are the legends told in connection with them. Though they have human form, they are, at the same time, immortal, and adept in the magical arts. Sennin are frequently depicted in Japanese art: Chokoro releasing his magic horse from a gigantic gourd; Gama with his wizard toad; Tekkai blowing his soul into space; Roko balancing himself on a flying tortoise; and Kume, who fell from his chariot of cloud because, contrary to his holy calling, he loved the image of a fair girl reflected in a stream.

The first great Japanese sennin was Yosho, who was born at Noto AD 870. Just before his birth his mother dreamt that she had swallowed the sun, a dream that foretold the miraculous power of her child. Yosho was studious and devout, and spent most of his time in studying the 'Lotus of the Law'. He lived very simply indeed, and at length reduced his diet to a single grain of millet a day. He departed from the earth AD 901, having attained much supernatural power. He left his mantle hanging on the branch of a tree, together with a scroll bearing these words: 'I bequeath my mantle to Emmei of Dogen-ji.' In due time, Emmei became a sennin, and, like his master, was able to perform many marvels. Shortly after Yosho's disappearance, his father became seriously ill, and he prayed most ardently that he might see his well-loved son again. In reply to his prayers, Yosho's voice was heard overhead reciting the 'Lotus of the Law'.

Baku

In Japan, among superstitious people, evil dreams are believed to be the result of evil spirits, and the supernatural creature called baku is known as Eater of Dreams. The baku, like so many mythological beings, is a curious mingling of various animals. It has the face of a lion, the body of a horse, the tail of a cow, the forelock of a rhinoceros, and the feet of a tiger. Several evil dreams are mentioned in an old Japanese book, such as two snakes twined together, a fox with the voice of a man, blood-stained garments, a talking rice-pot, and so on. When a Japanese peasant awakens from an evil nightmare, he cries: 'Devour, O Baku! devour my evil dream.' At one time pictures of the baku were hung up in Japanese houses and its name written upon pillows. It was believed that if the baku could be induced to eat a horrible dream, the creature had the power to change it into good fortune.

The Dragon

The dragon is undoubtedly the most famous of mythical beasts, but, though Chinese in origin, it has become intimately associated with Japanese mythology. The creature lives for the most part in oceans, rivers or lakes, but it has the power of flight and rules over clouds and tempests. The dragons of China and Japan resemble each other, with the exception that the Japanese variety has three claws, while that of China has five. The dragon generally has the head of a camel, horns of a deer, eyes of a hare, scales of a carp, paws of a tiger, and claws resembling those of an eagle. This, of course, does not apply to all dragons: some have heads of so extraordinary a kind that they cannot be compared with anything in the animal kingdom. In addition the dragon usually has whiskers, a bright jewel under its chin, and a measure on the top of its head that enables it to ascend to Heaven at will. Its breath changes into clouds from which come either rain or fire. It is able to expand or contract its body, and in addition it has the power of transformation and invisibility. In both Chinese and Japanese mythology the dragon is associated with water.

Inari, the Fox God

The fox takes an important place in Japanese legend, and the subject is of a far-reaching and complex kind. Inari was originally the God of Rice, but in the eleventh century he became associated with the Fox God, with attributes for good and evil, mostly for evil, so profuse and so manifold in their application that they cause no little confusion to the Western reader. All foxes possess supernatural powers to an almost limitless degree. They have the power of infinite vision; they can hear everything and understand the secret thoughts of mankind generally, and in addition, they possess the power of transformation and of transmutation. The chief attribute of the bad fox is the power to delude human beings, and for this purpose it will take the form of a beautiful woman, and many are the legends told in this connection. If the shadow of a fox-woman chance to fall upon water, only the fox, and not the fair woman, is revealed. It is said that if a dog sees a fox-woman the feminine form vanishes immediately, and the fox alone remains.

Butterflies

Japanese poets and artists were fond of choosing for their professional appellation such names as 'Butterfly-Dream', 'Solitary Butterfly', 'Butterfly-Help' and so on. Though probably of Chinese origin, such ideas naturally appealed to the aesthetic taste of the Japanese people, and no doubt they played in early days the romantic game of butterflies. Emperor Genso used to make butterflies choose his loves for him. At a wine-party in his garden fair ladies would set caged butterflies free. These bright-coloured insects would fly and settle upon the fairest damsels, and those maidens immediately received royal favours.

In Japan the butterfly was at one time considered to be the soul of a living man or woman. If it entered a guest room and pitched behind the bamboo screen, it was a sure sign that the person whom it represented would shortly appear in the house. The presence of a butterfly in the house was regarded as a good omen, though of course everything depended on the individual typified by the butterfly.

Ed. by Gouranga Charan Pradhan

TALES OF GOD AND CREATION

We are told that in the very beginning "Heaven and Earth were not yet separated, and the *In* and *Yo* not yet divided." The *In* and *Yo*, corresponding to the Chinese *Yang* and *Yin*, were the male and female principles. It was more convenient for the old Japanese writers to imagine the coming into being of creation in terms not very remote from their own manner of birth. We are told in the *Nihon Shoki* that these male and female principles "formed a chaotic mass like an egg which was of obscurely defined limits and contained germs." Eventually this egg was quickened into life, and the purer and clearer part was drawn out and formed Heaven, while the heavier element settled down and became Earth, which was "compared to the floating of a fish sporting on the surface of the water." A mysterious form resembling a reed-shoot suddenly appeared between Heaven and Earth, and as suddenly became transformed into a God called Kunitokotachi, ('Land-eternal-stand-of-august-thing').

We may pass over the other divine births until we come to the important deities known as Izanagi and Izanami ('Male-who-invites' and 'Female-who-invites'). About these beings has been woven an entrancing myth, the first in this section. We also present some tales and exploits of other gods, including Amaterasu, Susanoo, Ninigi, Uzume, Ko-no-Hana, the Sea God, Kwannon, Benten and the Thunder God.

IZANAGI AND IZANAMI

Izanagi and Izanami stood on the Floating Bridge of Heaven and looked down into the abyss. They inquired of each other if there were a country far, far below the great Floating Bridge. They were determined to find out. In order to do so they thrust down a jewel-spear, and found the ocean. Raising the spear a little, water dripped from it, coagulated, and became the island of Onogoro-jima ('Spontaneously-congeal-island').

Upon this island the two deities descended. Shortly afterwards they desired to become husband and wife, though as a matter of fact they were brother and sister; but such a relationship in the East has never precluded marriage. These deities accordingly set up a pillar on the island. Izanagi walked round one way, and Izanami the other. When they met, Izanami said: "How delightful! I have met with a lovely youth." One would have thought that this naive remark would have pleased Izanagi; but it made him, extremely angry, and he retorted: "I am a man, and by that right should have spoken first. How is it that on the contrary thou, a woman, shouldst have been the first to speak? This is unlucky. Let us go round again." So it happened that the two deities started afresh. Once again they met, and this time Izanagi remarked: "How delightful! I have met a lovely maiden." Shortly after this very ingenuous proposal Izanagi and Izanami were married.

When Izanami had given birth to islands, seas, rivers, herbs, and trees, she and her lord consulted together, saying: "We have now produced the Great-Eight-Island country, with the mountains, rivers, herbs, and trees. Why should we not produce someone who shall be the Lord of the Universe?"

The wish of these deities was fulfilled, for in due season Amaterasu, the Sun Goddess, was born. She was known as 'Heaven-Illumine-of-Great-Deity', and was so extremely beautiful that her parents determined to send her up the Ladder of Heaven, and in the high sky above to cast for ever her glorious sunshine upon the earth.

Their next child was the Moon God, Tsuki-yumi. His silver radiance was not so fair as the golden effulgence of his sister, the Sun Goddess, but he was, nevertheless, deemed worthy to be her consort. So up the Ladder of Heaven climbed the Moon God. They soon quarrelled, and Amaterasu said: "Thou art a wicked deity. I must not see thee face to face." They were therefore separated by a day and night, and dwelt apart.

The next child of Izanagi and Izanami was Susanoo ('The Impetuous Male'). We shall return to Susanoo and his doings later on, and content ourselves for the present with confining our attention to his parents.

Izanami gave birth to the Fire God, Kagutsuchi. The birth of this child made her extremely ill. Izanagi knelt on the ground, bitterly weeping and lamenting. But his sorrow availed nothing, and Izanami crept away into the Land of Yomi (Hades).

Her lord, however, could not live without her, and he too went into the Land of Yomi. When he discovered her, she said regretfully: "My lord and husband, why is thy coming so late? I have already eaten of the cooking-furnace of Yomi. Nevertheless, I am about to lie down to rest. I pray thee do not look at me."

Izanagi, moved by curiosity, refused to fulfil her wish. It was dark in the Land of Yomi, so he secretly took out his many-toothed comb, broke off a piece, and lighted it. The sight that greeted him was ghastly and horrible in the extreme. His once beautiful wife had now become a swollen and festering creature. Eight varieties of Thunder Gods rested upon her. The Thunder of the Fire, Earth, and Mountain were all there leering upon him, and roaring with their great voices.

Izanagi grew frightened and disgusted, saying: "I have come unawares to a hideous and polluted land." His wife retorted: "Why didst thou not observe that which I charged thee? Now am I put to shame."

Izanami was so angry with her lord for ignoring her wish and breaking in upon her privacy that she sent the Eight Ugly Females of Yomi to pursue him. Izanagi drew his sword and fled down the dark regions of the Underworld. As he ran he took off his headdress, and flung it to the ground. It immediately became a bunch of grapes. When the Ugly Females saw it, they bent down and ate the luscious fruit. Izanami saw them pause, and deemed it wise to pursue her lord herself.

By this time Izanagi had reached the Even Pass of Yomi. Here he placed a huge rock, and eventually came face to face with Izanami. One would scarcely have thought that amid such exciting adventures Izanagi would have solemnly declared a divorce. But this is just what he did do. To this proposal his wife replied: "My dear lord and husband, if thou sayest so, I will strangle to death the people in one day." This plaintive and threatening speech in no way influenced

Izanagi, who readily replied that he would cause to be born in one day no less than fifteen hundred.

The above remark must have proved conclusive, for when we next hear of Izanagi he had escaped from the Land of Yomi, from an angry wife, and from the Eight Ugly Females. After his escape he was engaged in copious ablutions, by way of purification, from which numerous deities were born. We read in the *Nihon Shoki*: "After this, Izanagi, his divine task having been accomplished, and his spirit-career about to suffer a change, built himself an abode of gloom in the island of Ahaji, where he dwelt for ever in silence and concealment."

AMATERASU AND SUSANOO

Susanoo, or 'The Impetuous Male', was the brother of Amaterasu, the Sun Goddess. Now Susanoo was a very undesirable deity indeed, and he figured in the Realm of the Japanese Gods as a decidedly disturbing element. His character has been clearly drawn in the *Nihon Shoki*, more clearly perhaps than that of any other deity mentioned in these ancient records. Susanoo had a very bad temper, which often resulted in many cruel and ungenerous acts. Moreover, in spite of his long beard, he had a habit of continually weeping and wailing. Where a child in a tantrum would crush a toy to pieces, the Impetuous Male, when in a towering rage, and without a moment's warning, would wither the once fair greenery of mountains, and in addition bring many people to an untimely end.

His parents, Izanagi and Izanami, were much troubled by his doings, and, after consulting together, they decided to banish their unruly son to the Land of Yomi. Susa, however, had a word to say in the matter. He made the following petition, saying: "I will now obey thy instructions and proceed to the Nether-Land (Yomi). Therefore I wish for a short time to go to the Plain of High Heaven and meet with my elder sister (Amaterasu), after which I will go away for ever." This apparently harmless request was granted, and Susanoo ascended to Heaven. His departure occasioned a great commotion of the sea, and the hills and mountains groaned aloud.

Now Amaterasu heard these noises, and perceiving that they denoted the near approach of her wicked brother Susanoo, she said to herself: "Is my younger brother coming with good intentions? I think it must be his purpose to rob me of my kingdom. By the charge which our parents gave to their children, each of us has his own allotted limits. Why, therefore, does he reject the kingdom to which he should proceed, and make bold to come spying here?"

Amaterasu then prepared for warfare. She tied her hair into knots and hung jewels upon it, and round her wrists "an august string of five hundred Yasaka jewels." She presented a very formidable appearance when in addition she slung over her back "a thousand-arrow quiver and a five-hundred-arrow quiver," and protected her arms with pads to deaden the recoil of the bowstring. Having arrayed herself for deadly combat, she brandished her bow, grasped her sword-hilt, and stamped on the ground till she had made a hole sufficiently large to serve as a fortification.

All this elaborate and ingenious preparation was in vain. The Impetuous Male adopted the manner of a penitent. "From the beginning," he said, "my heart has not been black. But as, in obedience to the stern behest of our parents, I am about to depart for ever to the Nether-Land, how could I bear to depart without having seen face to face thee my elder sister? It is for this reason that I have traversed on foot the clouds and mists and have come hither from afar. I am surprised that my elder sister should, on the contrary, put on so stern a countenance."

Amaterasu regarded these remarks with a certain amount of suspicion. Susanoo's filial piety and Susanoo's cruelty were not easily to be reconciled. She thereupon resolved to test his sincerity by a remarkable proceeding we need not describe. Suffice it to say that for the time being the test proved the Impetuous Male's purity of heart and general sincerity towards his sister.

But Susanoo's good behaviour was a very short-lived affair indeed. It happened that Amaterasu had made a number of excellent rice-fields in Heaven. Some were narrow and some were long, and Amaterasu was justly proud of these rice-fields. No sooner had she sown the seed in the spring than Susanoo broke down the divisions between the plots, and in the autumn let loose a number of piebald colts.

One day when he saw his sister in the sacred Weaving Hall, weaving the garments of the Gods, he made a hole through the roof and flung down a flayed horse. Amaterasu was so frightened that she accidentally wounded herself with the shuttle. Extremely angry, she determined to leave her abode; so, gathering her shining robes about her, she crept down the blue sky, entered a cave, fastened it securely, and there dwelt in seclusion.

Now the world was in darkness, and the alternation of night and day was unknown. When this dreadful catastrophe had taken place the Eighty Myriads of Gods assembled together on the bank of the River of Heaven and discussed how they might best persuade Amaterasu to grace Heaven once more with her shining glory. No less a God than 'Thought-combining', after much profound reasoning, gathered together a number of singing-birds from the Eternal Land. After sundry divinations with a deer's leg-bone, over a fire of cherry-bark, the Gods made a number of tools, bellows, and forges. Stars were welded together to form a mirror, and jewellery and musical instruments were eventually fashioned.

When all these things had been duly accomplished the Eighty Myriads of Gods came down to the rock-cavern where the Sun Goddess lay concealed, and gave an elaborate entertainment. On the upper branches of the True Sakaki Tree they hung the precious jewels, and on the middle branches the mirror. From every side there was a great singing of birds, which was only the prelude to what followed. Now Uzume ('Heavenly-alarming-female') took in her hand a spear wreathed with Eulalia grass, and made a headdress of the True Sakaki Tree. Then she placed a tub upside down, and proceeded to dance in a very immodest manner, till the Eighty Myriad Gods began to roar with laughter.

Such extraordinary proceedings naturally awakened the curiosity of Amaterasu, and she peeped forth. Once more the world became golden with her presence. Once more she dwelt in the Plain of High Heaven, and Susanoo was duly chastised and banished to the Yomi Land.

SUSANOO AND THE SERPENT

Susanoo, having descended from Heaven, arrived at the river Hi, in the province of Idzumo. Here he was disturbed by a sound of weeping. It was so unusual to hear any other than himself weep that he went in search of the cause of the sorrow. He discovered an old man and an old woman. Between them was a young girl, whom they fondly caressed and gazed at with pitiful eyes, as if they were reluctantly bidding her a last farewell. When Susanoo asked the old couple who they were and why they lamented, the old man replied: "I am an Earthly Deity, and my name is Ashinadzuchi ('Foot-stroke-elder'). My wife's name is Tenadzuchi ('Hand-stroke-elder'). This girl is our daughter, and her name is Kushinadahime ('Wondrous-Inada-Princess'). The reason of our weeping is that formerly we had eight children, daughters; but they have been devoured year by year by an eight-forked serpent, and now the time approaches for this girl to be devoured. There is no means of escape for her, and therefore do we grieve exceedingly."

The Impetuous Male listened to this painful recital with profound attention, and, perceiving that the maiden was extremely beautiful, he offered to slay the eight-forked serpent if her parents would give her to him in marriage as a fitting reward for his services. This request was readily granted.

Susanoo now changed Kushinadahime into a many-toothed comb and stuck it in his hair. Then he bade the old couple brew a quantity of *sake*. When the *sake* was ready, he poured it into eight tubs, and awaited the coming of the dreadful monster.

Eventually the serpent came. It had eight heads, and the eyes were red, "like winter-cherry." Moreover it had eight tails, and firs and cypress-trees grew on its back. It was in length the space of eight hills and eight valleys. Its lumbering progress was necessarily slow, but finding the *sake*, each head eagerly drank the tempting beverage till the serpent became extremely drunk, and fell asleep. Then Susanoo, having little to fear, drew his ten-span sword and chopped the great monster into little pieces. When he struck one of the tails his weapon became notched, and bending down he discovered a sword called the Murakumo-no-Tsurugi. Perceiving it to be a divine sword, he gave it to the Gods of Heaven.

Having successfully accomplished his task, Susanoo converted the many-toothed comb into Kushinadahime again, and at length came to Suga, in the province of Idzumo, in order that he might celebrate his marriage. Here he composed the following verse:

> "Many clouds arise,
> On all sides a manifold fence,
> To receive within it the spouses,
> They form a manifold fence:
> Ah! that manifold fence!"

THE DIVINE MESSENGERS

Now at that time the Gods assembled in the High Plain of Heaven were aware of continual disturbances in the Central Land of Reed-Plains (Idzumo). We are told that "Plains, the rocks, tree-stems, and herbage have still the power of speech. At night they make a clamour like that of flames of fire; in the day-time they swarm up like flies in the fifth month." In addition certain deities made themselves objectionable. The Gods determined to put an end to these disturbances, and after a consultation Takamimusubi decided to send his grandchild Ninigi to govern the Central Land of Reed-Plains, to wipe out insurrection, and to bring peace and prosperity to the country. It was deemed necessary to send messengers to prepare the way in advance. The first envoy was Ama-no-ho; but as he spent three years in the country without reporting to the Gods, his son was sent in his place. He adopted the same course as his father, and defied the orders of the Heavenly Ones. The third messenger was Ame-waka ('Heaven-young-Prince'). He, too, was disloyal, in spite of his noble weapons, and instead of going about his duties he fell in love and took to wife Shita-teru-hime ('Lower-shine-Princess').

Now the assembled Gods grew angry at the long delay, and sent a pheasant down to ascertain what was going on in Idzumo. The pheasant perched on the top of a cassia-tree before Ame-waka's gate. When Ame-waka saw the bird he immediately shot it. The arrow went through the bird, rose into the Place of Gods, and was hurled back again, so that it killed the disloyal and idle Ame-waka.

The weeping of Lower-shine-Princess reached Heaven, for she loved her lord and failed to recognise in his sudden death the just vengeance of the Gods. She wept so loud and so pitifully that the Heavenly Ones heard her. A swift wind descended, and the body of Ame-waka floated up into the High Plain of Heaven. A mortuary house was made, in which the deceased was laid. Mr Frank Rinder writes: "For eight days and eight nights there was wailing and lamentation. The wild goose of the river, the heron, the kingfisher, the sparrow, and the pheasant mourned with a great mourning."

Now it happened that a friend of Ame-waka, Aji-shi-ki by name, heard the sad dirges proceeding from Heaven. He therefore offered his condolence. He so resembled the deceased that when Ame-waka's parents, relations, wife, and children saw him, they exclaimed: "Our lord is still alive!" This greatly angered Aji-shi-ki, and he drew his sword and cut down the mortuary house, so that it fell to the Earth and became the mountain of Moyama.

We are told that the glory of Aji-shi-ki was so effulgent that it illuminated the space of two hills and two valleys. Those assembled for the mourning celebrations uttered the following song:

> "Like the string of jewels
> Worn on the neck
> Of the Weaving-maiden,
> That dwells in Heaven:
> Oh! the lustre of the jewels
> Flung across two valleys
> From Aji-suki-taka-hiko-ne!

> "To the side-pool:
> The side-pool
> Of the rocky stream
> Whose narrows are crossed
> By the country wenches
> Afar from Heaven,
> Come hither, come hither!
> (The women are fair)
> And spread across thy net
> In the side-pool
> Of the rocky stream."

Two more Gods were sent to the Central Land of Reed-Plains, and these Gods were successful in their mission. They returned to Heaven with a favourable report, saying that all was now ready for the coming of the August Grandchild.

The Coming of the August Grandchild

Amaterasu presented her grandson Ninigi, or Prince Rice-Ear-Ruddy-Plenty, with many gifts. She gave him precious stones from the mountain-steps of Heaven, white crystal balls, and, most valuable gift of all, the divine sword that Susanoo had discovered in the serpent. She also gave him the star-mirror into which she had gazed when peeping out of her cave. Several deities accompanied Ninigi, including that lively maiden of mirth and dance Uzume, whose dancing, it will be remembered, so amused the Gods.

Ninigi and his companions had hardly broken through the clouds and arrived at the eight-forked road of Heaven, when they discovered, much to their alarm, a gigantic creature with large and brightly shining eyes. So formidable was his aspect that Ninigi and all his companions, except the merry and bewitching Uzume, started to turn back with intent to abandon their mission. But Uzume went up to the giant and demanded who it was that dared to impede their progress. The giant replied: "I am the Deity of the Field-paths. I come to pay my homage to Ninigi, and beg to have the honour to be his guide. Return to your master, O fair Uzume, and give him this message."

So Uzume returned and gave her message to the Gods, who had so ignominiously retreated. When they heard the good news they greatly rejoiced, burst once more through the clouds, rested on the Floating Bridge of Heaven, and finally reached the summit of Takachihi.

The August Grandchild, with the Deity of the Field-paths for guide, travelled from end to end of the kingdom over which he was to rule. When he had reached a particularly charming spot, he built a palace.

Ninigi was so pleased with the service the Deity of the Field-paths had rendered him that he gave that giant the merry Uzume to wife.

Ninigi, after having romantically rewarded his faithful guide, began to feel the stirring of love himself, when one day, while walking along the shore, he saw an extremely lovely maiden. "Who are you, most beautiful lady?" inquired Ninigi. She replied: "I am the daughter of the Great-Mountain-Possessor. My name is Ko-no-Hana, the Princess who makes the Flowers of the Trees Blossom."

Ninigi fell in love with Ko-no-Hana. He went with all haste

to her father, Oho-yama, and begged that he would favour him with his daughter's hand.

Oho-yama had an elder daughter, Iha-naga, Princess Long-as-the-Rocks. As her name implies, she was not at all beautiful; but her father desired that Ninigi's children should have life as eternal as the life of rocks. He therefore presented both his daughters to Ninigi, expressing the hope that the suitor's choice would fall upon Iha-naga. Just as Cinderella, and not her ugly sisters, is dear to children of our own country, so did Ninigi remain true to his choice, and would not even look upon Iha-naga. This neglect made Princess Long-as-the-Rocks extremely angry. She cried out, with more vehemence than modesty: "Had you chosen me, you and your children would have lived long in the land. Now that you have chosen my sister, you and yours will perish as quickly as the blossom of trees, as quickly as the bloom on my sister's cheek."

However, Ninigi and Ko-no-Hana lived happily together for some time; but one day jealousy came to Ninigi and robbed him of his peace of mind. He had no cause to be jealous, and Ko-no-Hana much resented his treatment. She retired to a little wooden hut, and set it on fire. From the flames came three baby boys. We need only concern ourselves with two of them – Hoderi ('Fire-shine') and Hoori ('Fire-fade'). Hoori, as we shall see later on, was the grandfather of the first Mikado of Japan.

IN THE PALACE OF THE SEA GOD

Hoderi **was a great fisherman**, while his younger brother, Hoori, was an accomplished hunter. One day they exclaimed: "Let us for a trial exchange gifts." This they did, but the elder brother, who could catch fish to some purpose, came home without any spoil when he went a-hunting. He therefore returned the bow and arrows, and asked his younger brother for the fish-hook. Now it so happened that Hoori had lost his brother's fish-hook. The generous offer of a new hook to take the place of the old one was scornfully refused. He also refused to accept a heaped-up tray of fish-hooks. To this offer the elder brother replied: "These are not my old fish-hook: though they are many, I will not take them." Now Hoori was sore troubled by his brother's harshness, so he went down to the sea-shore and there gave way to his grief. A kind old man by the name of Shiko-tsutsu no Oji ('Salt-sea-elder') said: "Why dost thou grieve here?" When the sad tale was told, the old man replied: "Grieve no more. I will arrange this matter for thee."

True to his word, the old man made a basket, set Hoori in it, and then sank it in the sea. After descending deep down in the water Hoori came to a pleasant strand rich with all manner of fantastic seaweed. Here he abandoned the basket and eventually arrived at the Palace of the Sea God.

Now this palace was extremely imposing. It had battlements and turrets and stately towers. A well stood at the gate, and over the well there was a cassia-tree. Here Hoori loitered in the pleasant shade. He had not stood there long before a beautiful woman appeared. As she was about to draw water, she raised her eyes, saw the stranger, and immediately returned, with much alarm, to tell her mother and father what she had seen.

The God of the Sea, when he had heard the news, "prepared an eightfold cushion" and led the stranger in, asking his visitor why he had been honoured by his presence. When Hoori explained the sad loss of his brother's fish-hook the Sea God assembled all the fishes of his kingdom, "broad of fin and narrow of fin." And when the thousands upon thousands of fishes were assembled, the Sea God asked them if they knew anything about the missing fish-hook. "We know not," answered the fishes. "Only the Red-woman (the *tai*) has had a sore mouth for some time past, and has not come." She was accordingly summoned, and on her mouth being opened the lost fish-hook was discovered.

Hoori then took to wife the Sea God's daughter, Toyotama ('Rich-jewel'), and they dwelt together in the palace under the sea. For three years all went well, but after a time Hoori hungered for a sight of his own country, and possibly he may have remembered that he had yet to restore the fish-hook to his elder brother. These not unnatural feelings troubled the heart of the loving Toyotama, and she went to her father and told him of her sorrow. But the Sea God, who was always urbane and courteous, in no way resented his son-in-law's behaviour. On the contrary he gave him the fish-hook, saying: "When thou givest this fish-hook to thy elder brother, before giving it to him, call to it secretly, and say, 'A poor hook!'" He also presented Hoori with the Jewel of the Flowing Tide and the Jewel of the Ebbing Tide, saying: "If thou dost dip the Tide-flowing Jewel, the tide will suddenly flow, and therewithal thou shalt drown thine elder brother. But in case thy elder brother should repent and beg forgiveness, if, on the contrary, thou dip the Tide-ebbing

Jewel, the tide will spontaneously ebb, and therewithal thou shalt save him. If thou harass him in this way thy elder brother will of his own accord render submission."

Just before Hoori was about to depart his wife came to him and told him that she was soon to give him a child. Said she: "On a day when the winds and waves are raging I will surely come forth to the seashore. Build for me a house, and await me there."

Hoderi and Hoori Reconciled

When Hoori reached his own home he found his elder brother, who admitted his offence and begged for forgiveness, which was readily granted.

Toyotama and her younger sister bravely confronted the winds and waves, and came to the sea-shore. There Hoori had built a hut roofed with cormorant feathers, and there in due season she gave birth to a son. When Toyotama had blessed her lord with offspring, she turned into a dragon and slipped back into the sea. Hoori's son married his aunt, and was the father of four children, one of whom was Kamu-Yamato-Iware-Biko, who is said to have been the first human Emperor of Japan, and is now known as Jimmu Tenno.

KWANNON AND THE DEER

An old hermit named Saion Zenji took up his abode on Mount Nariai in order that he might be able to gaze upon the beauty of Ama-no-Hashidate, a narrow fir-clad promontory dividing Lake Iwataki and Miyazu Bay. Ama-no-Hashidate is still regarded as one of the *Sankei*, or 'Three Great Sights', of Japan, and still Mount Nariai is considered the best spot from which to view this charming scene. On Mount Nariai this gentle and holy recluse erected a little shrine to Kwannon not far from a solitary pine-tree. He spent his happy days in looking upon Ama-no-Hashidate and in chanting the Buddhist Scriptures, and his charming disposition and holy ways were much appreciated by the people who came to pray at the little shrine he had so lovingly erected for his own joy and for the joy of others.

The hermit's abode, delightful enough in mild and sunny weather, was dreary in the winter-time, for when it snowed the good old man was cut off from human intercourse. On one occasion the snow fell so heavily that it was piled up in some places to a height of twenty feet.

Day after day the severe weather continued, and at last the poor old hermit found that he had no food of any kind. Chancing to look out one morning, he saw that a deer was lying dead in the snow. As he gazed upon the poor creature, which had been frozen to death, he remembered that it was unlawful in the sight of Kwannon to eat the flesh of animals; but on thinking over the matter more carefully it seemed to him that he could do more good to his fellow creatures by partaking of this deer than by observing the strict letter of the law and allowing himself to starve in sight of plenty.

When Saion Zenji had come to this wise decision he went out and cut off a piece of venison, cooked it, and ate half, with many prayers of thanksgiving for his deliverance. The rest of the venison he left in his cooking-pot.

Eventually the snow melted, and several folk hastily wended their way from the neighbouring village, and ascended Mount Nariai, expecting to see that their good and much-loved hermit had forever passed away from this world. As they approached the shrine, however, they were rejoiced to hear the old man chanting, in a clear and ringing voice, the sacred Buddhist Scriptures.

The folk from the village gathered about the hermit while he narrated the story of his deliverance. When, out of curiosity, they chanced to peep into his cooking-pot, they saw, to their utter amazement, that it contained no venison, but a piece of wood covered with gold foil. Still wondering what it all meant, they looked upon the image of Kwannon in the little shrine, and found that a piece had been cut from her loins, and when they inserted the piece of wood the wound was healed. Then it was that the old hermit and the folk gathered about him realised that the deer had been none other than Kwannon, who, in her boundless love and tender mercy, had made a sacrifice of her own divine flesh.

BENTEN AND THE DRAGON

In a certain cave there lived a formidable dragon, which devoured the children of the village of Koshigoe. In the sixth century Benten was determined to put a stop to this monster's unseemly behaviour, and having caused a great earthquake she hovered in the clouds over the cave where the dread dragon had taken up his abode.

Benten then descended from the clouds, entered the cavern, married the dragon, and was thus able, through her good influence, to put an end to the slaughter of little children. With the coming of Benten there arose from the sea the famous Island of Enoshima, which has remained to this day sacred to the Goddess of the Sea.

DAIKOKU'S RAT

According to a certain old legend, the Buddhist Gods grew jealous of Daikoku. They consulted together, and finally decided that they would get rid of the too popular Daikoku, to whom the Japanese offered prayers and incense. Emma-O, the Lord of the Dead, promised to send his most cunning and clever *oni*, Shiro, who, he said, would have no difficulty in conquering the God of Wealth.

Shiro, guided by a sparrow, went to Daikoku's castle, but though he hunted high and low he could not find its owner. Finally Shiro discovered a large storehouse, in which he saw the God of Wealth seated. Daikoku called his Rat and bade him find out who it was who dared to disturb him. When the Rat saw Shiro he ran into the garden and brought back a branch of holly, with which he drove the *oni* away, and Daikoku remains to this day one of the most popular of the Japanese Gods. This incident is said to be the origin of the New Year's Eve charm, consisting of a holly leaf and a skewer, or a sprig of holly fixed in the lintel of the door of a house to prevent the return of the *oni*.

THE CHILD OF THE THUNDER GOD

Near Mount Hakuzan there once lived a very poor farmer named Bimbo. His plot of land was extremely small, and though he worked upon it from dawn till sunset he had great difficulty in growing sufficient rice for himself and his wife.

One day, after a protracted drought, Bimbo dismally surveyed his dried-up rice sprouts. As he thus stood fearing starvation in the near future, rain suddenly descended, accompanied by loud claps of thunder. Just as Bimbo was about to take shelter from the storm he was nearly blinded by a vivid flash of lightning, and he prayed fervently to Buddha for protection. When he had done so he looked about him, and to his amazement saw a little baby boy laughing and crooning as he lay in the grass.

Bimbo took the infant in his arms, and gently carried him to his humble dwelling, where his wife greeted him with surprise and pleasure. The child was called Raitaro, the Child of Thunder, and lived with his foster-parents a happy and dutiful boy. He never played with other children, for he loved to roam in the fields, to watch the stream and the swift flight of clouds overhead.

With the coming of Raitaro there came prosperity to Bimbo, for Raitaro could beckon to clouds and bid them throw down their rain-drops only on his foster-father's field.

When Raitaro had grown into a handsome youth of eighteen he once again thanked Bimbo and his wife for all they had done for him, and told them that he must now bid farewell to his benefactors.

Almost before the youth had finished speaking, he suddenly turned into a small white dragon, lingered a moment, and then flew away.

The old couple ran to the door. As the white dragon ascended into the sky it grew bigger and bigger, till it was hidden behind a great cloud.

When Bimbo and his wife died a white dragon was carved upon their tomb in memory of Raitaro, the Child of Thunder.

SHOKURO AND THE THUNDER GOD

Shokuro, in order to stand well with Tom, the magistrate of his district, promised him that he would catch the Thunder God. "If," said Shokuro, "I were to tie a human navel to the end of a kite, and fly it during a stormy day, I should be sure to catch Raiden, for the Thunder God would not be able to resist such a repast. The most difficult part of the whole business is to secure the meal."

With this scheme in view Shokuro set out upon a journey in quest of food for the Thunder God. On reaching a wood he chanced to see a beautiful woman named Chiyo. The ambitious Shokuro, without the least compunction, killed the maid, and, having secured his object, flung her corpse into a deep ditch. He then proceeded on his way with a light heart.

Raiden, while sitting on a cloud, happened to notice the woman's body lying in a ditch. He descended quickly, and, being fascinated by the beauty of Chiyo, he took from his mouth a navel, restored her to life, and together they flew away into the sky.

Some days later Shokuro was out hunting for the Thunder God, his kite, with its gruesome relic, soaring high over the trees as it flew hither and thither in a strong wind. Chiyo saw the kite, and descended nearer and nearer to the earth. At last she held it in her hands and saw what was attached. Filled with indignation, she looked down in order to see who was flying the kite, and was much astonished to recognise her murderer. At this juncture Raiden descended in a rage, only to receive severe chastisement at the hands of Shokuro, who then made his peace with Chiyo, and afterwards became a famous man in the village. Truly an astonishing story!

HEROES, WARRIORS
& ADVENTURE

Early heroes and warriors are always regarded as minor divinities, and the very nature of Shinto, associated with ancestor worship, has enriched those of Japan with many a fascinating legend. For strength, skill, endurance, and a happy knack of overcoming all manner of difficulties by a subtle form of quick-witted enterprise, the Japanese hero must necessarily take a high position among the famous warriors of other countries. There is something eminently chivalrous about the heroes of Japan. The most valiant men are those who champion the cause of the weak or redress evil and tyranny of every kind, and we trace in the Japanese hero, who is very far from being a crude swashbuckler, these most excellent qualities. He is not always above criticism, and sometimes we find in him a touch of cunning, but such a characteristic is extremely rare, and very far from being a national trait. An innate love of poetry and the beautiful has had its refining influence upon the Japanese hero, with the result that his strength is combined with gentleness.

YORIMASA

A long time ago a certain Emperor became seriously ill. He was unable to sleep at night owing to a most horrible and unaccountable noise he heard proceeding from the roof of the palace, called the Purple Hall of the North Star. A number of his courtiers decided to lie in wait for this strange nocturnal visitor. As soon as the sun set they noticed that a dark cloud crept from the eastern horizon, and alighted on the roof of the august palace. Those who waited in the imperial bed-chamber heard extraordinary scratching sounds, as if what had at first appeared to be a cloud had suddenly changed into a beast with gigantic and powerful claws. Night after night this terrible visitant came, and night after night the Emperor grew worse. He at last became so ill that it was obvious to all those in attendance upon him that unless something could be done to destroy this monster the Emperor would certainly die.

At last it was decided that Yorimasa was the one knight in the kingdom valiant enough to relieve his Majesty of these terrible hauntings. Yorimasa accordingly made elaborate preparations for the fray. He took his best bow and steel-headed arrows, donned his armour, over which he wore a hunting-dress, and a ceremonial cap instead of his usual helmet.

At sunset he lay in concealment outside the palace. While he thus waited thunder crashed overhead, lightning blazed in the sky, and the wind shrieked like a pack of wild demons. But Yorimasa was a brave man, and the fury of the elements in no way daunted him. When midnight came he saw a black cloud rush through the sky and rest upon the roof of the palace. At the north-east corner it stopped. Once more the lightning flashed in the sky, and this time he saw the gleaming eyes of a large animal. Noting the exact position of this strange monster, he pulled at his bow till it became as round as the full moon. In another moment his steel-headed arrow hit its mark. There was an awful roar of anger, and then a heavy thud as the huge monster rolled from the palace roof to the ground.

Yorimasa and his retainer ran forward and despatched the fearful creature they saw before them. This evil monster of the night was as large as a horse. It had the head of an ape, and the body and claws were like those of a tiger, with a serpent's tail, wings of a bird, and the scales of a dragon.

It was no wonder that the Emperor gave orders that the skin of this monster should be kept for all time as a curiosity in the Imperial treasure-house. From the very moment the creature died the Emperor's health rapidly improved, and Yorimasa was rewarded for his services by being presented with a sword called Shishi-wo, which means "the King of Lions." He was also promoted at Court, and finally married the Lady Ayame, the most beautiful of ladies-in-waiting at the Imperial Court.

YOSHITSUNE AND BENKEI

Yoshitsune's father, Yoshitomo, had been killed in a great battle with the Taira. At that time the Taira clan was all-powerful, and its cruel leader, Kiyomori, did all he could to destroy Yoshitomo's children. But the mother of these children, Tokiwa, fled into hiding, taking her little ones with her. With characteristic Japanese fortitude, she finally consented to become the wife of the hated Kiyomori. She did so because it was the only way to save the lives of her children. She was allowed to keep Yoshitsune with her, and she daily whispered to him: "Remember thy father, Minamoto Yoshitomo! Grow strong and avenge his death, for he died at the hands of the Taira!"

When Yoshitsune was seven years of age he was sent to a monastery to be brought up as a monk. Though diligent in his studies, the young boy ever treasured in his heart the dauntless words of his brave, self-sacrificing mother. They stirred and quickened him to action. He used to go to a certain valley, where he would flourish his little wooden sword, and, singing fragments of war-songs, hit out at rocks and stones, desiring that he might one day become a great warrior, and right the wrongs so heavily heaped upon his family by the Taira clan.

One night, while thus engaged, he was startled by a great thunderstorm, and saw before him a mighty giant with a long red nose and enormous glaring eyes, bird-like claws, and feathered wings. Bravely standing his ground, Yoshitsune inquired who this giant might be, and was informed that he was King of the Tengu – that is, King of the elves of the mountains, sprightly little beings who were frequently engaged in all manner of fantastic tricks.

The King of the Tengu was very kindly disposed towards Yoshitsune. He explained that he admired his perseverance, and told him that he had appeared upon the scene with the meritorious intention of teaching him all that was to be learnt in the art of swordsmanship. The lessons progressed in a most satisfactory manner, and it was not long before Yoshitsune could vanquish as many as twenty small *tengu*, and this extreme agility stood Yoshitsune in very good stead, as we shall see later on in the story.

Now when Yoshitsune was fifteen years old he heard that there lived on Mount Hiei a very wild *bonze* (priest) by the name of Benkei. Benkei had for some time waylaid knights who happened to cross the Gojo Bridge of Kyoto. His idea was to obtain a thousand swords, and he was so brave, although such a rascal, that he had won from knights no less than nine hundred and ninety-nine swords by his lawless behaviour. When the news of these doings reached the ears of Yoshitsune he determined to put the teaching of the King of the Tengu to good use and slay this Benkei, and so put an end to one who had become a terror in the land.

One evening Yoshitsune started out, and, in order to establish the manner and bearing of absolute indifference, he played upon his flute till he came to the Gojo Bridge. Presently he saw coming towards him a gigantic man clad in black armour, who was none other than Benkei. When Benkei saw the youth he considered it to be beneath his dignity to attack what appeared to him to be a mere weakling, a dreamer who could play excellently, and no doubt write a pretty poem about the moon, which was then shining in the sky, but one who was in no way a warrior. This affront naturally angered Yoshitsune, and he suddenly kicked Benkei's halberd out of his hand.

Yoshitsune and Benkei Fight

Benkei gave a growl of rage, and cut about indiscriminately with his weapon. But the sprightliness of the *tengu* teaching favoured Yoshitsune. He jumped from side to side, from the front to the rear, and from the rear to the front again, mocking the giant with many a jest and many a peal of ringing laughter. Round and round went Benkei's weapon, always striking either the air or the ground, and ever missing its adversary.

At last Benkei grew weary, and once again Yoshitsune knocked the halberd out of the giant's hand. In trying to regain his weapon Yoshitsune tripped him up, so that he stumbled upon his hands and knees, and the hero, with a cry of triumph, mounted upon the now four-legged Benkei. The giant was utterly amazed at his defeat, and when he was told that the victor was none other than the son of Lord Yoshitomo he not only took his defeat in a manly fashion, but begged that he might henceforth become a retainer of the young conqueror.

From this time we find the names of Yoshitsune and Benkei linked together, and in all the stories of warriors, whether in Japan or elsewhere, never was there a more valiant and harmonious union of strength and friendship. We hear of them winning numerous victories over the Taira, finally driving them to the sea, where they perished at Dan-no-ura.

We get one more glimpse of Dan-no-ura from a legendary point of view. Yoshitsune and his faithful henchman arranged to cross in a ship from the province of Settsu to Saikoku. When they reached Dan-no-ura a great storm arose. Mysterious noises came from the towering waves, a far-away echo of the din of battle, of the rushing of ships and the whirling of arrows, of the footfall of a thousand men. Louder and louder the noise grew, and from the lashing crests of the waves there arose a ghostly company of the Taira clan. Their armour was torn and blood-stained, and they thrust out their vaporous arms and tried to stop the boat in which Yoshitsune and Benkei sailed. It was a ghostly reminiscence of the battle of Dan-no-ura, when the Taira had suffered a terrible and permanent defeat. Yoshitsune, when he saw this great phantom host, cried out for revenge even upon the ghosts of the Taira dead; but Benkei, always shrewd and circumspect, bade his master lay aside the sword, and took out a rosary and recited a number of Buddhist prayers. Peace came to the great company of ghosts, the wailing ceased, and gradually they faded into the sea which now became calm.

Legend tells us that fishermen still see from time to time ghostly armies come out of the sea and wail and shake their long arms. They explain that the crabs with dorsal markings are the wraiths of the Taira warriors. Later on we shall introduce another legend relating to these unfortunate ghosts, who seem never to tire of haunting the scene of their defeat.

THE GOBLIN OF OEYAMA

In the reign of the Emperor Ichijo many dreadful stories were current in Kyoto in regard to a demon that lived on Mount Oye. This demon could assume many forms. Sometimes appearing as a human being, he would steal into Kyoto, and leave many a home destitute of well-loved sons and daughters.

These young men and women he took back to his mountain stronghold, and, sad to narrate, after making sport of them, he and his goblin companions made a great feast and devoured these poor young people. Even the sacred Court was not exempt from these awful happenings, and one day Kimitaka lost his beautiful daughter. She had been snatched away by the Goblin King, Shutendoji.

When this sad news reached the ears of the Emperor he called his council together and consulted how they might slay this dreadful creature. His ministers informed his Majesty that Raiko was a doughty knight, and advised that he should be sent with certain companions on this perilous but worthy adventure.

Raiko accordingly chose five companions and told them what had been ordained, and how they were to set out upon an adventurous journey, and finally to slay the King of the Goblins. He explained that subtlety of action was most essential if they wished for success in their enterprise, and that it would be well to go disguised as mountain priests, and to carry their armour and weapons on their backs, carefully concealed in unsuspicious-looking knapsacks. Before starting upon their journey two of the knights went to pray at the temple of Hachiman, the God of War, two at the shrine of Kwannon, the Goddess of Mercy, and two at the temple of Gongen.

When these knights had prayed for a blessing upon their undertaking they set out upon their journey, and in due time reached the province of Tamba, and saw immediately in front of them Mount Oye. The Goblin had certainly chosen the most formidable of mountains. Mighty rocks and great dark forests obstructed their path in every direction, while almost bottomless chasms appeared when least expected.

Just when these brave knights were beginning to feel just a little disheartened, three old men suddenly appeared before them. At first these newcomers were regarded with suspicion, but later on with the utmost friendliness and thankfulness. These old men were none other than the deities to whom the knights had prayed before setting out upon their journey. The old men presented Raiko with a jar of magical *sake* called Shimben-Kidoku-Shu ('a cordial for men, but poison for goblins'), advising him that he should by strategy get Shutendoji to drink it, whereupon he would immediately become paralysed and prove an easy victim for the final despatch. No sooner had these old men given the magical *sake* and proffered their valuable advice than a miraculous light shone round them, and they vanished into the clouds.

Once again Raiko and his knights, much cheered by what had happened, continued to ascend the mountain. Coming to a stream, they noticed a beautiful woman washing a blood-stained garment in the running water. She was weeping bitterly, and wiped away her tears with the long sleeve of her *kimono*. Upon Raiko asking who she was, she informed him that she was a princess, and one of the miserable captives of the Goblin King. When she was told that it was none other than the great Raiko who stood before her, and that he and his knights had come to kill the vile creature of that mountain, she was overcome with joy, and finally led the little band to a great palace of black iron, satisfying the sentinels by telling them that her followers were poor mountain priests who sought temporary shelter.

After passing through long corridors Raiko and his knights found themselves in a mighty hall. At one end sat the awful Goblin King. He was of gigantic stature, with bright red skin and a mass of white hair. When Raiko meekly informed him who they were, the Goblin King, concealing his mirth, bade them be seated and join the feast that was about to be set before them. Thereupon he clapped his red hands together, and immediately many beautiful damsels came running in with an abundance of food and drink, and as Raiko watched these women he knew that they had once lived in happy homes in Kyoto.

When the feast was in full progress Raiko took out the jar of magic *sake*, and politely begged the Goblin King to try it. The monster, without demur or suspicion, drank some of the *sake*, and found it so good that he asked for a second cup. All the goblins partook of the magic wine, and while they were drinking Raiko and his companions danced.

The power of this magical drink soon began to work. The Goblin King became drowsy, till finally he and his fellow goblins fell fast asleep. Then Raiko sprang to his feet, and he and his knights rapidly donned their armour and prepared for war. Once more the three deities appeared before them, and said to Raiko: "We have tied the hands and feet of the Demon fast, so you have nothing to fear. While your knights cut off his limbs do you cut off his head: then kill the rest of the *oni* (evil spirits) and your work will be done." Then these divine beings suddenly disappeared.

Raiko Slays the Goblin

Raiko and his knights, with their swords drawn, cautiously approached the sleeping Goblin King. With a mighty sweep

Raiko's weapon came crashing down on the Goblin's neck.
No sooner was the head severed than it shot up into the air,
and smoke and fire poured out from the nostrils, scorching the
valiant Raiko. Once more he struck out with his sword, and
this time the horrible head fell to the floor, and never moved
again. It was not long before these brave knights despatched
the Demon's followers also.

There was a joyful exit from the great iron palace. Raiko's
five knights carried the monster head of the Goblin King,
and this grim spectacle was followed by a company of happy
maidens released at last from their horrible confinement, and
eager to walk once again in the streets of Kyoto.

THE GOBLIN SPIDER

Some time after the incident mentioned in the previous
legend had taken place the brave Raiko became seriously
ill, and was obliged to keep to his room. At about midnight
a little boy always brought him some medicine. This boy was
unknown to Raiko, but as he kept so many servants it did
not at first awaken suspicion. Raiko grew worse instead of
better, and always worse immediately after he had taken the
medicine, so he began to think that some supernatural force
was the cause of his illness.

At last Raiko asked his head servant if he knew anything
about the boy who came to him at midnight. Neither the
head servant nor anyone else seemed to know anything about
him. By this time Raiko's suspicions were fully awakened, and
he determined to go carefully into the matter.

When the small boy came again at midnight, instead of taking the medicine, Raiko threw the cup at his head, and drawing his sword attempted to kill him. A sharp cry of pain rang through the room, but as the boy was flying from the apartment he threw something at Raiko. It spread outward into a huge white sticky web, which clung so tightly to Raiko that he could hardly move. No sooner had he cut the web through with his sword than another enveloped him. Raiko then called for assistance, and his chief retainer met the miscreant in one of the corridors and stopped his further progress with extended sword. The Goblin threw a web over him too. When he at last managed to extricate himself and was able to run into his master's room, he saw that Raiko had also been the victim of the Goblin Spider.

The Goblin Spider was eventually discovered in a cave writhing with pain, blood flowing from a sword-cut on the head. He was instantly killed, and with his death there passed away the evil influence that had caused Raiko's serious illness. From that hour the hero regained his health and strength, and a sumptuous banquet was prepared in honour of the happy event.

Another Version

There is another version of this legend, written by Kenko Hoshi, which differs so widely in many of its details from the one we have already given that it almost amounts to a new story altogether. To dispense with this version would be to rob the legend of its most sinister aspect, which has not hitherto been accessible to the general reader.

On one occasion Raiko left Kyoto with Tsuna, the most worthy of his retainers. As they were crossing the plain of

Rendai they saw a skull rise in the air, and fly before them as if driven by the wind, until it finally disappeared at a place called Kagura ga Oka.

Raiko and his retainer had no sooner noticed the disappearance of the skull than they perceived before them a mansion in ruins. Raiko entered this dilapidated building, and saw an old woman of strange aspect. She was dressed in white, and had white hair; she opened her eyes with a small stick, and the upper eyelids fell back over her head like a hat; then she used the rod to open her mouth, and let her breast fall forward upon her knees. Thus she addressed the astonished Raiko:

"I am two hundred and ninety years old. I serve nine masters, and the house in which you stand is haunted by demons."

Having listened to these words, Raiko walked into the kitchen, and, catching a glimpse of the sky, he perceived that a great storm was brewing. As he stood watching the dark clouds gather he heard a sound of ghostly footsteps, and there crowded into the room a great company of goblins. Nor were these the only supernatural creatures which Raiko encountered, for presently he saw a being dressed like a nun. Her very small body was naked to the waist, her face was two feet in length, and her arms were white as snow and thin as threads. For a moment this dreadful creature laughed, and then vanished like a mist.

Raiko heard the welcome sound of a cock crowing, and imagined that the ghostly visitors would trouble him no more; but once again he heard footsteps, and this time he saw no hideous hag, but a lovely woman, more graceful than the willow branches as they wave in the breeze. As he gazed upon this lovely maiden his eyes became blinded for a moment on account of her radiant beauty. Before he could recover his sight he found himself enveloped in countless cobwebs. He struck at her with his sword, when she disappeared, and he found that he had but cut through the planks of the floor, and broken the foundation-stone beneath.

At this moment Tsuna joined his master, and they perceived that the sword was covered with *white* blood, and that the point had been broken in the conflict.

After much search Raiko and his retainer discovered a den in which they saw a monster with many legs and a head of enormous size covered with downy hair. Its mighty eyes shone like the sun and moon, as it groaned aloud: "I am sick and in pain!"

As Raiko and Tsuna drew near they recognised the broken sword-point projecting from the monster. The heroes then dragged the creature out of its den and cut off its head. Out of the deep wound in the creature's stomach gushed nineteen hundred and ninety skulls, and in addition many spiders as large as children. Raiko and his follower realised that the monster before them was none other than the Mountain Spider. When they cut open the great carcass they discovered, within the entrails, the ghostly remains of many human corpses.

THE OGRE OF RASHOMON, OR WATANABE DEFEATS THE IBARAKI-DOJI

Long, long ago in Kyoto, the people of the city were terrified by accounts of a dreadful ogre, who, it was said, haunted the Gate of Rashomon at twilight and seized whoever passed by. The missing victims were never seen again, so it was whispered that the ogre was a horrible cannibal, who not only killed the unhappy victims but ate them also. Now everybody in the town and neighbourhood was in great fear, and no one durst venture out after sunset near the Gate of Rashomon.

Now at this time there lived in Kyoto a general named Raiko, who had made himself famous for his brave deeds. Some time before this he made the country ring with his name, for he had attacked Oeyama, where a band of ogres lived with their chief, who instead of wine drank the blood of human beings. He had routed them all and cut off the head of the chief monster.

This brave warrior was always followed by a band of faithful knights. In this band there were five knights of great valour. One evening as the five knights sat at a feast quaffing *sake* in their rice bowls and eating all kinds of fish, raw, and stewed, and broiled, and toasting each other's healths and exploits, the first knight, Hojo, said to the others:

"Have you all heard the rumour that every evening after sunset there comes an ogre to the Gate of Rashomon, and that he seizes all who pass by?"

The second knight, Watanabe, answered him, saying:

"Do not talk such nonsense! All the ogres were killed by our chief Raiko at Oeyama! It cannot be true, because even if any ogres did escape from that great killing they would not dare to show themselves in this city, for they know that our brave master would at once attack them if he knew that any of them were still alive!"

"Then do you disbelieve what I say, and think that I am telling you a falsehood?"

"No, I do not think that you are telling a lie," said Watanabe; "but you have heard some old woman's story which is not worth believing."

"Then the best plan is to prove what I say, by going there yourself and finding out yourself whether it is true or not," said Hojo.

Watanabe, the second knight, could not bear the thought that his companion should believe he was afraid, so he answered quickly:

"Of course, I will go at once and find out for myself!"

So Watanabe at once got ready to go – he buckled on his long sword and put on a coat of armor, and tied on his large helmet. When he was ready to start he said to the others:

"Give me something so that I can prove I have been there!"

Then one of the men got a roll of writing paper and his box of Indian ink and brushes, and the four comrades wrote their names on a piece of paper.

"I will take this," said Watanabe, "and put it on the Gate of Rashomon, so tomorrow morning will you all go and look at it? I may be able to catch an ogre or two by then!" and he mounted his horse and rode off gallantly.

It was a very dark night, and there was neither moon nor star to light Watanabe on his way. To make the darkness worse a storm came on, the rain fell heavily and the wind howled like wolves in the mountains. Any ordinary man would have trembled at the thought of going out of doors, but Watanabe was a brave warrior and dauntless, and his honour and word were at stake, so he sped on into the night, while his companions listened to the sound of his horse's hoofs dying away in the distance, then shut the sliding shutters close and gathered round the charcoal fire and wondered what would happen – and whether their comrade would encounter one of those horrible Oni.

At last Watanabe reached the Gate of Rashomon, but peer as he might through the darkness he could see no sign of an ogre.

"It is just as I thought," said Watanabe to himself; "there are certainly no ogres here; it is only an old woman's story. I will stick this paper on the gate so that the others can see I have been here when they come tomorrow, and then I will take my way home and laugh at them all."

He fastened the piece of paper, signed by all his four companions, on the gate, and then turned his horse's head towards home.

As he did so he became aware that someone was behind him, and at the same time a voice called out to him to wait. Then his helmet was seized from the back. "Who are you?" said Watanabe fearlessly. He then put out his hand and groped around to find out who or what it was that held him by the helmet. As he did so he touched something that felt like an arm – it was covered with hair and as big round as the trunk of a tree!

Watanabe knew at once that this was the arm of an ogre, so he drew his sword and cut at it fiercely.

There was a loud yell of pain, and then the ogre dashed in front of the warrior.

Watanabe's eyes grew large with wonder, for he saw that the ogre was taller than the great gate, his eyes were flashing like mirrors in the sunlight, and his huge mouth was wide open, and as the monster breathed, flames of fire shot out of his mouth.

The ogre thought to terrify his foe, but Watanabe never flinched. He attacked the ogre with all his strength, and thus they fought face to face for a long time. At last the ogre, finding that he could neither frighten nor beat Watanabe and that he might himself be beaten, took to flight. But Watanabe, determined not to let the monster escape, put spurs to his horse and gave chase.

But though the knight rode very fast the ogre ran faster, and to his disappointment he found himself unable to overtake the monster, who was gradually lost to sight.

Watanabe returned to the gate where the fierce fight had taken place, and got down from his horse. As he did so he stumbled upon something lying on the ground.

Stooping to pick it up he found that it was one of the ogre's huge arms which he must have slashed off in the fight. His joy was great at having secured such a prize, for this was the best of all proofs of his adventure with the ogre. So he took it up carefully and carried it home as a trophy of his victory.

When he got back, he showed the arm to his comrades, who one and all called him the hero of their band and gave him a great feast. His wonderful deed was soon noised abroad in Kyoto, and people from far and near came to see the ogre's arm.

Watanabe now began to grow uneasy as to how he should keep the arm in safety, for he knew that the ogre to whom it belonged was still alive. He felt sure that one day or other, as soon as the ogre got over his scare, he would come to try to get his arm back again. Watanabe therefore had a box made of the strongest wood and banded with iron. In this he placed the arm, and then he sealed down the heavy lid, refusing to open it for anyone. He kept the box in his own room and took charge of it himself, never allowing it out of his sight.

Now one night he heard someone knocking at the porch, asking for admittance.

When the servant went to the door to see who it was, there was only an old woman, very respectable in appearance. On being asked who she was and what was her business, the old woman replied with a smile that she had been nurse to the master of the house when he was a little baby. If the lord of the house were at home she begged to be allowed to see him.

The servant left the old woman at the door and went to tell his master that his old nurse had come to see him. Watanabe thought it strange that she should come at that time of night, but at the thought of his old nurse, who had been like a foster-mother to him and whom he had not seen for a long time, a very tender feeling sprang up for her in his heart. He ordered the servant to show her in.

The old woman was ushered into the room, and after the customary bows and greetings were over, she said:

"Master, the report of your brave fight with the ogre at the Gate of Rashomon is so widely known that even your poor old nurse has heard of it. Is it really true, what everyone says, that you cut off one of the ogre's arms? If you did, your deed is highly to be praised!"

"I was very disappointed," said Watanabe, "that I was not able take the monster captive, which was what I wished to do, instead of only cutting off an arm!"

"I am very proud to think," answered the old woman, "that my master was so brave as to dare to cut off an ogre's arm. There is nothing that can be compared to your courage.

Before I die it is the great wish of my life to see this arm," she added pleadingly.

"No," said Watanabe, "I am sorry, but I cannot grant your request."

"But why?" asked the old woman.

"Because," replied Watanabe, "ogres are very revengeful creatures, and if I open the box there is no telling but that the ogre may suddenly appear and carry off his arm. I have had a box made on purpose with a very strong lid, and in this box I keep the ogre's arm secure; and I never show it to anyone, whatever happens."

"Your precaution is very reasonable," said the old woman. "But I am your old nurse, so surely you will not refuse to show me the arm. I have only just heard of your brave act, and not being able to wait till the morning I came at once to ask you to show it to me."

Watanabe was very troubled at the old woman's pleading, but he still persisted in refusing. Then the old woman said:

"Do you suspect me of being a spy sent by the ogre?"

"No, of course I do not suspect you of being the ogre's spy, for you are my old nurse," answered Watanabe.

"Then you cannot surely refuse to show me the arm any longer." entreated the old woman; "for it is the great wish of my heart to see for once in my life the arm of an ogre!"

Watanabe could not hold out in his refusal any longer, so he gave in at last, saying:

"Then I will show you the ogre's arm, since you so earnestly wish to see it. Come, follow me!" and he led the way to his own room, the old woman following.

When they were both in the room Watanabe shut the door carefully, and then going towards a big box which stood in a corner of the room, he took off the heavy lid. He then called to the old woman to come near and look in, for he never took the arm out of the box.

"What is it like? Let me have a good look at it," said the old nurse, with a joyful face.

She came nearer and nearer, as if she were afraid, till she stood right against the box. Suddenly she plunged her hand into the box and seized the arm, crying with a fearful voice which made the room shake:

"Oh, joy! I have got my arm back again!"

And from an old woman she was suddenly transformed into the towering figure of the frightful ogre!

Watanabe sprang back and was unable to move for a moment, so great was his astonishment; but recognizing the ogre who had attacked him at the Gate of Rashomon, he determined with his usual courage to put an end to him this time. He seized his sword, drew it out of its sheath in a flash, and tried to cut the ogre down.

So quick was Watanabe that the creature had a narrow escape. But the ogre sprang up to the ceiling, and bursting through the roof, disappeared in the mist and clouds.

In this way the ogre escaped with his arm. The knight gnashed his teeth with disappointment, but that was all he could do. He waited in patience for another opportunity to dispatch the ogre. But the latter was afraid of Watanabe's great strength and daring, and never troubled Kyoto again. So once more the people of the city were able to go out without fear even at night time, and the brave deeds of Watanabe have never been forgotten!

THE ADVENTURES OF PRINCE YAMATO TAKE

King Keiko bade his youngest son, Prince Yamato, go forth and slay a number of brigands. Before his departure the Prince prayed at the shrines of Ise, and begged that Amaterasu, the Sun Goddess, would bless his enterprise. Prince Yamato's aunt was high-priestess of one of the Ise temples, and he told her about the task his father had entrusted to him. This good lady was much pleased to hear the news, and presented her nephew with a rich silk robe, saying that it would bring him luck, and perhaps be of service to him later on.

When Prince Yamato had returned to the palace and taken leave of his father, he left the court accompanied by his wife, the Princess Ototachibana, and a number of staunch followers, and proceeded to the Southern Island of Kiushiu, which was infested by brigands. The country was so rough and impassable that Prince Yamato saw at once that he must devise some cunning scheme by which he might take the enemy unawares.

Having come to this conclusion, he bade the Princess Ototachibana bring him the rich silk robe his aunt had given him. This he put on under the direction, no doubt, of his wife. He let down his hair, stuck a comb in it, and adorned himself with jewels. When he looked into a mirror he saw that the disguise was perfect, and that he made quite a handsome woman.

Thus gorgeously apparelled, he entered the enemy's tent, where Kumaso and Takeru were sitting. It happened that they were discussing the King's son and his efforts to exterminate their band. When they chanced to look up they saw a fair woman coming towards them.

Kumaso was so delighted that he beckoned to the disguised Prince and bade him serve wine as quickly as possible. Yamato was only too delighted to do so. He affected feminine shyness. He walked with very minute steps, and glanced out of the corner of his eyes with all the timidity of a bashful maiden.

Kumaso drank far more wine than was good for him. He still went on drinking just to have the pleasure of seeing this lovely creature pouring it out for him.

When Kumaso became drunk Prince Yamato flung down the wine-jar, whipped out his dagger, and stabbed him to death.

Takeru, when he saw what had happened to his brother, attempted to escape, but Prince Yamato leapt upon him. Once more his dagger gleamed in the air, and Takeru fell to the earth.

"Stay your hand a moment," gasped the dying brigand. "I would fain know who you are and whence you have come. Hitherto I thought that my brother and I were the strongest men in the kingdom. I am indeed mistaken."

"I am Yamato," said the Prince, "and son of the King who bade me kill such rebels as you!"

"Permit me to give you a new name," said the brigand politely. "From henceforth you shall be called Yamato Take, because you are the bravest man in the land."

Having thus spoken Takeru fell back dead.

The Wooden Sword

When the Prince was on his way to the capital he encountered another outlaw named Idzumo Takeru. Again resorting to strategy, he professed to be extremely friendly with this fellow.

He cut a sword of wood and rammed it tightly into the sheath of his own steel weapon. He wore this whenever he expected to meet Takeru.

On one occasion Prince Yamato invited Takeru to swim with him in the river Hinokawa. While the brigand was swimming down-stream the Prince secretly landed, and, going to Takeru's clothes, lying on the bank, he managed to change swords, putting his wooden one in place of the keen steel sword of Takeru.

When Takeru came out of the water and put on his clothes the Prince asked him to show his skill with the sword. "We will prove," said he, "which is the better swordsman of the two."

Nothing loath, Takeru tried to unsheath his sword. It stuck fast, and as it happened to be of wood it was, of course, useless in any case. While the brigand was thus struggling Yamato cut off his head. Once again cunning had served him, and when he had returned to the palace he was feasted, and received many costly gifts from the King his father.

The 'Grass-Cleaving-Sword'

Prince Yamato did not long remain idle in the palace, for his father commanded him to go forth and quell an Ainu rising in the eastern provinces.

When the Prince was ready to depart the King gave him a spear made from a holly-tree called the 'Eight-Arms-Length-Spear'. With this precious gift Prince Yamato visited the temples of Ise. His aunt, the high-priestess, again greeted him. She listened with interest to all her nephew told her, and was especially delighted to know how well the robe she had given him had served in his adventures.

When she had listened to his story she went into the temple and brought forth a sword and a bag containing flints. These she gave to Yamato as a parting gift.

The sword was the sword of Murakumo, belonging to the insignia of the Imperial House of Japan. The Prince could not have received a more auspicious gift. This sword, it will be remembered, once belonged to the Gods, and was discovered by Susanoo.

After a long march Prince Yamato and his men found themselves in the province of Suruga. The governor hospitably received him, and by way of entertainment organised a deer-hunt. Our hero for once in a way was utterly deceived, and joined the hunt without the least misgiving.

The Prince was taken to a great and wild plain covered with high grass. While he was engaged in hunting down the deer he suddenly became aware of fire. In another moment he saw flames and clouds of smoke shooting up in every direction. He was surrounded by fire, from which there was, apparently, no escape. Too late the guileless warrior realised that he had fallen into a trap, and a very warm trap too!

Our hero opened the bag his aunt had given him, set fire to the grass near him, and with the sword of Murakumo he cut down the tall green blades on either side as quickly as possible. No sooner had he done so than the wind suddenly changed and blew the flames away from him, so that eventually the Prince made good his escape without the slightest burn of any kind. And thus it was that the sword of Murakumo came to be known as the 'Grass-Cleaving-Sword'.

The Sacrifice of Ototachibana

In all these adventures the Prince had been followed by his faithful wife, the Princess Ototachibana. Sad to say, our hero, so praiseworthy in battle, was not nearly so estimable in his love. He looked down on his wife and treated her with indifference. She, poor loyal soul, had lost her beauty in serving her lord. Her skin was burnt with the sun, and her garments were soiled and torn. Yet she never complained, and though her face became sad she made a brave effort to maintain her usual sweetness of manner.

Now Prince Yamato happened to meet the fascinating Princess Miyadzu. Her robes were charming, her skin delicate as cherry-blossom. It was not long before he fell desperately in love with her. When the time came for him to depart he swore that he would return again and make the beautiful Princess Miyadzu his wife. He had scarcely made this promise when he looked up and saw Ototachibana, and on her face was a look of intense sadness. But Prince Yamato hardened his heart, and rode away, secretly determined to keep his promise.

When Prince Yamato, his wife and men, reached the sea-shore of Idzu, his followers desired to secure a number of boats in order that they might cross the Straits of Kadzusa.

The Prince cried haughtily: "Bah! this is only a brook! Why so many boats? I could jump across it!"

When they had all embarked and started on their journey a great storm arose. The waves turned into water-mountains, the wind shrieked, the lightning blazed in the dark clouds, and the thunder roared. It seemed that the boat that carried the Prince and his wife must needs sink, for this storm was the work of Rin-Jin, King of the Sea, who was angry with the proud and foolish words of Prince Yamato.

When the crew had taken down the sails in the hope of steadying the vessel the storm grew worse instead of better. At last Ototachibana arose, and, forgiving all the sorrow her lord had caused her, she resolved to sacrifice her life in order to save her much-loved husband.

Thus spoke the loyal Ototachibana: "Oh, Rin-Jin, the Prince, my husband, has angered you with his boasting. I, Ototachibana, give you my poor life in the place of Yamato Take. I now cast myself into your great surging kingdom, and do you in return bring my lord safely to the shore."

Having uttered these words, Ototachibana leapt into the seething waves, and in a moment they dragged that brave woman out of sight. No sooner had this sacrifice been made than the storm abated and the sun shone forth in a cloudless sky.

Yamato Take safely reached his destination, and succeeded in quelling the Ainu rising.

Our hero had certainly erred in his treatment of his faithful wife. Too late he learnt to appreciate her goodness; but let it be said to his credit that she remained a loving memory till his death, while the Princess Miyadzu was entirely forgotten.

The Slaying of the Serpent

Now that Yamato Take had carried out his father's instructions, he passed through the province of Owari until he came to the province of Omi.

The province of Omi was afflicted with a great trouble. Many were in mourning, and many wept and cried aloud in their sorrow. The Prince, on making inquiries, was informed that a great serpent every day came down from the mountains and entered the villages, making a meal of many of the unfortunate inhabitants.

Prince Yamato at once started to climb up Mount Ibaki, where the great serpent was said to live. About half-way up he encountered the awful creature. The Prince was so strong that he killed the serpent by twisting his bare arms about it. He had no sooner done so than sudden darkness came over the land, and rain fell heavily. However, eventually the weather improved, and our hero was able to climb down the mountain.

When he reached home he found that his feet burned with a strange pain, and, moreover, that he felt very ill. He realised that the serpent had stung him, and, as he was too ill to move, he was carried to a famous mineral spring. Here he finally regained his accustomed health and strength, and for these blessings gave thanks to Amaterasu, the Sun Goddess.

THE ADVENTURES OF MOMOTARO

One day, while an old woman stood by a stream washing her clothes, she chanced to see an enormous peach floating on the water. It was quite the largest she had ever seen, and as this old woman and her husband were extremely poor she immediately thought what an excellent meal this extraordinary peach would make. As she could find no stick with which to draw the fruit to the bank, she suddenly remembered the following verse:

> "Distant water is bitter,
> The near water is sweet;
> Pass by the distant water
> And come into the sweet."

This little song had the desired effect. The peach came nearer and nearer till it stopped at the old woman's feet. She stooped down and picked it up. So delighted was she with her discovery that she could not stay to do any more washing, but hurried home as quickly as possible.

When her husband arrived in the evening, with a bundle of grass upon his back, the old woman excitedly took the peach out of a cupboard and showed it to him. The old man, who was tired and hungry, was equally delighted at the thought of so delicious a meal. He speedily brought a knife and was about to cut the fruit open, when it suddenly opened of its own accord, and the prettiest child imaginable tumbled out with a merry laugh.

"Don't be afraid," said the little fellow. "The Gods have heard how much you desired a child, and have sent me to be a solace and a comfort in your old age."

The old couple were so overcome with joy that they scarcely knew what to do with themselves. Each in turn nursed the child, caressed him, and murmured many sweet and affectionate words. They called him Momotaro, or 'Son of a Peach'.

When Momotaro was fifteen years old he was a lad far taller and stronger than boys of his own age. The making of a great hero stirred in his veins, and it was a knightly heroism that desired to right the wrong.

One day Momotaro came to his foster-father and asked him if he would allow him to take a long journey to a certain island in the North-Eastern Sea where dwelt a number of devils, who had captured a great company of innocent people, many of whom they ate. Their wickedness was beyond description, and Momotaro desired to kill them, rescue the unfortunate captives, and bring back the plunder of the island that he might share it with his foster-parents.

The old man was not a little surprised to hear this daring scheme. He knew that Momotaro was no common child. He had been sent from heaven, and he believed that all the devils in the world could not harm him. So at length the old man gave his consent, saying: "Go, Momotaro, slay the devils and bring peace to the land."

When the old woman had given Momotaro a number of rice-cakes the youth bade his foster-parents farewell, and started out upon his journey.

The Triumph of Momotaro

While Momotaro was resting under a hedge eating one of the rice-cakes, a great dog came up to him, growled, and showed his teeth. The dog, moreover, could speak, and threateningly begged that Momotaro would give him a cake. "Either you give me a cake," said he, "or I will kill you!"

When, however, the dog heard that the famous Momotaro stood before him, his tail dropped between his legs and he bowed with his head to the ground, requesting that he might follow 'Son of a Peach', and render to him all the service that lay in his power.

Momotaro readily accepted the offer, and after throwing the dog half a cake they proceeded on their way.

They had not gone far when they encountered a monkey, who also begged to be admitted to Momotaro's service. This was granted, but it was some time before the dog and the monkey ceased snapping at each other and became good friends.

Proceeding upon their journey, they came across a pheasant. Now the innate jealousy of the dog was again awakened, and he ran forward and tried to kill the bright-plumed creature. Momotaro separated the combatants, and in the end the pheasant was also admitted to the little band, walking decorously in the rear.

At length Momotaro and his followers reached the shore of the North-Eastern Sea. Here our hero discovered a boat, and after a good deal of timidity on the part of the dog, monkey, and pheasant, they all got aboard, and soon the little vessel was spinning away over the blue sea.

After many days upon the ocean they sighted an island. Momotaro bade the bird fly off, a winged herald to announce his coming, and bid the devils surrender.

The pheasant flew over the sea and alighted on the roof of a great castle and shouted his stirring message, adding that the devils, as a sign of submission, should break their horns.

The devils only laughed and shook their horns and shaggy red hair. Then they brought forth iron bars and hurled them furiously at the bird. The pheasant cleverly evaded the missiles, and flew at the heads of many devils.

In the meantime Momotaro had landed with his two companions. He had no sooner done so than he saw two beautiful damsels weeping by a stream, as they wrung out blood-soaked garments.

"Oh!" said they pitifully, "we are daughters of *daimyōs*, and are now the captives of the Demon King of this dreadful island. Soon he will kill us, and alas! there is no one to come to our aid." Having made these remarks the women wept anew.

"Ladies," said Momotaro, "I have come for the purpose of slaying your wicked enemies. Show me a way into yonder castle."

So Momotaro, the dog, and the monkey entered through a small door in the castle. Once inside this fortification they fought tenaciously. Many of the devils were so frightened that they fell off the parapets and were dashed to pieces, while others were speedily killed by Momotaro and his companions. All were destroyed except the Demon King himself, and he wisely resolved to surrender, and begged that his life might be spared.

"No," said Momotaro fiercely. "I will not spare your wicked life. You have tortured many innocent people and robbed the country for many years."

Having said these words he gave the Demon King into the monkey's keeping, and then proceeded through all the rooms of the castle, and set free the numerous prisoners he found there. He also gathered together much treasure.

The return journey was a very joyous affair indeed. The dog and the pheasant carried the treasure between them, while Momotaro led the Demon King.

Momotaro restored the two daughters or *daimyōs* to their homes, and many others who had been made captives in the island. The whole country rejoiced in his victory, but no one more than Momotaro's foster-parents, who ended their days in peace and plenty, thanks to the great treasure of the devils which Momotaro bestowed upon them.

MY LORD BAG OF RICE

One day the great Hidesato came to a bridge that spanned the beautiful Lake Biwa. He was about to cross it when he noticed a great serpent-dragon fast asleep obstructing his progress. Hidesato, without a moment's hesitation, climbed over the monster and proceeded on his way.

He had not gone far when he heard someone calling to him. He looked back and saw that in the place of the dragon a man stood bowing to him with much ceremony. He was a strange-looking fellow with a dragon-shaped crown resting upon his red hair.

"I am the Dragon King of Lake Biwa," explained the red-haired man. "A moment ago I took the form of a horrible monster in the hope of finding a mortal who would not be afraid of me. You, my lord, showed no fear, and I rejoice exceedingly. A great centipede comes down from yonder mountain, enters my palace, and destroys my children and grandchildren. One by one they have become food for this dread creature, and I fear soon that unless something can be done to slay this centipede I myself shall become a victim. I have waited long for a brave mortal. All men who have hitherto seen me in my dragon-shape have run away. You are a brave man, and I beg that you will kill my bitter enemy."

Hidesato, who always welcomed an adventure, the more so when it was a perilous one, readily consented to see what he could do for the Dragon King.

When Hidesato reached the Dragon King's palace he found it to be a very magnificent building indeed, scarcely less beautiful than the Sea King's palace itself. He was feasted with crystallised lotus leaves and flowers, and ate the delicacies spread before him with choice ebony chopsticks. While he feasted ten little goldfish danced, and just behind the goldfish ten carp made sweet music on the *koto* and *samisen*. Hidesato was just thinking how excellently he had been entertained, and how particularly good was the wine, when they all heard an awful noise like a dozen thunderclaps roaring together.

Hidesato and the Dragon King hastily rose and ran to the balcony. They saw that Mount Mikami was scarcely recognisable, for it was covered from top to bottom with the great coils of the centipede. In its head glowed two balls of fire, and its hundred feet were like a long winding chain of lanterns.

Hidesato fitted an arrow to his bowstring and pulled it back with all his might. The arrow sped forth into the night and struck the centipede in the middle of the head, but glanced off immediately without inflicting any wound. Again Hidesato sent an arrow whirling into the air, and again it struck the monster and fell harmlessly to the ground. Hidesato had only one arrow left. Suddenly remembering the magical effect of human saliva, he put the remaining arrow-head into his mouth for a moment, and then hastily adjusted it to his bow and took careful aim.

The last arrow struck its mark and pierced the centipede's brain. The creature stopped moving; the light in its eyes and legs darkened and then went out, and Lake Biwa, with its palace beneath, was shrouded in awful darkness. Thunder rolled, lightning flashed, and it seemed for the moment that the Dragon King's palace would topple to the ground.

The next day, however, all sign of storm had vanished. The sky was clear. The sun shone brightly. In the sparkling blue lake lay the body of the great centipede.

The Dragon King and those about him were overjoyed when they knew that their dread enemy had been destroyed. Hidesato was again feasted, even more royally than before. When he finally departed he did so with a retinue of fishes suddenly converted into men. The Dragon King bestowed upon our hero five precious gifts – two bells, a bag of rice, a roll of silk, and a cooking-pot.

The Dragon King accompanied Hidesato as far as the bridge, and then he reluctantly allowed the hero and the procession of servants carrying the presents to proceed on their way.

When Hidesato reached his home the Dragon King's servants put down the presents and suddenly disappeared.

The presents were no ordinary gifts. The rice-bag was inexhaustible, there was no end to the roll of silk, and the cooking-pot would cook without fire of any kind. Only the bells were without magical properties, and these were presented to a temple in the vicinity. Hidesato grew rich, and his fame spread far and wide. People now no longer called him Hidesato, but Tawara Toda, or 'My Lord Bag of Rice'.

THE TRANSFORMATION OF ISSUNBOSHI

An old married couple went to the shrine of the deified Empress Jingo, and prayed that they might be blessed with a child, even if it were no bigger than one of their fingers. A voice was heard from behind the bamboo curtain of the shrine, and the old people were informed that their wish would be granted.

In due time the old woman gave birth to a child, and when she and her husband discovered that this miniature piece of humanity was no bigger than a little finger, they became extremely angry, and thought that the Empress Jingo had treated them very meanly indeed, though, as a matter of fact, she had fulfilled their prayer to the letter.

'One-Inch Priest'

The little fellow was called Issunboshi ('One-Inch Priest'), and every day his parents expected to see him suddenly grow up as other boys; but at thirteen years of age he still remained the same size as when he was born. Gradually his parents became exasperated, for it wounded their vanity to hear the neighbours describe their son as Little Finger, or Grain-of-Corn. They were so much annoyed that at last they determined to send Issunboshi away.

The little fellow did not complain. He requested his mother to give him a needle, a small soup-bowl, and a chop-stick, and with these things he set off on his adventures.

Issunboshi becomes a Page

His soup-bowl served as a boat, which he propelled along the river with his chop-stick. In this fashion he finally reached Kyoto. Issunboshi wandered about this city until he saw a large roofed gate. Without the least hesitation he walked in, and having reached the porch of a house, he cried out in a very minute voice: "I beg an honourable inquiry!"

Prince Sanjo himself heard the little voice, and it was some time before he could discover where it came from. When he did so he was delighted with his discovery, and on the little fellow begging that he might live in the Prince's house, his request was readily granted. The boy became a great favourite, and was at once made the Princess Sanjo's page. In this capacity he accompanied his mistress everywhere, and though so very small, he fully appreciated the honour and dignity of his position.

An Encounter with Oni

One day the Princess Sanjo and her page went to the Temple of Kwannon, the Goddess of Mercy, "under whose feet are dragons of the elements and the lotuses of Purity." As they were leaving the temple two *oni* (evil spirits) sprang upon them. Issunboshi took out his needle-sword from its hollow straw, and loudly denouncing the *oni*, he flourished his small weapon in their evil-looking faces.

One of the creatures laughed. "Why," said he scornfully, "I could swallow you, as a cormorant swallows a trout, and what is more, my funny little bean-seed, I will do so!"

The *oni* opened his mouth, and Issunboshi found himself slipping down a huge throat until he finally stood in the creature's great dark stomach. Issunboshi, nothing daunted, began boring away with his needle-sword. This made the evil spirit cry out and give a great cough, which sent the little fellow into the sunny world again. The second *oni*, who had witnessed his companion's distress, was extremely angry, and tried to swallow the remarkable little page, but was not successful. This time Issunboshi climbed up the creature's nostril, and when he had reached the end of what seemed to him to be a very long and gloomy tunnel, he began piercing the *oni's* eyes. The creature, savage with pain, ran off as fast as he could, followed by his yelling companion.

Needless to say, the Princess was delighted with her page's bravery, and told him that she was sure her father would reward him when he was told about the terrible encounter.

The Magic Mallet

On their way home the Princess happened to pick up a small wooden mallet. "Oh!" said she, "this must have been dropped by the wicked *oni*, and it is none other than a lucky mallet. You have only to wish and then tap it upon the ground, and your wish, no matter what, is always granted. My brave Issunboshi, tell me what you would most desire, and I will tap the mallet on the ground."

After a pause the little fellow said: "Honourable Princess, I should like to be as big as other people."

The Princess tapped the mallet on the ground, calling aloud the wish of her page. In a moment Issunboshi was transformed from a bijou creature to a lad just like other youths of his age.

These wonderful happenings excited the curiosity of the Emperor, and Issunboshi was summoned to his presence. The Emperor was so delighted with the youth that he gave him many gifts and made him a high official. Finally, Issunboshi became a great lord and married Prince Sanjo's youngest daughter.

KINTARO, THE GOLDEN BOY

Sakata Kurando was an officer of the Emperor's bodyguard, and though he was a brave man, well versed in the art of war, he had a gentle disposition, and during his military career chanced to love a beautiful lady named Yaegiri. Kurando eventually fell into disgrace, and was forced to leave the Court and to become a travelling tobacco merchant. Yaegiri, who was much distressed by her lover's flight, succeeded in escaping from her home, and wandered up and down the country in the hope of meeting Kurando. At length she found him, but the unfortunate man, who, no doubt, felt deeply his disgrace and his humble mode of living, put an end to his humiliation by taking his miserable life.

Animal Companions

When Yaegiri had buried her lover she went to the Ashigara Mountain, where she gave birth to a child, called Kintaro, or the Golden Boy. Now Kintaro was remarkable for his extreme strength. When only a few years old his mother gave him an axe, with which he felled trees as quickly and easily as an experienced woodcutter. Ashigara Mountain was a lonely and desolate spot, and as there were no children with whom Kintaro could play, he made companions of the bear, deer, hare, and monkey, and in a very short time was able to speak their strange language.

One day, when Kintaro was sitting on the mountain, with his favourites about him, he sought to amuse himself by getting his companions to join in a friendly wrestling match. A kindly old bear was delighted with the proposal, and at once set to work to dig up the earth and arrange it in the form of a small dais. When this had been made a hare and a monkey wrestled together, while a deer stood by to give encouragement and to see that the sport was conducted fairly. Both animals proved themselves to be equally strong, and Kintaro tactfully rewarded them with tempting rice-cakes.

After spending a pleasant afternoon in this way, Kintaro proceeded to return home, followed by his devoted friends. At length they came to a river, and the animals were wondering how they should cross such a wide stretch of water, when Kintaro put his strong arms round a tree which was growing on the bank, and pulled it across the river so that it formed a bridge. Now it happened that the famous hero, Yorimitsu, and his retainers witnessed this extraordinary feat of strength, and said to Watanabe Tsuna: "This child is truly remarkable. Go and find out where he lives and all about him."

A Famous Warrior

So Watanabe Tsuna followed Kintaro and entered the house where he lived with his mother. "My master," said he, "Lord Yorimitsu, bids me find out who your wonderful son is." When Yaegiri had narrated the story of her life and informed her visitor that her little one was the son of Sakata Kurando, the retainer departed and told Yorimitsu all he had heard.

Yorimitsu was so pleased with what Watanabe Tsuna told him that he went himself to Yaegiri, and said: "If you will give me your child I will make him my retainer." The woman gladly consented, and the Golden Boy went away with the great hero, who named him Sakata Kintoki. He eventually became a famous warrior, and the stories of his wonderful deeds are recited to this day. Children regard him as their favourite hero, and little boys, who would fain emulate the strength and bravery of Sakata Kintoki, carry his portrait in their bosoms.

A JAPANESE GULLIVER

Shikaiya **Wasobioye** was a man of Nagasaki, and possessed considerable learning, but disliked visitors. On the eighth day of the eighth month, in order to escape the admirers of the full moon, he set off in his boat, and had proceeded some distance, when the sky looked threatening, and he attempted to return, but the wind tore his sail and broke his mast. The poor man was tossed for three months on the waves, until at last he came to the Sea of Mud, where he nearly died of hunger, for there were no fishes to be caught.

At length he reached a mountainous island, where the air was sweet with the fragrance of many flowers, and in this island he found a spring, the waters of which revived him. At length Wasobioye met Jofuku, who led him through the streets of the main city, where all the inhabitants were spending their time in pursuit of pleasure. There was no death or disease on this island; but the fact that here life was eternal was regarded by many as a burden, which they tried to shake off by studying the magic art of death and the power of poisonous food, such as globe-fish sprinkled with soot and the flesh of mermaids.

When twenty years had passed by Wasobioye grew weary of the island, and as he had failed in his attempts to take his life, he started upon a journey to the Three Thousand Worlds mentioned in Buddhist Scriptures. He then visited the Land of Endless Plenty, the Land of Shams, the Land of the Followers of the Antique, the Land of Paradoxes, and, finally, the Land of Giants.

After Wasobioye had spent five months riding on the back of a stork through total darkness, he at length reached a country where the sun shone again, where trees were hundreds of feet in girth, where weeds were as large as bamboos, and men sixty feet in height. In this strange land a giant picked up Wasobioye, took him to his house, and fed him from a single grain of monster rice, with chopsticks the size of a small tree. For a few weeks Wasobioye attempted to catechise his host in regard to the doctrines of the old world whence he came, but the giant laughed at him and told him that such a small man could not be expected to understand the ways of big people, for their intelligences were in like proportion to their size.

LEADING LADIES & AFFAIRS OF THE HEART

Self-less heroines, doomed lovers and romance feature heavily in Japanese myth and folkore, often as a device to illustrate the importance of filial piety. 'The Bamboo Cutter and the Moon Maiden' is adapted from a tenth-century story called *Taketori Monogatari*, and is the earliest example of the Japanese romance. All the characters in this very charming legend are Japanese, but most of the incidents have been borrowed from China. Mr F.V. Dickins wrote concerning the *Taketori Monogatari*: "The art and grace of the story of the Lady Kaguya are native, its unstrained pathos, its natural sweetness, are its own, and in simple charm and purity of thought and language it has no rival in the fiction of either the Middle Kingdom or of the Dragonfly Land."

One of the most romantic of the old Japanese festivals is the Festival of Tanabata. The story that inspired it is the famous one of 'The Star Lovers', Tanabata (more often known as Orihime) and Hikoboshi, from the Chinese tale of 'The Cowherd and the Weaver Girl', in which the lovers are punished for their disrespect by being separated, only to be allowed to meet once a year.

Snow-time in Japan has a beauty peculiarly its own, and it is a favourite theme of Japanese poets and artists. Because it is so particularly beautiful it is surprising to find that Yuki-Onna, the Lady of the Snow, is very far from being a benevolent and attractive spirit. But Japan is full of sharp and surprising contrasts, and the delicate and beautiful jostle with the ugly and horrible.

THE BAMBOO CUTTER AND THE MOON MAIDEN

Long ago there lived an old bamboom cutter by the name of Sanugi no Miyakko. One day, while he was busy with his hatchet in a grove of bamboos, he suddenly perceived a miraculous light, and on closer inspection discovered in the heart of a reed a very small creature of exquisite beauty. He gently picked up the tiny girl, only about four inches in height, and carried her home to his wife. So delicate was this little maiden that she had to be reared in a basket.

Now it happened that the Bamboo Cutter continued to set about his business, and night and day, as he cut down the reeds, he found gold, and, once poor, he now amassed a considerable fortune.

The child, after she had been but three months with these simple country folk, suddenly grew in stature to that of a full-grown maid; and in order that she should be in keeping with such a pleasing, if surprising, event, her hair, hitherto allowed to flow in long tresses about her shoulders, was now fastened in a knot on her head. In due season the Bamboo Cutter named the girl the Lady Kaguya, or 'Precious-Slender-Bamboo-of-the-Field-of-Autumn'. When she had been named a great feast was held, in which all the neighbours participated.

The Wooing of the 'Precious-Slender-Bamboo-of-the-Field-of-Autumn'

Now the Lady Kaguya was of all women the most beautiful, and immediately after the feast the fame of her beauty spread throughout the land. Would-be lovers gathered around the fence and lingered in the porch with the hope of at least getting a glimpse of this lovely maiden. Night and day these forlorn suitors waited, but in vain. Those who were of humble origin gradually began to recognise that their love-making was useless. But five wealthy suitors still persisted, and would not relax their efforts. They were Prince Ishizukuri and Prince Kuramochi, the Sadaijin Dainagon Abe no Miushi, the Chiunagon Otomo no Miyuki, and Morotada, the Lord of Iso. These ardent lovers bore "the ice and snow of winter and the thunderous heats of midsummer with equal fortitude." When these lords finally asked the Bamboo Cutter to bestow his daughter upon one of them, the old man politely explained that the maiden was not really his daughter, and as that was so she could not be compelled to obey his own wishes in the matter.

At last the lords returned to their mansions, but still continued to make their supplications more persistently than ever. Even the kindly Bamboo Cutter began to remonstrate with the Lady Kaguya, and to point out that it was becoming for so handsome a maid to marry, and that among the five noble suitors she could surely make a very good match. To this the wise Kaguya replied: "Not so fair am I that I may be certain of a man's faith, and were I to mate with one whose heart proved fickle what a miserable fate were mine! Noble lords, without doubt, are these of whom thou speakest, but I would not wed a man whose heart should be all untried and unknown."

It was finally arranged that Kaguya should marry the suitor who proved himself the most worthy. This news brought momentary hope to the five great lords, and when night came they assembled before the house where the maiden dwelt "with flute music and with singing, with chanting to accompaniments and piping, with cadenced tap and clap of fan." Only the Bamboo Cutter went out to thank the lords for their serenading. When he had come into the house again, Kaguya thus set forth her plan to test the suitors:

"In Tenjiku (Northern India) is a beggar's bowl of stone, which of old the Buddha himself bore, in quest whereof let Prince Ishizukuri depart and bring me the same. And on the mountain Horai, that towers over the Eastern ocean, grows a tree with roots of silver and trunk of gold and fruitage of pure white jade, and I bid Prince Kuramochi fare thither and break off and bring me a branch thereof. Again, in the land of Morokoshi men fashion fur-robes of the pelt of the Flame-proof Rat, and I pray the Dainagon to find me one such. Then of the Chiunagon I require the rainbow-hued jewel that hides its sparkle deep in the dragon's head; and from the hands of the Lord Iso would I fain receive the cowry-shell that the swallow brings hither over the broad sea-plain."

The Begging-bowl of the Lord Buddha

The Prince Ishizukuri, after pondering over the matter of going to distant Tenjiku in search of the Lord Buddha's begging-bowl, came to the conclusion that such a proceeding would be futile. He decided, therefore, to counterfeit the bowl in question. He laid his plans cunningly, and took good care that the Lady Kaguya was informed that he had actually undertaken the journey. As a matter

of fact this artful suitor hid in Yamato for three years, and after that
time discovered in a hill-monastery in Tochi a bowl of extreme
age resting upon an altar of Binzuru (the Succourer in Sickness).
This bowl he took away with him, and wrapped it in brocade, and
attached to the gift an artificial branch of blossom.

When the Lady Kaguya looked upon the bowl she found
inside a scroll containing the following:

> *"Over seas, over hills*
> *hath thy servant fared, and weary*
> *and wayworn he perisheth:*
> *O what tears hath cost this*
> *bowl of stone,*
> *what floods of streaming tears!"*

But when the Lady Kaguya perceived that no light shone
from the vessel she at once knew that it had never belonged
to the Lord Buddha. She accordingly sent back the bowl with
the following verse:

> *"Of the hanging dewdrop*
> *not even the passing sheen*
> *dwells herein:*
> *On the Hill of Darkness, the Hill*
> *of Ogura,*
> *what couldest thou hope to find?"*

The Prince, having thrown away the bowl, sought to turn
the above remonstrance into a compliment to the lady who
wrote it.

> *"Nay, on the Hill of Brightness*
> *what splendour*
> *will not pale?*
> *Would that away from the light*
> *of thy beauty*
> *the sheen of yonder Bowl might*
> *prove me true!"*

It was a prettily turned compliment by a suitor who was an utter humbug. This latest poetical sally availed nothing, and the Prince sadly departed.

The Jewel-bearing Branch of Mount Horai

Prince Kuramochi, like his predecessor, was equally wily, and made it generally known that he was setting out on a journey to the land of Tsukushi in quest of the Jewel-bearing Branch. What he actually did was to employ six men of the Uchimaro family, celebrated craftsmen, and secure for them a dwelling hidden from the haunts of men, where he himself abode, for the purpose of instructing the craftsmen as to how they were to make a Jewel-bearing Branch identical with the one described by the Lady Kaguya.

When the Jewel-bearing Branch was finished, he set out to wait upon the Lady Kaguya, who read the following verse attached to the gift:

> *"Though it were at the peril*
> *of my very life,*
> *without the Jewel-laden Branch*
> *in my hands never again*
> *would I have dared to return!"*

The Lady Kaguya looked sadly upon this glittering branch, and listened without interest to the Prince's purely imaginative story of his adventures. The Prince dwelt upon the terrors of the sea, of strange monsters, of acute hunger, of disease, which were their trials upon the ocean. Then this incorrigible story-teller went on to describe how they came to a high mountain rising out of the sea, where they were greeted by a woman bearing a silver vessel which she filled with water. On the mountain were wonderful flowers and trees, and a stream "rainbow-hued, yellow as gold, white as silver, blue as precious *ruri* (lapis lazuli); and the stream was spanned by bridges built up of divers gems, and by it grew trees laden with dazzling jewels, and from one of these I broke off the branch which I venture now to offer to the Lady Kaguya."

No doubt the Lady Kaguya would have been forced to believe this ingenious tale had not at that very moment the six craftsmen appeared on the scene, and by loudly demanding payment for the ready-made Jewel-Branch, exposed the treachery of the Prince, who made a hasty retreat. The Lady Kaguya herself rewarded the craftsmen, happy, no doubt, to escape so easily.

The Flameproof Fur-Robe

The Sadaijin (Left Great Minister) Abe no Miushi commissioned a merchant, by the name of Wokei, to obtain for him a fur-robe made from the Flame-proof Rat, and when the merchant's ship had returned from the land of Morokoshi it bore a fur-robe, which the sanguine Sadaijin imagined to be the very object of his desire. The Fur-Robe rested in a casket, and the Sadaijin, believing in the honesty of the merchant, described it as being "of a sea-green colour, the hairs tipped with shining gold, a treasure indeed of incomparable loveliness, more to be admired for its pure excellence than even for its virtue in resisting the flame of fire."

The Sadaijin, assured of success in his wooing, gaily set out to present his gift to the Lady Kaguya, offering in addition the following verse:

> *"Endless are the fires of love*
> *that consume me, yet unconsumed*
> *is the Robe of Fur:*
> *dry at last are my sleeves,*
> *for shall I not see her face this day!"*

At last the Sadaijin was able to present his gift to the Lady Kaguya. Thus she addressed the Bamboo Cutter, who always seems to have been conveniently on the scene at such times: "If this Robe be thrown amid the flames and be not burnt up, I shall know it is in very truth the Flame-proof Robe, and may no longer refuse this lord's suit." A fire was lighted, and the Robe thrown into the flames, where it perished immediately. "When the Sadaijin saw this his face grew green as grass, and he stood there astonished." But the Lady Kaguya discreetly rejoiced, and returned the casket with the following verse:

> *"Without a vestige even left*
> *thus to burn utterly away,*
> *had I dreamt it of this Robe of Fur.*
> *Alas the pretty thing! far otherwise*
> *would I have dealt with it."*

The Jewel in the Dragon's Head

The Chiunagon Otomo no Miyuki assembled his household and informed his retainers that he desired them to bring him the Jewel in the Dragon's head.

After some demur they pretended to set off on this quest. In the meantime the Chiunagon was so sure of his servants' success that he had his house lavishly adorned throughout with exquisite lacquer-work, in gold and silver. Every room was hung with brocade, the panels rich with pictures, and over the roof were silken cloths.

Weary of waiting, the Chiunagon after a time journeyed to Naniwa and questioned the inhabitants if any of his servants had taken boat in quest of the Dragon. The Chiunagon learnt that none of his men had come to Naniwa, and, considerably displeased at the news, he himself embarked with a helmsman.

Now it happened that the Thunder God was angry and the sea ran high. After many days the storm grew so severe and the boat was so near sinking that the helmsman ventured to remark: "The howling of the wind and the raging of the waves and the mighty roar of the thunder are signs of the wrath of the God whom my lord offends, who would slay the Dragon of the deep, for through the Dragon is the storm raised, and well it were if my lord offered a prayer."

As the Chiunagon had been seized with a terrible sickness, it is not surprising to find that he readily took the helmsman's advice. He prayed no less than a thousand times, enlarging on his folly in attempting to slay the Dragon, and solemnly vowed that he would leave the Ruler of the deep in peace.

The thunder ceased and the clouds dispersed, but the wind was as fierce and strong as ever. The helmsman, however, told his master that it was a fair wind and blew towards their own land.

At last they reached the strand of Akashi, in Harima. But the Chiunagon, still ill and mightily frightened, vowed that they had been driven upon a savage shore, and lay full length in the boat, panting heavily, and refusing to rise when the governor of the district presented himself.

When the Chiunagon at last realised that they had not been blown upon some savage shore he consented to land. No wonder the governor smiled when he saw the wretched appearance of the discomfited lord, chilled to the very bone, with swollen belly and eyes lustreless as sloes.

At length the Chiunagon was carried in a litter to his own home. When he had arrived his cunning servants humbly told their master how they had failed in the quest. Thus the Chiunagon greeted them: "Ye have done well to return empty-handed. Yonder Dragon, assuredly, has kinship with the Thunder God, and whoever shall lay hands on him to take the jewel that gleams in his head shall find himself in peril. Myself am sore spent with toil and hardship, and no guerdon have I won. A thief of men's souls and a destroyer of their bodies is the Lady Kaguya, nor ever will I seek her abode again, nor ever bend ye your steps thitherward."

When the women of his household heard of their lord's adventure they laughed till their sides were sore, while the silken cloths he had caused to be drawn over the roof of his mansion were carried away, thread by thread, by the crows to line their nests with.

The Royal Hunt

Now the fame of the Lady Kaguya's beauty reached the court, and the Mikado, anxious to gaze upon her, sent one of his palace ladies, Fusago, to go and see the Bamboo Cutter's daughter, and to report to his Majesty of her excellences.

However, when Fusago reached the Bamboo Cutter's house the Lady Kaguya refused to see her. So the palace lady returned to court and reported the matter to the Mikado. His Majesty, not a little displeased, sent for the Bamboo Cutter, and made him bring the Lady Kaguya to court that he might see her, adding: "A hat of nobility, perchance, shall be her father's reward."

The old Bamboo Cutter was an admirable soul, and mildly discountenanced his daughter's extraordinary behaviour. Although he loved court favours and probably hankered after so distinguished a hat, it must be said of him that he was first of all true to his duty as a father.

When, on returning to his home, he discussed the matter with the Lady Kaguya, she informed the old man that if she were compelled to go to court it would certainly cause her death, adding: "The price of my father's hat of nobility will be the destruction of his child."

The Bamboo Cutter was deeply affected by these words, and once more set out on a journey to the court, where he humbly made known his daughter's decision.

The Mikado, not to be denied even by an extraordinarily beautiful woman, hit on the ingenious plan of ordering a Royal Hunt, so arranged that he might unexpectedly arrive at the Bamboo Cutter's dwelling, and perchance see the lady who could set at defiance the desires of an emperor.

On the day appointed for the Royal Hunt, therefore, the Mikado entered the Bamboo Cutter's house. He had no sooner done so than he was surprised to see in the room in which he stood a wonderful light, and in the light none other than the Lady Kaguya.

His Majesty advanced and touched the maiden's sleeve, whereupon she hid her face, but not before the Mikado had caught a glimpse of her beauty. Amazed by her extreme loveliness, and taking no notice of her protests, he ordered a palace litter to be brought; but on its arrival the Lady Kaguya suddenly vanished. The Emperor, perceiving that he was dealing with no mortal maid, exclaimed: "It shall be as thou desirest, maiden; but 'Tis prayed that thou resume thy form, that once more thy beauty may be seen."

So the Lady Kaguya resumed her fair form again. As his Majesty was about to be borne away he composed the following verse:

> *"Mournful the return*
> *of the Royal Hunt,*
> *and full of sorrow the*
> *brooding heart;*
> *for she resists and stays behind,*
> *the Lady Kaguya!"*

The Lady Kaguya thus made answer:

> *"Under the roof o'ergrown*
> *with hopbine*
> *long were the years*
> *she passed.*
> *How may she dare to look upon*
> *The Palace of Precious Jade?"*

The Celestial Robe of Feathers

In the third year after the Royal Hunt, and in the spring-time, the Lady Kaguya continually gazed at the moon. On the seventh month, when the moon was full, the Lady Kaguya's sorrow increased so that her weeping distressed the maidens who served her. At last they came to the Bamboo Cutter, and said: "Long has the Lady Kaguya watched the moon, waxing in melancholy with the waxing thereof, and her woe now passes all measure, and sorely she weeps and wails; wherefore we counsel thee to speak with her."

When the Bamboo Cutter communed with his daughter, he requested that she should tell him the cause of her sorrow, and was informed that the sight of the moon caused her to reflect upon the wretchedness of the world.

During the eighth month the Lady Kaguya explained to her maids that she was no ordinary mortal, but that her birthplace was the Capital of Moonland, and that the time was now at hand when she was destined to leave the world and return to her old home.

Not only was the Bamboo Cutter heart-broken at this sorrowful news, but the Mikado also was considerably troubled when he heard of the proposed departure of the Lady Kaguya. His Majesty was informed that at the next full moon a company would be sent down from that shining orb to take this beautiful lady away, whereupon he determined to put a check upon this celestial invasion. He ordered that a guard of soldiers should be stationed about the Bamboo Cutter's house, armed and prepared, if need be, to shoot their arrows upon those Moonfolk, who would fain take the beautiful Lady Kaguya away.

The old Bamboo Cutter naturally thought that with such a guard to protect his daughter the invasion from the moon would prove utterly futile. The Lady Kaguya attempted to correct the old man's ideas on the subject, saying: "Ye cannot prevail over the folk of yonder land, nor will your artillery harm them nor your defences avail against them, for every door will fly open at their approach, nor may your valour help, for be ye never so stout-hearted, when the Moonfolk come vain will be your struggle with them." These remarks made the Bamboo Cutter exceedingly angry. He asserted that his nails would turn into talons – in short, that he would completely annihilate such impudent visitors from the moon.

Now while the royal guard was stationed about the Bamboo Cutter's house, on the roof and in every direction, the night wore away. At the hour of the Rata great glory, exceeding the splendour of the moon and stars, shone around. While the light still continued a strange cloud approached, bearing upon it a company of Moonfolk. The cloud slowly descended until it came near to the ground, and the Moonfolk assembled themselves in order. When the royal guard perceived them every soldier grew afraid at the strange spectacle; but at length some of their number summoned up sufficient courage to bend their bows and send their arrows flying; but all their shafts went astray.

On the cloud there rested a canopied car, resplendent with curtains of finest woollen fabric, and from out the car a mighty voice sounded, saying: "Come thou forth, Miyakko Maro!"

The Bamboo Cutter tottered forth to obey the summons, and received for his pains an address from the chief of the Moonfolk commencing with, "Thou fool," and ending up with a command that the Lady Kaguya should be given up without further delay.

The car floated upward upon the cloud till it hovered over the roof. Once again the same mighty voice shouted: "Ho there, Kaguya! How long wouldst thou tarry in this sorry place?"

Immediately the outer door of the storehouse and the inner lattice-work were opened by the power of the Moonfolk, and revealed the Lady Kaguya and her women gathered about her. The Lady Kaguya, before taking her departure, greeted the prostrate Bamboo Cutter and gave him a scroll bearing these words: "Had I been born in this land, never should I have quitted it until the time came for my father to suffer no sorrow for his child; but now, on the contrary, must I pass beyond the boundaries of this world, though sorely against my will. My silken mantle I leave behind me as a memorial, and when the moon lights up the night let my father gaze upon it. Now my eyes must take their last look and I must mount to yonder sky, whence I fain would fall, meteorwise, to earth."

Now the Moonfolk had brought with them, in a coffer, a Celestial Feather Robe and a few drops of the Elixir of Life. One of them said to the Lady Kaguya: "Taste, I pray you, of this Elixir, for soiled has your spirit become with the grossnesses of this filthy world."

The Lady Kaguya, after tasting the Elixir, was about to wrap up some in the mantle she was leaving behind for the benefit of the old Bamboo Cutter, who had loved her so well, when one of the Moonfolk prevented her, and attempted to throw over her shoulders the Celestial Robe, when the Lady Kaguya exclaimed: "Have patience yet awhile; who dons yonder robe changes his heart, and I have still somewhat to say ere I depart." Then she proceeded to write the following to the Mikado:

"Your Majesty deigned to send a host to protect your servant, but it was not to be, and now is the misery at hand of departing with those who have come to bear her away with them. Not permitted was it to her to serve your Majesty, and despite her will was it that she yielded not obedience to the Royal command, and wrung with grief is her heart thereat, and perchance your Majesty may have thought the Royal will was not understood, and was opposed by her, and so will she appear to your Majesty lacking in good manners, which she would not your Majesty deemed her to be, and therefore humbly she lays this writing at the Royal Feet. And now must she don the Feather Robe and mournfully bid her lord farewell."

Having delivered this scroll into the hands of the captain of the host, together with a bamboo joint containing the Elixir, the Feather Robe was thrown over her, and in a moment all memory of her earthly existence departed.

Then the Lady Kaguya entered the car, surrounded by the company of Moonfolk, and the cloud rapidly rose skyward till it was lost to sight.

The sorrow of the Bamboo Cutter and of the Mikado knew no bounds. The latter held a Grand Council, and inquired which was the highest mountain in the land. One of the councillors answered: "In Suruga stands a mountain, not remote from the capital, that towers highest towards heaven among all the mountains of the land." Whereupon his Majesty composed the following verse:

> *"Never more to see her!*
> *Tears of grief overwhelm me,*
> *and as for me,*
> *with the Elixir of Life*
> *what have I to do?"*

Then the scroll, which the Lady Kaguya had written, together with the Elixir, was given to Tsuki no Iwakasa. These he was commanded to take to the summit of the highest mountain in Suruga, and, standing upon the highest peak, to burn the scroll and the Elixir of Life.

So Tsuki no Iwakasa heard humbly the Royal command, and took with him a company of warriors, and climbed the mountain and did as he was bidden. And it was from that time forth that the name of Fuji (*Fuji-yama*, 'Never Dying') was given to yonder mountain, and men say that the smoke of that burning still curls from its high peak to mingle with the clouds of heaven.

THE STAR LOVERS

The God of the Firmament had a lovely daughter, Tanabata by name, and she spent her time in weaving for her august father. One day, while she sat at her loom, she chanced to see a handsome lad leading an ox, and she immediately fell in love with him. Tanabata's father, reading her secret thoughts, speedily consented to their marriage.

Unfortunately, however, the couple loved not wisely, but too well, with the result that Tanabata neglected her weaving, and Hikoboshi's ox was allowed to wander at large over the High Plain of Heaven. The God of the Firmament became extremely angry, and commanded that these too ardent lovers should henceforth be separated by the Celestial River. On the seventh night of the seventh month, provided the weather was favourable, a great company of birds formed a bridge across the river, and by this means the lovers were able to meet. Their all too brief visit was not even a certainty, for if there were rain the Celestial River would become too wide for even a great bridge of magpies to span, and the lovers would be compelled to wait another weary year before there was even a chance of meeting each other again.

No wonder that on the Festival of the Weaving Maiden little children should sing, *"Tenki ni nari"* ("Oh, weather, be clear!"). When the weather is fine and the Star Lovers meet each other after a weary year's waiting it is said that the stars, possibly Lyra and Aquila, shine with five different colours – blue, green, red, yellow, and white – and that is why the poems are written on paper of these colours.

THE ROBE OF FEATHERS

It was spring-time, and along Mio's pine-clad shore there came a sound of birds. The blue sea danced and sparkled in the sunshine, and Hairukoo, a fisherman, sat down to enjoy the scene. As he did so he chanced to see, hanging on a pine-tree, a beautiful robe of pure white feathers.

As Hairukoo was about to take down the robe he saw coming toward him from the sea an extremely lovely maiden, who requested that the fisherman would restore the robe to her.

Hairukoo gazed upon the lady with considerable admiration. Said he: "I found this robe, and I mean to keep it, for it is a marvel to be placed among the treasures of Japan. No, I cannot possibly give it to you."

"Oh," cried the maiden pitifully, "I cannot go soaring into the sky without my robe of feathers, for if you persist in keeping it I can never more return to my celestial home. Oh, good fisherman, I beg of you to restore my robe!"

The fisherman, who must have been a hard-hearted fellow, refused to relent. "The more you plead," said he, "the more determined I am to keep what I have found."

Thus the maiden made answer:

> *"Speak not, dear fisherman! speak not that word!*
> *Ah! know'st thou not that, like the hapless bird*
> *Whose wings are broke, I seek, but seek in vain,*
> *Reft of my wings, to soar to heav'n's blue plain?"*

After further argument on the subject the fisherman's heart softened a little. "I will restore your robe of feathers," said he, "if you will at once dance before me."

Then the maiden replied: "I will dance it here – the dance that makes the Palace of the Moon turn round, so that even poor transitory man may learn its mysteries. But I cannot dance without my feathers."

"No", said the fisherman suspiciously. "If I give you this robe you will fly away without dancing before me."

This remark made the maiden extremely angry. "The pledge of mortals may be broken," said she, "but there is no falsehood among the Heavenly Beings."

These words put the fisherman to shame, and, without more ado, he gave the maiden her robe of feathers.

The Moon-Lady's Song

When the maiden had put on her pure white garment she struck a musical instrument and began to dance, and while she danced and played she sang of many strange and beautiful things concerning her far-away home in the Moon. She sang of the mighty Palace of the Moon, where thirty monarchs ruled, fifteen in robes of white when that shining orb was full, and fifteen robed in black when the Moon was waning. As she sang and played and danced she blessed Japan, "that earth may still her proper increase yield!"

The fisherman did not long enjoy this kindly exhibition of the Moon-Lady's skill, for very soon her dainty feet ceased to tap upon the sand. She rose into the air, the white feathers of her robe gleaming against the pine-trees or against the blue sky itself. Up, up she went, still playing and singing, past the summits of the mountains, higher and higher, until her song was hushed, until she reached the glorious Palace of the Moon.

YUKI-ONNA, THE SNOW-BRIDE

Mosaku and his apprentice Minokichi journeyed to a forest, some little distance from their village. It was a bitterly cold night when they neared their destination, and saw in front of them a cold sweep of water. They desired to cross this river, but the ferryman had gone away, leaving his boat on the other side of the water, and as the weather was too inclement to admit of swimming across the river they were glad to take shelter in the ferryman's little hut.

Mosaku fell asleep almost immediately he entered this humble but welcome shelter. Minokichi, however, lay awake for a long time listening to the cry of the wind and the hiss of the snow as it was blown against the door.

Minokichi at last fell asleep, to be soon awakened by a shower of snow falling across his face. He found that the door had been blown open, and that standing in the room was a fair woman in dazzlingly white garments. For a moment she stood thus; then she bent over Mosaku, her breath coming forth like white smoke. After bending thus over the old man for a minute or two she turned to Minokichi and hovered over him. He tried to cry out, for the breath of this woman was like a freezing blast of wind. She told him that she had intended to treat him as she had done the old man at his side, but forbore on account of his youth and beauty. Threatening Minokichi with instant death if he dared to mention to anyone what he had seen, she suddenly vanished.

Then Minokichi called out to his beloved master: "Mosaku, Mosaku, wake! Something very terrible has happened!" But there was no reply. He touched the hand of his master in the dark, and found it was like a piece of ice. Mosaku was dead!

During the next winter, while Minokichi was returning home, he chanced to meet a pretty girl by the name of Yuki. She informed him that she was going to Edo, where she desired to find a situation as a servant. Minokichi was charmed with this maiden, and he went so far as to ask if she were betrothed, and hearing that she was not, he took her to his own home, and in due time married her.

Yuki presented her husband with ten fine and handsome children, fairer of skin than the average. When Minokichi's mother died her last words were in praise of Yuki, and her eulogy was echoed by many of the country folk in the district.

One night, while Yuki was sewing, the light of a paper lamp shining upon her face, Minokichi recalled the extraordinary experience he had had in the ferryman's hut. "Yuki," said he, "you remind me so much of a beautiful white woman I saw when I was eighteen years old. She killed my master with her ice-cold breath. I am sure she was some strange spirit, and yet tonight she seems to resemble you!"

Yuki flung down her sewing. There was a horrible smile on her face as she bent close to her husband and shrieked: "It was I, Yuki-Onna, who came to you then, and silently killed your master! Oh, faithless wretch, you have broken your promise to keep the matter secret, and if it were not for our sleeping children I would kill you now! Remember, if they have aught to complain of at your hands I shall hear, I shall know, and on a night when the snow falls I *will* kill you!"

Then Yuki-Onna, the Lady of the Snow, changed into a white mist, and, shrieking and shuddering, passed through the smoke-hole, never to return again.

KYUZAEMON'S GHOSTLY VISITOR

Kyuzaemon, a poor farmer, had closed the shutters of his humble dwelling and retired to rest. Shortly before midnight he was awakened by loud tapping. Going to the door, he exclaimed: "Who are you? What do you want?"

The strange visitor made no attempt to answer these questions, but persistently begged for food and shelter. The cautious Kyuzaemon refused to allow the visitor to enter, and, having seen that his dwelling was secure, he was about to retire to bed again, when he saw standing beside him a woman in white flowing garments, her hair falling over her shoulders.

"Where did you leave your *geta?*" demanded the frightened farmer.

The white woman informed him that she was the visitor who had tapped upon his door. "I need no *geta,*" she said, "for I have no feet! I fly over the snow-capped trees, and should have proceeded to the next village, but the wind was blowing strongly against me, and I desired to rest awhile."

The farmer expressed his fear of spirits, whereupon the woman inquired if her host had a *butsudan* (a family altar). Finding that he had, she bade him open the *butsudan* and light a lamp. When this was done the woman prayed before the ancestral tablets, not forgetting to add a prayer for the still much-agitated Kyuzaemon.

Having paid her respects at the *butsudan,* she informed the farmer that her name was Oyasu, and that she had lived with her parents and her husband, Isaburo. When she died her husband left her parents, and it was her intention to try to persuade him to go back again and support the old people.

Kyuzaemon began to understand as he murmured to himself: "Oyasu perished in the snow, and this is her spirit I see before me." However, in spite of this recollection he still felt much afraid. He sought the family altar with trembling footsteps, repeating over and over again: "Namu Amida Butsu!" ("Hail, Omnipotent Buddha!")

At last the farmer went to bed and fell asleep. Once he woke up to hear the white creature murmur farewell; but before he could make answer she had disappeared.

The following day Kyuzaemon went to the next village, and called upon Isaburo, whom he now found living with his father-in-law again. Isaburo informed him that he had received numerous visits from the spirit of his wife in the guise of Yuki-Onna. After carefully considering the matter Kyuzaemon found that this Lady of the Snow had appeared before Isaburo almost immediately after she had paid him such a mysterious visit. On that occasion Isaburo had promised to fulfil her wish, and neither he nor Kyuzaemon were again troubled with her who travels in the sky when the snow is falling fast.

THE MAIDEN OF UNAI

The Maiden Unai dwelt with her parents in the village of Ashinoya. She was extremely beautiful, and it so happened that she had two most ardent and persistent lovers – Mubara, who was a native of the same countryside, and Chinu; who came from Izumi. These two lovers might very well have been twins, for they resembled each other in age, face, figure, and stature. Unfortunately, however, they both loved her with an equal passion, so that it was impossible to distinguish between them. Their gifts were the same, and there appeared to be no difference in their manner of courting. We get a good idea of the formidable aspect of these two lovers in the following, taken from Mushimaro's poem on the subject:

"With jealous love these champions twain
The beauteous girl did woo;
Each had his hand on the hilt of his sword,
And a full-charged quiver, too,

"Was slung o'er the back of each champion fierce,
And a bow of snow-white wood
Did rest in the sinewy hand of each;
And the twain defiant stood."

In the meantime, the Maiden of Unai grew sick at heart. She never accepted the gifts of either Mubara or Chinu, and yet it distressed her to see them standing at the gate month after month, never relaxing for a moment the ardent expression of their feeling toward her.

The Maiden of Unai's parents do not seem to have appreciated the complexity of the situation, for they said to her: "Sad it is for us to have to bear the burden of thine unseemly conduct in thus carelessly from month to month, and from year to year, causing others to sorrow. If thou wilt accept the one, after a little time the other's love will cease."

These well-meant words brought no consolation or assistance to the poor Maiden of Unai, so her parents sent for the lovers, explained the pitiful situation, and decided that he who should shoot a water-bird swimming in the river Ikuta, which flowed by the platform on which the house was built, should have their daughter in marriage. The lovers were delighted at this decision, and anxious to put an end to this cruel suspense. They pulled their bow-strings at the same instant, and together their arrows struck the bird, one in the head and the other in the tail, so that neither could claim to be the better marksman. When the Maiden of Unai saw how entirely hopeless the whole affair was, she exclaimed:

> "Enough, enough! yon swiftly flowing wave
> Shall free my soul from her long anxious strife:
> Men call fair Settsu's stream the stream of life,
> But in that stream shall be the maiden's grave!"

With these melodramatic words she flung herself from the platform into the surging water beneath.

The maid's parents, who witnessed the scene, shouted and raved on the platform, while the devoted lovers sprang into the river. One held the maiden's foot, and the other her hand, and in a moment the three sank and perished. In due time the maiden was buried with her lovers on either side, and to this day the spot is known as the 'Maiden's Grave'. In the grave of Mubara there was a hollow bamboo-cane, together with a bow, a quiver, and a long sword; but nothing had been placed in the grave of Chinu.

Some time afterwards a stranger happened to pass one night in the neighbourhood of the grave, and he was suddenly disturbed by hearing the sound of fighting. He sent his retainers to inquire into the matter, but they returned to him saying they could hear or see nothing of an unusual nature. While the stranger pondered over the love-story of the Maiden of Unai he fell asleep. He had no sooner done so than he saw before him, kneeling on the ground, a blood-stained man, who told him that he was much harassed by the persecutions of an enemy, and begged that the stranger would lend him his sword. This request was reluctantly granted. When the stranger awoke he was inclined to think the whole affair a dream; but it was no passing fantasy of the night, for not only was his sword missing, but he heard near at hand the sound of a great combat. Then the clash of weapons suddenly ceased, and once more the blood-stained man stood before him, saying: "By thine honourable assistance have I slain the foe that had oppressed me during these many years." So we may infer that in the spirit world Chinu fought and slew his rival, and after many years of bitter jealousy was finally able to call the Maiden of Unai his own.

THE MAIDEN WITH THE WOODEN BOWL

In ancient days there lived an old couple with their only child, a girl of remarkable charm and beauty. When the old man fell sick and died his widow became more and more concerned for her daughter's future welfare.

One day she called her child to her, and said: "Little one, your father lies in yonder cemetery, and I, being old and feeble, must needs follow him soon. The thought of leaving you alone in the world troubles me much, for you are beautiful, and beauty is a temptation and a snare to men. Not all the purity of a white flower can prevent it from being plucked and dragged down in the mire. My child, your face is all too fair. It must be hidden from the eager eyes of men, lest it cause you to fall from your good and simple life to one of shame."

Having said these words, she placed a lacquered bowl upon the maiden's head, so that it veiled her attractions. "Always wear it, little one," said the mother, "for it will protect you when I am gone."

Shortly after this loving deed had been performed the old woman died, and the maiden was forced to earn her living by working in the rice-fields. It was hard, weary work, but the girl kept a brave heart and toiled from dawn to sunset without a murmur. Over and over again her strange appearance created considerable comment, and she was known throughout the country as the "Maiden with the Bowl on her Head." Young men laughed at her and tried to peep under the vessel, and not a few endeavoured to pull off the wooden covering; but it could not be removed, and laughing and jesting, the young men had to be content with a glimpse of the lower part of the fair maiden's face. The poor girl bore this rude treatment with a patient but heavy heart, believing that out of her mother's love and wisdom would come some day a joy that would more than compensate for all her sorrow.

One day a rich farmer watched the maiden working in his rice-fields. He was struck by her diligence and the quick and excellent way she performed her tasks. He was pleased with that bent and busy little figure, and did not laugh at the wooden bowl on her head. After observing her for some time, he came to the maiden, and said: "You work well and do not chatter to your companions. I wish you to labour in my rice-fields until the end of the harvest."

When the rice harvest had been gathered and winter had come the wealthy farmer, still more favourably impressed with the maiden, and anxious to do her a service, bade her become an inmate of his house. "My wife is ill," he added, "and I should like you to nurse her for me."

The maiden gratefully accepted this welcome offer. She tended the sick woman with every care, for the same quiet diligence she displayed in the rice-fields was characteristic of her gentle labour in the sick-room. As the farmer and his wife had no daughter they took very kindly to this orphan and regarded her as a child of their own.

At length the farmer's eldest son returned to his old home. He was a wise young man who had studied much in gay Kyoto, and was weary of a merry life of feasting and frivolous pleasure. His father and mother expected that their son would soon grow tired of his father's house and its quiet surroundings, and every day they feared that he would come to them, bid farewell, and return once more to the city of the Mikado. But to the surprise of all the farmer's son expressed no desire to leave his old home.

One day the young man came to his father, and said: "Who is this maiden in our house, and why does she wear an ugly black bowl upon her head?"

When the farmer had told the sad story of the maiden his son was deeply moved; but, nevertheless, he could not refrain from laughing a little at the bowl. The young man's laughter, however, did not last long. Day by day the maiden became more fascinating to him. Now and again he peeped at the girl's half-hidden face, and became more and more impressed by her gentleness of manner and her nobility of nature. It was not long before his admiration turned into love, and he resolved that he would marry the Maiden with the Bowl on her Head. Most of his relations were opposed to the union. They said: "She is all very well in her way, but she is only a common servant. She wears that bowl in order to captivate the unwary, and we do not think it hides beauty, but rather ugliness. Seek a wife elsewhere, for we will not tolerate this ambitious and scheming maiden."

From that hour the maiden suffered much. Bitter and spiteful things were said to her, and even her mistress, once so good and kind, turned against her. But the farmer did not change his opinion. He still liked the girl, and was quite willing that she should become his son's wife, but, owing to the heated remarks of his wife and relations, he dared not reveal his wishes in the matter.

All the opposition, none too kindly expressed, only made the young man more desirous to achieve his purpose. At length his mother and relations, seeing that their wishes were useless, consented to the marriage, but with a very bad grace.

The young man, believing that all difficulties had been removed, joyfully went to the Maiden with the Bowl on her Head, and said: "All troublesome opposition is at an end, and now nothing prevents us from getting married."

"No," replied the poor maiden, weeping bitterly, "I cannot marry you. I am only a servant in your father's house, and therefore it would be unseemly for me to become your bride."

The young man spoke gently to her. He expressed his ardent love over and over again, he argued, he begged; but the maiden would not change her mind. Her attitude made the relations extremely angry. They said that the woman had made fools of them all, little knowing that she dearly loved the farmer's son, and believed, in her loyal heart, that marriage could only bring discord in the home that had sheltered her in her poverty.

That night the poor girl cried herself to sleep, and in a dream her mother came to her, and said: "My dear child, let your good heart be troubled no more. Marry the farmer's son and all will be well again." The maiden woke next morning full of joy, and when her lover came to her and asked once more if she would become his bride, she yielded with a gracious smile.

Great preparations were made for the wedding, and when the company assembled, it was deemed high time to remove the maiden's wooden bowl. She herself tried to take it off, but it remained firmly fixed to her head. When some of the relations, with not a few unkind remarks, came to her assistance, the bowl uttered strange cries and groans. At length the bridegroom approached the maiden, and said: "Do not let this treatment distress you. You are just as dear to me with or without the bowl," and having said these words, he commanded that the ceremony should proceed.

Then the wine-cups were brought into the crowded apartment and, according to custom, the bride and bridegroom were expected to drink together the 'Three times three' in token of their union. Just as the maiden put the wine-cup to her lips the bowl on her head broke with a great noise, and from it fell gold and silver and all manner of precious stones, so that the maiden who had once been a beggar now had her marriage portion. The guests were amazed as they looked upon the heap of shining jewels and gold and silver, but they were still more surprised when they chanced to look up and see that the bride was the most beautiful woman in all Japan.

GHOSTS & SUPERNATURAL CREATURES

Some of the legends in this chapter were adapted by Frederick Hadland Davis from stories in Lafcadio Hearn's *Kwaidan* and *Glimpses of Unfamiliar Japan*. In its widest sense, the word *kaidan* can indicate any ghost or horror story, but these tales tend to originate from or evoke the folklore and world of Edo period Japan. Classic *kaidan* usually include some element of vengeance on the part of the spirit for mistreatment in their lifetime – two long sagas that, alas, we did not have space for in this collection (*The Yotsuya Kwaidan* or *O'Iwa Inari* and *The Bancho Sarayashiki* or *The Lady of The Plates* – see our larger collection, *Japanese Myths & Tales*) are famous *kaidan* – the poor maidservant who haunts a well in the latter story is familiar to fans of the horror film *Ring*.

Supernatural beings populate many a Japanese tale. In addition to the fearsome demons or ogres known as *oni*, whom we have already encountered in some of the heroes' exploits, in the following stories we meet the *tengu* and other species of (often man-eating) goblin, *kappas*, fire ghosts, sea monsters and all manner of spirits and demons.

A KAKEMONO GHOST

Sawara was a pupil in the house of the artist Tenko, who was a kind and able master, while Sawara, even at the commencement of his art studies, showed considerable promise. Kimi, Tenko's niece, devoted her time to her uncle and in directing the affairs of the household generally. Kimi was beautiful, and it was not long before she fell desperately in love with Sawara. This young pupil regarded her as very charming, one to die for if need be, and in his heart he secretly loved her. His love, however, unlike Kimi's, was not demonstrative, for he had his work to attend to, and so, to be sure, had Kimi; but work with Sawara came before his love, and with Kimi it was only love that mattered.

One day, when Tenko was paying a visit, Kimi came to Sawara, and, unable to restrain her feelings any longer, told him of her love, and asked him if he would like to marry her. Having made her request, she set tea before her lover, and awaited his answer.

Sawara returned her affection, and said that he would be delighted to marry her, adding, however, that marriage was not possible until after two or three years, when he had established a position for himself and had become a famous artist.

Sawara, in order to add to his knowledge of art, decided to study under a celebrated painter named Myokei, and, everything having been arranged, he bade farewell to his old master and Kimi, promising that he would return as soon as he had made a name for himself and become a great artist.

Two years went by and Tenko and Kimi heard no news of Sawara. Many admirers of Kimi came to her uncle with offers of marriage, and Tenko was debating as to what he should do in the matter, when he received a letter from Myokei, saying that Sawara was doing good work, and that he desired that his excellent pupil should marry his daughter.

Tenko imagined, perhaps not without some reason, that Sawara had forgotten all about Kimi, and that the best thing he could do was to give her in marriage to Yorozuya, a wealthy merchant, and also to fulfil Miyokei's wish that Sawara should marry the great painter's daughter. With these intentions Tenko resolved to employ strategy, so he called Kimi to him, and said:

"Kimi, I have had a letter from Myokei, and I am afraid the sad news which it contains will distress you. Myokei wishes Sawara to marry his daughter, and I have told him that I fully approve of the union. I feel sure that Sawara has neglected you, and I therefore wish that you should marry Yorozuya, who will make, I am sure, a very good husband."

When Kimi heard these words she wept bitterly, and without a word went to her room.

In the morning Tenko entered Kimi's apartment, but his niece had gone, and the protracted search that followed failed to discover her whereabouts.

When Myokei had received Tenko's letter he told the promising young artist that he wished him to marry his daughter, and thus establish a family of painters; but Sawara was amazed to hear this extraordinary news, and explained that he could not accept the honour of becoming his son-in-law because he was already engaged to Tenko's niece.

Sawara, all too late, sent letters to Kimi, and, receiving no reply, he set out for his old home, shortly after the death of Myokei.

When he reached the little house where he had received his first lessons in the art of painting he learnt with anger that Kimi had left her old uncle, and in due time he married Kiku ('Chrysanthemum'), the daughter of a wealthy farmer.

Shortly after Sawara's marriage the Lord of Aki bade him paint the seven scenes of the Islands of Kabakari-jima, which were to be mounted on gold screens. He at once set out for these islands, and made a number of rough sketches. While thus employed he met along the shore a woman with a red cloth round her loins, her hair loose and falling about her shoulders. She carried shell-fish in her basket, and as soon as she saw Sawara she recognised him.

"You are Sawara and I am Kimi," said she, "to whom you are engaged. It was a false report about your marriage with Myokei's daughter, and my heart is full of joy, for now nothing prevents our union."

"Alas! poor, much-wronged Kimi, that cannot be!" replied Sawara. "I thought that you deserted Tenko, and that you had forgotten me, and believing these things to be true I have married Kiku, a farmer's daughter."

Kimi, without a word, sprang forward like a hunted animal, ran along the shore, and entered her little hut, Sawara running after her and calling her name over and over again. Before his very eyes he saw Kimi take a knife and thrust it into her throat, and in another moment she lay dead upon the ground. Sawara wept as he gazed upon her still form, noticed the wistful beauty of Death upon her cheek, and saw a new glory in her wind-blown hair. So fair and wonderful was her presence now that when he had controlled his weeping he made a sketch of the woman who had loved him so well, but so pitifully. Above the mark of the tide he buried her, and when he reached his own home he took out the rough sketch, painted a picture of Kimi, and hung the *kakemono* on the wall.

Kimi Finds Peace

That very night he awoke to find that the figure on the *kakemono* had come to life, that Kimi with the wound in her throat, the dishevelled hair, stood beside him. Night after night she came, a silent, pitiful figure, until at last Sawara, unable to bear these visitations any longer, presented the *kakemono* to the Korinji Temple and sent his wife back to her parents. The priests of the Korinji Temple prayed every day for the soul of Kimi, and by and by Kimi found peace and troubled Sawara no more.

THE PEONY LANTERN

Tsuyu ('Morning Dew') was the only daughter of Iijima. When her father married again she found she could not live happily with her stepmother, and a separate house was built for her, where she lived with her servant-maid Yone.

One day Tsuyu received a visit from the family physician, Yamamoto Shijo accompanied by a handsome young *samurai* named Hagiwara Shinzaburo. These young people fell in love with each other, and at parting Tsuyu whispered to Shinzaburo: *"Remember! if you do not come to see me again I shall certainly die!"*

Shinzaburo had every intention of seeing the fair Tsuyu as frequently as possible. Etiquette, however, would not allow him to visit her alone, so that he was compelled to rely on the old doctor's promise to take him to the villa where his loved one lived. The old doctor, however, having seen more than the young people had supposed, purposely refrained from keeping his promise.

Tsuyu, believing that the handsome young *samurai* had proved unfaithful, slowly pined away and died. Her faithful servant Yone also died soon afterwards, being unable to live without her mistress, and they were buried side by side in the cemetery of Shin-Banzui-In.

Shortly after this sad event had taken place the old doctor called upon Shinzaburo and gave him full particulars of the death of Tsuyu and her maid.

Shinzaburo felt the blow keenly. Night and day the girl was in his thoughts. He inscribed her name upon a mortuary tablet, placed offerings before it, and repeated many prayers.

The Dead Return

When the first day of the Festival of the Dead arrived he set food on the Shelf of Souls and hung out lanterns to guide the spirits during their brief earthly sojourn. As the night was warm and the moon at her full, he sat in his verandah and waited. He felt that all these preparations would not be in vain, and in his heart he believed that the soul of Tsuyu would come to him.

Suddenly the stillness was broken by the sound of *kara-kon*, *kara-kon*, the soft patter of women's *geta*. There was something strange and haunting about the sound. Shinzaburo rose and peeped over the hedge. He saw two women. One was carrying a long-shaped lantern with silk peonies stuck in at the upper end; the other wore a lovely robe covered with designs of autumnal blossom. In another moment he recognised the sweet figure of Tsuyu and her maid Yone.

When Yone had explained that the wicked old doctor had told them that Shinzaburo was dead, and the young *samurai* had likewise informed his visitors that he, too, had learnt from the same source that his loved one and her maid had departed this life, the two women entered the house, and remained there that night, returning home a little before sunrise. Night after night they came in this mysterious manner, and always Yone carried the shining peony-lantern, always she and her mistress departed at the same hour.

A Spy

One night Tomozo, one of Shinzaburo's servants, who lived next door to his master, chanced to hear the sound of a woman's voice in his lord's apartment. He peeped through a crack in one of the sliding doors, and perceived by the night-lantern within the room that his master was talking with a strange woman under the mosquito-net. Their conversation was so extraordinary that Tomozo was determined to see the woman's face. When he succeeded in doing so his hair stood on end and he trembled violently, for he saw the face of a dead woman, a woman long dead. There was no flesh on her fingers, for what had once been fingers were now a bunch of jangling bones. Only the upper part of her body had substance; below her waist there was but a dim, moving shadow. While Tomozo gazed with horror upon such a revolting scene a second woman's figure sprang up from within the room. She made for the chink and for Tomozo's eye behind it. With a shriek of terror the spying Tomozo fled to the house of Hakuodo Yusai.

Yusai's Advice

Now Yusai was a man well versed in all manner of mysteries; but nevertheless Tomozo's story made considerable impression upon him, and he listened to every detail with the utmost amazement. When the servant had finished his account of the affair Yusai informed him that his master was a doomed man if the woman proved to be a ghost, that love between the living and the dead ended in the destruction of the living.

However, apart from critically examining this strange event, Yusai took practical steps to rescue this young *samurai* from so horrible a fate. The next morning he discussed the matter with Shinzaburo, and told him pretty clearly that he had been loving a ghost, and that the sooner he got rid of that ghost the better it would be for him. He ended his discourse by advising the youth to go to the district of Shitaya, in Yanaka-no-Sasaki, the place where these women had said they lived.

The Mystery is Revealed

Shinzaburo carried out Yusai's advice, but nowhere in the quarter of Yanaka-no-Sasaki could he find the dwelling-place of Tsuyu. On his return home he happened to pass through the temple Shin-Banzui-In. There he saw two tombs placed side by side, one of no distinction, and the other large and handsome, adorned with a peony-lantern swinging gently in the breeze. Shinzaburo remembered that this lantern and the one carried by Yone were identical, and an acolyte informed him that the tombs were those of Tsuyu and Yone. Then it was that he realised the strange meaning of Yone's words: "*We went away, and found a very small house in Yanaka-no-Sasaki. There we are now just barely able to live by doing a little private work.*" Their house, then, was a grave. The ghost of Yone carried the peony-lantern, and the ghost of Tsuyu wound her fleshless arms about the neck of the young *samurai*.

Holy Charms

Shinzaburo, now fully aware of the horror of the situation, hastily retraced his steps and sought counsel from the wise, far-seeing Yusai. This learned man confessed his inability to help him further in the matter, but advised him to go to the high-priest Ryoseki, of Shin-Banzui-In, and gave him a letter explaining what had taken place.

Ryoseki listened unmoved to Shinzaburo's story, for he had heard so many bearing on the same theme, the evil power of Karma. He gave the young man a small gold image of Buddha, which he instructed him to wear next his skin, telling him that it would protect the living from the dead. He also gave him a holy *sutra*, called "Treasure-Raining Sutra," which he was commended to recite in his house every night; and lastly he gave him a bundle of sacred texts. Each holy strip he was to paste over an opening in his house.

By nightfall everything was in order in Shinzaburo's house. All the apertures were covered with sacred texts, and the air resounded with the recitation of the 'Treasure-Raining Sutra', while the little gold Buddha swayed upon the *samurai's* breast. But somehow or other peace did not come to Shinzaburo that night. Sleep refused to close his weary eyes, and just as a temple bell ceased booming he heard the old *karan-koron*, *karan-koron* – the patter of ghostly *geta*! Then the sound ceased. Fear and joy battled within Shinzaburo's heart. He stopped reciting the holy *sutra* and looked forth into the night. Once more he saw Tsuyu and her maid with the peony-lantern. Never before had Tsuyu looked so beautiful or so alluring; but a nameless terror held him back. He heard with bitter anguish the women speaking together. He heard Yone tell her mistress that his love had changed because his doors had been made fast against them, followed by the plaintive weeping of Tsuyu. At last the women wandered round to the back of the house. But back and front alike prevented their entry, so potent were the sacred words of the Lord Buddha.

The Betrayal

As all the efforts of Yone to enter Shinzaburo's house were of no avail, she went night after night to Tomozo and begged him to remove the sacred texts from his master's dwelling. Over and over again, out of intense fear, Tomozo promised to do so, but with the coming of daylight he grew brave and decided not to betray one to whom he owed so much. One night, however, Yone refused to be trifled with. She threatened Tomozo with awful hatred if he did not take away one of the sacred texts, and in addition she pulled such a terrible face that Tomozo nearly died of fright.

Tomozo's wife Mine happened to awake and hear the voice of a strange woman speaking to her husband. When the ghost-woman had vanished Mine gave her lord cunning counsel to the effect that he should consent to carry out Yone's request provided that she would reward him with a hundred *ryō*.

Two nights later, when this wicked servant had received his reward, he gave Yone the little gold image of Buddha, took down from his master's house one of the sacred texts, and buried in a field the *sutra* which his master used to recite.

This enabled Yone and her mistress to enter the house of Shinzaburo once more, and with their entry began again this horrible love of the dead, presided over by the mysterious power of Karma.

When Tomozo came the next morning to call his master as usual, he obtained no response to his knocking. At last he entered the apartment, and there, under the mosquito-net, lay his master dead, and beside him were the white bones of a woman. The bones of 'Morning Dew' were twined round the neck of one who had loved her too well, of one who had loved her with a fierce passion that at the last had been his undoing.

HOICHI-THE-EARLESS

It is said that for seven hundred years after this great battle the sea and coast in the vicinity have been haunted by the ghosts of the Taira clan. Mysterious fires shone on the waves, and the air was filled with the noise of warfare. In order to pacify the unfortunate spirits the temple of Amidaji was built at Akamagaseki, and a cemetery was made close by, in which were various monuments inscribed with the names of the drowned Emperor and his principal followers. This temple and cemetery pacified the ghostly visitants to a certain extent, but from time to time many strange things happened, as we shall gather from the following legend.

There once lived at the Amidaji temple a blind priest named Hōichi. He was famous for his recitation and for his marvellous skill in playing upon the *biwa* (a four-stringed lute), and he was particularly fond of reciting stories in connection with the protracted war between the Taira and Minamoto clans.

One night Hōichi was left alone in the temple, and as it was a very warm evening he sat out on the verandah, playing now and again upon his *biwa*. While thus occupied he heard someone approaching, someone stepping across the little back garden of the temple. Then a deep voice cried out from below the verandah: "Hōichi!" Yet again the voice sounded: "Hōichi!"

Hōichi, now very much alarmed, replied that he was blind, and would be glad to know who his visitor might be.

"My lord," began the stranger, "is now staying at Akamagaseki with many noble followers, and he has come for the purpose of viewing the scene of the battle of Dan-no-ura. He has heard how excellently you recite the story of the conflict, and has commanded me to escort you to him in order that you may show him your skill. Bring your *biwa* and follow me. My lord and his august assembly now await your honourable presence."

Hōichi, deeming that the stranger was some noble *samurai*, obeyed immediately. He donned his sandals and took his *biwa*. The stranger guided him with an iron hand, and they marched along very quickly. Hōichi heard the clank of armour at his side; but all fear left him, and he looked forward to the honour of showing his skill before a distinguished company.

Arriving at a gate, the stranger shouted: "*Kaimon!*" Immediately the gate was unbarred and opened, and the two men passed in. Then came the sound of many hurrying feet, and a rustling noise as of screens being opened. Hōichi was assisted in mounting a number of steps, and, arriving at the top, he was commanded to leave his sandals. A woman then led him forward by the hand till he found himself in a vast apartment, where he judged that a great company of people were assembled. He heard the subdued murmur of voices and the soft movement of silken garments. When Hōichi had seated himself on a cushion the woman who had led him bade him recite the story of the great battle of Dan-no-ura.

Hōichi began to chant to the accompaniment of his *biwa*. His skill was so great that the strings of his instrument seemed to imitate the sound of oars, the movement of ships, the shouting of men, the noise of surging waves, and the whirring of arrows. A low murmur of applause greeted Hōichi's wonderful performance. Thus encouraged, he continued to sing and play with even greater skill. When he came to chant of the perishing of the women and children, the plunge of Niidono into the sea with the infant Emperor in her arms, the company began to weep and wail.

When the performance was over the woman who had led Hōichi told him that her lord was well pleased with his skill, and that he desired him to play before him for the six following nights. "The retainer," added she, "who brought you tonight will visit your temple at the same hour tomorrow. You must keep these visits secret, and may now return to your abode."

Once more the woman led Hōichi through the apartment, and having reached the steps the same retainer led him back to the verandah at the back of the temple where he lived.

The next night Hōichi was again led forth to entertain the assembly, and he met with the same success. But this time his absence was detected, and upon his return his fellow priest questioned him in regard to the matter. Hōichi evaded his friend's question, and told him that he had merely been out to attend some private business.

His questioner was by no means satisfied. He regretted Hōichi's reticence and feared that there was something wrong, possibly that, the blind priest had been bewitched by evil spirits. He bade the men-servants keep a strict watch upon Hōichi, and to follow him if he should again leave the temple during the night.

Once more Hōichi left his abode. The men-servants hastily lit their lanterns and followed him with all speed; but though they walked quickly, looked everywhere, and made numerous inquiries, they failed to discover Hōichi, or learn anything concerning him. On their return, however, they were alarmed to hear the sound of a *biwa* in the cemetery of the temple, and on entering this gloomy place they discovered the blind priest. He sat at the tomb of Antoku Tenno, the infant Emperor, where he twanged his *biwa* loudly, and as loudly chanted the story of the battle of Dan-no-ura. About him on every side mysterious fires glowed, like a great gathering of lighted candles.

"Hōichi! Hōichi!" shouted the men. "Stop your playing at once! You are bewitched, Hōichi!" But the blind priest continued to play and sing, rapt, it seemed, in a strange and awful dream.

The men-servants now resorted to more extreme measures. They shook him, and shouted in his ear: "Hōichi, come back with us at once!"

The blind priest rebuked them, and said that such an interruption would not be tolerated by the noble assembly about him.

The men now dragged Hōichi away by force. When he reached the temple his wet clothes were taken off and food and drink set before him.

By this time Hōichi's fellow priest was extremely angry, and he not unjustly insisted upon a full explanation of his extraordinary behaviour. Hōichi, after much hesitation, told his friend all that had happened to him. When he had narrated his strange adventures, the priest said:

"My poor fellow! You ought to have told me this before. You have not been visiting a great house of a noble lord, but you have been sitting in yonder cemetery before the tomb of Antoku Tenno. Your great skill has called forth the ghosts of the Taira clan. Hōichi, you are in great danger, for by obeying these spirits you have assuredly put yourself in their power, and sooner or later they will kill you. Unfortunately I am called away tonight to perform a service, but before I go I will see that your body is covered with sacred texts."

Before night approached Hōichi was stripped, and upon his body an acolyte inscribed, with writing-brushes, the text of the *sutra* known as *Hannya-Shin-Kyō*. These texts were written upon Hōichi's breast, head, back, face, neck, legs, arms, and feet, even upon the soles thereof.

Then the priest said: "Hōichi, you will be called again tonight. Remain silent, sit very still, and continually meditate. If you do these things no harm will befall you."

That night Hōichi sat alone in the verandah, scarcely moving a muscle and breathing very softly.

Once more he heard the sound of footsteps. "Hōichi!" cried a deep voice. But the blind priest made no answer. He sat very still, full of a great fear.

His name was called over and over again, but to no effect. "This won't do," growled the stranger. "I must see where the fellow is." The stranger sprang into the verandah and stood beside Hōichi, who was now shaking all over with the horror of the situation.

"Ah!" said the stranger. "This is the *biwa*, but in place of the player I see – only two ears! Now I understand why he did not answer. He has no mouth, only his two ears! Those ears I will take to my lord!"

In another moment Hōichi's ears were torn off, but in spite of the fearful pain the blind priest remained mute. Then the stranger departed, and when his footsteps had died away the only sound Hōichi heard was the trickling of blood upon the verandah, and thus the priest found the unfortunate man upon his return.

"Poor Hōichi!" cried the priest. "It is all my fault. I trusted my acolyte to write sacred texts on every part of your body. He failed to do so on your ears. I ought to have seen that he carried out my instructions properly. However, you will never be troubled with those spirits in future." From that day the blind priest was known as *Mimi-nashi-Hōichi*, 'Hōichi-the-Earless'.

THE CORPSE-EATER

Muso Kokushi, a priest, lost his way while travelling through the province of Mino. Despairing of finding a human abode, he was about to sleep out in the open, when he chanced to discover a little hermitage, called *anjitsu*. An aged priest greeted him, and Muso requested that he would give him shelter for the night. "No," replied the old priest angrily, "I never give shelter to anyone. In yonder valley you will find a certain hamlet; seek a night's repose there."

With these rather uncivil words, Muso took his departure, and reaching the hamlet indicated he was hospitably received at the headman's dwelling. On entering the principal apartment, the priest saw a number of people assembled together. He was shown into a separate room, and was about to fall asleep, when he heard the sound of lamentation, and shortly afterwards a young man appeared before him, holding a lantern in his hand.

"Good priest," said he, "I must tell you that my father has recently died. We did not like to explain the matter upon your arrival, because you were tired and much needed rest. The number of people you saw in the principal apartment had come to pay their respects to the dead. Now we must all go away, for that is the custom in our village when anyone dies, because strange and terrible things happen to corpses when they are left alone; but perhaps, being a priest, you will not be afraid to remain with my poor father's body."

Muso replied that he was in no way afraid, and told the young man that he would perform a service, and watch by the deceased during the company's absence. Then the young man, together with the other mourners, left the house, and Muso remained to perform his solitary night vigil.

After Muso had undertaken the funeral ceremonies, he sat meditating for several hours. When the night had far advanced, he was aware of the presence of a strange Shape, so terrible in aspect that the priest could neither move nor speak. The Shape advanced, raised the corpse, and quickly devoured it. Not content with this horrible meal, the mysterious form also ate the offerings, and then vanished.

The next morning the villagers returned, and they expressed no surprise, on hearing that the corpse had disappeared. After Muso had narrated his strange adventure he inquired if the priest on the hill did not sometimes perform the funeral service. "I visited him last night at his *anjitsu*, and though he refused me shelter, he told me where I might rest."

The villagers were amazed at these words, and informed Muso that there was certainly no priest and no *anjitsu* on yonder hill. They were positive in their assertion, and assured Muso that he had been deluded in the matter by some evil spirit. Muso did not reply, and shortly afterwards he took his departure, determined if possible to unravel the mystery.

Muso had no difficulty in finding the *anjitsu* again. The old priest came out to him, bowed, and exclaimed that he was sorry for his former rudeness. "I am ashamed," added he, "not only because I gave you no shelter, but because you have seen my real shape. You have seen me devour a corpse and the funeral offerings. Alas! good sir, I am a *jikininki* (man-eating goblin), and if you will bear with me I will explain my wretched condition.

"Many years ago I used to be a priest in this district, and I performed a great number of burial services; but I was not a good priest, for I was not influenced by true religion in performing my tasks, and thought only of the good and fine clothes I could get out of my calling. For that reason I was reborn a *jikininki*, and have ever since devoured the corpses of all those who died in this district. I beg that you will have pity on my miserable plight, and repeat certain prayers on my behalf, that I may speedily find peace and make an end of my great wickedness."

Immediately after these words had been spoken, the recluse and his hermitage suddenly vanished, and Muso found himself kneeling beside a moss-covered tomb, which was probably the tomb of the unfortunate priest.

THE GHOST MOTHER

A pale-faced woman crept down a street called Nakabaramachi, entered a certain shop, and purchased a small quantity of *midzu-ame*. Every night, at a late hour, she came, always haggard of countenance and always silent. The shopkeeper, who took a kindly interest in her, followed her one night, but seeing that she entered a cemetery, he turned back, puzzled and afraid.

Once again the mysterious woman came to the little shop, and this time she did not buy *midzu-ame*, but beckoned the shopkeeper to follow her. Down the street went the pale-faced woman, followed by the seller of amber syrup and some of his friends. When they reached the cemetery the woman disappeared into a tomb, and those without heard the weeping of a child. When the tomb was opened they saw the corpse of the woman they had followed, and by her side a living child, laughing at the lantern-light and stretching forth its little hands towards a cup of *midzu-ame*. The woman had been prematurely buried and her babe born in the tomb. Every night the silent mother went forth from the cemetery in order that she might bring back nourishment for her child.

THE FUTON OF TOTTORI

In Tottori there was a small and modest inn. It was a new inn, and as the landlord was poor he had been compelled to furnish it with goods purchased from a second-hand shop in the vicinity. His first guest was a merchant, who was treated with extreme courtesy and given much warm *sake*. When the merchant had drunk the refreshing rice wine he retired to rest and soon fell asleep. He had not slumbered long when he heard the sound of children's voices in his room, crying pitifully: "Elder Brother probably is cold?" "Nay, thou probably art cold?" Over and over again the children repeated these plaintive words. The merchant, thinking that children had strayed into his room by mistake, mildly rebuked them and prepared to go to sleep again. After a moment's silence the children again cried: "Elder Brother probably is cold?" "Nay, thou probably art cold?"

The guest arose, lit the *andon* (night-light), and proceeded to examine the room. But there was no one in the apartment; the cupboards were empty, and all the *shōji* (paper-screens) were closed. The merchant, lay down again, puzzled and amazed. Once more he heard the cry, close to his pillow: "Elder Brother probably is cold?" "Nay, thou probably art cold?" The cries were repeated, and the guest, cold with horror, found that the voices proceeded from his *futon* (quilt).

He hurriedly descended the stairs and told the innkeeper what had happened. The landlord was angry. "You have drunk too much warm *sake*," said he. "Warm *sake* has brought you evil dreams." But the guest paid his bill and sought lodging elsewhere.

On the following night another guest, slept in the haunted room, and he, too, heard the same mysterious voices, rated the innkeeper, and hastily took his departure. The landlord then entered the apartment himself. He heard the pitiful cries of children coming from one *futon*, and now was forced to believe the strange story his two guests had told him.

The next day the landlord went to the second-hand shop where he had purchased the *futon*, and made inquiries. After going from one shop to another, he finally heard the following story of the mysterious *futon*:

There once lived in Tottori a poor man and his wife, with two children, boys of six and eight years respectively. The parents died, and the poor children were forced to sell their few belongings, until one day they were left with only a thin and much-worn *futon* to cover them at night. At last they had no money to pay the rent, and not even the wherewithal to purchase food of any kind.

When the period of the greatest cold came, the snow gathered so thickly about the humble dwelling that the children could do nothing but wrap the *futon* about them, and murmur to each other in their sweet, pathetic way: "Elder Brother probably is cold?" "Nay, thou probably art cold?" And sobbing forth these words they clung together, afraid of the darkness and of the bitter, shrieking wind.

While their poor little bodies nestled together, striving to keep each other warm, the hard-hearted landlord entered, and finding that there was no one to pay the rent, he turned the children out of the house, each clad only in one thin *kimono*. They tried to reach a temple of Kwannon, but the snow was too heavy, and they hid behind their old home. A *futon* of snow covered them and they fell asleep on the merciful bosom of the Gods, and were finally buried in the cemetery of the Temple of Kwannon-of-the-Thousand-Arms.

When the innkeeper heard this sad story he gave the *futon* to the priests of the Kwannon temple, prayers were recited for the children's souls, and from that hour the *futon* ceased to murmur its plaintive cries.

THE RETURN

In the village of Mochida-no-ura there lived a peasant. He was extremely poor, but, notwithstanding, his wife bore him six children. Directly a child was born, the cruel father flung it into a river and pretended that it had died at birth, so that his six children were murdered in this horrible way.

At length, as years went by, the peasant found himself in a more prosperous position, and when a seventh child was born, a boy, he was much gratified and loved him dearly.

One night the father took the child in his arms, and wandered out into the garden, murmuring ecstatically: "What a beautiful summer night!"

The babe, then only five months old, for a moment assumed the speech of a man, saying: "The moon looks just as it did when you last threw me in the river!"

When the infant had uttered these words he became like other children; but the peasant, now truly realising the enormity of his crime, from that day became a priest.

A TEST OF LOVE

There **was once** a certain fair maiden who, contrary to Japanese custom, was permitted to choose her own husband. Many suitors sought her hand, and they brought her gifts and fair poems, and said many loving words to her. She spoke kindly to each suitor, saying: "I will marry the man who is brave enough to bear a certain test I shall impose upon him, and whatever that test of love may be, I expect him, on the sacred honour of a *samurai*, not to divulge it." The suitors readily complied with these conditions, but one by one they left her, with horror upon their faces, ceased their wooing, but breathed never a word concerning the mysterious and awful secret.

At length a poor *samurai*, whose sword was his only wealth, came to the maiden, and informed her that he was prepared to go through any test, however severe, in order that he might make her his wife.

When they had supped together the maiden left the apartment, and long after midnight returned clad in a white garment. They went out of the house together, through innumerable streets where dogs howled, and beyond the city, till they came to a great cemetery. Here the maiden led the way while the *samurai* followed, his hand upon his sword.

When the wooer was able to penetrate the darkness he saw that the maiden was digging the ground with a spade. She dug with extreme haste, and eventually tore off the lid of a coffin. In another moment she snatched up the corpse of a child, tore off an arm, broke it, and commenced to eat one piece, flinging the other to her wooer, crying: "If you love me, eat what I eat!"

Without a moment's hesitation the *samurai* sat down by the grave and began to eat one half of the arm. "Excellent!" he cried, "I pray you give me more!" At this point of the legend the horror happily disappears, for neither the *samurai* nor the maiden ate a corpse – the arm was made of delicious confectionery!

The maiden, with a cry of joy, sprang to her feet, and said: "At last I have found a brave man! I will marry you, for you are the husband I have ever longed for, and until this night have never found."

THE KAPPA'S PROMISE

In Izumo the village people refer to the *Kappa* as *Kawako* ('The Child of the River'). Near Matsue there is a little hamlet called Kawachi-mura, and on the bank of the river Kawachi there is a small temple known as Kawako-no-miya, that is, the temple of the *Kawako* or *Kappa*, said to contain a document signed by this river goblin. Concerning this document the following legend is recorded.

In ancient days a *Kappa* dwelt in the river Kawachi, and he made a practice of seizing and destroying a number of villagers, and in addition many of their domestic animals. On one occasion a horse went into the river, and the *Kappa*, in trying to capture it, in some way twisted his neck, but in spite of considerable pain he refused to let his victim go. The frightened horse sprang up the river bank and ran into a neighbouring field with the Kappa still holding on to the terrified animal. The owner of the horse, together with many villagers, securely bound the Child of the River. "Let us kill this horrible creature," said the peasants, "for he has assuredly committed many horrible crimes, and we should do well to be rid of such a dreadful monster." "No," replied the owner of the horse, "we will not kill him. We will make him swear never to destroy any of the inhabitants or the domestic animals of this village." A document was accordingly prepared, and the *Kappa* was asked to peruse it, and when he had done so to sign his name. "I cannot write," replied the penitent *Kappa*, "but I will dip my hand in ink and press it upon the document." When the creature had made his inky mark, he was released and allowed to return to the river, and from that day to this the *Kappa* has remained true to his promise.

TOBIKAWA IMITATES A TENGU

Tobikawa, an ex-wrestler who lived in Matsue, spent his time in hunting and killing foxes. He did not believe in the various superstitions concerning this animal, and it was generally believed that his great strength made him immune from the witchcraft of foxes. However, there were some people of Matsue who prophesied that Tobikawa would come to an untimely end as the result of his daring deeds and disbelief in supernatural powers.

Tobikawa was extremely fond of practical jokes, and on one occasion he had the hardihood to imitate the general appearance of a *Tengu*, feathers, long nose, claws, and all. Having thus disguised himself he climbed up into a tree belonging to a sacred grove. Presently the peasants observed him, and deeming the creature they saw to be a *Tengu*, they began to worship him and to place many offerings about the tree. Alas! the dismal prophecy came true, for while the merry Tobikawa was trying to imitate the acrobatic antics of a *Tengu*, he slipped from a branch and was killed.

THE ADVENTURES OF KIUCHI HEIZAYEMON

One evening, Kiuchi Heizayemon, a retainer, mysteriously disappeared. Kiuchi's friends, when they heard of what had taken place, searched for him in every direction. Eventually they discovered the missing man's clogs, scabbard, and sword; but the sheath was bent like the curved handle of a tea-kettle. They had no sooner made this lamentable discovery than they also perceived Kiuchi's girdle, which had been cut into three pieces. At midnight, those who searched heard a strange cry, a voice calling for help. Suzuki Shichiro, one of the party, chanced to look up, and he saw a strange creature with wings standing upon the roof of a temple. When the rest of the band had joined their comrade, they all looked upon the weird figure, and one said: "I believe it is nothing but an umbrella flapping in the wind." "Let us make quite sure," replied Suzuki Shichiro, and with these words he lifted up his voice, and cried loudly: "Are you the lost Kiuchi?" "Yes," was the reply, "and I pray that you will take me down from this temple as speedily as possible."

When Kiuchi had been brought down from the temple roof, he fainted, and remained in a swoon for three days. At length, gaining consciousness, he gave the following account of his strange adventure:

"The evening when I disappeared I heard someone shouting my name over and over again, and going out I discovered a black-robed monk, bawling 'Heizayemon!' Beside the monk stood a man of great stature; his face was red, and his dishevelled hair fell upon the ground. 'Climb up on yonder roof,' he shouted fiercely. I refused to obey such an evil-faced villain, and drew my sword, but in a moment he bent the blade and broke my scabbard into fragments. Then my girdle was roughly torn off and cut into three pieces. When these things had been done, I was carried to a roof, and there severely chastised. But this was not the end of my trouble, for after I had been beaten, I was forced to seat myself on a round tray. In a moment I was whirled into the air, and the tray carried me with great speed to many regions. When it appeared to me that I had travelled through space for ten days, I prayed to the Lord Buddha, and found myself on what appeared to be the summit of a mountain, but in reality it was the roof of the temple whence you, my comrades, rescued me."

A GLOBE OF FIRE

From the beginning of March to the end of June there may be seen in the province of Settsu a globe of fire resting on the top of a tree, and within this globe there is a human face. In ancient days there once lived in Nikaido district of Settsu province a priest named Nikobo, famous for his power to exorcise evil spirits and evil influences of every kind. When the local governor's wife fell sick, Nikobo was requested to attend and see what he could do to restore her to health again. Nikobo willingly complied, and spent many days by the bedside of the suffering lady. He diligently practised his art of exorcism, and in due time the governor's wife recovered.

But the gentle and kind-hearted Nikobo was not thanked for what he had done; on the contrary, the governor became jealous of him, accused him of a foul crime, and caused him to be put to death. The soul of Nikobo flashed forth in its anger and took the form of a miraculous globe of fire, which hovered over the murderer's house. The strange light, with the justly angry face peering from it, had its effect, for the governor was stricken with a fever that finally killed him. Every year, at the time already indicated, Nikobo's ghost pays a visit to the scene of its suffering and revenge.

THE GHOSTLY WRESTLERS

In Omi province, at the base of the Katada hills, there is a lake. During the cloudy nights of early autumn a ball of fire emerges from the margin of the lake, expanding and contracting as it floats toward the hills. When it rises to the height of a man it reveals two shining faces, to develop slowly into the torsos of two naked wrestlers, locked together and struggling furiously. The ball of fire, with its fierce combatants, floats slowly away to a recess in the Katada hills. It is harmless so long as no one interferes with it, but it resents any effort to retard its progress.

According to a legend concerning this phenomenon, we are informed that a certain wrestler, who had never suffered a defeat, waited at midnight for the coming of this ball of fire. When it reached him he attempted to drag it down by force, but the luminous globe proceeded on its way, and hurled the foolish wrestler to a considerable distance.

THE SHŌJŌ'S WHITE SAKE

The Shōjō is a sea monster with bright red hair, and is extremely fond of drinking large quantities of sacred white *sake*. The following legend will give some account of this creature and the nature of his favourite beverage.

We will refer later to the miraculous appearance of Mount Fuji. On the day following this alleged miracle a poor man named Yurine, who lived near this mountain, became extremely ill, and feeling that his days were numbered, he desired to drink a cup of *sake* before he died. But there was no rice wine in the little hut, and his boy, Koyuri, desiring if possible to fulfil his father's dying wish, wandered along the shore with a gourd in his hand. He had not gone far when he heard someone calling his name. On looking about him he discovered two strange-looking creatures with long red hair and skin the colour of pink cherry-blossom, wearing green seaweed girdles about their loins. Drawing nearer, he perceived that these beings were drinking white *sake* from large flat cups, which they continually replenished from a great stone jar.

"My father is dying," said the boy, "and he much desires to drink a cup of *sake* before he departs this life. But alas! we are poor, and I know not how to grant him his last request."

"I will fill your gourd with this white *sake*," replied one of the creatures, and when he had done so Koyuri ran with haste to his father.

The old man drank the white *sake* eagerly. "Bring me more," he cried, "for this is no common wine. It has given me strength, and already I feel new life flowing through my old veins."

So Koyuri returned to the seashore, and the red-haired creatures gladly gave him more of their wine; indeed, they supplied him with the beverage for five days, and by the end of that time Yurine was restored to health again.

Now Yurine's neighbour was a man called Mamikiko, and when he heard that Yurine had recently obtained a copious supply of *sake* he grew jealous, for above all things he loved a cup of rice wine. One day he called Koyuri and questioned him in regard to the matter, saying: "Let me taste the *sake*." He roughly snatched the gourd from the boy's hand and began to drink, making a wry face as he did so. "This is not *sake*!" he exclaimed fiercely; "it is filthy water," and having said these words, he began to beat the boy, crying: "Take me to those red people you have told me about. I will get from them fine *sake*, and let the beating I have given you warn you never again to play a trick upon me."

Koyuri and Mamikiko went along the shore together, and presently they came to where the red-haired creatures were drinking. When Koyuri saw them he began to weep.

"Why are you crying?" said one of the creatures. "Surely your good father has not drunk all the *sake* already?"

"No," replied the boy, "but I have met with misfortune. This man I bring with me, Mamikiko by name, drank some of the *sake*, spat it out immediately, and threw the rest away, saying that I had played a trick upon him and given him foul water to drink. Be so good as to let me have some more *sake* for my father."

The red-haired man filled the gourd, and chuckled over Mamikiko's unpleasant experience.

"I should also like a cup or *sake*" said Mamikiko. "Will you let me have some?"

Permission having been granted, the greedy Mamikiko filled the largest cup he could find, smiling over the delicious fragrance. But directly he tasted the *sake* he felt sick, and angrily remonstrated with the red-haired creature.

The red man thus made answer: "You are evidently not aware that I am a *Shōjō*, and that I live near the Sea Dragon's Palace. When I heard of the sudden appearance of Mount Fuji I came here to see it, assured that such an event was a good omen and foretold of the prosperity and perpetuity of Japan. While enjoying the beauty of this fair mountain I met Koyuri, and had the good fortune to save his honest father's life by giving him some of our sacred white *sake* that restores youth to human beings, together with an increase in years, while to *Shōjō* it vanquishes death. Koyuri's father is a good man, and the *sake* was thus able to exert its full and beneficent power upon him; but you are greedy and selfish, and to all such this *sake* is poison."

"*Poison?*" groaned the now contrite Mamikiko. "Good *Shōjō*, have mercy upon me and spare my life!"

The *Shōjō* gave him a powder, saying: "Swallow this in *sake* and repent of your wickedness."

Mamikiko did so, and this time he found that the white *sake* was delicious. He lost no time in making friends with Yurine, and some years later these men took up their abode on the southern side of Mount Fuji, brewed the *Shōjō's* white *sake*, and lived for three hundred years.

HOW AN OLD MAN LOST HIS WEN

There was once an old man who had a wen on his right cheek. This disfigurement caused him a good deal of annoyance, and he had spent a considerable sum of money in trying to get rid of it. He took various medicines and applied many lotions, but instead of the wen disappearing or even diminishing, it increased in size.

One night, while the old man was returning home laden with firewood, he was overtaken by a terrible thunderstorm, and was forced to seek shelter in a hollow tree. When the storm had abated, and just as he was about to proceed on his journey, he was surprised to hear a sound of merriment close at hand. On peeping out from his place of retreat, he was amazed to see a number of demons dancing and singing and drinking. Their dancing was so strange that the old man, forgetting caution, began to laugh, and eventually left the tree in order that he might see the performance better. As he stood watching, he saw that a demon was dancing by himself, and, moreover, that the chief of the company was none too pleased with his very clumsy antics. At length the leader of the demons said: "Enough! Is there no one who can dance better than this fellow?"

When the old man heard these words, it seemed that his youth returned to him again, and having at one time been an expert dancer, he offered to show his skill. So the old man danced before that strange gathering of demons, who congratulated him on his performance, offered him a cup of *sake*, and begged that he would give them the pleasure of several other dances.

The old man was extremely gratified by the way he had been received, and when the chief of the demons asked him to dance before them on the following night, he readily complied. "That is well," said the chief, "but you must leave some pledge behind you. I see that you have a wen on your right cheek, and that will make an excellent pledge. Allow me to take it off for you." Without inflicting any pain, the chief removed the wen, and having accomplished this extraordinary feat, he and his companions suddenly vanished.

The old man, as he walked towards his home, kept on feeling his right cheek with his hand, and could scarcely realise that after many years of disfigurement he had at last the good fortune to lose his troublesome and unsightly wen. At length he entered his humble abode, and his old wife was none the less pleased with what had taken place.

A wicked and cantankerous old man lived next door to this good old couple. For many years he had been afflicted with a wen on his left cheek, which had failed to yield to all manner of medical treatment. When he heard of his neighbour's good fortune, he called upon him and listened to the strange adventures with the demons. The good old man told his neighbour where he might find the hollow tree, and advised him to hide in it just before sunset.

The wicked old man found the hollow tree and entered it. He had not remained concealed more than a few minutes when he rejoiced to see the demons. Presently one of the company said: "The old man is a long time coming. I made sure he would keep his promise."

At these words the old man crept out of his hiding-place, flourished his fan, and began to dance; but, unfortunately, he knew nothing about dancing, and his extraordinary antics caused the demons to express considerable dissatisfaction. "You dance extremely ill," said one of the company, "and the sooner you stop the better we shall be pleased; but before you depart we will return the pledge you left with us last night." Having uttered these words, the demon flung the wen at the right cheek of the old man, where it remained firmly fixed, and could not be removed. So the wicked old man, who had tried to deceive the demons, went away with a wen on either side of his face.

ZENROKU'S GHOST

About ten years ago there lived a fishmonger, named Zenroku, in the Mikawa-street, at Kanda, in Edo. He was a poor man, living with his wife and one little boy. His wife fell sick and died, so he engaged an old woman to look after his boy while he himself went out to sell his fish. It happened, one day, that he and the other hucksters of his guild were gambling; and this coming to the ears of the authorities, they were all thrown into prison. Although their offence was in itself a light one, still they were kept for some time in durance while the matter was being investigated; and Zenroku, owing to the damp and foul air of the prison, fell sick with fever. His little child, in the meantime, had been handed over by the authorities to the charge of the petty officers of the ward to which his father belonged, and was being well cared for; for Zenroku was known to be an honest fellow, and his fate excited much compassion.

One night Zenroku, pale and emaciated, entered the house in which his boy was living; and all the people joyfully congratulated him on his escape from jail. "Why, we heard that you were sick in prison. This is, indeed, a joyful return." Then Zenroku thanked those who had taken care of the child, saying that he had returned secretly by the favour of his jailers that night; but that on the following day his offence would be remitted, and he should be able to take possession of his house again publicly. For that night, he must return to the prison. With this he begged those present to continue their good offices to his babe; and, with a sad and reluctant expression of countenance, he left the house.

On the following day, the officers of that ward were sent for by the prison authorities. They thought that they were summoned that Zenroku might be handed back to them a free man, as he himself had said to them; but to their surprise, they were told that he had died the night before in prison, and were ordered to carry away his dead body for burial. Then they knew that they had seen Zenroku's ghost; and that when he said that he should be returned to them on the morrow, he had alluded to his corpse. So they buried him decently, and brought up his son, who is alive to this day.

THE MONEY-LENDER'S GHOST

About thirty years ago there stood a house at Mitsume, in the Honjo of Edo, which was said to be nightly visited by ghosts, so that no man dared to live in it, and it remained untenanted on that account. However, a man called Miura Takeshi, a native of the province of Oshiu, who came to Edo to set up in business as a fencing-master, but was too poor to hire a house, hearing that there was a haunted house, for which no tenant could be found, and that the owner would let any man live in it rent free, said that he feared neither man nor devil, and obtained leave to occupy the house. So he hired a fencing-room, in which he gave his lessons by day, and after midnight returned to the haunted house.

One night, his wife, who took charge of the house in his absence, was frightened by a fearful noise proceeding from a pond in the garden, and, thinking that this certainly must be the ghost that she had heard so much about, she covered her head with the bed-clothes and remained breathless with terror. When her husband came home, she told him what had happened; and on the following night he returned earlier than usual, and waited for the ghostly noise. At the same time as before, a little after midnight, the same sound was heard – as though a gun had been fired inside the pond. Opening the shutters, he looked out, and saw something like a black cloud floating on the water, and in the cloud was the form of a bald man. Thinking that there must be some cause for this, he instituted careful inquiries, and learned that the former tenant, some ten years previously, had borrowed money from a blind shampooer, and, being unable to pay the debt, had murdered his creditor, who began to press him for his money, and had thrown his head into the pond.

The fencing-master accordingly collected his pupils and emptied the pond, and found a skull at the bottom of it; so he called in a priest, and buried the skull in a temple, causing prayers to be offered up for the repose of the murdered man's soul. Thus the ghost was laid, and appeared no more.

HOW TAJIMA SHUME WAS TORMENTED BY A DEVIL OF HIS OWN CREATION

Once upon a time, a certain Ronin, Tajima Shume by name, an able and well-read man, being on his travels to see the world, went up to Kiyoto by the Tokaido. One day, in the neighbourhood of Nagoya, in the province of Owari, he fell in with a wandering priest, with whom he entered into conversation. Finding that they were bound for the same place, they agreed to travel together, beguiling their weary way by pleasant talk on divers matters; and so by degrees, as they became more intimate, they began to speak without restraint about their private affairs; and the priest, trusting thoroughly in the honour of his companion, told him the object of his journey.

"For some time past," said he, "I have nourished a wish that has engrossed all my thoughts; for I am bent on setting up a molten image in honour of Buddha; with this object I have wandered through various provinces collecting alms and (who knows by what weary toil?) we have succeeded in amassing two hundred ounces of silver – enough, I trust, to erect a handsome bronze figure."

What says the proverb? "He who bears a jewel in his bosom bears poison." Hardly had the Ronin heard these words of the priest than an evil heart arose within him, and he thought to himself, "Man's life, from the womb to the grave, is made up of good and of ill luck. Here am I, nearly forty years old, a wanderer, without a calling, or even a hope of advancement in the world. To be sure, it seems a shame; yet if I could steal the money this priest is boasting about, I could live at ease for the rest of my days;" and so he began casting about how best he might compass his purpose. But the priest, far from guessing the drift of his comrade's thoughts, journeyed cheerfully on, till they reached the town of Kuana. Here there is an arm of the sea, which is crossed in ferry-boats, that start as soon as some twenty or thirty passengers are gathered together; and in one of these boats the two travellers embarked. About half-way across, the priest was taken with a sudden necessity to go to the side of the boat; and the Ronin, following him, tripped him up whilst no one was looking, and flung him into the sea. When the boatmen and passengers heard the splash, and saw the priest struggling in the water, they were afraid, and made every effort to save him; but the wind was fair, and the boat running swiftly under the bellying sails, so they were soon a few hundred yards off from the drowning man, who sank before the boat could be turned to rescue him.

When he saw this, the Ronin feigned the utmost grief and dismay, and said to his fellow-passengers, "This priest, whom we have just lost, was my cousin: he was going to Kiyoto, to visit the shrine of his patron; and as I happened to have business there as well, we settled to travel together. Now, alas! by this misfortune, my cousin is dead, and I am left alone."

He spoke so feelingly, and wept so freely, that the passengers believed his story, and pitied and tried to comfort him. Then the Ronin said to the boatmen:

"We ought, by rights, to report this matter to the authorities; but as I am pressed for time, and the business might bring trouble on yourselves as well, perhaps we had better hush it up for the present; and I will at once go on to Kiyoto and tell my cousin's patron, besides writing home about it. What think you, gentlemen?" added he, turning to the other travellers.

They, of course, were only too glad to avoid any hindrance to their onward journey, and all with one voice agreed to what the Ronin had proposed; and so the matter was settled. When, at length, they reached the shore, they left the boat, and every man went his way; but the Ronin, overjoyed in his heart, took the wandering priest's luggage, and, putting it with his own, pursued his journey to Kiyoto.

On reaching the capital, the Ronin changed his name from Shume to Tokubei, and, giving up his position as a Samurai, turned merchant, and traded with the dead man's money. Fortune favouring his speculations, he began to amass great wealth, and lived at his ease, denying himself nothing; and in course of time he married a wife, who bore him a child.

Thus the days and months wore on, till one fine summer's night, some three years after the priest's death, Tokubei stepped out on to the verandah of his house to enjoy the cool air and the beauty of the moonlight. Feeling dull and lonely, he began musing over all kinds of things, when on a sudden the deed of murder and theft, done so long ago, vividly recurred to his memory, and he thought to himself, "Here am I, grown rich and fat on the money I wantonly stole. Since then, all has gone well with me; yet, had I not been poor, I had never turned assassin nor thief. Woe betide me! what a pity it was!" and as he was revolving the matter in his mind, a feeling of remorse came over him, in spite of all he could do. While his conscience thus smote him, he suddenly, to his utter amazement, beheld the faint outline of a man standing near a fir-tree in the garden: on looking more attentively, he perceived that the man's whole body was thin and worn and the eyes sunken and dim; and in the poor ghost that was before him he recognized the very priest whom he had thrown into the sea at Kuana. Chilled with horror, he looked again, and saw that the priest was smiling in scorn. He would have fled into the house, but the ghost stretched forth its withered arm, and, clutching the back of his neck, scowled at him with a vindictive glare, and a hideous ghastliness of mien, so unspeakably awful that any ordinary man would have swooned with fear. But Tokubei, tradesman though he was, had once been a soldier, and was not easily matched for daring; so he shook off the ghost, and, leaping into the room for his dirk, laid about him boldly enough; but, strike as he would, the spirit, fading into the air, eluded his blows, and suddenly reappeared only to vanish again: and from that time forth Tokubei knew no rest, and was haunted night and day.

At length, undone by such ceaseless vexation, Tokubei fell ill, and kept muttering, "Oh, misery! misery! – the wandering priest is coming to torture me!" Hearing his moans and the disturbance he made, the people in the house fancied he was mad, and called in a physician, who prescribed for him. But neither pill nor potion could cure Tokubei, whose strange frenzy soon became the talk of the whole neighbourhood.

Now it chanced that the story reached the ears of a certain wandering priest who lodged in the next street. When he heard the particulars, this priest gravely shook his head, as though he knew all about it, and sent a friend to Tokubei's house to say that a wandering priest, dwelling hard by, had heard of his illness, and, were it never so grievous, would undertake to heal it by means of his prayers; and Tokubei's wife, driven half wild by her husband's sickness, lost not a moment in sending for the priest, and taking him into the sick man's room.

But no sooner did Tokubei see the priest than he yelled out, "Help! help! Here is the wandering priest come to torment me again. Forgive! forgive!" and hiding his head under the coverlet, he lay quivering all over. Then the priest turned all present out of the room, put his mouth to the affrighted man's ear, and whispered:

"Three years ago, at the Kuana ferry, you flung me into the water; and well you remember it."

But Tokubei was speechless, and could only quake with fear.

"Happily," continued the priest, "I had learned to swim and to dive as a boy; so I reached the shore, and, after wandering through many provinces, succeeded in setting up a bronze figure to Buddha, thus fulfilling the wish of my heart. On my journey homewards, I took a lodging in the next street, and there heard of your marvellous ailment. Thinking I could divine its cause, I came to see you, and am glad to find I was not mistaken. You have done a hateful deed; but am I not a priest, and have I not forsaken the things of this world? and would it not ill become me to bear malice? Repent, therefore, and abandon your evil ways. To see you do so I should esteem the height of happiness. Be of good cheer, now, and look me in the face, and you will see that I am really a living man, and no vengeful goblin come to torment you."

Seeing he had no ghost to deal with, and overwhelmed by the priest's kindness, Tokubei burst into tears, and answered, "Indeed, indeed, I don't know what to say. In a fit of madness I was tempted to kill and rob you. Fortune befriended me ever after; but the richer I grew, the more keenly I felt how wicked I had been, and the more I foresaw that my victim's vengeance would some day overtake me. Haunted by this thought, I lost my nerve, till one night I beheld your spirit, and from that time forth fell ill. But how you managed to escape, and are still alive, is more than I can understand."

"A guilty man," said the priest, with a smile, "shudders at the rustling of the wind or the chattering of a stork's beak: a murderer's conscience preys upon his mind till he sees what is not. Poverty drives a man to crimes which he repents of in his wealth. How true is the doctrine of Moshi, that the heart of man, pure by nature, is corrupted by circumstances."

Thus he held forth; and Tokubei, who had long since repented of his crime, implored forgiveness, and gave him a large sum of money, saying, "Half of this is the amount I stole from you three years since; the other half I entreat you to accept as interest, or as a gift."

The priest at first refused the money; but Tokubei insisted on his accepting it, and did all he could to detain him, but in vain; for the priest went his way, and bestowed the money on the poor and needy. As for Tokubei himself, he soon shook off his disorder, and thenceforward lived at peace with all men, revered both at home and abroad, and ever intent on good and charitable deeds.

LITTLE SILVER'S DREAM OF THE SHOJO

Ko Gin San (Miss Little Silver) was a young maid who did not care for strange stories of animals, so much as for those of wonder-creatures in the form of human beings. Even of these, however, she did not like to dream, and when the foolish old nurse would tell her ghost stories at night, she was terribly afraid they would appear to her in her sleep.

To avoid this, the old nurse told her to draw pictures of a tapir, on the sheet of white paper, which, wrapped round the tiny pillow, makes the pillow-case of every young lady, who rests her head on two inches of a bolster in order to keep her well-dressed hair from being mussed or rumpled.

Old grannies and country folks believe that if you have a picture of a tapir under the bed or on the paper pillow-case, you will not have unpleasant dreams, as the tapir is said to eat them.

So strongly do some people believe this that they sleep under quilts figured with the device of this long-snouted beast. If in spite of this precaution one should have a bad dream, he must cry out on awaking, "tapir, come eat, tapir, come eat"; when the tapir will swallow the dream, and no evil results will happen to the dreamer.

Little Silver listened with both eyes and open mouth to this account of the tapir, and then making the picture and wrapping it around her pillow, she fell asleep. I suspect that the kowameshi (red rice) of which she had eaten so heartily at supper time, until her waist strings tightened, had something to do with her travels in dream-land.

She thought she had gone down to Osaka, and there got on a junk and sailed far away to the southwest, through the Inland sea. One night the water seemed full of white ghosts of men and women. Some of them were walking on, and in, the water. Some were running about. Here and there groups appeared to be talking together. Once in a while the junk would run against one of them; and when Little Silver looked to see if he were hurt or knocked over, she could see nothing until the junk passed by, when the ghost would appear standing in the same place, as though the ship had gone through empty air.

Occasionally a ghost would come up to the side of the ship, and in a squeaky voice ask for a dipper. While she would be wondering what a ghost wanted to do with a dipper, a sailor would quietly open a locker, take out a dipper having no bottom, and give one every time he was asked for them. Little Silver noticed a large bundle of these dippers ready. The ghosts would then begin to bail up water out of the sea to empty it in the boat. All night they followed the junk, holding on with one hand to the gunwale, while they vainly dipped up water with the other, trying to swamp the boat. If dippers with bottoms in them had been given them, the sailors said, the boat would have been sunk. When daylight appeared the shadowy host of people vanished.

In the morning they passed an island, the shores of which were high rocks of red coral. A great earthen jar stood on the beach, and around it lay long-handled ladles holding a half-gallon or more, and piles of very large shallow red lacquered wine cups, which seemed as big as the full moon. After the sun had been risen some time, there came down from over the hills a troop of the most curious looking people. Many were short, little wizen-faced folks, that looked very old; or rather, they seemed old before they ought to be. Some were very aged and crooked, with hickory-nut faces, and hair of a reddish gray tint. All the others had long scarlet locks hanging loose over their heads, and streaming down their backs. Their faces were flushed as if by hard drinking, and their pimpled noses resembled huge red barnacles. No sooner did they arrive at the great earthen jar than they ranged themselves round it. The old ones dipped out ladles full, and drank of the wine till they reeled. The younger ones poured the liquor into cups and drank. Even the little infants guzzled quantities of the yellow sake from the shallow cups of very thin red-lacquered wood.

Then began the dance, and wild and furious it was. The leather-faced old sots tossed their long reddish-grey locks in the air, and pirouetted round the big sake jar. The younger ones of all ages clapped their hands, knotted their handkerchiefs over their foreheads, waved their dippers or cups or fans, and practiced all kinds of antics, while their scarlet hair streamed in the wind or was blown in their eyes.

The dance over, they threw down their cups and dippers, rested a few minutes and then took another heavy drink all around.

"Now to work" shouted an old fellow whose face was redder than his half-bleached hair, and who having only two teeth like tusks left looked just like an *oni* (imp.) As for his wife, her teeth had long ago fallen out and the skin of her face seemed to have added a pucker for every year since a half century had rolled over her head.

Then Little Silver looked and saw them scatter. Some gathered shells and burned them to make lime. Others carried water and made mortar, which they thickened by a pulp made of paper, and a glue made by boiling fish skin. Some dived under the sea for red coral, which they hauled up by means of straw ropes, in great sprigs as thick as the branches of a tree. They quickly ran up a scaffold, and while some of the scarlet-headed plasterers smeared the walls, others below passed up the tempered mortar on long shell shovels, to the hand mortar-boards. Even at work they had casks and cups of sake at hand, while children played in the empty kegs and licked the gummy sugar left in some of them.

"What is that house for?" asked Little Silver of the sailors.

"Oh, that is the Kura (storehouse) in which the King of the Shōjō stores the treasures of life, and health, and happiness, and property, which men throw away, or exchange for the sake, which he gives them, by making funnels of themselves."

"Oh, Yes," said Little Silver to herself, as she remembered how her father had said of a certain neighbour who had lately been drinking hard, "he swills sake like a Shōjō."

She also understood why picnic or "chow-chow" boxes were often decorated with pictures of Shōjō, with their cups and dippers. For, at these picnics, many men get drunk; so much so indeed, that after a while the master of the feast orders very poor and cheap wine to be served to the guests.

He also replaces the delicate wine cups of egg-shell porcelain, with big thick tea-cups or wooden bowls, for the guests when drunk, do not know the difference.

She also now understood why it was commonly said of a Mr Matsu, who had once been very rich but was now a poor sot, "His property has all gone to the Shōjō."

Just then the ship in which she was sailing struck a rock, and the sudden jerk woke up Little Silver, who cried out, "Tapir, come eat; tapir, come eat."

No tapir came, but if he had I fear Little Silver would have been more frightened than she was by her dream of the ghosts; for next morning she laughed to think how they had all their work a-dipping water for nothing, and at her old nurse for thinking a picture of a tapir could keep off dreams.

THE GOBLIN OF ADACHIGAHARA

Long, long ago there was a large plain called Adachigahara, in the province of Mutsu in Japan. This place was said to be haunted by a cannibal goblin who took the form of an old woman. From time to time many travelers disappeared and were never heard of more, and the old women round the charcoal braziers in the evenings, and the girls washing the household rice at the wells in the mornings, whispered dreadful stories of how the missing folk had been lured to the goblin's cottage and devoured, for the goblin lived only on human flesh. No one dared to venture near the haunted spot after sunset, and all those who could, avoided it in the daytime, and travelers were warned of the dreaded place.

One day as the sun was setting, a priest came to the plain. He was a belated traveler, and his robe showed that he was a Buddhist pilgrim walking from shrine to shrine to pray for some blessing or to crave for forgiveness of sins. He had apparently lost his way, and as it was late he met no one who could show him the road or warn him of the haunted spot.

He had walked the whole day and was now tired and hungry, and the evenings were chilly, for it was late autumn, and he began to be very anxious to find some house where he could obtain a night's lodging. He found himself lost in the midst of the large plain, and looked about in vain for some sign of human habitation.

At last, after wandering about for some hours, he saw a clump of trees in the distance, and through the trees he caught sight of the glimmer of a single ray of light. He exclaimed with joy:

"Oh. surely that is some cottage where I can get a night's lodging!"

Keeping the light before his eyes he dragged his weary, aching feet as quickly as he could towards the spot, and soon came to a miserable-looking little cottage. As he drew near he saw that it was in a tumble-down condition, the bamboo fence was broken and weeds and grass pushed their way through the gaps. The paper screens which serve as windows and doors in Japan were full of holes, and the posts of the house were bent with age and seemed scarcely able to support the old thatched roof. The hut was open, and by the light of an old lantern an old woman sat industriously spinning.

The pilgrim called to her across the bamboo fence and said:

"O Baa San (old woman), good evening! I am a traveler! Please excuse me, but I have lost my way and do not know what to do, for I have nowhere to rest tonight. I beg you to be good enough to let me spend the night under your roof."

The old woman as soon as she heard herself spoken to stopped spinning, rose from her seat and approached the intruder.

"I am very sorry for you. You must indeed be distressed to have lost your way in such a lonely spot so late at night. Unfortunately I cannot put you up, for I have no bed to offer you, and no accommodation whatsoever for a guest in this poor place!"

"Oh, that does not matter," said the priest; "all I want is a shelter under some roof for the night, and if you will be good enough just to let me lie on the kitchen floor I shall be grateful. I am too tired to walk further tonight, so I hope you will not refuse me, otherwise I shall have to sleep out on the cold plain." And in this way he pressed the old woman to let him stay.

She seemed very reluctant, but at last she said:

"Very well, I will let you stay here. I can offer you a very poor welcome only, but come in now and I will make a fire, for the night is cold."

The pilgrim was only too glad to do as he was told. He took off his sandals and entered the hut. The old woman then brought some sticks of wood and lit the fire, and bade her guest draw near and warm himself.

"You must be hungry after your long tramp," said the old woman. "I will go and cook some supper for you." She then went to the kitchen to cook some rice.

After the priest had finished his supper the old woman sat down by the fire-place, and they talked together for a long time. The pilgrim thought to himself that he had been very lucky to come across such a kind, hospitable old woman. At last the wood gave out, and as the fire died slowly down he began to shiver with cold just as he had done when he arrived.

"I see you are cold," said the old woman; "I will go out and gather some wood, for we have used it all. You must stay and take care of the house while I am gone."

"No, no," said the pilgrim, "let me go instead, for you are old, and I cannot think of letting you go out to get wood for me this cold night!"

The old woman shook her head and said:

"You must stay quietly here, for you are my guest." Then she left him and went out.

In a minute she came back and said:

"You must sit where you are and not move, and whatever happens don't go near or look into the inner room. Now mind what I tell you!"

"If you tell me not to go near the back room, of course I won't," said the priest, rather bewildered.

The old woman then went out again, and the priest was left alone. The fire had died out, and the only light in the hut was that of a dim lantern. For the first time that night he began to feel that he was in a weird place, and the old woman's words, "Whatever you do don't peep into the back room," aroused his curiosity and his fear.

What hidden thing could be in that room that she did not wish him to see? For some time the remembrance of his promise to the old woman kept him still, but at last he could no longer resist his curiosity to peep into the forbidden place.

He got up and began to move slowly towards the back room. Then the thought that the old woman would be very angry with him if he disobeyed her made him come back to his place by the fireside.

As the minutes went slowly by and the old woman did not return, he began to feel more and more frightened, and to wonder what dreadful secret was in the room behind him. He must find out.

"She will not know that I have looked unless I tell her. I will just have a peep before she comes back," said the man to himself.

With these words he got up on his feet (for he had been sitting all this time in Japanese fashion with his feet under him) and stealthily crept towards the forbidden spot. With trembling hands he pushed back the sliding door and looked in. What he saw froze the blood in his veins. The room was full of dead men's bones and the walls were splashed and the floor was covered with human blood. In one corner skull upon skull rose to the ceiling, in another was a heap of arm bones, in another a heap of leg bones. The sickening smell made him faint. He fell backwards with horror, and for some time lay in a heap with fright on the floor, a pitiful sight. He trembled all over and his teeth chattered, and he could hardly crawl away from the dreadful spot.

"How horrible!" he cried out. "What awful den have I come to in my travels? May Buddha help me or I am lost. Is it possible that that kind old woman is really the cannibal goblin? When she comes back she will show herself in her true character and eat me up at one mouthful!"

With these words his strength came back to him and, snatching up his hat and staff, he rushed out of the house as fast as his legs could carry him. Out into the night he ran, his one thought to get as far as he could from the goblin's haunt. He had not gone far when he heard steps behind him and a voice crying: "Stop! stop!"

He ran on, redoubling his speed, pretending not to hear. As he ran he heard the steps behind him come nearer and nearer, and at last he recognized the old woman's voice which grew louder and louder as she came nearer.

"Stop! stop, you wicked man, why did you look into the forbidden room?"

The priest quite forgot how tired he was and his feet flew over the ground faster than ever. Fear gave him strength, for he knew that if the goblin caught him he would soon be one of her victims. With all his heart he repeated the prayer to Buddha:

"Namu Amida Butsu, Namu Amida Butsu."

And after him rushed the dreadful old hag, her hair flying in the wind, and her face changing with rage into the demon that she was. In her hand she carried a large blood-stained knife, and she still shrieked after him, "Stop! stop!"

At last, when the priest felt he could run no more, the dawn broke, and with the darkness of night the goblin vanished and he was safe. The priest now knew that he had met the Goblin of Adachigahara, the story of whom he had often heard but never believed to be true. He felt that he owed his wonderful escape to the protection of Buddha to whom he had prayed for help, so he took out his rosary and bowing his head as the sun rose he said his prayers and made his thanksgiving earnestly. He then set forward for another part of the country, only too glad to leave the haunted plain behind him.

LEGENDS OF THE SEA

As an island nation, it is only natural that the sea holds much significance for Japan. In bygone years, on the last day of the Festival of the Dead the sea would be covered with countless *shōrōbune* (soul-ships), for on that day, called *Hotoke-umi*, which means Buddha-Flood, or the Tide of the Returning Ghosts, the souls go back to their spirit world again. No superstitious human being would dream of putting out to sea amid such sacred company, for the sea that night belongs to the dead; it is their long pathway to the realm where Emma-O reigns supreme. It sometimes happened, however, that a vessel would fail to come to port before the departure of the soul-ships, and on such occasions it is said that the dead would arise from the deep, stretch forth their arms, and implore that buckets may be given them. Sailors would present the ghosts with one that has no bottom, for if they gave the dead sound buckets, the angry spirits would use them for the purpose of sinking the vessel.

"The legend of Urashima," wrote Professor B.H. Chamberlain in *Japanese Poetry*, "is one of the oldest in the language, and traces of it may even be found in the official annals." Indeed, the popular version, which we give in this section, was included in standard school reading books in the first half of the twentieth century and has become one of the 'core' fairy tales of Japan. In that tale we are taken to the Dragon Palace, while elsewhere in this section we encounter a Serpent God, the spirit of a magical abalone and a 'shark person'.

URASHIMA AND THE TORTOISE

One day Urashima, who lived in a little fishing village called Midzunoe, in the province of Tango, went out to fish. It so happened that he caught a tortoise, and as tortoises are said to live many thousands of years, the thoughtful Urashima allowed the creature to return to the sea, rebaited his hook, and once more waited for the bite of a fish. Only the sea gently waved his line to and fro. The sun beat down upon his head till at last Urashima fell asleep.

He had not been sleeping long when he heard someone calling his name: "Urashima, Urashima!"

It was such a sweet, haunting voice that the fisher-lad stood up in his boat and looked around in every direction, till he chanced to see the very tortoise he had been kind enough to restore to its watery home. The tortoise, which was able to speak quite fluently, profusely thanked Urashima for his kindness, and offered to take him to the *ryūkyū*, or Palace of the Dragon King.

The invitation was readily accepted, and getting on the tortoise's back, Urashima found himself gliding through the sea at a tremendous speed, and the curious part about it was he discovered that his clothes remained perfectly dry.

In the Sea King's Palace

Arriving at the Sea King's Palace, red bream, flounder, sole, and cuttlefish came out to give Urashima a hearty welcome. Having expressed their pleasure, these vassals of the Dragon King escorted the fisher-lad to an inner apartment, where the beautiful Princess Otohime and her maidens were seated. The Princess was arrayed in gorgeous garments of red and gold, all the colours of a wave with the sunlight upon it.

This Princess explained that she had taken the form of a tortoise by way of testing his kindness of heart. The test had happily proved successful, and as a reward for his virtue she offered to become his bride in a land where there was eternal youth and everlasting summer.

Urashima bashfully accepted the high honour bestowed upon him. He had no sooner spoken than a great company of fishes appeared, robed in long ceremonial garments, their fins supporting great coral trays loaded with rare delicacies. Then the happy couple drank the wedding cup of *sake*, and while they drank, some of the fishes played soft music, others sang, and not a few, with scales of silver and golden tails, stepped out a strange measure on the white sand.

After the festivities were over, Otohime showed her husband all the wonders of her father's palace. The greatest marvel of all was to see a country where all the seasons lingered together. Looking to the east, Urashima saw plum- and cherry-trees in full bloom, with bright-winged butterflies skimming over the blossom, and away in the distance it seemed that the pink petals and butterflies had suddenly been converted into the song of a wondrous nightingale. In the south he saw trees in their summer glory, and heard the gentle note of the cricket. Looking to the west, the autumn maples made a fire in the branches, so that if Urashima had been other than a humble fisher-lad he might have recalled the following poem:

> *"Fair goddess of the paling Autumn skies,*
> *Fain would I know how many looms she plies,*
> *Wherein through skilful tapestry she weaves*
> *Her fine brocade of fiery maple leaves:*
> *Since on each hill, with every gust that blows,*
> *In varied hues her vast embroidery glows?"*

It was, indeed, a 'vast embroidery', for when Urashima looked toward the north he saw a great stretch of snow and a mighty pond covered with ice. All the seasons lingered together in that fair country where Nature had yielded to the full her infinite variety of beauty.

After Urashima had been in the Sea King's Palace for three days, and seen many wonderful things, he suddenly remembered his old parents, and felt a strong desire to go and see them. When he went to his wife, and told her of his longing to return home, Otohime began to weep, and tried to persuade him to stop another day. But Urashima refused to be influenced in the matter. "I must go," said he, "but I will leave you only for a day. I will return again, dear wife of mine."

The Home-coming of Urashima

Then Otohime gave her husband a keepsake in remembrance of their love. It was called the *Tamate-Bako* ('Box of the Jewel Hand'). She explained that he was on no account to open the box, and Urashima, promising to fulfil her wish, said farewell, mounted a large tortoise, and soon found himself in his own country. He looked in vain for his father's home. Not a sign of it was to be seen. The cottage had vanished, only the little stream remained.

Still much perplexed, Urashima questioned a passer-by, and he learnt from him that a fisher-lad, named Urashima, had gone to sea three hundred years ago and was drowned, and that his parents, brothers, and their grandchildren had been laid to rest for a long time. Then Urashima suddenly remembered that the country of the Sea King was a divine land, where a day, according to mortal reckoning, was a hundred years.

Urashima's reflections were gloomy in the extreme, for all whom he had loved on earth were dead. Then he heard the murmur of the sea, and recalled the lovely Otohime, as well as the country where the seasons joined hands and made a fourfold pageant of their beauty – the land where trees had emeralds for leaves and rubies for berries, where the fishes wore long robes and sang and danced and played. Louder the sea sounded in Urashima's ears. Surely Otohime called him? But no path opened out before him, no obliging tortoise appeared on the scene to carry him to where his wife waited for him. "The box! the box!" said Urashima softly, "if I open my wife's mysterious gift, it may reveal the way."

Urashima untied the red silk thread and slowly, fearfully opened the lid of the box. Suddenly there rushed out a little white cloud; it lingered a moment, and then rolled away far over the sea. But a sacred promise had been broken, and

Urashima from a handsome youth became old and wrinkled. He staggered forward, his white hair and beard blowing in the wind. He looked out to sea, and then fell dead upon the shore.

THE SLAUGHTER OF THE SEA SERPENT

Oribe Shima had offended the great ruler Hojo Takatoki, and was in consequence banished to Kamishima, one of the Oki Islands, and forced to leave his beautiful daughter Tokoyo, whom he deeply loved.

At last Tokoyo was unable to bear the separation any longer, and she was determined to find her father. She therefore set out upon a long journey, and arriving at Akasaki, in the province of Hoki, from which coast town the Oki Islands are visible on a fine day, she besought many a fisherman to row her to her destination. But the fisher-folk laughed at Tokoyo, and bade her relinquish her foolish plan and return home. The maiden, however, would not listen to their advice, and at nightfall she got into the lightest vessel she could find, and by dint of a fair wind and persistent rowing the brave girl came to one of the rocky bays of the Oki Islands.

That night Tokoyo slept soundly, and in the morning partook of food. When she had finished her meal she questioned a fisherman as to where she might find her father. "I have never heard of Oribe Shima," replied the fisherman, "and if he has been banished, I beg that you will desist from further search, lest it lead to the death of you both."

That night the sorrowful Tokoyo slept beneath a shrine dedicated to Buddha. Her sleep was soon disturbed by the clapping of hands, and looking up she saw a weeping maiden clad in a white garment with a priest standing beside her. Just as the priest was about to push the maiden over the rocks into the roaring sea, Tokoyo sprang up and held the maiden's arm.

The priest explained that on that night, the thirteenth of June, the Serpent God, known as Yofune-Nushi, demanded the sacrifice of a young girl, and that unless this annual sacrifice was made the God became angry and caused terrible storms.

"Good sir," said Tokoyo, "I am glad that I have been able to save this poor girl's life. I gladly offer myself in her place, for I am sad of heart because I have been unable to find my father. Give him this letter, for my last words of love and farewell go to him."

Having thus spoken, Tokoyo took the maiden's white robe and clad herself in it, and having prayed to the image of Buddha, she placed a small dagger between her teeth and plunged into the tempestuous sea. Down she went through the moonlit water till she came to a mighty cave where she saw a statue of Hojo Takatoki, who had sent her poor father into exile. She was about to tie the image on her back when a great white serpent crept out from the cave with eyes gleaming angrily. Tokoyo, realising that this creature was none other than Yofune-Nushi, drew her dagger and thrust it through the right eye of the God. This unexpected attack caused the serpent to retire into the cave, but the brave Tokoyo followed and struck another blow, this time at the creature's heart. For a moment Yofune-Nushi blindly stumbled forward, then with a shriek of pain fell dead upon the floor of the cavern.

During this adventure the priest and the maiden stood on the rocks watching the spot where Tokoyo had disappeared, praying fervently for the peace of her sorrowful soul. As they watched and prayed they saw Tokoyo come to the surface of the water carrying an image and a mighty fish-like creature. The priest hastily came to the girl's assistance, dragged her upon the shore, placed the image on a high rock, and secured the body of the White Sea Serpent.

In due time the remarkable story was reported to Tameyoshi, lord of the island, who in turn reported the strange adventure to Hojo Takatoki. Now Takatoki had for some time been suffering from a disease which defied the skill of the most learned doctors; but it was observed that he regained his health precisely at the hour when his image, which had been cursed and thrown into the sea by some exile, had been restored. When Hojo Takatoki heard that the brave girl was the daughter of the exiled Oribe Shima, he sent him back with all speed to his own home, where he and his daughter lived in peace and happiness.

THE SPIRIT OF THE SWORD

One night a junk anchored off Fudo's Cape, and when various preparations had been made, the Captain, Tarada by name, and his crew fell asleep on deck. At about midnight Tarada was awakened by hearing an extraordinary rumbling sound that seemed to proceed from the bottom of the sea. Chancing to look in the direction of the bow of the vessel, he saw a fair girl clad in white and illumined by a dazzling light.

When Tarada had awakened his crew he approached the maiden, who said: "My only wish is to be back in the world again." Having uttered these words, she disappeared among the waves.

The next day Tarada went on shore and asked many who lived in Amakura if they had ever heard of a wondrous maiden bathed, as it were, in a phosphorescent light. One of the villagers thus made answer: "We have never seen the maiden you describe, but for some time past we have been disturbed by rumbling noises that seem to come from Fudo's Cape, and ever since, these mysterious sounds have prevented fish from entering our bay. It may be that the girl you saw was the ghost of some poor maiden drowned at sea, and the noise we hear none other than the anger of the Sea God on account of a corpse or human bones polluting the water."

It was eventually decided that the dumb Sankichi should dive into the sea and bring up any corpse he might find there. So Sankichi went on board Tarada's junk, and having said farewell to his friends, he plunged into the water. He searched diligently, but could see no trace of corpse or human bones. At length, however, he perceived what looked like a sword wrapped in silk, and on untying the wrapping he found that it was indeed a sword, of great brightness and without a flaw of any kind. Sankichi came to the surface and was quickly taken aboard. The poor fellow was gently laid on the deck, but he fainted from exhaustion. His cold body was rubbed vigorously and fires were lit. In a very short time Sankichi became conscious and was able to show the sword and give particulars of his adventure.

An official, by the name of Naruse Tsushimanokami, was of the opinion that the sword was a sacred treasure, and on his recommendation it was placed in a shrine and dedicated to Fudo. Sankichi faithfully guarded the precious weapon, and Fudo's Cape became known as the Cape of the Woman's Sword. To the delight of the fisher-folk, the spirit of the weapon now being satisfied, the fish came back into the bay again.

THE LOVE OF O CHO SAN

In the isolated Hatsushima Island, celebrated for its *suisenn* (jonquils), there once lived a beautiful maiden called Cho, and all the young men on the island were eager to marry her. One day the handsome Shinsaku, who was bolder than the rest, went to Gisuke, the brother of Cho, and told him that he much desired to marry his fair sister. Gisuke offered no objections, and calling Cho to him, when the suitor had gone, he said: "Shinsaku wishes to become your husband. I like the fisherman, and think that in him you will make an excellent match. You are now eighteen, and it is quite time that you got married."

O Cho San fully approved of what her brother had said, and the marriage was arranged to take place in three days' time. Unfortunately, those days were days of discord on the island, for when the other fishermen lovers heard the news they began to hate the once popular Shinsaku, and, moreover, they neglected their work and were continually fighting each other. These lamentable scenes cast such a gloom upon the once happy Hatsushima Island that O Cho

San and her lover decided that for the peace of the many they would not marry after all.

This noble sacrifice, however, did not bring about the desired effect, for the thirty lovers still fought each other and still neglected their fishing. O Cho San determined to perform a still greater sacrifice. She wrote loving letters of farewell to her brother and Shinsaku, and having left them by the sleeping Gisuke, she softly crept out of the house on a stormy night on the 10th of June. She dropped big stones into her pretty sleeves, and then flung herself into the sea.

The next day Gisuke and Shinsaku read their letters from O Cho San, and, overcome by grief, they searched the shore, where they found the straw sandals of Cho. The two men realised that the fair maid had indeed taken her precious life, and shortly after her body was taken from the sea and buried, and over her tomb Shinsaku placed many flowers and wept continually.

One evening, Shinsaku, unable to bear his sorrow any longer decided to take his life, believing that by doing so he would meet the spirit of O Cho San. As he lingered by the girl's grave, he seemed to see her white ghost, and, murmuring her name over and over again, he rushed toward her. At this moment Gisuke, awakened by the noise, came out of his house, and found Shinsaku clinging to his lover's gravestone.

When Shinsaku told his friend that he had seen the spirit of O Cho San, and intended to take his life in order to be with her for ever, Gisuke made answer thus: "Shinsaku, great is your love for my poor sister, but you can love her best by serving her in this world. When the great Gods call, you will meet her, but await with hope and courage till that hour comes, for only a brave, as well as a loving, heart is worthy of O Cho San. Let us together build a shrine and dedicate it to my sister, and keep your love strong and pure by never marrying anyone else."

The thirty lovers who had shown such unmanly feeling now fully realised the sorrow they had caused, and in order to show their contrition they too helped to build the shrine of the unfortunate maiden, where to this day a ceremony takes place on the 10th of June, and it is said that the spirit of O Cho San comes in the rain.

THE SPIRIT OF THE GREAT AWABI

The morning after a great earthquake had devastated the fishing village of Nanao, it was observed that about two miles from the shore a rock had sprung up as the result of the seismic disturbance and, moreover, that the sea had become muddy. One night a number of fishermen were passing by the rock, when they observed, near at hand, a most extraordinary light that appeared to float up from the bottom of the sea with a glory as bright as the sun. The fishermen shipped their oars and gazed upon the wonderful spectacle with considerable surprise, but when the light was suddenly accompanied by a deep rumbling sound, the sailors feared another earthquake and made all speed for Nanao.

On the third day the wondrous rays from the deep increased in brilliance, so that folk standing on the shore of Nanao could see them distinctly, and the superstitious fishermen became more and more frightened. Only Kansuke and his son Matakichi had sufficient courage to go fishing. On their return journey they reached the Rock Island, and were drawing in their line when Kansuke lost his balance and fell into the sea.

Though old Kansuke was a good swimmer, he went down like a stone and did not rise to the surface. Matakichi, deeming this strange, dived into the water, almost blinded by the mysterious rays we have already described. When he at length reached the bottom he discovered innumerable *awabi* (ear-shells or abalone), and in the middle of the group one of vast size. From all these shells there poured forth a brilliant light, and though it was like day under the water, Matakichi could find no trace of his father. Eventually he was forced to rise to the surface, only to find that the rough sea had broken his boat. However, scrambling upon a piece of wreckage, with the aid of a favourable wind and current he at last reached the shore of Nanao, and gave the villagers an account of his remarkable adventure, and of the loss of his old father.

Matakichi, grieving sorely over the death of his parent, went to the old village priest and begged that worthy that he would make him one of his disciples in order that he might pray the more efficaciously for the spirit of his father. The priest readily consented, and about three weeks later they took boat to the Rock Island, where both prayed ardently for the soul of Kansuke.

That night the old priest awoke with a start and saw an ancient man standing by his bedside. With a profound bow the stranger thus spoke: "I am the Spirit of the Great Awabi, and I am more than one thousand years old. I live in the sea near the Rock Island, and this morning I heard you praying for the soul of Kansuke. Alas! good priest, your prayers have deeply moved me, but in shame and sorrow I confess that I ate Kansuke. I have bade my followers depart elsewhere, and in order to atone for my sin I shall take my own wretched life, so that the pearl that is within me may be given to Matakichi." And having uttered these words, the Spirit of the Great Awabi suddenly disappeared.

When Matakichi awoke next morning and opened the shutters he discovered the enormous *awabi* he had seen near the Rock Island. He took it to the old priest, who, after listening to his disciple's story, gave an account of his own experience. The great pearl and shell of the *awabi* were placed in the temple, and the body was reverently buried.

THE JEWEL-TEARS OF SAMEBITO

One day, while Totaro was crossing the Long Bridge of Seta, he saw a strange-looking creature. It had the body of a man, with a skin blacker than that of a negro; its eyes glowed like emeralds, and its beard was like the beard of a dragon. Totaro was not a little startled at seeing such an extraordinary being; but there was so much pathos in its green eyes that Totaro ventured to ask questions, to which the strange fellow replied:

"I am Samebito ('shark person'), and quite recently I was in the service of the Eight Great Dragon Kings as a subordinate officer in the Dragon Palace. I was dismissed from this glorious dwelling for a very slight fault, and I was even banished from the sea. Ever since I have been extremely miserable, without a place of shelter, and unable to get food. Pity me, good sir! Find me shelter, and give me something to eat!"

Totaro's heart was touched by Samebito's humility, and he took him to a pond in his garden and there gave him a liberal supply of food. In this quiet and secluded spot this strange creature of the sea remained for nearly half a year.

Now in the summer of that year there was a great female pilgrimage to the temple called Miidera, situated in the neighbouring town of Otsu. Totaro attended the festival, and there saw an extremely charming girl. "Her face was fair and pure as snow; and the loveliness of her lips assured the beholder that their very utterance would sound 'as sweet as the voice of a nightingale singing upon a plum-tree.'"

Totaro at once fell in love with this maiden. He discovered that her name was Tamana, that she was unmarried, and would remain so unless a young man could present her with a betrothal gift of a casket containing no fewer than ten thousand jewels.

When Totaro learnt that this fair girl was only to be won by what seemed to him an impossible gift, he returned home with a heavy heart. The more he thought about the beautiful Tamana, the more he fell in love with her. But alas! no one less wealthy than a prince could make such a betrothal gift – ten thousand jewels!

Totaro worried himself into an illness, and when a physician came to see him, he shook his head, and said: "I can do nothing for you, for no medicine will cure the sickness of love." And with these words he left him.

Now Samebito gained tidings of the sickness of his master, and when the sad news reached him, he left the garden pond and entered Totaro's chamber.

Totaro did not speak about his own troubles. He was full of concern for the welfare of this creature of the sea. "Who will feed you, Samebito, when I am gone?" said he mournfully.

When Samebito saw that his good master was dying, he uttered a strange cry, and began to weep. He wept great tears of blood, but when they touched the floor they suddenly turned into glowing rubies.

When Totaro saw these jewel-tears he shouted for joy, and new life came back to him from that hour. "I shall live! I shall live!" he cried with great delight. "My good friend, you have more than repaid me for the food and shelter I have given you. Your wonderful tears have brought me untold happiness."

Then Samebito stopped weeping, and asked his master to be so good as to explain the nature of his speedy recovery.

So Totaro told the Shark-Man of his love-affair and of the marriage-gift demanded by the family of Tamana. "I thought," added Totaro, "that I should never be able to get ten thousand jewels, and it was that thought that brought me so near to death. Now your tears have turned into jewels, and with these the maid will become my wife."

Totaro proceeded to count the jewels with great eagerness. "Not enough! Not enough!" he exclaimed with considerable disappointment. "Oh, Samebito, be so good as to weep a little more!"

These words made Samebito angry. "Do you think," said he, "I can weep at will like women? My tears come from the heart, the outward sign of true and deep sorrow. I can weep no longer, for you are well again. Surely the time has come for laughter and merrymaking, and not for tears."

"Unless I get ten thousand jewels, I cannot marry the fair Tamana," said Totaro. "What am I to do? Oh, good friend, weep, weep!"

Samebito was a kindly creature. After a pause, he said: "I can shed no more tears today. Let us go tomorrow to the Long Bridge of Seta, and take with us a good supply of wine and fish. It may be that as I sit on the bridge and gaze toward the Dragon Palace, I shall weep again, thinking of my lost home, and longing to return once more."

On the morrow they went to the Seta Bridge, and after Samebito had taken a good deal of wine, he gazed in the direction of the Dragon Kingdom. As he did so his eyes filled with tears, red tears that turned into rubies as soon as they touched the bridge. Totaro, without very much concern for his friend's sorrow, picked up the jewels, and found at last that he had ten thousand lustrous rubies.

Just at that moment they heard a sound of sweet music, and from the water there rose a cloud-like palace, with all the colours of the setting sun shining upon it. Samebito gave a shout of joy and sprang upon the parapet of the bridge, saying: "Farewell, my master! The Dragon Kings are calling!" With these words he leaped from the bridge and returned to his old home again.

Totaro lost no time in presenting the casket containing ten thousand jewels to Tamana's parents, and in due season he married their lovely daughter.

FOX & ANIMAL LEGENDS

Many of the following stories are the tales a Japanese parent narrates to their child, for animal stories make a universal appeal to the child-mind. They are generally regarded as fairy stories, but they contain so much legendary material that it is necessary to include them in a book of this kind, for they tend to illustrate our subject in a lighter vein, where the miraculous is mingled with the humorous. Legends regarding the fox come first in this section, on account of the importance of the subject, but it must be borne in mind that the supernatural characteristics of this animal apply also to the badger and cat, for in Japanese legend all three animals have been associated with an incalculable amount of mischief.

Inari or other fox beings not infrequently reward human beings for any act of kindness to a fox. Only a part of his reward, however, is real; at least one tempting coin is bound to turn very quickly into grass! The little good done by Inari – and we have tried to do him justice – is altogether weighed down by his countless evil actions, often of an extremely cruel nature. The subject of the fox in Japan was aptly described by Lafcadio Hearn as 'ghostly zoology'.

As we have learnt earlier, many other animals feature in Japanese legend and folklore, whether as representations of spirits and deities, to act as vehicles for didactic messages, or even in origin tales (see 'The Jelly-fish and the Monkey'). So in this section you will encounter, in addition to the fox, hare, badger and cat, everything from a boar to a butterfly.

THE DEATH-STONE

> "The Death-Stone stands on Nasu's moor
> Through winter snows and summer heat;
> The moss grows grey upon its sides,
> But the foul demon haunts it yet.

> "Chill blows the blast: the owl's sad choir
> Hoots hoarsely through the moaning pines;
> Among the low chrysanthemums
> The skulking fox, the jackal whines,
> As o'er the moor the autumn light declines."

The Buddhist priest Genno, after much weary travel, came to the moor of Nasu, and was about to rest under the shadow of a great stone, when a spirit suddenly appeared, and said: "Rest not under this stone. This is the Death-Stone. Men, birds, and beasts have perished by merely touching it!"

These mysterious and warning remarks naturally awakened Genno's curiosity, and he begged that the spirit would favour him with the story of the Death-Stone.

Thus the spirit began: "Long ago there was a fair girl living at the Japanese Court. She was so charming that she was called the Jewel Maiden. Her wisdom equalled her beauty, for she understood Buddhist lore and the Confucian classics, science, and the poetry of China."

"One night," went on the spirit, "the Mikado gave a great feast in the Summer Palace, and there he assembled the wit, wisdom, and beauty of the land. It was a brilliant gathering; but while the company ate and drank, accompanied by the strains of sweet music, darkness crept over the great apartment. Black clouds raced across the sky, and there was not a star to be seen. While the guests sat rigid with fear a mysterious wind arose. It howled through the Summer Palace and blew out all the lanterns. The complete darkness produced a state of panic, and during the uproar someone cried out, 'A light! A light!'"

> *"And lo! from out the Jewel Maiden's frame*
> *There's seen to dart a weirdly lustrous flame!*
> *It grows, it spreads, it fills th' imperial halls;*
> *The painted screens, the costly panell'd walls,*
> *Erst the pale viewless damask of the night*
> *Sparkling stand forth as in the moon's full light."*

"From that very hour the Mikado sickened," continued the spirit. "He grew so ill that the Court Magician was sent for, and this worthy soul speedily ascertained the cause of his Majesty's decline. He stated, with much warmth of language, that the Jewel Maiden was a harlot and a fiend, 'who, with insidious art, the State to ravage, captivates thy heart!'"

"The Magician's words turned the Mikado's heart against the Jewel Maiden. When this sorceress was spurned she resumed her original shape, that of a fox, and ran away to this very stone on Nasu moor."

The priest looked at the spirit critically. "Who are you?" he said at length.

"I am the demon that once dwelt in the breast of the Jewel Maiden! Now I inhabit the Death-Stone for evermore!"

The good Genno was much horrified by this dreadful confession, but, remembering his duty as a priest, he said: "Though you have sunk low in wickedness, you shall rise to virtue again. Take this priestly robe and begging-bowl, and reveal to me your fox form."

Then this wicked spirit cried pitifully:

> "In the garish light of day
> I hide myself away,
> Like pale Asama's fires:
> With the night I'll come again,
> Confess my guilt with pain
> And new-born pure desires."

With these words the spirit suddenly vanished.

Genno did not relinquish his good intentions. He strove more ardently than ever for this erring soul's salvation. In order that she might attain Nirvana, he offered flowers, burnt incense, and recited the sacred Scriptures in front of the stone.

When Genno had performed these religious duties, he said: "Spirit of the Death-Stone, I conjure thee! what was it in a former world that did cause thee to assume in this so foul a shape?"

Suddenly the Death-Stone was rent and the spirit once more appeared, crying:

> "In stones there are spirits,
> In the waters is a voice heard:
> The winds sweep across the firmament!"

Genno saw a lurid glare about him and, in the shining light, a fox that suddenly turned into a beautiful maiden.

Thus spoke the spirit of the Death-Stone: "I am she who first, in Ind, was the demon to whom Prince Hazoku paid homage.... In Great Cathay I took the form of Hoji, consort of the Emperor Iuwao; and at the Court of the Rising Sun I became the Flawless Jewel Maiden, concubine to the Emperor Toba."

The spirit confessed to Genno that in the form of the Jewel Maiden she had desired to bring destruction to the Imperial line. "Already," said the spirit, "I was making my plans, already I was gloating over the thought of the Mikado's death, and had it not been for the power of the Court Magician I should have succeeded in my scheme. As I have told you, I was driven from the Court. I was pursued by dogs and arrows, and finally sank exhausted into the Death-Stone. From time to time I haunted the moor. Now the Lord Buddha has had compassion upon me, and he has sent his priest to point out the way of true religion and to bring peace."

The legend concludes with the following pious utterances poured forth by the now contrite spirit:

> "'I swear, O man of God! I swear,' she cries,
> 'To thee whose blessing wafts me to the skies,

> I swear a solemn oath, that shall endure
> Firm as the Death-Stone standing on the moor,
> That from this hour I'm virtue's child alone!'
> Thus spake the ghoul, and vanished 'neath the Stone."

HOW A MAN WAS BEWITCHED AND HAD HIS HEAD SHAVED BY FOXES

In the village of Iwahara, in the province of Shinshiu, there dwelt a family which had acquired considerable wealth in the wine trade. On some auspicious occasion it happened that a number of guests were gathered together at their house, feasting on wine and fish; and as the wine-cup went round, the conversation turned upon foxes. Among the guests was a certain carpenter, Tokutaro by name, a man about thirty years of age, of a stubborn and obstinate turn, who said:

"Well, sirs, you've been talking for some time of men being bewitched by foxes; surely you must be under their influence yourselves, to say such things. How on earth can foxes have such power over men? At any rate, men must be great fools to be so deluded. Let's have no more of this nonsense."

Upon this a man who was sitting by him answered:

"Tokutaro little knows what goes on in the world, or he would not speak so. How many myriads of men are there who have been bewitched by foxes? Why, there have been at least twenty or thirty men tricked by the brutes on the Maki Moor alone. It's hard to disprove facts that have happened before our eyes."

"You're no better than a pack of born idiots," said Tokutaro. "I will engage to go out to the Maki Moor this very night and prove it. There is not a fox in all Japan that can make a fool of Tokutaro."

Thus he spoke in his pride; but the others were all angry with him for boasting, and said:

"If you return without anything having happened, we will pay for five measures of wine and a thousand copper cash worth of fish; and if you are bewitched, you shall do as much for us."

Tokutaro took the bet, and at nightfall set forth for the Maki Moor by himself. As he neared the moor, he saw before him a small bamboo grove, into which a fox ran; and it instantly occurred to him that the foxes of the moor would try to bewitch him. As he was yet looking, he suddenly saw the daughter of the headman of the village of Upper Horikane, who was married to the headman of the village of Maki.

"Pray, where are you going to, Master Tokutaro?" said she.

"I am going to the village hard by."

"Then, as you will have to pass my native place, if you will allow me, I will accompany you so far."

Tokutaro thought this very odd, and made up his mind that it was a fox trying to make a fool of him; he accordingly determined to turn the tables on the fox, and answered – "It is a long time since I have had the pleasure of seeing you; and as it seems that your house is on my road, I shall be glad to escort you so far."

With this he walked behind her, thinking he should certainly see the end of a fox's tail peeping out; but, look as he might, there was nothing to be seen. At last they came to the village of Upper Horikane; and when they reached the cottage of the girl's father, the family all came out, surprised to see her.

"Oh dear! oh dear! here is our daughter come: I hope there is nothing the matter."

And so they went on, for some time, asking a string of questions.

In the meanwhile, Tokutaro went round to the kitchen door, at the back of the house, and, beckoning out the master of the house, said:

"The girl who has come with me is not really your daughter. As I was going to the Maki Moor, when I arrived at the bamboo grove, a fox jumped up in front of me, and when it had dashed into the grove it immediately took the shape of your daughter, and offered to accompany me to the village; so I pretended to be taken in by the brute, and came with it so far."

On hearing this, the master of the house put his head on one side, and mused a while; then, calling his wife, he repeated the story to her, in a whisper.

But she flew into a great rage with Tokutaro, and said:

"This is a pretty way of insulting people's daughters. The girl is our daughter, and there's no mistake about it. How dare you invent such lies?"

"Well," said Tokutaro, "you are quite right to say so; but still there is no doubt that this is a case of witchcraft."

Seeing how obstinately he held to his opinion, the old folks were sorely perplexed, and said:

"What do you think of doing?"

"Pray leave the matter to me: I'll soon strip the false skin off, and show the beast to you in its true colours. Do you two go into the store-closet, and wait there."

With this he went into the kitchen, and, seizing the girl by the back of the neck, forced her down by the hearth.

"Oh! Master Tokutaro, what means this brutal violence? Mother! father! help!"

So the girl cried and screamed; but Tokutaro only laughed, and said:

"So you thought to bewitch me, did you? From the moment you jumped into the wood, I was on the look-out for you to play me some trick. I'll soon make you show what you really are;" and as he said this, he twisted her two hands behind her back, and trod upon her, and tortured her; but she only wept, and cried:

"Oh! it hurts, it hurts!"

"If this is not enough to make you show your true form, I'll roast you to death;" and he piled firewood on the hearth, and, tucking up her dress, scorched her severely.

"Oh! oh! this is more than I can bear;" and with this she expired.

The two old people then came running in from the rear of the house, and, pushing aside Tokutaro, folded their daughter in their arms, and put their hands to her mouth to feel whether she still breathed; but life was extinct, and not the sign of a fox's tail was to be seen about her. Then they seized Tokutaro by the collar, and cried:

"On pretence that our true daughter was a fox, you have roasted her to death. Murderer! Here, you there, bring ropes and cords, and secure this Tokutaro!"

So the servants obeyed, and several of them seized Tokutaro and bound him to a pillar. Then the master of the house, turning to Tokutaro, said:

"You have murdered our daughter before our very eyes. I shall report the matter to the lord of the manor, and you will assuredly pay for this with your head. Be prepared for the worst."

And as he said this, glaring fiercely at Tokutaro, they carried the corpse of his daughter into the store-closet. As they were sending to make the matter known in the village of Maki, and taking other measures, who should come up but the priest of the temple called Anrakuji, in the village of Iwahara, with an acolyte and a servant, who called out in a loud voice from the front door:

"Is all well with the honourable master of this house? I have been to say prayers today in a neighbouring village, and on my way back I could not pass the door without at least inquiring after your welfare. If you are at home, I would fain pay my respects to you."

As he spoke thus in a loud voice, he was heard from the back of the house; and the master got up and went out, and, after the usual compliments on meeting had been exchanged, said:

"I ought to have the honour of inviting you to step inside this evening; but really we are all in the greatest trouble, and I must beg you to excuse my impoliteness."

"Indeed! Pray, what may be the matter?" replied the priest. And when the master of the house had told the whole story, from beginning to end, he was thunderstruck, and said:

"Truly, this must be a terrible distress to you." Then the priest looked on one side, and saw Tokutaro bound, and exclaimed, "Is not that Tokutaro that I see there?"

"Oh, your reverence," replied Tokutaro, piteously, "it was this, that, and the other: and I took it into my head that the young lady was a fox, and so I killed her. But I pray your reverence to intercede for me, and save my life;" and as he spoke, the tears started from his eyes.

"To be sure," said the priest, "you may well bewail yourself; however, if I save your life, will you consent to become my disciple, and enter the priesthood?"

"Only save my life, and I'll become your disciple with all my heart."

When the priest heard this, he called out the parents, and said to them:

"It would seem that, though I am but a foolish old priest, my coming here today has been unusually well timed. I have a request to make of you. Your putting Tokutaro to death won't bring your daughter to life again. I have heard his story, and there certainly was no malice prepense on his part to kill your daughter. What he did, he did thinking to do a service to your family; and it would surely be better to hush the matter up. He wishes, moreover, to give himself over to me, and to become my disciple."

"It is as you say," replied the father and mother, speaking together. "Revenge will not recall our daughter. Please dispel our grief, by shaving his head and making a priest of him on the spot."

"I'll shave him at once, before your eyes," answered the priest, who immediately caused the cords which bound Tokutaro to be untied, and, putting on his priest's scarf, made him join his hands together in a posture of prayer. Then the reverend man stood up behind him, razor in hand, and, intoning a hymn, gave two or three strokes of the razor, which he then handed to his acolyte, who made a clean shave of

Tokutaro's hair. When the latter had finished his obeisance to the priest, and the ceremony was over, there was a loud burst of laughter; and at the same moment the day broke, and Tokutaro found himself alone, in the middle of a large moor. At first, in his surprise, he thought that it was all a dream, and was much annoyed at having been tricked by the foxes. He then passed his hand over his head, and found that he was shaved quite bald. There was nothing for it but to get up, wrap a handkerchief round his head, and go back to the place where his friends were assembled.

"Hallo, Tokutaro! so you've come back. Well, how about the foxes?"

"Really, gentlemen," replied he, bowing, "I am quite ashamed to appear before you."

Then he told them the whole story, and, when he had finished, pulled off the kerchief, and showed his bald pate.

"What a capital joke!" shouted his listeners, and amid roars of laughter, claimed the bet of fish, and wine. It was duly paid; but Tokutaro never allowed his hair to grow again, and renounced the world, and became a priest under the name of Sainen.

INARI ANSWERS A WOMAN'S PRAYER

Inari is often extremely benevolent. One legend informs us that a woman who had been married many years and had not been blessed with a child prayed at Inari's shrine. At the conclusion of her supplication the stone foxes wagged their tails, and snow began to fall. She regarded these phenomena as favourable omens.

When the woman reached her home a *yeta* (beggar) accosted her, and begged for something to eat. The woman good-naturedly gave this unfortunate wayfarer some red bean rice, the only food she had in the house, and presented it to him in a dish.

The next day her husband discovered this dish lying in front of the shrine where she had prayed. The beggar was none other than Inari himself, and the woman's generosity was rewarded in due season by the birth of a child.

THE MEANNESS OF RAIKO

Raiko was a wealthy man living in a certain village. In spite of his enormous wealth, which he carried in his *obi* (girdle), he was extremely mean. As he grew older his meanness increased till at last he contemplated dismissing his faithful servants who had served him so well.

One day Raiko became very ill, so ill that he almost wasted away, on account of a terrible fever. On the tenth night of his illness a poorly dressed *bozu* (priest) appeared by his pillow, inquired how he fared, and added that he had expected the *oni* to carry him off long ago.

These home truths, none too delicately expressed, made Raiko very angry, and he indignantly demanded that the priest should take his departure. But the *bozu*, instead of departing, told him that there was only one remedy for his illness. The remedy was that Raiko should loosen his *obi* and distribute his money to the poor.

Raiko became still more angry at what he considered the

gross impertinence of the priest. He snatched a dagger from his robe and tried to kill the kindly *bozu*. The priest, without the least fear, informed Raiko that he had heard of his mean intention to dismiss his worthy servants, and had nightly come to the old man to drain his life-blood. "Now," said the priest, "my object is attained!" and with these words he blew out the light.

The now thoroughly frightened Raiko felt a ghostly creature advance towards him. The old man struck out blindly with his dagger, and made such a commotion that his loyal servants ran, into the room with lanterns, and the light revealed the horrible claw of a monster lying by the side of the old man's mat.

Carefully following the little spots of blood, Raiko's servants came to a miniature mountain at the extreme end of the garden, and in the mountain was a large hole, from whence protruded the upper part of an enormous spider. This creature begged the servants to try to persuade their master not to attack the Gods, and in future to refrain from meanness.

When Raiko heard these words from his servants he repented, and gave large sums of money to the poor. Inari had assumed the shape of a spider and priest in order to teach the once mean old man a lesson.

THE FOXES' WEDDING

Once upon a time there was a young white fox, whose name was Fukuyemon. When he had reached the fitting age, he shaved off his forelock and began to think of taking to himself a beautiful bride. The old fox, his father, resolved to give up his inheritance to his son, and retired into private life; so the young fox, in gratitude for this, laboured hard and earnestly to increase his patrimony.

Now it happened that in a famous old family of foxes there was a beautiful young lady-fox, with such lovely fur that the fame of her jewel-like charms was spread far and wide. The young white fox, who had heard of this, was bent on making her his wife, and a meeting was arranged between them. There was not a fault to be found on either side; so the preliminaries were settled, and the wedding presents sent from the bridegroom to the bride's house, with congratulatory speeches from the messenger, which were duly acknowledged by the person deputed to receive the gifts; the bearers, of course, received the customary fee in copper cash.

When the ceremonies had been concluded, an auspicious day was chosen for the bride to go to her husband's house, and she was carried off in solemn procession during a shower of rain, the sun shining all the while. After the ceremonies of drinking wine had been gone through, the bride changed her dress, and the wedding was concluded, without let or hindrance, amid singing and dancing and merry-making.

The bride and bridegroom lived lovingly together, and a litter of little foxes were born to them, to the great joy of the old grandsire, who treated the little cubs as tenderly as if they had been butterflies or flowers. "They're the very image of their old grandfather," said he, as proud as possible. "As for medicine, bless them, they're so healthy that they'll never need a copper coin's worth!"

As soon as they were old enough, they were carried off to the temple of Inari Sama, the patron saint of foxes, and the old grand-parents prayed that they might be delivered from dogs and all the other ills to which fox flesh is heir.

In this way the white fox by degrees waxed old and prosperous, and his children, year by year, became more and more numerous around him; so that, happy in his family and his business, every recurring spring brought him fresh cause for joy.

THE WHITE HARE OF INABA

In ancient days there were eighty-one brothers, who were Princes in Japan. With the exception of one brother they were quarrelsome fellows, and spent their time in showing all manner of petty jealousy, one toward the other. Each wanted to reign over the whole kingdom, and, in addition, each had the misfortune to wish to marry the Princess of Yakami, in Inaba. Although these eighty Princes were at variance in most things, they were at one in persistently hating the brother who was gentle and peaceful in all his ways.

At length, after many angry words, the eighty brothers decided to go to Inaba in order to visit the Princess of Yakami, each brother fully resolved that he and he alone should be the successful suitor. The kind and gentle brother accompanied them, not, indeed, as a wooer of the fair Princess, but as a servant who carried a large and heavy bag upon his back.

At last the eighty Princes, who had left their much-wronged brother far behind, arrived at Cape Keta. They were about to continue their journey when they saw a white hare lying on the ground looking very miserable and entirely divested of fur.

The eighty Princes, who were much amused by the sorry plight of the hare, said: "If you want your fur to grow again, bathe in the sea, and, when you have done so, run to the summit of a high mountain and allow the wind to blow upon you." With these words the eighty heartless Princes proceeded on their way.

The hare at once went down to the sea, delighted at the prospect of regaining his handsome white fur. Having bathed, he ran up to the top of a mountain and lay down upon it; but he quickly perceived that the cold wind blowing on a skin recently immersed in salt water was beginning to crack and split. In addition to the humiliation of having no fur he now suffered considerable physical pain, and he realised that the eighty Princes had shamefully deceived him.

While the hare was lying in pain upon the mountain the kind and gentle brother approached, slowly and laboriously, owing to the heavy bag he carried. When he saw the weeping hare he inquired how it was that the poor animal had met with such a misfortune.

"Please stop a moment," said the hare, "and I will tell you how it all happened. I wanted to cross from the Island of Oki to Cape Keta, so I said to the crocodiles: 'I should very much like to know how many crocodiles there are in the sea, and how many hares on land. Allow me first of all to count you.' And having said these words the crocodiles formed themselves into a long line, stretching from the Island of Oki to Cape Keta. I ran across their horny bodies, counting each as I passed. When I reached the last crocodile, I said: 'O foolish crocodiles, it doesn't matter to me how many there are of you in the sea, or how many hares on land! I only wanted you for a bridge in order that I might reach my destination.' Alas! my miserable boast cost me dear, for the last crocodile raised his head and snapped off all my fur!"

"Well," said the gentle brother, "I must say you were in the wrong and deserved to suffer for your folly. Is that the end of your story?"

"No," continued the hare. "I had no sooner suffered this indignity than the eighty Princes came by, and lyingly told me that I might be cured by salt water and wind. Alas! not knowing that they deceived me, I carried out their instructions, with the result that my body is cracked and extremely sore."

"Bathe in fresh water, my poor friend," said the good brother, "and when you have done so scatter the pollen of sedges upon the ground and roll yourself in it. This will indeed heal your sores and cause your fur to grow again."

The hare walked slowly to the river, bathed himself, and then rolled about in sedge pollen. He had no sooner done so than his skin healed and he was covered once more with a thick coat of fur.

The grateful hare ran back to his benefactor. "Those eighty wicked and cruel brothers of yours," said he, "shall never win the Princess of Inaba. It is you who shall marry her and reign over the country."

The hare's prophecy came true, for the eighty Princes failed in their mission, while the brother who was good and kind to the white hare married the fair Princess and became King of the country.

THE CRACKLING MOUNTAIN

An old man and his wife kept a white hare. One day a badger came and ate the food provided for the pet. The mischievous animal was about to scamper away when the old man, seeing what had taken place, tied the badger to a tree, and then went to a neighbouring mountain to cut wood.

When the old man had gone on his journey the badger began to weep and to beg that the old woman would untie the rope. She had no sooner done so than the badger proclaimed vengeance and ran away.

When the good white hare heard what had taken place he set out to warn his master; but during his absence the badger returned, killed the old woman, assumed her form, and converted her corpse into broth.

"I have made such excellent broth," said the badger, when the old man returned from the mountain. "You must be hungry and tired: pray sit down and make a good meal!"

The old man, not suspecting treachery of any kind, consumed the broth and pronounced it excellent.

"Excellent?" sneered the badger. "You have eaten your wife! Her bones lie over there in that corner," and with these words he disappeared.

While the old man was overcome with sorrow, and while he wept and bewailed his fate, the hare returned, grasped the situation, and scampered off to the mountain fully resolved to avenge the death of his poor old mistress.

When the hare reached the mountain he saw the badger carrying a bundle of sticks on his back. Softly the hare crept up, and, unobserved, set light to the sticks, which began to crackle immediately.

"This is a strange noise," said the badger. "What is it?"

"The Crackling Mountain," replied the hare.

The fire began to burn the badger, so he sprang into a river and extinguished the flames; but on getting out again he found that his back was severely burnt, and the pain he suffered was increased by a cayenne poultice which the delighted hare provided for that purpose.

When the badger was well again he chanced to see the hare standing by a boat he had made.

"Where are you going in that vessel?" inquired the badger.

"To the moon," replied the hare. "Perhaps you would like to come with me?"

"Not in your boat!" said the badger. "I know too well your tricks on the Crackling Mountain. But I will build a boat of clay for myself, and we will journey to the moon."

Down the river went the wooden boat of the hare and the clay boat of the badger. Presently the badger's vessel began to come to pieces. The hare laughed derisively, and killed his enemy with his oar. Later on, when the loyal animal returned to the old man, he justly received much praise and loving care from his grateful master.

THE FOX AND THE BADGER

There is a certain mountainous district in Shikoku in which a skillful hunter had trapped or shot so many foxes and badgers that only a few were left. These were an old grey badger and a female fox with one cub. Though hard pressed by hunger, neither dared to touch a loose piece of food, lest a trap might be hidden under it. Indeed they scarcely stirred out of their holes except at night, lest the hunter's arrow should strike them. At last the two animals held a council together to decide what to do, whether to emigrate or to attempt to outwit their enemy. They thought a long while, when finally the badger having hit upon a good plan, cried out:

"I have it. Do you transform yourself into a man. I'll pretend to be dead. Then you can bind me up and sell me in the town. With the money paid you can buy some food. Then I'll get loose and come back. The next week I'll sell you and you can escape."

"Ha! ha! ha! *yoroshiu, yoroshiu*," (good, good,) cried both together. "It's a capital plan," said Mrs Fox.

So the Fox changed herself into a human form, and the badger, pretending to be dead, was tied up with straw ropes.

Slinging him over her shoulder, the fox went to town, sold the badger, and buying a lot of *tofu* (bean-cheese) and one or two chickens, made a feast. By this time the badger had got loose, for the man to whom he was sold, thinking him dead, had not watched him carefully. So scampering away to the mountains he met the fox, who congratulated him, while both feasted merrily.

The next week the badger took human form, and going to town sold the fox, who made believe to be dead. But the badger being an old skin-flint, and very greedy, wanted all the money and food for himself. So he whispered in the man's ear to watch the fox well as she was only feigning to be dead. So the man taking up a club gave the fox a blow on the head, which finished her. The badger, buying a good dinner, ate it all himself, and licked his chops, never even thinking of the fox's cub.

The cub after waiting a long time for its mother to come back, suspected foul play, and resolved on revenge. So going to the badger he challenged him to a trial of skill in the art of transformation. The badger accepted right off, for he despised the cub and wished to be rid of him.

"Well what do you want to do first? said Sir Badger."

"I propose that you go and stand on the Big Bridge leading to the city," said the cub, "and wait for my appearance. I shall come in splendid garments, and with many followers in my train. If you recognize me, you win, and I lose. If you fail, I win."

So the badger went and waited behind a tree. Soon a daimyo riding in a palanquin, with a splendid retinue of courtiers appeared, coming up the road. Thinking this was the fox-cub changed into a nobleman, although wondering at the skill of the young fox, the badger went up to the palanquin and told the person inside that he was recognized and had lost the game.

"What!" said the daimyo's followers, who were real men, and surrounding the badger, they beat him to death.

The fox-cub, who was looking on from a hill near by, laughed in derision, and glad that treachery was punished, scampered away.

KADZUTOYO AND THE BADGER

On one occasion Kadzutoyo and his retainer went fishing. They had had excellent sport, and were about to return home, when a violent shower came on, and they were forced to take shelter under a willow-tree. After waiting for some time the rain showed no sign of abating, and as it was already growing dark they decided to continue their journey in spite of the inclement weather. They had not proceeded far when they perceived a young girl weeping bitterly. Kadzutoyo regarded her with suspicion, but his retainer was charmed by the maiden's great beauty, and inquired who she was and why she lingered on such a stormy night.

"Alas! good sir," said the maiden, still weeping, "my tale is a sad one. I have long endured the taunts and cruelties of my wicked stepmother, who hates me. Tonight she spat upon me and beat me. I could bear the bitter humiliation no longer, and I was on the way to my aunt, who lives in yonder village, there to receive peace and shelter, when I was stricken down with a strange malady, and compelled to remain here until the pain subsided."

These words much affected the kind-hearted retainer, and he fell desperately in love with this fair maiden; but Kadzutoyo, after carefully considering the matter, drew his sword and cut off her head.

"Oh! my lord," said the retainer, "what awful deed is this? How can you kill a harmless girl? Believe me, you will have to pay for your folly."

"You do not understand," replied Kadzutoyo, "but all I ask is that you keep silence in the matter."

When they reached home Kadzutoyo soon fell asleep; but his retainer, after brooding over the murder of the fair maiden, went to his lord's parents and told them the whole pitiful story.

Kadzutoyo's father was stricken with anger when he heard the dreadful tale. He at once went to his son's room, roused him, and said: "Oh, miserable murderer! How could you slay an innocent girl without the least provocation? You have shamed the honourable name of *samurai*, a name that stands for true chivalry and for the defence of the weak and helpless. You have brought dishonour upon our house, and it is my duty to take your life." Having said these words, he drew his sword.

"Sir," replied Kadzutoyo, without flinching at the shining weapon, "you, like my retainer, do not understand. It has been given me to solve certain mysteries, and with that knowledge I assure you that I have not been guilty of so foul a crime as you suppose, but have been loyal to the fair calling of a *samurai*. The girl I cut down with my sword was no mortal. Be pleased to go tomorrow with your retainers to the spot where this scene occurred. If you find the corpse of a girl you will have no need to take my life, for I will disembowel myself."

Early next day, when the sun had scarce risen in the sky, Kadzutoyo's father, together with his retainers, set out upon the journey. When they reached the place where the tragedy had taken place the father saw lying by the roadside, not the corpse of a fair maiden as he had feared, but the body of a great headless badger.

When the father reached home again he questioned his son: "How is it," said he, "that what appeared to be a girl to your retainer seemed to you to be a badger?"

"Sir," replied Kadzutoyo, "the creature I saw last night appeared to me as a girl; but her beauty was strange, and not like the beauty of earthly women. Moreover, although it was raining hard, I observed that the garments of this being did not get wet, and having noticed this weird occurrence, I knew at once that the woman was none other than some wicked goblin. The creature took the form of a lovely maiden with the idea of bewitching us with her many charms, in the hope that she might get our fish."

The old Prince was filled with admiration for his son's cleverness. Having discovered so much foresight and prudence, he resolved to abdicate, and proclaim Kadzutoyo Prince of Tosa in his stead.

THE MIRACULOUS TEA-KETTLE

One day a priest of the Morinji temple put his old tea-kettle on the fire in order that he might make himself a cup of tea. No sooner had the kettle touched the fire than it suddenly changed into the head, tail, and legs of a badger. The novices of the temple were called in to see the extraordinary sight. While they gazed in utter astonishment, the badger, with the body of a kettle, rushed nimbly about the room, and finally flew into the air. Round and round the room went the merry badger, and the priests, after many efforts, succeeded in capturing the animal and thrusting it into a box.

Shortly after this event had taken place a tinker called at the temple, and the priest thought it would be an excellent idea if he could induce the good man to buy his extraordinary tea-kettle. He therefore took the kettle out of its box, for it had now resumed its ordinary form, and commenced to bargain, with the result that the unsuspecting tinker purchased the kettle, and took it away with him, assured that he had done a good day's work in buying such a useful article at so reasonable a price.

That night the tinker was awakened by hearing a curious sound close to his pillow. He looked out from behind his quilts and saw that the kettle he had purchased was not a kettle at all, but a very lively and clever badger.

When the tinker told his friends about his remarkable companion, they said: "You are a fortunate fellow, and we advise you to take this badger on show, for it is clever enough to dance and walk on the tight-rope. With song and music you certainly have in this very strange creature a series of novel entertainments which will attract considerable notice, and bring you far more money than you would earn by all the tinkering in the world."

The tinker accordingly acted upon this excellent advice, and the fame of his performing badger spread far and wide. Princes and princesses came to see the show, and from royal patronage and the delight of the common people he amassed a great fortune. When the tinker had made his money he restored the kettle to the Morinji temple, where it was worshipped as a precious treasure.

THE BADGER'S MONEY

It is a common saying among men, that to forget favours received is the part of a bird or a beast: an ungrateful man will be ill spoken of by all the world. And yet even birds and beasts will show gratitude; so that a man who does not requite a favour is worse even than dumb brutes. Is not this a disgrace?

Once upon a time, in a hut at a place called Namekata, in Hitachi, there lived an old priest famous neither for learning nor wisdom, but bent only on passing his days in prayer and meditation. He had not even a child to wait upon him, but prepared his food with his own hands. Night and morning he recited the prayer "Namu Amida Butsu," intent upon that alone. Although the fame of his virtue did not reach far, yet his neighbours respected and revered him, and often brought him food and raiment; and when his roof or his walls fell out of repair, they would mend them for him; so for the things of this world he took no thought.

One very cold night, when he little thought anyone was outside, he heard a voice calling "Your reverence! your reverence!" So he rose and went out to see who it was, and there he beheld an old badger standing. Any ordinary man would have been greatly alarmed at the apparition; but the priest, being such as he has been described above, showed no sign of fear, but asked the creature its business. Upon this the badger respectfully bent its knees, and said:

"Hitherto, sir, my lair has been in the mountains, and of snow or frost I have taken no heed; but now I am growing old, and this severe cold is more than I can bear. I pray you to let me enter and warm myself at the fire of your cottage, that I may live through this bitter night."

When the priest heard what a helpless state the beast was reduced to, he was filled with pity, and said:

"That's a very slight matter: make haste and come in and warm yourself."

The badger, delighted with so good a reception, went into the hut, and squatting down by the fire began to warm itself; and the priest, with renewed fervour, recited his prayers and struck his bell before the image of Buddha, looking straight before him. After two hours the badger took its leave, with profuse expressions of thanks, and went out; and from that time forth it came every night to the hut. As the badger would collect and bring with it dried branches and dead leaves from the hills for firewood, the priest at last became very friendly with it, and got used to its company; so that if ever, as the night wore on, the badger did not arrive, he used to miss it, and wonder why it did not come. When the winter was over, and the spring-time came at the end of the second month, the Badger gave up its visits, and was no more seen; but, on the return of the winter, the beast resumed its old habit of coming to the hut. When this practice had gone on for ten years, one day the badger said to the priest, "Through your reverence's kindness for all these years, I have been able to pass the winter nights in comfort. Your favours are such, that during all my life, and even after my death, I must remember them. What can I do to requite them? If there is anything that you wish for, pray tell me."

The priest, smiling at this speech, answered, "Being such as I am, I have no desire and no wishes. Glad as I am to hear your kind intentions, there is nothing that I can ask you to do for me. You need feel no anxiety on my account. As long as I live, when the winter comes, you shall be welcome here." The badger, on hearing this, could not conceal its admiration of the depth of the old man's benevolence; but having so much to be grateful for, it felt hurt at not being able to requite it. As this subject was often renewed between them, the priest at last, touched by the goodness of the badger's heart, said, "Since I have shaven my head, renounced the world, and forsaken the pleasures of this life, I have no desire to gratify, yet I own I should like to possess three riyos in gold. Food and raiment I receive by the favour of the villagers, so I take no heed for those things. Were I to die tomorrow, and attain my wish of being born again into the next world, the same kind folk have promised to meet and bury my body. Thus, although I have no other reason to wish for money, still if I had three riyos I would offer them up at some holy shrine, that masses and prayers might be said for me, whereby I might enter into salvation. Yet I would not get this money by violent or unlawful means; I only think of what might be if I had it. So you see, since you have expressed such kind feelings towards me, I have told you what is on my mind."

When the priest had done speaking, the badger leant its head on one side with a puzzled and anxious look, so much so that the old man was sorry he had expressed a wish which seemed to give the beast trouble, and tried to retract what he had said. "Posthumous honours, after all, are the wish of ordinary men. I, who am a priest, ought not to entertain such thoughts, or to want money; so pray pay no attention to what I have said;" and the badger, feigning assent to what the priest had impressed upon it, returned to the hills as usual.

From that time forth the badger came no more to the hut. The priest thought this very strange, but imagined either that the badger stayed away because it did not like to come without the money, or that it had been killed in an attempt to steal it; and he blamed himself for having added to his sins for no purpose, repenting when it was too late: persuaded, however, that the badger must have been killed, he passed his time in putting up prayers upon prayers for it.

After three years had gone by, one night the old man heard a voice near his door calling out, "Your reverence! your reverence!"

As the voice was like that of the badger, he jumped up as soon as he heard it, and ran out to open the door; and there, sure enough, was the badger. The priest, in great delight, cried out, "And so you are safe and sound, after all! Why have you been so long without coming here? I have been expecting you anxiously this long while."

So the badger came into the hut, and said, "If the money which you required had been for unlawful purposes, I could easily have procured as much as ever you might have wanted; but when I heard that it was to be offered to a temple for masses for your soul, I thought that, if I were to steal the hidden treasure of some other man, you could not apply to a sacred purpose money which had been obtained at the expense of his sorrow. So I went to the island of Sado, and gathering the sand and earth which had been cast away as worthless by the miners, fused it afresh in the fire; and at this work I spent months and days." As the badger finished speaking, the priest looked at the money which it had produced, and sure enough he saw that it was bright and new and clean; so he took the money, and received it respectfully, raising it to his head.

"And so you have had all this toil and labour on account of a foolish speech of mine? I have obtained my heart's desire, and am truly thankful."

As he was thanking the badger with great politeness and ceremony, the beast said, "In doing this I have but fulfilled my own wish; still I hope that you will tell this thing to no man."

"Indeed," replied the priest, "I cannot choose but tell this story. For if I keep this money in my poor hut, it will be stolen by thieves: I must either give it to someone to keep for me, or else at once offer it up at the temple. And when I do this, when people see a poor old priest with a sum of money quite unsuited to his station, they will think it very suspicious, and I shall have to tell the tale as it occurred; but as I shall say that the badger that gave me the money has ceased coming to my hut, you need not fear being waylaid, but can come, as of old, and shelter yourself from the cold." To this the badger nodded assent; and as long as the old priest lived, it came and spent the winter nights with him.

THE VAMPIRE CAT

The Prince of Hizen, a distinguished member of the Nabeshima family, lingered in the garden with O Toyo, the favourite among his ladies. When the sun set they retired to the palace, but failed to notice that they were being followed by a large cat.

O Toyo went to her room and fell asleep. At midnight she awoke and gazed about her, as if suddenly aware of some dreadful presence in the apartment. At length she saw, crouching close beside her, a gigantic cat, and before she could cry out for assistance the animal sprang upon her and strangled her. The animal then made a hole under the verandah, buried the corpse, and assumed the form of the beautiful O Toyo.

The Prince, who knew nothing of what had happened, continued to love the false O Toyo, unaware that in reality he was caressing a foul beast. He noticed, little by little, that his strength failed, and it was not long before he became dangerously ill. Physicians were summoned, but they could do nothing to restore the royal patient. It was observed that he suffered most during the night, and was troubled by horrible dreams. This being so his councillors arranged that a hundred retainers should sit with their lord and keep watch while he slept.

The watch went into the sick-room, but just before ten o'clock it was overcome by a mysterious drowsiness. When all the men were asleep the false O Toyo crept into the apartment and disturbed the Prince until sunrise. Night after night the retainers came to guard their master, but always they fell asleep at the same hour, and even three loyal councillors had a similar experience.

During this time the Prince grew worse, and at length a priest named Ruiten was appointed to pray on his behalf. One night, while he was engaged in his supplications, he heard a strange noise proceeding from the garden. On looking out of the window he saw a young soldier washing himself. When he had finished his ablutions he stood before an image of Buddha, and prayed most ardently for the recovery of the Prince.

Ruiten, delighted to find such zeal and loyalty, invited the young man to enter his house, and when he had done so inquired his name.

"I am Ito Soda," said the young man, "and serve in the infantry of Nabeshima. I have heard of my lord's sickness and long to have the honour of nursing him; but being of low rank it is not meet that I should come into his presence. I have, nevertheless, prayed to the Buddha that my lord's life may be spared. I believe that the Prince of Hizen is bewitched, and if I might remain with him I would do my utmost to find and crush the evil power that is the cause of his illness."

Ruiten was so favourably impressed with these words that he went the next day to consult with one of the councillors, and after much discussion it was arranged that Ito Soda should keep watch with the hundred retainers.

When Ito Soda entered the royal apartment he saw that his master slept in the middle of the room, and he also observed the hundred retainers sitting in the chamber quietly chatting together in the hope that they would be able to keep off approaching drowsiness. By ten o'clock all the retainers, in spite of their efforts, had fallen asleep. Ito Soda tried to keep his eyes open, but a heaviness was gradually overcoming him, and he realised that if he wished to keep awake he must resort to extreme measures. When he had carefully spread oil-paper over the mats he stuck his dirk into his thigh. The sharp pain he experienced warded off sleep for a time, but eventually he felt his eyes closing once more. Resolved to outwit the spell which had proved too much for the retainers, he twisted the knife in his thigh, and thus increased the pain and kept his loyal watch, while blood continually dripped upon the oil-paper.

While Ito Soda watched he saw the sliding doors drawn open and a beautiful woman creep softly into the apartment. With a smile she noticed the sleeping retainers, and was about to approach the Prince when she observed Ito Soda. After she had spoken curtly to him she approached the Prince and inquired how he fared, but the Prince was too ill to make a reply. Ito Soda watched every movement, and believed she tried to bewitch the Prince, but she was always frustrated in her evil purpose by the dauntless eyes of Ito Soda, and at last she was compelled to retire.

In the morning the retainers awoke, and were filled with shame when they learnt how Ito Soda had kept his vigil. The councillors loudly praised the young soldier for his loyalty and enterprise, and he was commanded to keep watch again that night. He did so, and once more the false O Toyo entered the sick-room, and, as on the previous night, she was compelled to retreat without being able to cast her spell over the Prince.

It was discovered that immediately the faithful Soda had kept guard the Prince was able to obtain peaceful slumber, and, moreover, that he began to get better, for the false O Toyo, having been frustrated on two occasions, now kept away altogether, and the guard was not troubled with mysterious drowsiness. Soda, impressed by these strange circumstances, went to one of the councillors and informed him that the so-called O Toyo was a goblin of some kind.

That night Soda planned to go to the creature's room and try to kill her, arranging that in case she should escape there should be eight retainers outside waiting to capture her and despatch her immediately.

At the appointed hour Soda went to the creature's apartment, pretending that he bore a message from the Prince.

"What is your message?" inquired the woman.

"Kindly read this letter," replied Soda, and with these words he drew his dirk and tried to kill her.

The false O Toyo seized a halberd and endeavoured to strike her adversary. Blow followed blow, but at last perceiving that flight would serve her better than battle she threw away her weapon, and in a moment the lovely maiden turned into a cat and sprang on to the roof. The eight men waiting outside in case of emergency shot at the animal, but the creature succeeded in eluding them.

The cat made all speed for the mountains, and caused trouble among the people who lived in the vicinity, but was finally killed during a hunt ordered by the Prince Hizen. The Prince became well again, and Ito Soda received the honour and reward he so richly deserved.

SHIPPEITARO AND THE PHANTOM CATS

A certain knight took shelter in a lonely and dilapidated mountain temple. Towards midnight he was awakened by hearing a strange noise. Gazing about him, he saw a number of cats dancing and yelling and shrieking, and over and over again he heard these words: *"Tell it not to Shippeitaro!"*

At midnight the cats suddenly disappeared, stillness reigned in the ruined temple, and our warrior was able to resume his slumber.

The next morning the young knight left the haunted building, and came to one or two small dwellings near a village. As he passed one of these houses he heard great wailing and lamentation, and inquired the cause of the trouble.

"Alas!" said those who thronged about the knight, "well may you ask why we are so sorely troubled. This very night the mountain spirit will take away our fairest maiden in a great cage to the ruined temple where you have spent the night, and in the morning she will be devoured by the wicked spirit of the mountain. Every year we lose a girl in this way, and there is none to help us."

The knight, greatly moved by these pitiful words, and anxious to be of service, said: "Who or what is Shippeitaro? The evil spirits in the ruined temple used the name several times."

"Shippeitaro," said one of the people, "is a brave and very fine dog, and belongs to the head man of our Prince." The knight hastened off, was successful in securing Shippeitaro for one night, and took the dog back with him to the house of the weeping parents. Already the cage was prepared for the damsel, and into this cage he put Shippeitaro, and, with several young men to assist him, they reached the haunted temple. But the young men would not remain on the mountain, for they were full of fear, and, having performed their task, they took their departure, so that the knight and the dog were left alone.

At midnight the phantom cats again appeared, this time surrounding a tomcat of immense size and of great fierceness. When the monster cat saw the cage he sprang round it with screams of delight, accompanied by his companions.

The warrior, choosing a suitable opportunity, opened the cage, and Shippeitaro sprang out and held the great cat in his teeth. In another moment his master drew forth his sword and slew the wicked creature. The other cats were too amazed at what they had seen to make good their escape, and the valiant Shippeitaro soon made short work of them. Thus the village was no longer troubled with ravages of the mountain spirit, and the knight, in true courtly fashion, gave all the praise to the brave Shippeitaro.

THE STORY OF THE FAITHFUL CAT

Some years ago, in the summertime, a man went to pay a visit at a certain house at Osaka, and, in the course of conversation, said: "I have eaten some very extraordinary cakes today," and on being asked what he meant, he told the following story:

"I received the cakes from the relatives of a family who were celebrating the hundredth anniversary of the death of a cat that had belonged to their ancestors. When I asked the history of the affair, I was told that, in former days, a young girl of the family, when she was about sixteen years old, used always to be followed about by a tom-cat, who was reared in the house, so much so that the two were never separated for an instant. When her father perceived this, he was very angry, thinking that the tom-cat, forgetting the kindness with which he had been treated for years in the house, had fallen in love with his daughter, and intended to cast a spell upon her; so he determined that he must kill the beast. As he was planning this in secret, the cat overheard him, and that night went to his pillow, and, assuming a human voice, said to him:

"'You suspect me of being in love with your daughter; and although you might well be justified in so thinking, your suspicions are groundless. The fact is this: There is a very large old rat who has been living for many years in your granary. Now it is this old rat who is in love with my young mistress, and this is why I dare not leave her side for a moment, for fear the old rat should carry her off. Therefore I pray you to dispel your suspicions. But as I, by myself, am no match for the rat, there is a famous cat, named Buchi, at the house of

Mr So-and-so, at Ajikawa: if you will borrow that cat, we will soon make an end of the old rat.'

"When the father awoke from his dream, he thought it so wonderful, that he told the household of it; and the following day he got up very early and went off to Ajikawa, to inquire for the house which the cat had indicated, and had no difficulty in finding it; so he called upon the master of the house, and told him what his own cat had said, and how he wished to borrow the cat Buchi for a little while.

"'That's a very easy matter to settle,' said the other: 'pray take him with you at once;' and accordingly the father went home with the cat Buchi in charge. That night he put the two cats into the granary; and after a little while, a frightful clatter was heard, and then all was still again; so the people of the house opened the door, and crowded out to see what had happened; and there they beheld the two cats and the rat all locked together, and panting for breath; so they cut the throat of the rat, which was as big as either of the cats: then they attended to the two cats; but, although they gave them ginseng and other restoratives, they both got weaker and weaker, until at last they died. So the rat was thrown into the river; but the two cats were buried with all honours in a neighbouring temple."

THE OLD MAN WHO MADE THE TREES BLOSSOM

One day, while an old man and his wife were in the garden, their dog suddenly became very excited as he lowered his head and sniffed the ground in one particular place. The old people, believing that their pet had detected something good to eat, brought a spade and commenced to dig, and to their amazement they dug up a great number of gold and silver pieces and a variety of precious treasures as well. With this newly acquired wealth the old couple lost no time in distributing alms among the poor.

When the people next door heard about their neighbours' good fortune they borrowed the dog, and spread before him all manner of delicacies in the hope that the animal would do them a good turn too. But the dog, who had been on previous occasions ill-treated by his hosts, refused to eat, and at length the angry couple dragged him into the garden. Immediately the dog began to sniff, and exactly where he sniffed the greedy couple began to dig; but they dug up no treasure, and all they could find was very objectionable refuse. The old couple, angry and disappointed, killed the dog and buried him under a pine-tree.

The good old man eventually learnt what had befallen his faithful dog, and, full of sorrow, he went to the place where his pet was buried, and arranged food and flowers on the grave, weeping as he did so.

That night the spirit of the dog came to his master, and said: "Cut down the tree where I am buried, and from the wood fashion a mortar, and think of me whenever you use it."

The old man carried out these instructions, and he found that when he ground the grains of rice in the pine mortar every grain turned into a precious treasure.

The wicked old couple, having borrowed the dog, had no compunction in borrowing the mortar too, but with these wicked people the rice immediately turned into filth, so that in their anger they broke and burnt the precious vessel.

Once again the spirit of the dog appeared before his master, and informed him what had taken place, adding: "If you will sprinkle the ashes of the mortar over withered trees they will immediately become full of blossom," and having uttered these words the spirit departed.

The kind-hearted old man secured the ashes, and, placing them in a basket, journeyed from village to village and from town to town, and over withered trees he threw the ashes, and, as the dog had promised, they suddenly came into flower. A prince heard of these wonders, and commanded the old man to appear before him, requesting that he would give an exhibition of his miraculous power. The old man did so, and joyfully departed with the many royal gifts bestowed upon him.

The old man's neighbours, hearing of these miracles, collected together the remaining ashes of the wonderful mortar, and the wicked fellow went about the country claiming to be able to revive withered or dead trees. Like the original worker of wonders, the greedy old man appeared in the palace, and was commanded to restore a withered tree. The old man climbed up into a tree and scattered the ashes, but the tree still remained withered, and the ashes almost blinded and suffocated the Prince. Upon this the old impostor was almost beaten to death, and he went away in a very miserable state indeed.

The kind old man and his wife, after rebuking their neighbours for their wickedness, allowed them to share in their wealth, and the once mean, cruel, and crafty couple led good and virtuous lives.

THE JELLY-FISH AND THE MONKEY

Rin-Jin, the King of the Sea, took to wife a young and beautiful Dragon Princess. They had not been married long when the fair Queen fell ill, and all the advice and attention of the great physicians availed nothing.

"Oh," sobbed the Queen, "there is only one thing that will cure me of my illness!"

"What is that?" inquired Rin-Jin.

"If I eat the liver of a live monkey I shall immediately recover. Pray get me a monkey's liver, for I know that nothing else will save my life."

So Rin-Jin called a jelly-fish to his side, and said: "I want you to swim to the land and return with a live monkey on your back, for I wish to use his liver that our Queen may be restored to health again. You are the only creature who can perform this task, for you alone have legs and are able to walk about on shore. In order to induce the monkey to come you must tell him of the wonders of the deep and of the rare beauties of my great palace, with its floor of pearl and its walls of coral."

The jelly-fish, delighted to think that the health and happiness of his mistress depended upon the success of his enterprise, lost no time in swimming to an island. He had no sooner stepped on shore than he observed a fine-looking monkey playing about in the branches of a pine-tree.

"Hello!" said the jelly-fish, "I don't think much of this island. What a dull and miserable life you must lead here! I come from the Kingdom of the Sea, where Rin-Jin reigns in a palace of great size and beauty. It may be that you would like to see a new country where there is plenty of fruit and where the weather is always fine. If so, get on my back, and I shall have much pleasure in taking you to the Kingdom of the Sea."

"I shall be delighted to accept your invitation," said the monkey, as he got down from the tree and comfortably seated himself on the thick shell of the jelly-fish.

"By the way," said the jelly-fish, when he had accomplished about half of the return journey, "I suppose you have brought your liver with you, haven't you?"

"What a personal question!" replied the monkey. "Why do you ask?"

"Our Sea Queen is dangerously ill," said the foolish jelly-fish, "and only the liver of a live monkey will save her life. When we reach the palace a doctor will make use of your liver and my mistress will be restored to health again."

"Dear me!" exclaimed the monkey, "I wish you had mentioned this matter to me before we left the island."

"If I had done so," replied the jelly-fish, "you would most certainly have refused my invitation."

"Believe me, you are quite mistaken, my dear jelly-fish. I have several livers hanging up on a pine-tree, and I would gladly have spared one in order to save the life of your Queen. If you will bring me back to the island again I will get it. It was most unfortunate that I should have forgotten to bring a liver with me."

So the credulous jelly-fish turned round and swam back to the island. Directly the jelly-fish reached the shore the monkey sprang from his back and danced about on the branches of a tree.

"*Liver*" said the monkey, chuckling, "did you say *liver*? You silly old jelly-fish, you'll certainly never get mine!"

The jelly-fish at length reached the palace, and told Rin-Jin his dismal tale. The Sea King fell into a great passion. "Beat him to a jelly!" he cried to those about him. "Beat this stupid fellow till he hasn't a bone left in his body!"

So the jelly-fish lost his shell from that unfortunate hour, and all the jelly-fishes that were born in the sea after his death were also without shells, and have remained nothing but jelly to this day.

THE SAGACIOUS MONKEY AND THE BOAR

Long, long ago, there lived in the province of Shinshin in Japan, a traveling monkey-man, who earned his living by taking round a monkey and showing off the animal's tricks.

One evening the man came home in a very bad temper and told his wife to send for the butcher the next morning.

The wife was very bewildered and asked her husband:

"Why do you wish me to send for the butcher?"

"It's no use taking that monkey round any longer, he's too old and forgets his tricks. I beat him with my stick all I know how, but he won't dance properly. I must now sell him to the butcher and make what money out of him I can. There is nothing else to be done."

The woman felt very sorry for the poor little animal, and pleaded for her husband to spare the monkey, but her pleading was all in vain, the man was determined to sell him to the butcher.

Now the monkey was in the next room and overheard every word of the conversation. He soon understood that he was to be killed, and he said to himself:

"Barbarous, indeed, is my master! Here I have served him faithfully for years, and instead of allowing me to end my days comfortably and in peace, he is going to let me be cut up by the butcher, and my poor body is to be roasted and stewed and eaten? Woe is me! What am I to do. Ah! a bright thought has struck me! There is, I know, a wild bear living in the forest near by. I have often heard tell of his wisdom. Perhaps if I go to him and tell him the strait I am in he will give me his counsel. I will go and try."

There was no time to lose. The monkey slipped out of the house and ran as quickly as he could to the forest to find the boar. The boar was at home, and the monkey began his tale of woe at once.

"Good Mr Boar, I have heard of your excellent wisdom. I am in great trouble, you alone can help me. I have grown old in the service of my master, and because I cannot dance properly now he intends to sell me to the butcher. What do you advise me to do? I know how clever you are!"

The boar was pleased at the flattery and determined to help the monkey. He thought for a little while and then said:

"Hasn't your master a baby?"

"Oh, yes," said the monkey, "he has one infant son."

"Doesn't it lie by the door in the morning when your mistress begins the work of the day? Well, I will come round early and when I see my opportunity I will seize the child and run off with it."

"What then?" said the monkey.

"Why the mother will be in a tremendous scare, and before

your master and mistress know what to do, you must run after me and rescue the child and take it home safely to its parents, and you will see that when the butcher comes they won't have the heart to sell you."

The monkey thanked the boar many times and then went home. He did not sleep much that night, as you may imagine, for thinking of the morrow. His life depended on whether the boar's plan succeeded or not. He was the first up, waiting anxiously for what was to happen. It seemed to him a very long time before his master's wife began to move about and open the shutters to let in the light of day. Then all happened as the boar had planned. The mother placed her child near the porch as usual while she tidied up the house and got her breakfast ready.

The child was crooning happily in the morning sunlight, dabbing on the mats at the play of light and shadow. Suddenly there was a noise in the porch and a loud cry from the child. The mother ran out from the kitchen to the spot, only just in time to see the boar disappearing through the gate with her child in its clutch. She flung out her hands with a loud cry of despair and rushed into the inner room where her husband was still sleeping soundly.

He sat up slowly and rubbed his eyes, and crossly demanded what his wife was making all that noise about. By the time that the man was alive to what had happened, and they both got outside the gate, the boar had got well away, but they saw the monkey running after the thief as hard as his legs would carry him.

Both the man and wife were moved to admiration at the plucky conduct of the sagacious monkey, and their gratitude knew no bounds when the faithful monkey brought the child safely back to their arms.

"There!" said the wife. "This is the animal you want to kill – if the monkey hadn't been here we should have lost our child forever."

"You are right, wife, for once," said the man as he carried the child into the house. "You may send the butcher back when he comes, and now give us all a good breakfast and the monkey too."

When the butcher arrived he was sent away with an order for some boar's meat for the evening dinner, and the monkey was petted and lived the rest of his days in peace, nor did his master ever strike him again.

THE BATTLE OF THE APE AND THE CRAB

Once upon a time there was a crab who lived in a marsh in a certain part of the country. It fell out one day that, the crab having picked up a rice cake, an ape, who had got a nasty hard persimmon-seed, came up, and begged the crab to make an exchange with him. The crab, who was a simple-minded creature, agreed to this proposal; and they each went their way, the ape chuckling to himself at the good bargain which he had made.

When the crab got home, he planted the persimmon-seed in his garden, and, as time slipped by, it sprouted, and by degrees grew to be a big tree. The crab watched the growth of his tree with great delight; but when the fruit ripened, and he was going to pluck it, the ape came in, and offered to gather it for him. The crab consenting, the ape climbed up into the tree, and began eating all the ripe fruit himself, while he only threw down the sour persimmons to the crab, inviting him, at the same time, to eat heartily. The crab, however, was not pleased at this arrangement, and thought that it was his turn to play a trick upon the ape; so he called out to him to come down head foremost. The ape did as he was bid; and as he crawled down, head foremost, the ripe fruit all came tumbling out of his pockets, and the crab, having picked up the persimmons, ran off and hid himself in a hole. The ape, seeing this, lay in ambush, and as soon as the crab crept out of his hiding-place gave him a sound drubbing, and went home. Just at this time a friendly egg and a bee, who were the apprentices of a certain rice-mortar, happened to pass that way, and, seeing the crab's piteous condition, tied up his wounds, and, having escorted him home, began to lay plans to be revenged upon the cruel ape.

Having agreed upon a scheme, they all went to the ape's house, in his absence; and each one having undertaken to play a certain part, they waited in secret for their enemy to come home. The ape, little dreaming of the mischief that was brewing, returned home, and, having a fancy to drink a cup of tea, began lighting the fire in the hearth, when, all of a sudden, the egg, which was hidden in the ashes, burst with. the heat, and bespattered the frightened ape's face, so that he fled, howling with pain, and crying, "Oh! what an unlucky beast I am!" Maddened with the heat of the burst egg, he tried to go to the back of the house, when the bee darted out of a cupboard, and a piece of seaweed, who had joined the party, coming up at the same time, the ape was surrounded by enemies. In despair, he seized the clothes-rack, and fought valiantly for awhile; but he was no match for so many, and was obliged to run away, with the others in hot pursuit after him. Just as he was making his escape by a back door, however, the piece of seaweed tripped him up, and the rice-mortar, closing with him from behind, made an end of him.

So the crab, having punished his enemy, went home in triumph, and lived ever after on terms of brotherly love with the seaweed and the mortar. Was there ever such a fine piece of fun!

THE TRAVELS OF TWO FROGS

Long, long ago, in the good old days before the hairy-faced and pale-cheeked men from over the Sea of Great Peace (Pacific Ocean) came to Japan; before the black coal-smoke and snorting engine scared the white heron from the rice-fields; before black crows and fighting sparrows, which fear not man, perched on telegraph wires, or ever a railway was thought of, there lived two frogs – one in a well in Kyoto, the other in a lotus-pond in Osaka.

Now it is a common proverb in the Land of the Gods (Japan) that "the frog in the well knows not the great ocean," and the Kyoto frog had so often heard this scornful sneer from the maids who came to draw out water, with their long bamboo-handled buckets that he resolved to travel abroad and see the world, and especially the *tai kai* (the great ocean).

"I'll see for myself," said Mr Frog, as he packed his wallet and wiped his spectacles, "what this great ocean is that they talk about. I'll wager it isn't half as deep or wide as well, where I can see the stars even at daylight."

Now the truth was, a recent earthquake had greatly reduced the depth of the well and the water was getting very shallow. Mr Frog informed his family of his intentions. Mrs Frog wept a great deal; but, drying her eyes with her paper handkerchief, she declared she would count the hours on her fingers till he came back, and at every morning and evening meal would set out his table with food on it, just as if he were home. She tied up a little lacquered box full ofboiled rice and snails for his journey, wrapped it around with a silk napkin, and, putting his extra clothes in a bundle, swung it on his back. Tying it over his neck, he seized his staff and was ready to go.

"*Sayonara*" ("Good-bye") cried he, as, with a tear in his eye, he walked away.

"*Sayonara. Oshidzukani*" ("Good-bye. Walk slowly"), croaked Mrs Frog and the whole family of young frogs in a chorus.

Two of the froggies were still babies, that is, they were yet polywogs, with a half inch of tail still on them; and, of course, were carried about by being strapped on the back of their older brothers.

Mr Frog being now on land, out of his well, noticed that the other animals did not leap, but walked on their legs. And, not wishing to be eccentric, he likewise began briskly walking upright on his hind legs or waddling on all fours.

Now it happened that about the same time the Osaka father frog had become restless and dissatisfied with life on the edges of his lotus-ditch. He had made up his mind to "cast the lion's cub into the valley."

"Why! that *is* tall talk for a frog, I must say," exclaims the reader. "What did he mean?"

I must tell you that the Osaka frog was a philosopher. Right at the edge of his lotus-pond was a monastery, full of Buddhist monks, who every day studied their sacred rolls and droned over the books of Confucius, to learn them by heart. Our frog had heard them so often that he could (in frog language, of course) repeat many of their wise sentences and intone responses to their evening prayers put up by the great idol Amida. Indeed, our frog had so often listened to their debates on texts from the classics that he had himself become a sage and a philosopher. Yet, as the proverb says, "the sage is not happy."

Why not? In spite of a soft mud-bank, plenty of green scum, stagnant water, and shady lotus leaves, a fat wife and a numerous family; in short, everything to make a frog happy, his forehead, or rather gullet, was wrinkled with care from long pondering of knotty problems, such as the following:

The monks often come down to the edge of the pond to look at the pink and white lotus. One summer day, as a little frog, hardly out of his tadpole state, with a small fragment of tail still left, sat basking on a huge round leaf, one monk said to the other:

"Of what does that remind you?"

"The babies of frogs will become but frogs," said one shaven pate, laughing.

"What think you?"

"The white lotus flower springs out of the black mud," said the other, solemnly, as both walked away.

The old frog, sitting near by, overheard them and began to philosophize: "Humph! The babies of frogs will become but frogs, hey? If mud becomes lotus, why shouldn't a frog become a man? Why not? If my pet son should travel abroad and see the world – go to Kyoto, for instance – why shouldn't he be as wise as those shining-headed men, I wonder? I shall try it, anyhow. I'll send my son on a journey to Kyoto. I'll 'cast the lion's cub into the valley' (send the pet son abroad in the world, to see and study) at once. I'll deny myself for the sake of my offspring."

Flump! splash! sounded the water, as a pair of webby feet disappeared. The "lion's cub" was soon ready, after much paternal advice, and much counsel to beware of being gobbled up by long-legged storks, and trod on by impolite men, and struck at by bad boys. *"Kio ni no inaka"* ("Even in the capital there are boors") said Father Frog.

Now it so happened that the old frog from Kyoto and the "lion's cub" from Osaka started each from his home at the same time. Nothing of importance occurred to either of them until, as luck would have it, they met on a hill near Hashimoto, which is half way between the two cities. Both were footsore, and websore, and very tired, especially about the hips, on account of the unfroglike manner of walking, instead of hopping, as they had been used to.

"Ohio gozarimasu" ("Good-morning") said the 'lion's cub' to the old frog, as he fell on all fours and bowed his head to the ground three times, squinting up over his left eye, to see if the other frog was paying equal deference in return.

"He, konnichi wa" ("Yes, good-day") replied the Kyoto frog.

"*O tenki*" ('It is rather fine weather today') said the "cub."

"*He, yoi tenki gozence*" ("Yes, it is very fine") replied the old fellow.

"I am Gamataro, from Osaka, the oldest son of Hiki Dono, Sensui no Kami" (Lord Bullfrog, Prince of the Lotus-Ditch).

"Your Lordship must be weary with your journey. I am Kayeru San of Idomidzu (Sir Frog of the Well) in Kyoto. I started out to see the 'great ocean' from Osaka; but, I declare, my hips are so dreadfully tired that I believe that I'll give up my plan and content myself with a look from this hill."

The truth must be owned that the old frog was not only on his hind legs, but also on his last legs, when he stood up to look at Osaka; while the "cub" was tired enough to believe anything. The old fellow, wiping his face, spoke up:

"Suppose we save ourselves the trouble of the journey. This hill is half way between the two cities, and while I see Osaka and the sea you can get a good look of the Kio" (Capital, or Kyoto).

"Happy thought!" said the Osaka frog.

Then both reared themselves upon their hind-legs, and stretching upon their toes, body to body, and neck to neck, propped each other up, rolled their goggles and looked steadily, as they supposed, on the places which they each wished to see. Now everyone knows that a frog has eyes mounted in that part of his head which is front when he is down and back when he stands up. They are set like a compass on gimbals.

Long and steadily they gazed, until, at last, their toes being tired, they fell down on all fours.

"I declare!" said the old *yaze* (daddy) "Osaka looks just like Kyoto; and as for 'the great ocean' those stupid maids talked about, I don't see any at all, unless they mean that strip of river that looks for all the world like the Yodo. I don't believe there is any 'great ocean'!"

"As for my part," said the 'cub', "I am satisfied that it's all folly to go further; for Kyoto is as like Osaka as one grain of rice is like another." Then he said to himself: "Old Totsu San (my father) is a fool, with all his philosophy."

Thereupon both congratulated themselves upon the happy labor-saving expedient by which they had spared themselves a long journey, much leg-weariness, and some danger. They departed, after exchanging many compliments; and, dropping again into a frog's hop, they leaped back in half the time – the one to his well and the other to his pond. There each told the story of both cities looking exactly alike; thus demonstrating the folly of those foolish folks called men. As for the old gentleman in the lotus-pond, he was so glad to get the "cub" back again that he never again tried to reason out the problems of philosophy. And to this day the frog in the well knows not and believes not in the "great ocean." Still do the babies of frogs become but frogs. Still is it vain to teach the reptiles philosophy; for all such labor is "like pouring water in a frog's face." Still out of the black mud springs the glorious white lotus in celestial purity, unfolding its stainless petals to the smiling heavens, the emblem of life and resurrection.

JIRAIYA, OR THE MAGIC FROG

Ogata was the name of a castle-lord who lived in the Island of the Nine Provinces, (Kiushiu). He had but one son, an infant, whom the people in admiration nicknamed Jiraiya (Young Thunder.) During one of the civil wars, this castle was taken, and Ogata was slain; but by the aid of a faithful retainer, who hid Jiraiya in his bosom, the boy escaped and fled northward to Echigo. There he lived until he grew up to manhood.

At that time Echigo was infested with robbers. One day the faithful retainer of Jiraiya being attacked, made resistance, and was slain by the robbers. Jiraiya now left alone in the world went out from Echigo and led a wandering life in several provinces.

All this time he was consumed with the desire to revive the name of his father, and restore the fortunes of his family. Being exceedingly brave, and an expert swordsman, he became chief of a band of robbers and plundered many wealthy merchants, and in a short time he was rich in men, arms and booty. He was accustomed to disguise himself, and go in person into the houses and presence of men of wealth, and thus learn all about their gates and guards, where they slept, and in what rooms their treasures were stored, so that success was easy.

Hearing of an old man who lived in Shinano, he started to rob him, and for this purpose put on the disguise of a pilgrim. Shinano is a very high table-land, full of mountains, and the snow lies deep in winter. A great snow storm coming on, Jiraiya took refuge in a humble house by the way. Entering, he found a very beautiful woman, who treated him with great kindness. This, however, did not change the robber's nature. At midnight, when all was still, he unsheathed his sword, and going noiselessly to her room, he found the lady absorbed in reading.

Lifting his sword, he was about to strike at her neck, when, in a flash, her body changed into that of a very old man, who seized the heavy steel blade and broke it in pieces as though it were a stick. Then he tossed the bits of steel away, and thus spoke to Jiraiya, who stood amazed but fearless:

"I am a man named Senso Dojin, and I have lived in these mountains many hundred years, though my true body is that of a huge frog. I can easily put you to death but I have another purpose. So I shall pardon you and teach you magic instead."

Then the youth bowed his head to the floor, poured out his thanks to the old man and begged to be received as his pupil.

Remaining with the old man of the mountain for several weeks, Jiraiya learned all the arts of the mountain spirits; how to cause a storm of wind and rain, to make a deluge, and to control the elements at will.

He also learned how to govern the frogs, and at his bidding they assumed gigantic size, so that on their backs he could stand up and cross rivers and carry enormous loads.

When the old man had finished instructing him he said "Henceforth cease from robbing, or in any way injuring the poor. Take from the wicked rich, and those who acquire money dishonestly, but help the needy and the suffering." Thus speaking, the old man turned into a huge frog and hopped away.

What this old mountain spirit bade him do, was just what Jiraiya wished to accomplish. He set out on his journey with a light heart. "I can now make the storm and the waters obey me, and all the frogs are at my command; but alas! the magic of the frog cannot control that of the serpent. I shall beware of his poison."

From that time forth the oppressed poor people rejoiced many a time as the avaricious merchants and extortionate money lenders lost their treasures. For when a poor farmer, whose crops failed, could not pay his rent or loan on the date promised, these hard-hearted money lenders would turn him out of his house, seize his beds and mats and rice-tub, and even the shrine and images on the god-shelf, to sell them at auction for a trifle, to their minions, who resold them at a high price for the money-lender, who thus got a double benefit. Whenever a miser was robbed, the people said, "The young thunder has struck," and then they were glad, knowing that it was Jiraiya, (Young Thunder.) In this manner his name soon grew to be the poor people's watchword in those troublous times.

Yet Jiraiya was always ready to help the innocent and honest, even if they were rich. One day a merchant named Fukutaro was sentenced to death, though he was really not guilty. Jiraiya hearing of it, went to the magistrate and said that he himself was the very man who committed the robbery. So the man's life was saved, and Jiraiya was hanged on a large oak tree. But during the night, his dead body changed into a bull-frog which hopped away out of sight, and off into the mountains of Shinano.

At this time, there was living in this province, a young and beautiful maiden named Tsunade. Her character was very lovely. She was always obedient to her parents and kind to her friends. Her daily task was to go to the mountains and cut brushwood for fuel. One day while thus busy singing at the task, she met a very old man, with a long white beard sweeping his breast, who said to her:

"Do not fear me. I have lived in this mountain many hundred years, but my real body is that of a snail. I will teach you the powers of magic, so that you can walk on the sea, or cross a river however swift and deep, as though it were dry land."

Gladly the maiden took daily lessons of the old man, and soon was able to walk on the waters as on the mountain paths. One day the old man said, "I shall now leave you and resume my former shape. Use your power to destroy wicked robbers. Help those who defend the poor. I advise you to marry the celebrated man Jiraiya, and thus you will unite your powers."

Thus saying, the old man shrivelled up into a snail and crawled away.

"I am glad," said the maiden to herself, "for the magic of the snail can overcome that of the serpent. When Jiraiya, who has the magic of the frog, shall marry me, we can then destroy the son of the serpent, the robber named Dragon-coil (Orochimaru)."

By good fortune, Jiraiya met the maiden Tsunade, and being charmed with her beauty, and knowing her power of magic, sent a messenger with presents to her parents, asking them to give him their daughter to wife. The parents agreed, and so the young and loving couple were married.

Hitherto when Jiraiya wished to cross a river he changed himself into a frog and swam across; or, he summoned a bull-frog before him, which increased in size until as large as an elephant. Then standing erect on his warty back, even though the wind blew his garments wildly, Jiraiya reached the opposite shore in safety. But now, with his wife's powers, the two, without any delay, walked over as though the surface was a hard floor.

Soon after their marriage, war broke out in Japan between the two famous clans of Tsukikage and Inukage. To help them fight their battles, and capture the castles of their enemies, the Tsukikage family besought the aid of Jiraiya, who agreed to serve them and carried their banner in his back. Their enemies, the Inukage, then secured the services of Dragon-coil.

This Orochimaru, or Dragon-coil, was a very wicked robber whose father was a man, and whose mother was a serpent that lived in the bottom of Lake Takura. He was perfectly skilled in the magic of the serpent, and by spurting venom on his enemies, could destroy the strongest warriors.

Collecting thousands of followers, he made great ravages in all parts of Japan, robbing and murdering good and bad, rich and poor alike. Loving war and destruction he joined his forces with the Inukage family.

Now that the magic of the frog and snail was joined to the one army, and the magic of the serpent aided the other, the conflicts were bloody and terrible, and many men were slain on both sides.

On one occasion, after a hard fought battle, Jiraiya fled and took refuge in a monastery, with a few trusty vassals, to rest a short time. In this retreat a lovely princess named Tagoto was dwelling. She had fled from Orochimaru, who wished her for his bride. She hated to marry the offspring of a serpent, and hoped to escape him. She lived in fear of him continually. Orochimaru hearing at one time that both Jiraiya and the princess were at this place, changed himself into a serpent, and distilling a large mouthful of poisonous venom, crawled up to the ceiling in the room where Jiraiya and his wife were sleeping, and reaching a spot directly over them, poured the poisonous venom on the heads of his rivals. The fumes of the prison so stupefied Jiraiya's followers, and even the monks, that Orochimaru, instantly changing himself to a man, profited by the opportunity to seize the princess Tagoto, and make off with her.

Gradually the faithful retainers awoke from their stupor to find their master and his beloved wife delirious, and near the point of death, and the princess gone.

"What can we do to restore our dear master to life?" This was the question each one asked of the others, as with sorrowful faces and weeping eyes they gazed at the pallid forms of their unconscious master and his consort. They called in the venerable abbot of the monastery to see if he could suggest what could be done.

"Alas!" said the aged priest, "there is no medicine in Japan to cure your lord's disease, but in India there is an elixir which is a sure antidote. If we could get that, the master would recover."

"Alas! alas!" and a chorus of groans showed that all hope had fled, for the mountain in India, where the elixir was made, lay five thousand miles from Japan.

Just then a youth named Rikimatsu, one of the pages of Jiraiya, arose to speak. He was but fourteen years old, and served Jiraiya out of gratitude, for he had rescued his father from many dangers and saved his life. He begged permission to say a word to the abbot, who, seeing the lad's eager face, motioned to him with his fan to speak.

"How long can our lord live," asked the youth.

"He will be dead in thirty hours," answered the abbot, with a sigh.

"I'll go and procure the medicine, and if our master is still living when I come back, he will get well."

Now Rikimatsu had learned magic and sorcery from the Tengus, or long-nosed elves of the mountains, and could fly high in the air with incredible swiftness. Speaking a few words of incantation, he put on the wings of a Tengu, mounted a white cloud and rode on the east wind to India, bought the elixir of the mountain spirits, and returned to Japan in one day and a night.

On the first touch of the elixir on the sick man's face he drew a deep breath, perspiration glistened on his forehead, and in a few moments more he sat up.

Jiraiya and his wife both got well, and the war broke out again. In a great battle Dragon-coil was killed and the princess rescued. For his prowess and aid Jiraiya was made daimyo of Idzu.

Being now weary of war and the hardships of active life, Jiraiya was glad to settle down to tranquil life in the castle and rear his family in peace. He spent the remainder of his days in reading the books of the sages, in composing verses, in admiring the flowers, the moon and the landscape, and occasionally going out hawking or fishing. There, amid his children and children's children, he finished his days in peace.

WHY THERE IS HATRED OF THE COCK

The God of Mionoseki (a town now part of the city of Matsue) detests cocks and hens and everything pertaining to these birds, and the inhabitants respect his very marked dislike. On one occasion a certain steamer, shortly after making for the open sea, encountered a severe storm, and it was thought that the God of Mionoseki, who is the God of Mariners, must have been seriously offended. At length the captain discovered that one of his passengers was smoking a pipe adorned with the figure of a crowing cock. The pipe was immediately thrown into the sea, and the storm abated.

We are able to gather the reason for the hatred of the cock from the following legend. In the *Kojiki* we are informed that the son of the Deity of Kitsuki spent many an hour at Mionoseki in catching birds and fish. At that time the cock was his trusted friend, and it was the duty of this bird to crow lustily when it was time for the God to return from his sport. On one occasion, however, the cock forgot to crow, and in consequence, in the God's hurry to go back in his boat he lost his oars, and was compelled to propel the vessel with his hands, which were severely bitten by fishes.

HOW YORITOMO WAS SAVED BY TWO DOVES

Yoritomo, having been defeated in a battle against Oba Kage-chika, was forced to retreat with six of his followers. They ran with all speed through a forest, and, finding a large hollow tree, crept inside for shelter.

In the meantime Oba Kage-chika said to his cousin, Oba Kagetoki: "Go and search for Yoritomo, for I have good reason to believe that he lies hidden in this forest. I will so arrange my men that the flight of our enemy will be impossible."

Oba Kagetoki departed, none too pleased with the mission, for he had once been on friendly terms with Yoritomo. When he reached the hollow tree and saw through a hole in the trunk that his old friend lay concealed within, he took pity on him, and returned to his cousin, saying: "I believe that Yoritomo, our enemy, is not in this wood."

When Oba Kage-chika heard these words he cried fiercely: "You lie! How could Yoritomo make his escape so soon and with my men standing on guard about the forest? Lead the way, and I and some of my men will follow you. No cunning this time, cousin, or you shall severely suffer for it."

In due time the party reached the hollow tree, and Kage-chika was about to enter it, when his cousin cried: "Stay! What folly is this? Cannot you see that there is a spider's web spun across the opening? How could anyone enter this tree without breaking it? Let us spend our time more profitably elsewhere."

Kage-chika, however, was still suspicious concerning his cousin, and he thrust his bow into the hollow trunk. It almost touched the crouching Yoritomo, when two white doves suddenly flew out of the cavity.

"Alas!" exclaimed Kage-chika, "you are right, our enemy cannot lie concealed here, for doves and a cobweb would not admit of such a thing."

By the timely aid of two doves and a spider's web the great hero Yoritomo made good his escape, and when, in later years, he became Shogun he caused shrines to be erected to

Hachiman, the God of War, in recognition of his deliverance, for the doves of Japan are recognised as the messengers of war, and not of peace, as is the case in our own country.

THE TONGUE-CUT SPARROW

A cross old woman was at her wash-tub when her neighbour's pet sparrow ate up all the starch, mistaking it for ordinary food. The old woman was so angry at what had happened that she cut out the sparrow's tongue, and the unfortunate bird flew away to a mountain.

When the old couple to whom the sparrow belonged heard what had taken place they left their home and journeyed a great distance until they had the good fortune to find their pet again.

The sparrow was no less delighted to meet his master and mistress, and begged them to enter his house. When they had done so they were feasted with an abundance of fish and *sake*, were waited upon by the sparrow's wife, children, and grandchildren, and, not content with these deeds of hospitality, the feathered host danced a jig called the Sparrow's Dance.

When it was time for the old couple to return home the sparrow brought forth two wicker baskets, saying: "One is heavy, and the other is light. Which would you rather have?"

"Oh, the light one," replied the old couple, "for we are aged and the journey is a long one."

When the old people reached their home they opened the basket, and to their delight and amazement discovered gold and silver, jewels and silk. As fast as they took the precious things out an inexhaustible supply came to their place, so that the wonderful basket of treasure could not be emptied, and the happy old couple grew rich and prosperous.

It was not long before the old woman who had cut out the sparrow's tongue heard about the good fortune of her neighbours, and she hastened to inquire where this wonderful sparrow was to be seen.

Having gained the information, she had no difficulty in finding the sparrow. When the bird saw her he asked which of two baskets she would prefer to take away with her, the heavy or light one? The cruel and greedy old woman chose the heavy one, believing that this basket would contain more treasure than the light one; but when, after much labour, she reached home and opened it, devils sprang upon her and tore her to pieces.

A NOBLE SACRIFICE

There was once a man who was extremely fond of shooting birds. He had two daughters, good Buddhists, and each in turn pointed out the folly of their father's cruel sport, and begged him not to destroy life wantonly. However, the man was obstinate and would not listen to his daughters' entreaties. One day a neighbour asked him to shoot two storks, and he promised to do so. When the women heard what their father was about to do, they said: "Let us dress in pure white garments and go down upon the shore tonight, for it is a place much frequented by storks. If our father should kill either of us in mistake for the birds, it will teach him a lesson, and he will surely repent his evil ways, which are contrary to the gentle teaching of the Lord Buddha."

That night the man went to the shore, and the cloudy sky made it difficult for him to discover any storks. At last, however, he saw two white objects in the distance. He fired; the bodies fell immediately, and he ran to where they lay, only to discover that he had shot both his noble, self-sacrificing daughters. Stricken with sorrow, the man erected a funeral pyre and burnt the bodies of his poor children. Having done these things, he shaved his head, went into the woods, and became a hermit.

TAMA'S RETURN

Kazariya Kyubei, a merchant, had a maid-servant called Tama. Tama worked well and cheerfully, but she was negligent in regard to her dress. One day, when she had been five years in Kyubei's house, her master said to her: "Tama, how is it that, unlike most girls, you seem to have no desire to look your best? When you go out you wear your working dress. Surely you should put on a pretty robe on such occasions."

"Good master," said Tama, "you do well to rebuke me, for you do not know why, during all these years, I have worn old clothes and have made no attempt to wear pretty ones. When my father and mother died I was but a child, and as I had no brothers or sisters it rested upon me to have Buddhist services performed on behalf of my parents. In order that this might come to pass I have saved the money you have given me, and spent as little upon myself as possible. Now my parents' mortuary tablets are placed in the Jorakuji temple, and, having given my money to the priests, the sacred rites have now been performed. I have fulfilled my wish, and, begging for your forgiveness, I will in future dress more becomingly."

Before Tama died she asked her mistress to keep the remaining money she had saved. Shortly after her death a large fly entered Kyubei's house. Now at that time of the year, the Period of the Greatest Cold, it was unusual for flies to appear, and the master of the house was considerably puzzled. He carefully put the insect outside the house; but it flew back immediately, and every time it was ejected it came back again. "This fly," said Kyubei's wife, "may be Tama." Kyubei cut a small piece out of the insect's wings, and this time carried it some distance from his abode. But the next day it returned once more, and this time the master painted the fly's wings and body with rouge, and took it even further away from his dwelling. Two days later the fly returned, and the nick in its wings and the rouge with which it was covered left no doubt in the minds of Kyubei and his wife that this persistent insect was indeed Tama.

"I believe," said Kyubei's wife, "that Tama has returned to us because she wants us to do something for her. I have the money she asked me to keep. Let us give it to the priests in order that they may pray for her soul." When these words had been spoken the fly fell dead upon the floor.

Kyubei and his wife placed the fly in a box, and with the girl's money they went to the priests. A *sutra* was recited over the body of the insect, and it was duly buried in the temple grounds.

A STRANGE DREAM

A young man of Matsue was returning home from a wedding-party when he saw, just in front of his house, a firefly. He paused a moment, surprised to see such an insect on a cold winter's night with snow on the ground. While he stood and meditated the firefly flew toward him, and the young man struck at it with his stick, but the insect flew away and entered the garden adjoining his own.

The next day he called at his neighbour's house, and was about to relate the experience of the previous night when the eldest daughter of the family entered the room, and exclaimed: "I had no idea you were here, and yet a moment ago you were in my mind. Last night I dreamt that I became a firefly. It was all very real and very beautiful, and while I was darting hither and thither I saw you, and flew toward you, intending to tell you that I had learnt to fly, but you thrust me aside with your stick, and the incident still frightens me."

The young man, having heard these words from the lips of his betrothed, held his peace.

THE VENGEANCE OF KANSHIRO

In the village of Funakami there lived a devout old farmer called Kanshiro. Every year the old man made various pilgrimages to certain shrines, where he prayed and asked the blessings of the deities. At last, however, he became so infirm that he realised that his earthly days were numbered, and that he would probably only have strength to pay one more visit to the great shrines at Ise. When the people of the village heard this noble resolution they generously gave him a sum of money in order that the respected old farmer might present it to the sacred shrines.

Kanshiro set off upon his pilgrimage carrying the money in a bag, which he hung round his neck. The weather was extremely hot, and the heat and fatigue of the journey made the old man so ill that he was forced to remain for a few days in the village of Myojo. He went to a small inn and asked Jimpachi, the innkeeper, to take care of his money, explaining that it was an offering to the Gods at Ise. Jimpachi took the money, and assured the old man that he would take great care of it, and, moreover, that he himself would attend upon him.

On the sixth day the old man, though still far from well, paid his bill, took the bag from the innkeeper, and proceeded on his journey. As Kanshiro observed many pilgrims in the vicinity he did not look into the bag, but carefully concealed it in the sack containing spare raiment and food.

When Kanshiro at length rested under a pine-tree he took out the bag and looked inside. Alas! the money had been stolen, and stones of the same weight inserted in its place. The old man hastily returned to the innkeeper and begged him to restore the money. Jimpachi grew extremely angry, and gave him a severe beating.

The poor old man crawled away from the village, and three days later, with indomitable courage, he succeeded in reaching the sacred shrines at Ise. He sold his property in order to refund the money his good neighbours had given him, and with what remained he continued his pilgrimage, till at last he was forced to beg for food.

Three years later Kanshiro went to the village of Myoto, and found that the innkeeper who had treated him so badly was now comparatively well off, and lived in a large house. The old man went to him, and said: "You have stolen sacred money from me, and I have sold my little property in order that I might refund it to those who had given it to me. Ever since that time I have been a beggar, but be assured vengeance shall fall upon you!"

Jimpachi cursed the old man and told him that he had not stolen his money. During the heated dispute a watchman seized Kanshiro, dragged him away from the house, and told him that he would be arrested if he dared to return. At the end of the village the old man died, and a kindly priest took his body to a temple, respectfully burnt it, and offered up many holy prayers for his good and loyal soul.

Immediately after Kanshiro's death Jimpachi grew afraid of what he had done, and became so ill that he was forced to take to his bed. When he had lost all power of movement a great company of fireflies flew out of the farmer's tomb and surrounded Jimpachi's mosquito-curtain, and tried to break it down. Many of the villagers came to Jimpachi's assistance and killed a number of fireflies, but the stream of shining insects that flew from Kanshiro's tomb never lessened. Hundreds were killed, but thousands came to take their place. The room was ablaze with firefly light, and the mosquito-curtain sank beneath their ever-increasing weight. At this remarkable sight some of the villagers murmured: "Jimpachi stole the old man's money after all. This is the vengeance of Kanshiro."

Even while they spoke the curtain broke and the fireflies rushed into the eyes, ears, mouth, and nose of the terrified

Jimpachi. For twenty days he screamed aloud for mercy; but no mercy came. Thicker and thicker grew the stream of flashing, angry insects, till at last they killed the wicked Jimpachi, when from that hour they completely disappeared.

THE FIREFLY'S LOVERS

On the southern and sunny side of the castle moats of the Fukui castle, in Echizen, the water had long ago become shallow so that lotus lilies grew luxuriantly. Deep in the heart of one of the great flowers whose petals were as pink as the lining of a sea-shell, lived the King of the Fireflies, Hi-o, whose only daughter was the lovely princess Hotaru-hime. While still a child the hime (princess) was carefully kept at home within the pink petals of the lily, never going even to the edges except to see her father fly off on his journey. Dutifully she waited until of age, when the fire glowed in her own body, and shone, beautifully illuminating the lotus, until its light at night was like a lamp within a globe of coral.

Every night her light grew brighter and brighter, until at last it was as mellow as gold. Then her father said:

"My daughter is now of age, she may fly abroad with me sometimes, and when the proper suitor comes she may marry whom she will."

So Hotaru-hime flew forth in and out among the lotus lilies of the moat, then into rich rice fields, and at last far off to the indigo meadows.

Whenever she went a crowd of suitors followed her, for she had the singular power of attracting all the night-flying insects to herself. But she cared for none of their attentions, and though she spoke politely to them all she gave encouragement to none. Yet some of the sheeny-winged gallants called her a coquette.

One night she said to her mother, the queen:

"I have met many admirers, but I don't wish a husband from any of them. Tonight I shall stay at home, and if any of them love me truly they will come and pay me court here. Then I shall lay an impossible duty on them. If they are wise they will not try to perform it; and if they love their lives more than they love me, I do not want any of them. Whoever succeeds may have me for his bride."

"As you will my child," said the queen mother, who arrayed her daughter in her most resplendent robes, and set her on her throne in the heart of the lotus.

Then she gave orders to her body-guard to keep all suitors at a respectful distance lest some stupid gallant, a horn-bug or a cockchafer dazzled by the light should approach too near and hurt the princess or shake her throne.

No sooner had twilight faded away, than forth came the golden beetle, who stood on a stamen and making obeisance, said:

"I am Lord Green-Gold, I offer my house, my fortune and my love to Princess Hotaru."

"Go and bring me fire and I will be your bride" said Hotaru-hime.

With a bow of the head the beetle opened his wings and departed with a stately whirr.

Next came a shining bug with wings and body as black as lamp-smoke, who solemnly professed his passion.

"Bring me fire and you may have me for your wife."

Off flew the bug with a buzz.

Pretty soon came the scarlet dragonfly, expecting so to dazzle the princess by his gorgeous colors that she would accept him at once.

"I decline your offer" said the princess, "but if you bring me a flash of fire, I'll become your bride."

Swift was the flight of the dragonfly on his errand, and in came the Beetle with a tremendous buzz, and ardently plead his suit.

"I'll say 'yes' if you bring me fire" said the glittering princess.

Suitor after suitor appeared to woo the daughter of the King of the Fireflies until every petal was dotted with them. One after another in a long troop they appeared. Each in his own way, proudly, humbly, boldly, mildly, with flattery, with boasting, even with tears, each proffered his love, told his rank or expatiated on his fortune or vowed his constancy, sang his tune or played his music. To everyone of her lovers the princess in modest voice returned the same answer:

"Bring me fire and I'll be your bride."

So without telling his rivals, each one thinking he had the secret alone sped away after fire.

But none ever came back to wed the princess. Alas for the poor suitors! The beetle whizzed off to a house near by through the paper windows of which light glimmered. So full was he of his passion that thinking nothing of wood or iron, he dashed his head against a nail, and fell dead on the ground.

The black bug flew into a room where a poor student was reading. His lamp was only a dish of earthenware full of rape seed oil with a wick made of pith. Knowing nothing of oil the love-lorn bug crawled into the dish to reach the flame and in a few seconds was drowned in the oil.

"Nan jaro?" (What's that?) said a thrifty housewife, sitting with needle in hand, as her lamp flared up for a moment, smoking the chimney, and then cracking it; while picking out the scorched bits she found a roasted dragonfly, whose scarlet wings were all burned off.

Mad with love the brilliant hawk-moth, afraid of the flame yet determined to win the fire for the princess, hovered round and round the candle flame, coming nearer and nearer each time. "Now or never, the princess or death," he buzzed, as he darted forward to snatch a flash of flame, but singeing his wings, he fell helplessly down, and died in agony.

"What a fool he was, to be sure," said the ugly clothes moth, coming on the spot, "I'll get the fire. I'll crawl up *inside* the candle." So he climbed up the hollow paper wick, and was nearly to the top, and inside the hollow blue part of the flame, when the man, snuffing the wick, crushed him to death.

Sad indeed was the fate of the lovers of Hi-o's daughter. Some hovered around the beacons on the headland, some fluttered about the great wax candles which stood eight feet high in their brass sockets in Buddhist temples; some burned their noses at the top of incense sticks, or were nearly choked by the smoke; some danced all night around the lanterns in the shrines; some sought the sepulchral lamps in the graveyard; one visited the cremation furnace; another the kitchen, where a feast was going on; another chased the sparks that flew out of the chimney; but none brought fire to the princess, or won the lover's prize. Many lost their feelers, had their shining bodies scorched or their wings singed, but most of them alas! lay dead, black and cold next morning.

As the priests trimmed the lamps in the shrines, and the servant maids the lanterns, each said alike:

"The Princess Hotaru must have had many lovers last night."

Alas! alas! poor suitors. Some tried to snatch a streak of green fire from the cat's eyes, and were snapped up for their pains. One attempted to get a mouthful of bird's breath, but was swallowed alive. A carrion beetle (the ugly lover) crawled off to the sea shore, and found some fish scales that emitted light. The stag-beetle climbed a mountain, and in a rotten tree stump found some bits of glowing wood like fire, but the distance was so great that long before they reached the castle moat it was daylight, and the fire had gone out; so they threw their fish scales and old wood away.

The next day was one of great mourning and there were so many funerals going on, that Hi-maro the Prince of the Fireflies on the north side of the castle moat inquired of his servants the cause. Then he learned for the first time of the glittering princess. Upon this the prince who had just succeeded his father upon the throne fell in love with the princess and resolved to marry her. He sent his chamberlain to ask of her father his daughter in marriage according to true etiquette. The father agreed to the prince's proposal, with the condition that the Prince should obey her behest in one thing, which was to come in person bringing her fire.

Then the Prince at the head of his glittering battalions came in person and filled the lotus palace with a flood of golden light. But Hotaru-hime was so beautiful that her charms paled not their fire even in the blaze of the Prince's glory. The visit ended in wooing, and the wooing in wedding. On the night appointed, in a palanquin made of the white lotus-petals, amid the blazing torches of the prince's battalions of warriors, Hotaru-hime was borne to the prince's palace and there, prince and princess were joined in the wedlock.

Many generations have passed since Hi-maro and Hotaru-hime were married, and still it is the whim of all Firefly princesses that their base-born lovers must bring fire as their love-offering or lose their prize. Else would the glittering fair ones be wearied unto death by the importunity of their lovers. Great indeed is the loss, for in this quest of fire many thousand insects, attracted by the firefly, are burned to death in the vain hope of winning the fire that shall gain the cruel but beautiful one that fascinates them. It is for this cause that each night insects hover around the lamp flame, and every morning a crowd of victims drowned in the oil, or scorched in the flame, must be cleaned from the lamp. This is the reason why young ladies catch and imprison the fireflies to watch the war of insect-love, in the hope that they may have human lovers who will dare as much, through fire and flood, as they.

THE WHITE BUTTERFLY

An old man named Takahama lived in a little house behind the cemetery of the temple of Sozanji. He was extremely amiable and generally liked by his neighbours, though most of them considered him to be a little mad. His madness, it would appear, entirely rested upon the fact that he had never married or evinced desire for intimate companionship with women.

One summer day he became very ill, so ill, in fact, that he sent for his sister-in-law and her son. They both came and did all they could to bring comfort during his last hours. While they watched Takahama fell asleep; but he had no sooner done so than a large white butterfly flew into the room, and rested on the old man's pillow. The young man tried to drive it away with a fan; but it came back three times, as if loth to leave the sufferer.

At last Takahama's nephew chased it out into the garden, through the gate, and into the cemetery beyond, where it lingered over a woman's tomb, and then mysteriously disappeared. On examining the tomb the young man found the name "Akiko" written upon it, together with a description narrating how Akiko died when she was eighteen. Though the tomb was covered with moss and must have been erected fifty years previously, the boy saw that it was surrounded with flowers, and that the little water-tank had been recently filled.

When the young man returned to the house he found that Takahama had passed away, and he returned to his mother and told her what he had seen in the cemetery.

"Akiko?" murmured his mother. "When your uncle was young he was betrothed to Akiko. She died of consumption shortly before her wedding-day. When Akiko left this world your uncle resolved never to marry and to live ever near her grave. For all these years he has remained faithful to his vow, and kept in his heart all the sweet memories of his one and only love. Every day Takahama went to the cemetery, whether the air was fragrant with summer breeze or thick with falling, snow. Every day he went to her grave and prayed for her happiness, swept the tomb and set flowers there. When Takahama was dying, and he could no longer perform his loving task, Akiko came for him. That white butterfly was her sweet and loving soul."

Just before Takahama passed away into the Land of the Yellow Spring he may have murmured words like those of Yone Noguchi:

> *"Where the flowers sleep,*
> *Thank God! I shall sleep tonight.*
> *Oh, come, butterfly!"*

FLOWERS & TREES

One of the most striking, and certainly one of the most pleasing, characteristics of the Japanese is their intense love of flowers and trees. Merry parties set out to see the azaleas bloom, or the splendour of the pink-white cherry-blossom, or the scarlet glory of the maple-trees. The love of flowers is only a small part of the Japanese love of Nature. The great Japanese designer of gardens, Kobori-Enshū, said that an ideal garden should be like "the sweet solitude of a landscape clouded by moonlight, with a half-gloom between the trees."

The pine-tree is the emblem of good fortune and longevity, symbolising the comradeship of love, the peaceful and mutual devotion of old married people in Japan. The chrysanthemum is Japan's national flower and is certainly a fitting symbolism for the Imperial standard. Once, like the English rose, it figured as a badge in the War of the Chrysanthemums, a protracted civil war that divided the nation into two hostile factions. Now the chrysanthemum stands for a united Empire. The supreme floral glory of Japan takes place in April with the coming of the cherry and plum blossom, which are regarded with the most favour. The poet Motoori wrote: "If one should ask you concerning the heart of a true Japanese, point to the wild cherry flower glowing in the sun".

CHRYSANTHEMUM-OLD-MAN

Kikuo ('Chrysanthemum-Old-Man') was the faithful retainer of Tsugaru. One day his lord's force was overthrown, and the castle and fine estates were taken away by the enemy; but fortunately Tsugaru and Kikuo were able to escape to the mountains.

Kikuo, knowing his master's love of flowers, especially that of the chrysanthemum, resolved to cultivate this flower to the best of his ability, and in so doing to lessen a little of his master's remorse and humiliation in exile.

His efforts pleased Tsugaru, but unfortunately that lord soon fell sick and died, and the faithful Kikuo wept over his master's grave. Then once more he returned to his work, and planted chrysanthemums about his master's tomb till he had made a border thirty yards broad, so that red, white, pink, yellow, and bronze blossoms scented the air, to the wonder of all who chanced to come that way.

When Kikuo was about eighty-two he caught cold and was confined to his humble dwelling, where he suffered considerable pain.

One autumn night, when he knew those beloved flowers dedicated to his master were at their best, he saw in the verandah a number of young children. As he gazed upon them he realised that they were not the children of this world.

Two of these little ones drew near to Kikuo, and said: "We are the spirits of your chrysanthemums, and have come to tell you how sorry we are to find you ill. You have guarded and loved us with such care. There was a man in China,

Hozo by name, who lived eight hundred years by drinking the dew from chrysanthemum blossoms. Gladly would we lengthen out your days, but, alas! the Gods ordain otherwise. Within thirty days you will die."

The old man expressed the wish that he might die in peace, and the regret that he must needs leave behind him all his chrysanthemums.

"Listen," said one of the ghostly children: "we have all loved you, Kikuo, for what you have done for us. When you die we shall die too." As soon as these words were spoken a puff of wind blew against the dwelling, and the spirits departed.

Kikuo grew worse instead of better, and on the thirtieth day he passed away. When visitors came to see the chrysanthemums he had planted, all had vanished. The villagers buried the old man near his master, and, thinking to please Kikuo, they planted chrysanthemums near his grave; but all died immediately they were put into the ground. Only grasses grow over the tombs now. The child-souls of the chrysanthemums chatter and sing and play with the spirit of Kikuo.

THE VIOLET WELL

Shinge and her waiting-maids were picnicking in the Valley of Shimizutani, that lies between the mountains of Yoshino and Tsubosaka. Shinge, full of the joy of spring, ran towards the Violet Well, where she discovered great clumps of purple, sweet-scented violets. She was about to pick the fragrant blossoms when a great snake darted forth, and she immediately fainted.

When the maidens found her they saw that her lips were purple, as purple as the violets that surrounded her, and when they saw the snake, still lurking in the vicinity, they feared that their mistress would die. Matsu, however, had sufficient presence of mind to throw her basket of flowers at the snake, which at once crawled away.

Just at that moment a handsome youth appeared, and, explaining to the maidens that he was a doctor, he gave Matsu some medicine, in order that she might give it to her mistress.

While Matsu forced the powder into Shinge's mouth the doctor took up a stick, disappeared for a few moments, and then returned with the dead snake in his hands.

By this time Shinge had regained consciousness, and asked the name of the physician to whom she was indebted for saving her life. But he politely bowed, evaded her question, and then took his departure. Only Matsu knew that the name of her mistress's rescuer was Yoshisawa.

When Shinge had been taken to her home she grew worse instead of better. All the cleverest doctors came to her bedside, but could do nothing to restore her to health.

Matsu knew that her mistress was gradually fading away for love of the handsome man who had saved her life, and she therefore talked the matter over with her master, Zembei. Matsu told him the story, and said that although Yoshisawa was of a low birth, belonging to the Outcasts, the lowest caste in Japan, who live by killing and skinning animals, yet nevertheless he was extremely courteous and had the manner and bearing of a *samurai*. "Nothing," said Matsu, "will restore your daughter to health unless she marries this handsome physician."

Both Zembei and his wife were dismayed at these words, for Zembei was a great *daimyō*, and could not for one moment tolerate the idea of his daughter marrying one of the Outcast class. However, he agreed to make inquiries concerning Yoshisawa, and Matsu returned to her mistress with something like good news. When Matsu had told Shinge what her father was doing on her behalf she rallied considerably, and was able to take food.

When Shinge was nearly well again Zembei called her to him and said that he had made careful inquiries concerning Yoshisawa, and could on no account agree to her marrying him.

Shinge wept bitterly, and brooded long over her sorrow with a weary heart. The next morning she was not to be found in the house or in the garden. Search was made in every direction; even Yoshisawa himself sought her everywhere; but those who sought her found her not. She had mysteriously disappeared, burdened with a sorrow that now made her father realise the effect of his harsh decree.

After three days she was found lying at the bottom of the Violet Well, and shortly after Yoshisawa, overcome with grief, sought a similar end to his troubles. It is said that on stormy nights the ghost of Shinge is to be seen floating over the well, while near by comes the sound of the weeping of Yoshisawa.

THE GHOST OF THE LOTUS LILY

A certain disease broke out in Kyoto from which many thousands of people died. It spread to Idzumi, where the

Lord of Koriyama lived, and Koriyama, his wife and child, were stricken down with the malady.

One day Tada Samon, a high official in Koriyama's castle, received a visit from a *yamabushi*, or mountain recluse. This man was full of concern for the illness of the Lord Koriyama, and, addressing Samon, he said: "All this trouble has come about through the entrance of evil spirits in the castle. They have come because the moats about the abode are dry and contain no lotus. If these moats were at once planted with this sacred flower the evil spirits would depart, and your lord, his wife and child, grow well again."

Samon was much impressed by these wise words, and permission was given for this recluse to plant lotus about the castle. When he had accomplished his task he mysteriously disappeared.

Within a week the Lord Koriyama, his wife and son, were able to get up and resume their respective duties, for by this time the walls had been repaired, the moats filled with pure water, which reflected the nodding heads of countless lotus.

Many years later, and after the Lord Koriyama had died, a young *samurai* chanced to pass by the castle moats. He was gazing admiringly at these flowers when he suddenly saw two extremely handsome boys playing on the edge of the water. He was about to lead them to a safer place when they sprang into the air and, falling, disappeared beneath the water.

The astonished *samurai*, believing that he had seen a couple of *kappas*, or river goblins, made a hasty retreat to the castle, and there reported his strange adventure. When he had told his story the moats were dragged and cleaned, but nothing could be found of the supposed *kappas*.

A little later on another *samurai*, Murata Ippai, saw near the same lotus a number of beautiful little boys. He drew his sword and cut them down, breathing in as he did so the heavy perfume of this sacred flower with every stroke of his weapon. When Ippai looked about him to see how many of these strange beings he had killed, there arose before him a cloud of many colours, a cloud that fell upon his face with a fine spray.

As it was too dark to ascertain fully the extent and nature of his onslaught, Ippai remained all night by the spot. When he awoke in the morning he found to his disgust that he had only struck off the heads of a number of lotus. Knowing that this beneficent flower had saved the life of the Lord Koriyama, and now protected that of his son, Ippai was filled with shame and remorse. Saying a prayer by the water's edge, he committed *hara-kiri*.

THE SPIRIT OF THE PEONY

It had been arranged that the Princess Aya should marry the second son of Lord Ako. The arrangements, according to Japanese custom, had been made entirely without the consent or approval of the actual parties concerned.

One night Princess Aya walked through the great garden of her home, accompanied by her waiting-maids. The moon shone brightly upon her favourite peony bed near a pond, and covered the sweet-scented blooms in a silver sheen. Here she lingered, and was stooping to breathe the fragrance of these flowers when her foot slipped, and she would have fallen had not a handsome young man, clad in a robe of embroidered peonies, rescued her just in time. He vanished as quickly and mysteriously as he had come, before, indeed, she had time to thank him.

It so happened that shortly after this event the Princess Aya became very ill, and in consequence the day for her marriage had to be postponed. All the medical aid available was useless to restore the feverish maiden to health again.

The Princess Aya's father asked his favourite daughter's maid, Sadayo, if she could throw any light upon this lamentable affair.

Sadayo, although hitherto bound to secrecy, felt that the time had come when it was wise, indeed essential, to communicate all she knew in the matter. She told her master that the Princess Aya was deeply in love with the young *samurai* wearing the robes embroidered with peonies, adding that if he could not be found she feared that her young mistress would die.

That night, while a celebrated player was performing upon the *biwa* in the hope of entertaining the sick Princess, there once more appeared behind the peonies the same young man in the same silk robe.

The next night, too, while Yae and Yakumo were playing on the flute and *koto*, the young man appeared again.

The Princess Aya's father now resolved to get at the root of the matter, and for this purpose he bade Maki Hiogo dress in black and lie concealed in the peony bed on the following night.

When the next night came Maki Hiogo lay hidden among the peonies, while Yae and Yakumo made sweet music. Not long after the music had sounded the mysterious young *samurai* again appeared. Maki Hiogo rose from his hiding-place with his arms tightly bound round this strange visitor. A cloud seemed to emanate from his captive. It made him dizzy, and he fell to the ground still tightly holding the handsome *samurai*.

Just as a number of guards came hurrying to the spot Maki Hiogo regained consciousness. He looked down expecting to see his captive. But all that he held in his arms was a large peony!

By this time Princess Aya and her father joined the astonished group, and the Lord Naizen-no-jo at once grasped the situation. "I see now," said he, "that the spirit of the peony flower had a moment ago, and on former occasions, taken the form of a young and handsome *samurai*. My daughter, you must take this flower and treat it with all kindness."

The Princess Aya needed to be told no more. She returned to the house, placed the peony in a vase, and stood it by her bedside. Day by day she got better, while the flower flourished exceedingly.

When the Princess Aya was quite well the Lord of Ako arrived at the castle, bringing with him his second son, whom she was to marry. In due time the wedding took place, but at that hour the beautiful peony suddenly died.

THE MIRACULOUS CHESTNUT

The Princess Hinako-Nai-Shinno begged that chestnuts should be brought to her; but she took but one, bit it, and threw it away.

It took root, and upon all the chestnuts that it eventually bore there were the marks of the Princess's small teeth. In honouring her death the chestnut had expressed its devotion in this strange way.

THE SILENT PINE

The **Emperor Go-Toba**, who strongly objected to the croaking of frogs, was on one occasion disturbed by a wind-blown pine-tree.

When his Majesty loudly commanded it to be still, the pine-tree never for a moment moved again. So greatly impressed was this obedient tree that the fiercest wind failed to stir its branches, or even its myriad pine-needles.

WILLOW WIFE

In a certain **Japanese village** there grew a great willow-tree. For many generations the people loved it. In the summer it was a resting-place, a place where the villagers might meet after the work and heat of the day were over, and there talk till the moonlight streamed through the branches. In winter it was like a great half-opened umbrella covered with sparkling snow.

Heitaro, a young farmer, lived quite near this tree, and he, more than any of his companions, had entered into a deep communion with the imposing willow. It was almost the first object he saw upon waking, and upon his return from work in the fields he looked out eagerly for its familiar form. Sometimes he would burn a joss-stick beneath its branches and kneel down and pray.

One day an old man of the village came to Heitaro and explained to him that the villagers were anxious to build a bridge over the river, and that they particularly wanted the great willow-tree for timber.

"For timber?" said Heitaro, hiding his face in his hands. "My dear willow-tree for a bridge, one to bear the incessant patter of feet? Never, never, old man!"

When Heitaro had somewhat recovered himself, he offered to give the old man some of his own trees, if he and the villagers would accept them for timber and spare the ancient willow.

The old man readily accepted this offer, and the willow-tree continued to stand in the village as it had stood for so many years.

One night while Heitaro sat under the great willow he suddenly saw a beautiful woman standing close beside him, looking at him shyly, as if wanting to speak.

"Honourable lady," said he, "I will go home. I see you wait for someone. Heitaro is not without kindness towards those who love."

"He will not come now," said the woman, smiling.

"Can he have grown cold? Oh, how terrible when a mock love comes and leaves ashes and a grave behind!"

"He has not grown cold, dear lord."

"And yet he does not come! What strange mystery is this?"

"He has come! His heart has been always here, here under this willow-tree." And with a radiant smile the woman disappeared.

Night after night they met under the old willow-tree. The woman's shyness had entirely disappeared, and it seemed that she could not hear too much from Heitaro's lips in praise of the willow under which they sat.

One night he said to her: "Little one, will you be my wife – you who seem to come from the very tree itself?"

"Yes," said the woman. "Call me Higo ('Willow') and ask no questions, for love of me. I have no father or mother, and some day you will understand."

Heitaro and Higo were married, and in due time they were blessed with a child, whom they called Chiyodo. Simple was their dwelling, but those it contained were the happiest people in all Japan.

While this happy couple went about their respective duties great news came to the village. The villagers were full of it, and it was not long before it reached Heitaro's ears. The ex-Emperor Toba wished to build a temple to Kwannon in Kyoto, and those in authority sent far and wide for timber. The villagers said that they must contribute towards building the sacred edifice by presenting their great willow-tree. All Heitaro's argument and persuasion and promise of other trees were ineffectual, for neither he nor anyone else could give as large and handsome a tree as the great willow.

Heitaro went home and told his wife. "Oh, wife," said he, "they are about to cut down our dear willow-tree! Before I married you I could not have borne it. Having you, little one, perhaps I shall get over it some day."

That night Heitaro was aroused by hearing a piercing cry. "Heitaro," said his wife, "it grows dark! The room is full of whispers. Are you there, Heitaro? Hark! They are cutting down the willow-tree. Look how its shadow trembles in the moonlight. I am the soul of the willow-tree! The villagers are killing me. Oh, how they cut and tear me to pieces! Dear Heitaro, the pain, the pain! Put your hands here, and here. Surely the blows cannot fall now?"

"My Willow Wife! My Willow Wife!" sobbed Heitaro.

"Husband," said Higo, very faintly, pressing her wet, agonised face close to his, "I am going now. Such a love as ours cannot be cut down, however fierce the blows. I shall wait for you and Chiyodo – – My hair is falling through the sky! My body is breaking!"

There was a loud crash outside. The great willow-tree lay green and dishevelled upon the ground. Heitaro looked round for her he loved more than anything else in the world. Willow Wife had gone!

THE TREE OF THE ONE-EYED PRIEST

In ancient days there stood on the summit of Oki-yama a temple dedicated to Fudo, a god surrounded by fire, with sword in one hand and rope in the other. For twenty years Yenoki had performed his office, and one of his duties was to guard Fudo, who sat in a shrine, only accessible to the high-priest himself. During the whole of this period Yenoki had rendered faithful service and resisted the temptation to take a peep at this extremely ugly god. One morning, finding that the door of the shrine was not quite closed, his curiosity overcame him and he peeped within. No sooner had he done so than he became stone-blind in one eye and suffered the humiliation of being turned into a *tengu*.

He lived for a year after these deplorable happenings, and then died. His spirit passed into a great cryptomeria-tree standing on the east side of the mountain, and from that day Yenoki's spirit was invoked by sailors who were harassed by storms on the Chinese Sea. If a light blazed from the tree in answer to their prayers, it was a sure sign that the storm would abate.

At the foot of Oki-yama there was a village, where, sad to relate, the young people were very lax in their morals. During the Festival of the Dead they performed a dance known as the Bon Odori. These dances were very wild affairs indeed, and were accompanied by flirtations of a violent and wicked nature. The dances became more unrestrained as years went by, and the village got a bad name for immoral practices among the young people.

After a particularly wild celebration of the Bon a young maiden named Kimi set out to find her lover, Kurosuke. Instead of finding him she saw an extremely good-looking youth, who smiled upon her and continually beckoned. Kimi forgot all about Kurosuke; indeed, from that moment she hated him and eagerly followed the enticing youth. Nine fair but wicked maidens disappeared from the village in a similar way, and always it was the same youth who lured them astray in this mysterious manner.

The elders of the village consulted together, and came to the conclusion that the spirit of Yenoki was angry with the excesses connected with the Bon festival, and had assumed the form of a handsome youth for the purpose of administering severe admonition. The Lord of Kishiwada accordingly summoned Sonobe to his presence, and bade him journey to the great cryptomeria-tree on Oki-yama.

When Sonobe reached his destination he thus addressed the ancient tree: "Oh, home of Yenoki's spirit, I upbraid you for carrying away our daughters. If this continues I shall cut down the tree, so that you will be compelled to seek lodging elsewhere."

Sonobe had no sooner spoken than rain began to fall, and he heard the rumblings of a mighty earthquake. Then from out of the tree Yenoki's spirit suddenly appeared. He explained that many of the young people of Sonobe's village had offended against the Gods by their misconduct, and that he had, as conjectured, assumed the form of a handsome youth in order to take away the principal offenders. "You will find them," added the spirit of Yenoki, "bound to trees on the second summit of this mountain. Go, release them, and allow them to return to the village. They have not only repented of their follies, but will now persuade others to live nobler and purer lives." And with these words Yenoki disappeared into his tree.

Sonobe set off to the second summit and released the maidens. They returned to their homes, good and dutiful daughters, and from that day to this the Gods have been well satisfied with the general behaviour of the village that nestles at the foot of Oki-yama.

THE PINE-TREE LOVER

In ancient days there lived at Takasago a fisherman, his wife, and little daughter Matsue. There was nothing that Matsue loved to do more than to sit under the great pine-tree. She was particularly fond of the pine-needles that never seemed tired of falling to the ground. With these she fashioned a beautiful dress and sash, saying: "I will not wear these pine-clothes until my wedding-day."

One day, while Matsue was sitting under the pine-tree, she sang the following song:

> *"No man so callous but he heaves a sigh*
> *When o'er his head the withered cherry flowers*
> *Come fluttering down. Who knows?*
> *the Spring's soft showers*
> *May be but tears shed by the sorrowing sky."*

While she thus sang Teoyo stood on the steep shore of Sumiyoshi watching the flight of a heron. Up, up it went into the blue sky, and Teoyo saw it fly over the village where the fisherfolk and their daughter lived.

Now Teoyo was a youth who dearly loved adventure, and he thought it would be very delightful to swim across the sea and discover the land over which the heron had flown. So one morning he dived into the sea and swam so hard and so long that the poor fellow found the waves spinning and dancing, and saw the great sky bend down and try to touch him. Then he lay unconscious on the water; but the waves were kind to him after all, for they pressed him on and on till he was washed up at the very place where Matsue sat under the pine-tree.

Matsue carefully dragged Teoyo underneath the sheltering branches, and then set him down upon a couch of pine-needles, where he soon regained consciousness, and warmly thanked Matsue for her kindness.

Teoyo did not go back to his own country, for after a few happy months had gone by he married Matsue, and on her wedding morn she wore her dress and sash of pine-needles.

When Matsue's parents died her loss only seemed to make her love Teoyo the more. The older they grew the more they loved each other. Every night, when the moon shone, they went hand in hand to the pine-tree, and with their little rakes they made a couch for the morrow.

One night the great silver face of the moon peered through the branches of the pine-tree and looked in vain for the old lovers sitting together on a couch of pine-needles. Their little rakes lay side by side, and still the moon waited for the slow and stumbling steps of the Pine-Tree Lovers. But that night they did not come. They had gone home to an everlasting resting-place on the River of Souls. They had loved so well and so splendidly, in old age as well as in youth, that the Gods allowed their souls to come back again and wander round the pine-tree that had listened to their love for so many years. When the moon is full they whisper and laugh and sing and draw the pine-needles together, while the sea sings softly upon the shore.

BELLS, MIRRORS & TEA

The bell of Enkakuji, which features in the first short tales, is the largest bell in the city of Kamakura and is designated a National Treasure. When rung, a great note quivers forth, "deep as thunder, rich as the bass of a mighty organ." The sheer physical presence of these great bells affirms their *spiritual* heft.

The great legendary idea underlying Japanese mirrors is that the mirror, through constant reflection of its owner's face, draws to itself the very soul of its possessor. Long before the Japanese mirror was a familiar object in the house it had a very deep religious significance in connection with Shintoism. The Divine Mirror into which the Sun Goddess gazed is said to repose at Ise. Other mirrors are to be found in Shinto shrines. The mirror is said to "typify the human heart, which, when perfectly placid and clear, reflects the very image of the deity." In the *Kojiki* we are told that Izanagi presented his children with a polished silver disc, and bade them kneel before it every morning and evening and examine their reflections. He told them to think of heavenly things, to stifle passion and all evil thought, so that the disc should reveal a pure and lovely soul.

Tea-drinking in Japan has been influenced most particularly by the Zen sect of Buddhism. The priests of this order drank tea from a single bowl before the image of Bodhidharma (Daruma). This Zen observance, strictly of a religious nature, finally developed into the Japanese tea ceremony. And so it is unsurprising that there are tales concerning legendary tea masters and even the origin of the plant itself.

TALES OF THE BELL OF ENKAKUJI

The Return of Ono-no-Kimi

When **Ono-no-Kimi died** he went before the Judgment Seat of Emma-O, the Judge of Souls, and was told by that dread deity that he had quitted earthly life too soon, and that he must at once return.

Ono-no-Kimi pleaded that he could not retrace his steps, as he did not know the way. Then Emma-O said: "By listening to the bell of Enkakuji you will be able to find your way into the world again." And Ono-no-Kimi went forth from the Judgment Seat, and, with the sound of the bell for guidance, once more found himself in his old home.

The Giant Priest

On one occasion it is said that a priest of giant stature was seen in the country, and no one knew his name or whence he had come. With unceasing zest he travelled up and down the land, from village to village, from town to town, exhorting the people to pray before the bell of Enkakuji.

It was eventually discovered that this giant priest was none other than a personification of the holy bell itself. This extraordinary news had its effect, for numerous people now flocked to the bell of Enkakuji, prayed, and returned with many a wish fulfilled.

Faith Rewarded

On another occasion this sacred bell is said to have sounded a deep note of its own accord. Those who were incredulous and laughed at the miracle met with calamity, and those who believed in the miraculous power of the sacred bell were rewarded with much prosperity.

A WOMAN AND THE BELL OF MIIDERA

In the ancient monastery of Miidera there was a great bronze bell. It rang out every morning and evening, a clear, rich note, and its surface shone like sparkling dew. The priests would not allow any woman to strike it, because they thought that such an action would pollute and dull the metal, as well as bring calamity upon them.

When a certain pretty woman who lived in Kyoto heard this she grew extremely inquisitive, and at last, unable to restrain her curiosity, she said: "I will go and see this wonderful bell of Miidera. I will make it sound forth a soft note, and in its shining surface, bigger and brighter than a thousand mirrors, I will paint and powder, my face and dress my hair."

At length this vain and irreverent woman reached the belfry in which the great bell was suspended at a time when all were absorbed in their sacred duties. She looked into the gleaming bell and saw her pretty eyes, flushed cheeks, and laughing dimples. Presently she stretched forth her little fingers, lightly touched the shining metal, and prayed that she might have as great and splendid a mirror for her own. When the bell felt this woman's fingers, the bronze that she touched shrank, leaving a little hollow, and losing at the same time all its exquisite polish.

BENKEI AND THE BELL

When Benkei, the faithful retainer of Yoshitsune, was a monk he very much desired to steal the bell of Miidera, and bring it to his own monastery. He accordingly visited Miidera, and, at an opportune moment, unhooked the great bell. Benkei's first thought was to roll it down the hill, and thus save himself the trouble of carrying such a huge piece of metal; but, thinking that the monks would hear the noise, he was forced to set about carrying it down the steep incline. He accordingly pulled out the crossbeam from the belfry, suspended the bell at one end, and – humorous touch – his paper lantern at the other, and in this manner he carried his mighty burden for nearly seven miles.

When Benkei reached his temple he at once demanded food. He managed to get through a concoction which filled an iron soup-pot five feet in diameter, and when he had finished he gave permission for a few priests to strike the stolen bell of Miidera. The bell was struck, but in its dying murmur it seemed to cry: "I want to go back to Miidera! I want to go back to Miidera!"

When the priests heard this they were amazed. The abbot, however, thought that if the bell were sprinkled with holy water it would become reconciled to its new abode; but in spite of holy water the bell still sobbed forth its plaintive and provoking cry. No one was more displeased by the sound than Benkei himself. It seemed that the bell mocked him and that arduous journey of his.

At last, exasperated beyond endurance, he rushed to the rope, strained it till the beam was far from the great piece of metal, then let it go, hoping that the force of the swift-rushing beam would crack such a peevish and ill-bred bell. The whirling wood reached the bell with a terrific crash; but it did not break. Through the air rang again: "I want to go back to Miidera!" and whether the bell was struck harshly or softly it always spoke the same words.

At last Benkei, now in a towering rage, shouldered the bell and beam, and, coming to the top of a mountain, he set down his burden, and, with a mighty kick, sent it rolling into the valley beneath. Some time later the Miidera priests found their precious bell, and joyfully hung it in its accustomed place, and from that time it failed to speak, and only rang like other temple bells.

A BELL AND THE POWER OF KARMA

Near the banks of the Hidaka there once stood a far-famed tea-house nestling amid lovely scenery beside a hill called the Dragon's Claw. The fairest girl in this tea-house was Kiyo, for she was like "the fragrance of white lilies, when the wind, sweeping down the mountain heights, comes perfume-laden to the traveller."

Across the river stood a Buddhist temple where the abbot and a number of priests lived a simple and devout life. In the belfry of this temple reposed a great bell, six inches thick and weighing several tons. It was one of the monastery rules that none of the priests should eat fish or meat or drink *sake*, and they were especially forbidden to stop at tea-houses, lest they should lose their spirituality and fall into the sinful ways of the flesh.

One of the priests, however, on returning from a certain shrine, happened to see the pretty Kiyo, flitting hither and thither in the tea-garden, like a large, bright-winged butterfly. He stood and watched her for a moment, sorely tempted to enter the garden and speak to this beautiful creature, but, remembering his priestly calling, he crossed the river and entered his temple.

That night, however, he could not sleep. The fever of a violent love had come upon him. He fingered his rosary and repeated passages from the Buddhist Scriptures, but these things brought him no peace of mind. Through all his pious thoughts there ever shone the winsome face of Kiyo, and it seemed to him that she was calling from that fair garden across the river.

His burning love grew so intense that it was not long before he stifled his religious feelings, broke one of the temple rules, and entered the forbidden tea-house. Here he entirely forgot his religion, or found a new one in contemplating the beautiful Kiyo, who brought him refreshment. Night after night he crept across the river and fell under the spell of this woman. She returned his love with equal passion, so that for the moment it appeared to this erring priest that he had found in a woman's charms something far sweeter than the possibility of attaining Nirvana.

After the priest had seen Kiyo on many nights conscience began to stir within him and to do battle with his unholy love. The power of Karma and the teaching of the Lord Buddha struggled within his breast. It was a fierce conflict, but in the end passion was vanquished, though, as we shall learn, not its awful consequences. The priest, having stamped out his carnal love, deemed it wise to deal with Kiyo as circumspectly as possible, lest his sudden change should make her angry.

When Kiyo saw the priest after his victory over the flesh she observed the far-away look in his eyes and the ascetic calm that now rested upon his face. She redoubled her feminine wiles, determined either to make the priest love her again, or, failing that, to put him to a cruel death by sorcery.

All Kiyo's blandishments failed to awaken love within the priest's heart, and, thinking only of vengeance, she set out, arrayed in a white robe, and went to a certain mountain where there was a Fudo shrine. Fudo sat, surrounded by fire, a sword in one hand and a small coil of rope in the other. Here Kiyo prayed with fearful vehemence that this hideous-looking God would show her how to kill the priest who had once loved her.

From Fudo she went to the shrine of Kompira, who has the knowledge of magic and is able to teach sorcery. Here she begged that she might have the power to turn herself at will into a dragon-serpent. After many visits a long-nosed sprite (probably a *tengu*), who waited upon Kompira, taught Kiyo all the mysteries of magic and sorcery. He taught this once sweet girl how to change herself into the awful creature she desired to be for the purpose of a cruel vengeance.

Still the priest visited Kiyo; but no longer was he the lover. By many exhortations he tried to stay the passion of this maiden he once loved; but these priestly discourses only made Kiyo more determined to win the victory in the end. She wept, she pleaded, she wound her fair arms about him; but none of her allurements had the slightest effect, except to drive away the priest for the last time.

Just as the priest was about to take his departure he was horrified to see Kiyo's eyes suddenly turn into those of a serpent. With a shriek of fear he ran out of the tea-garden, swam across the river, and hid himself inside the great temple bell.

Kiyo raised her magic wand, murmured a certain incantation, and in a moment the sweet face and form of this lovely maiden became transformed into that of a dragon-serpent, hissing and spirting fire. With eyes as large and luminous as moons she crawled over the garden, swam across the river, and entered the belfry. Her weight broke down the supporting columns, and the bell, with the priest inside, fell with a deafening crash to the ground.

Kiyo embraced the bell with a terrible lust for vengeance. Her coils held the metal as in a vice; tighter and tighter she hugged the bell, till the metal became red-hot. All in vain was the prayer of the captive priest; all in vain, too, were the earnest entreaties of his fellow brethren, who implored that

Buddha would destroy the demon. Hotter and hotter grew the bell, and it rang with the piteous shrieks of the priest within. Presently his voice was stilled, and the bell melted and ran down into a pool of molten metal. The great power of Karma had destroyed it, and with it the priest and the dragon-serpent that was once the beautiful Kiyo.

HIDARI JINGORO THE SCULPTOR

The famous sculptor **Hidari Jingoro** on one occasion happened to fall in love with a very attractive woman whom he met in the street on his return to his studio. He was so fascinated by her rare beauty that as soon as he had reached his destination he commenced to carve a statue of her.

Between the chiselled robes he placed a mirror, the mirror which the lovely woman had dropped, and which her eager lover had at once picked up. Because this mirror had reflected a thousand thousand times that fair face, it had taken to its shining surface the very body and soul of its owner, and because of these strange things the statue came to life, to the extreme happiness of sculptor and maid.

THE SOUL OF A MIRROR

The shrine of **Ogawachi-Myojin** fell into decay, and the Shinto priest in charge, Matsumura, journeyed to Kyoto in the hope of successfully appealing to the Shogun for a grant for the restoration of the temple.

Matsumura and his family resided in a house in Kyoto, said to be extremely unlucky, and many tenants had thrown themselves into the well on the north-east side of the dwelling. But Matsumura took no notice of these tales, and was not the least afraid of evil spirits.

During the summer of that year there was a great drought in Kyoto. Though the river-beds dried up and many wells failed for want of rain, the well in Matsumura's garden was full to overflowing. The distress elsewhere, owing to want of water, forced many poor people to beg for it, and for all their drawing the water in this particular well did not diminish.

One day, however, a dead body was found lying in the well, that of a servant who had come to fetch water. In his case suicide was out of the question, and it seemed impossible that he should have accidentally fallen in. When Matsumura heard of the fatality he went to inspect the well. To his surprise the water stirred with a strange rocking movement. When the motion lessened he saw reflected in the clear water the form of a fair young woman. She was touching her lips with *beni*. At length she smiled upon him. It was a strange smile that made Matsumura feel dizzy, a smile that blotted out everything else save the beautiful woman's face. He felt an almost irresistible desire to fling himself into the water in order that he might reach and hold this enchanting woman. He struggled against this strange feeling, however, and was able after a while to enter the house, where he gave orders that a fence should be built round the well, and that from thenceforth no one, on any pretext whatever, should draw water there.

Shortly afterwards the drought came to an end. For three days and nights there was a continuous downpour of rain, and the city shook with an earthquake. On the third night of the storm there was a loud knocking at Matsumura's door. The priest himself inquired who his visitor might be. He half opened the door, and saw once more the woman he had seen in the well. He refused her admission, and asked why she had been guilty of taking the lives of so many harmless and innocent people.

Thus the woman made answer: "Alas! good priest, I have never desired to lure human beings to their death. It is the Poison Dragon, who lived in that well, who forced me against my will to entice people to death. But now the Gods have compelled the Poison Dragon to live elsewhere, so that tonight I was able to leave my place of captivity. Now there is but little water in the well, and if you will search there you will find my body. Take care of it for me, and I shall not fail to reward your goodness." With these words she vanished as suddenly as she had appeared.

Next day well-cleaners searched the well, and discovered some ancient hair ornaments and an old metal mirror.

Matsumura, being a wise man, took the mirror and cleaned it, believing that it might reveal a solution to the mystery.

Upon the back of the mirror he discovered several characters. Many of the ideographs were too blurred to be legible, but he managed to make out "third month, the third day." In ancient time the third month used to be called *Yayoi*, or Month of Increase, and remembering that the woman had called herself Yayoi, Matsumura realised that he had probably received a visit from the Soul of the Mirror.

Matsumura took every care of the mirror. He ordered it to be resilvered and polished, and when this had been done he laid it in a box specially made for it, and mirror and box were placed in a particular room in the house.

One day, when Matsumura was sitting in the apartment where the mirror reposed, he once more saw Yayoi standing before him, looking more beautiful than ever, and the refulgence of her beauty was like summer moonlight. After she had saluted Matsumura she explained that she was indeed the Soul of the Mirror, and narrated how she had fallen into the possession of Lady Kamo, of the Imperial Court, and how she had become an heirloom of the Fujiwara House, until during the period of Hogen, when the Taira and Minamoto clans were engaged in conflict, she was thrown into a well, and there forgotten. Having narrated these things, and all the horrors she had gone through under the tyranny of the Poison Dragon, Yayoi begged that Matsumura would present the mirror to the Shogun, the Lord Yoshimasa, who was a descendant of her former possessors, promising the priest considerable good fortune if he did so. Before Yayoi departed she advised Matsumura to leave his home immediately, as it was about to be washed away by a great storm.

On the following day Matsumura left the house, and, as Yayoi had prophesied, almost immediately afterwards his late dwelling was swept away.

At length Matsumura was able to present, the mirror to the Shogun Yoshimasa, together with a written account of its strange history. The Shogun was so pleased with the gift that he not only gave Matsumura many personal presents, but he also presented the priest with a considerable sum of money for the rebuilding of his temple.

A MIRROR AND A BELL

When the priests of Mugenyama required a large bell for their temple they asked the women in the vicinity to contribute their old bronze mirrors for the purpose of providing the necessary metal.

Hundreds of mirrors were given for this purpose, and all were offered gladly, except the mirror presented by a certain farmer's wife. As soon as she had given her mirror to the priests she began to regret having parted with it. She remembered how old it was, how it had reflected her mother's laughter and tears, and even her great-grandmother's. Whenever this farmer's wife went to the temple she saw her coveted mirror lying in a great heap behind a railing. She recognised it by the design on the back known as the *Shō-Chiku-Bai*, or the three emblems of the Pine, Bamboo, and Plum-flower. She yearned to stretch forth her arm between the railings and to snatch back her beloved mirror. Her soul was in the shining surface, and it mingled with the souls of those who had gazed into it before she was born.

When the Mugenyama bell was in course of construction the bell-founders discovered that one mirror would not melt. The workers said that it refused to melt because the owner had afterwards regretted the gift, which had made the metal hard, as hard as the woman's selfish heart.

Soon everyone knew the identity of the giver of the mirror that would not melt, and, angry and ashamed, the farmer's wife drowned herself, first having written the following: "When I am dead you will be able to melt my mirror, and so cast the bell. My soul will come to him who breaks that bell by ringing it, and I will give him great wealth."

When the woman died her old mirror melted immediately, and the bell was cast and was suspended in its customary place. Many people having heard of the message written by the deceased farmer's wife, a great multitude came to the temple, and one by one rang the bell with the utmost violence in the hope of breaking it and winning great wealth. Day after day the ringing continued, till at last the noise became so unbearable that the priests rolled the bell into a swamp, where it lay hidden from sight.

THE PASSING OF RIKIU

Rikiu was one of the greatest of tea-masters, and for long he remained the friend of Taiko-Hideyoshi; but the age in which he lived was full of treachery. There were many who were jealous of Rikiu, many who sought his death. When a coldness sprang up between Hideyoshi and Rikiu, the enemies of the great tea-master made use of this breach of friendship by spreading the report that Rikiu intended to add poison to a cup of tea and present it to his distinguished patron. Hideyoshi soon heard of the rumour, and without troubling to examine the matter he condemned Rikiu to die by his own hand.

On the last day of the famous tea-master's life he invited many of his disciples to join with him in his final tea ceremony. As they walked up the garden path it seemed that ghosts whispered in the rustling leaves. When the disciples entered the tea-room they saw a *kakemono* hanging in the *tokonoma*, and when they raised their sorrowful eyes they saw that the writing described the passing of all earthly things. There was poetry in the singing of the tea-kettle, but it was a sad song like the plaintive cry of an insect. Rikiu came into the tea-room calm and dignified, and, according to custom, he allowed the chief guest to admire the various articles associated with the tea ceremony. When all the guests had gazed upon them, noting their beauty with a heavy heart, Rikiu presented each disciple with a souvenir. He took his own cup in his hand, and said: "Never again shall this cup, polluted by the lips of misfortune, be used by man." Having spoken these words, he broke the cup as a sign that the tea ceremony was over, and the guests bade a sad farewell and departed. Only one remained to witness, not the drinking of another cup of tea, but the passing of Rikiu. The great master took off his outer garment, and revealed the pure white robe of Death. Still calm and dignified, he looked upon his dagger, and then recited the following verse with unfaltering voice:

"Welcome to thee,
O sword of eternity!
Through Buddha
And through Daruma alike
Thou hast cleft thy way."

He who loved to quote the old poem, "To those who long only for flowers fain would I show the full-blown spring which abides in the toiling buds of snow-covered hills," has crowned the Japanese tea ceremony with an immortal flower.

THE LEGEND OF THE TEA-PLANT

Daruma was an Indian sage, whose image, as we have already seen, was associated with the ritualistic drinking of tea by the Zen sect in Japan. He is said to have been the son of a Hindu king, and received instruction from Panyatara. When he had completed his studies he retired to Lo Yang, where he remained seated in meditation for nine years.

During this period the sage was tempted after the manner of St. Anthony. He wrestled with these temptations by continually reciting sacred scriptures; but the frequent repetition of the word 'jewel' lost its spiritual significance, and became associated with the precious stone worn in the ear of a certain lovely woman. Even the word 'lotus', so sacred to all true Buddhists, ceased to be the symbol of the Lord Buddha and suggested to Daruma the opening of a girl's fair mouth. His temptations increased, and he was transported to an Indian city, where he found himself among a vast crowd of worshippers. He saw strange deities with horrible symbols upon their foreheads, and Rajahs and Princes riding upon elephants, surrounded by a great company of dancing-girls. The great crowd of people surged forward, and Daruma with them, till they came to a temple with innumerable pinnacles, a temple covered with a multitude of foul forms, and it seemed to Daruma that he met and kissed the woman who had changed the meaning of jewel and lotus. Then suddenly the vision departed, and Daruma awoke to find himself sitting under the Chinese sky.

The sage, who had fallen asleep during his meditation, was truly penitent for the neglect of his devotions, and, taking a knife from his girdle, he cut off his eyelids and cast them upon the ground, saying: "O Thou Perfectly Awakened!" The eyelids were transformed into the tea-plant, from which was made a beverage that would repel slumber and allow good Buddhist priests to their vigils.

A GENERAL
GLOSSARY OF
MYTHOLOGICAL TERMS

Aaru Heavenly paradise where the blessed went after death.

Ab Heart or mind.

Absál Nurse to Saláman, who died after their brief love affair.

Achilles The son of Peleus and the sea-nymph Thetis, who distinguished himself in the Trojan War. He was made almost immortal by his mother, who dipped him in the River Styx, and he was invincible except for a portion of his heel which remained out of the water.

Acropolis Citadel in a Greek city.

Adad-Ea Ferryman to Ut-Napishtim, who carried Gilgamesh to visit his ancestor.

Adapa Son of Ea and a wise sage.

Adar God of the sun, who is worshipped primarily in Nippur.

Aditi Sky goddess and mother of the gods.

Adityas Vishnu, children of Aditi, including Indra, Mitra, Rudra, Tvashtar, Varuna and Vishnu.

Aeneas The son of Anchises and the goddess Aphrodite, reared by a nymph. He led the Dardanian troops in the Trojan War According to legend, he became the founder of Rome.

Aengus Óg Son of Dagda and Boann (a woman said to have given the Boyne river its name), Aengus is the Irish god of love whose stronghold is reputed to have been at New Grange. The famous tale Dream of Aengus tells of how he fell in love with a maiden he had dreamt of. He eventually discovered that she was to be found at the Lake of the Dragon's Mouth in Co. Tipperary, but that she lived every alternate year in the form of a swan. Aengus pursues the woman of his dreams and plunges into the lake transforming himself also into the shape of a swan. Then the two fly back together to his palace on the Boyne where they live out their days as guardians of would-be lovers.

Aesir Northern gods who made their home in Asgard; there are twelve in number.

Afrásiyáb Son of Poshang, king of Túrán, who led an army against Nauder. Afrásiyáb became ruler of Persia on defeating Nauder.

Afterlife Life after death or paradise, reached only by the process of preserving the body from decay through embalming and preparing it for reincarnation.

Agamemnon A famous King of Mycenae. He married Helen of Sparta's sister Clytemnestra. When Paris abducted Helen, beginning the Trojan War, Menelaus called on Agamemnon to raise the Greek troops. He had to sacrifice his daughter Iphigenia in order to get a fair wind to travel to Troy.

Agastya A rishi (sage). Leads hermits to Rama.

Agemo (Yoruba) A chameleon who aided Olorun in outwitting Olokun, who was angry at him for letting Obatala create life on her lands without her permission. Agemo outwitted Olokun by changing colour, letting her think that he and Olorun were better cloth dyers than she was. She admitted defeat and there was peace between the gods once again.

Aghasur A dragon sent by Kans to destroy Krishna.

Aghríras Son of Poshang and brother of Afrásiyáb, who was killed by his brother.

Agni The god of fire.

Agora Greek marketplace.

Ahura-Mazda Supreme god of the Persians, god of the sky. Similar to the Hindu god Varuna.

Ajax Ajax of Locris was another warrior at Troy. When Troy was captured, he committed the ultimate sacrilege by seizing Cassandra from her sanctuary with the Palladium.

Ajax Ajax the Greater was the bravest, after Achilles, of all warriors at Troy, fighting Hector in single combat and distinguishing himself in the Battle of the Ships. He was not chosen as the bravest warrior and eventually went mad.

Aje (Igbo) Goddess of the earth and the underworld.

Aje (Yoruba) Goddess of the River Niger, daughter of Yemoja.

Akhet Season of the year when the River Nile traditionally flooded.

Akkadian Person of the first Mesopotamian empire, centred in Akkad.

Akwán Diw An evil spirit who appeared as a wild ass in the court of Kai-khosráu. Rustem fought and defeated the demon, presenting its head to Kai-khosráu.

Alberich King of the dwarfs.

Alcinous King of the Phaeacians.

Alf-heim Home of the elves, ruled by Frey.

All Hallowmass All Saints' Day.

Allfather Another name for Odin; Yggdrasill was created by Allfather.

Alsvider Steed of the moon (Mani) chariot.

Alsvin Steed of the sun (Sol) chariot.

Amado Outer panelling of a dwelling, usually made of wood.

Ama-no-uzume Goddess of the dawn, meditation and the arts, who showed courage when faced with a giant who scared the other deities, including Ninigi. Also known as Uzume.

Amaterasu Goddess of the sun and daughter of Izanagi after Izanami's death; she became ruler of the High Plains of Heaven on her father's withdrawal from the world. Sister of Tsuki-yomi and Susanoo.

Ambalika Daughter of the king of Benares.

Ambika Daughter of the king of Benares.

Ambrosia Food of the gods.

Amemet Eater of the dead, monster who devoured the souls of the unworthy.

Amen Original creator deity.

Amen-Ra A being created from the fusion of Ra and Osiris. He champions the poor and those in trouble. Similar to the Greek god Zeus.

Ananda Disciple of Buddha.

Anansi One of the most popular African animal myths, Anansi the spider is a clever and shrewd character who outwits his fellow animals to get his own way. He is an entertaining but morally dubious character. Many African countries tell Anansi stories.

Ananta Thousand-headed snake that sprang from Balarama's mouth, Vishnu's attendant, serpent of infinite time.

Andhrímnir Cook at Valhalla.

Andvaranaut Ring of Andvari, the King of the dwarfs.

Angada Son of Vali, one of the monkey host.

Anger-Chamber Room designated for an angry queen.

Angurboda Loki's first wife, and the mother of Hel, Fenris and Jormungander.

Aniruddha Son of Pradyumna.

Anjana Mother of Hanuman.

Anunnaki Great spirits or gods of Earth.

Ansar God of the sky and father of Ea and Anu. Brother-husband to Kishar. Also known as Anshar or Asshur.

Anshumat A mighty chariot fighter.

Anu God of the sky and lord of heaven, son of Ansar and Kishar.

Anubis Guider of souls and ruler of the underworld before Osiris.; he was one of the divinities who brought Osiris back to life. He is portrayed as a canid, African wolf or jackal.

Apep Serpent and emblem of chaos.

Apollo One of the twelve Olympian gods, son of Zeus and Leto. He is attributed with being the god of plague, music, song and prophecy.

Apsu Primeval domain of fresh water, originally part of Tiawath with whom he mated to have Mummu. The term is also used for the abyss from which creation came.

Aquila The divine eagle.

Arachne A Lydian woman with great skill in weaving. She was challenged in a competition by the jealous Athene who destroyed her work and when she killed herself, turned her into a spider destined to weave until eternity.

Aralu Goddess of the underworld, also known as Eres-ki-Gal. Married to Nergal.

Ares God of War, 'gold-changer of corpses', and the son of Zeus and Hera.

Argonauts Heroes who sailed with Jason on the ship Argo to fetch the golden fleece from Colchis.

Ariki A high chief, a leader, a master, a lord.

Arjuna The third of the Pandavas.

Aroha Affection, love.

Artemis The virgin goddess of the chase, attributed with being the moon goddess and the primitive mother-goddess. She was daughter of Zeus and Leto.

Arundhati The Northern Crown.

Asamanja Son of Sagara.

Asclepius God of healing who often took the form of a snake. He is the son of Apollo by Coronis.

Asgard Home of the gods, at one root of Yggdrasill.

Ashvatthaman Son of Drona.

Ashvins Twin horsemen, sons of the sun, benevolent gods and related to the divine.

Ashwapati Uncle of Bharata and Satrughna.

Asipû Wizard.

Asopus The god of the River Asopus.

Apsaras Dancing girls of Indra's court and heavenly nymphs.

Astrolabe Instrument for making astronomical measurements.

Asuras Titans, demons, and enemies of the gods possessing magical powers.

Atef crown White crown made up of the Hedjet, the white crown of Upper Egypt, and red feathers.

Atem The first creator-deity, he is also thought to be the finisher of the world. Also known as Tem.

Athene Virgin warrior-goddess, born from the forehead of Zeus when he swallowed his wife Metis. Plays a key role in the travels of Odysseus, and Perseus.

Atlatl Spear-thrower.

Atua A supernatural being, a god.

Atua-toko A small carved stick, the symbol of the god whom it represents. It was stuck in the ground whilst holding incantations to its presiding god.

Augeas King of Elis, one of the Argonauts.

Augsburg Tyr's city.

Avalon Legendary island where Excalibur was created and where Arthur went to recover from his wounds. It is said he will return from Avalon one day to reclaim his kingdom.

Ba Dead person or soul. Also known as ka.

Bairn Little child, also called bairnie.

Balarama Brother of Krishna.

Balder Son of Frigga; his murder causes Ragnarok.

Bali Brother of Sugriva and one of the five great monkeys in the Ramayana.

Balor The evil, one-eyed King of the Fomorians and also grandfather of Lugh of the Long Arm. It was prophesied that Balor would one day be slain by his own grandson so he locked his daughter away on a remote island where he intended that she would never fall pregnant. But Cian, father of Lugh, managed to reach the island disguised as a woman, and Balor's daughter eventually bore him a child. During the second battle of Mag Tured (or Moytura), Balor was killed by Lugh who slung a stone into his giant eye.

Ban King of Benwick, father of Lancelot and brother of King Bors.

Bannock Oat or barley cake.

Barû Seer.

Basswood Any of several North American linden trees with a soft light-coloured wood.

Bastet Goddess of love, fertility and sex and a solar deity. She is often portrayed with the head of a cat.

Bateta (Yoruba) The first human, created alongside Hanna by the Toad and reshaped into human form by the Moon.

Bau Goddess of humankind and the sick, and known as the 'divine physician'. Daughter of Anu.

Beaver Largest rodent in the United States of America, held in high esteem by the native American people. Although a land mammal, it spends a great deal of time in water and has a dense waterproof fur coat to protect it from harsh weather conditions.

Behula Daughter of Saha.

Bel Name for the god En-lil, the word Is also used as a title meaning 'lord'.

Belus Deity who helped form the heavens and earth and created animals and celestial beings. Similar to Zeus in Greek mythology.

Benten Goddess of the sea and one of the Seven Divinities of Luck. Also referred to as the goddess of love, beauty and eloquence and as being the personification of wisdom.

Bere Barley.

Berossus Priest of Bel who wrote a history of Babylon.

Bestla Giant mother of Aesir's mortal element.

Bhadra A mighty elephant.

Bhagavati Shiva's wife, also known as Parvati.

Bhagiratha Son of Dilipa.

Bharadhwaja Father of Drona and a hermit.

Bharata One of Dasharatha's four sons.

Bhaumasur A demon, slain by Krishna.

Bhima The second of the Pandavas.

Bhimasha King of Rajagriha and disciple of Buddha.

Bier Frame on which a coffin or dead body is placed before being carried to the grave.

Bifrost Rainbow bridge presided over by Heimdall.

Big-Belly One of Ravana's monsters.

Bilskirnir Thor's palace.

Bodach The term means 'old man'. The Highlanders believed that the Bodach crept down chimneys in order to steal naughty children. In other territories, he was a spirit who warned of death.

Boer Person of Dutch origin who settled in southern Africa in the late seventeenth century. The term means 'farmer'. Boer people are often called Afrikaners.

Book of the Dead Book for the dead, thought to be written by Thoth, texts from which were written on papyrus and buried with the dead, or carved on the walls of tombs, pyramids or sarcophagi.

Bors King of Gaul and brother of King Ban.

Brahma Creator of the world, mythical origin of colour (caste).

Brahmadatta King of Benares.

Brahman Member of the highest Hindu caste, traditionally a priest.

Bran In Scottish legend, Bran is the great hunting hound of Fionn Mac Chumail. In Irish mythology, he is a great hero.

Branstock Giant oak tree in the Volsung's hall; Odin placed a sword in it and challenged the guests of a wedding to withdraw it.

Brave Young warrior of native American descent, sometimes also referred to as a 'buck'.

Breidablik Balder's palace.

Brigit Scottish saint or spirit associated with the coming of spring.

Brisingamen Freyia's necklace.

Britomartis A Cretan goddess, also known as Dictynna.

Brocéliande Legendary enchanted forest and the supposed burial place of Merlin.

Brokki Dwarf who makes a deal with Loki, and who makes Miolnir, Draupnir and Gulinbursti.

Brollachan A shapeless spirit of unknown origin. One of the most frightening in Scottish mythology, it spoke only two words, 'Myself' and 'Thyself', taking the shape of whatever it sat upon.

Brownie A household spirit or creature which took the form of a small man (usually hideously ugly) who undertakes household chores, and mill or farm work, in exchange for a bowl of milk.

Brunhilde A Valkyrie found by Sigurd.

Buddha Founder of buddhism, Gautama, avatar of Vishnu in Hinduism.

Buddhism Buddhism arrived in China in the first century BC via the silk trading route from India and Central Asia. Its founder was

Guatama Siddhartha (the Buddha), a religious teacher in northern India. Buddhist doctrine declared that by destroying the causes of all suffering, mankind could attain perfect enlightenment. The religion encouraged a new respect for all living things and brought with it the idea of reincarnation; i.e. that the soul returns to the earth after death in another form, dictated by the individual's behaviour in his previous life. By the fourth century, Buddhism was the dominant religion in China, retaining its powerful influence over the nation until the mid-ninth century.

Buffalo A type of wild ox, once widely scattered over the Great Plains of North America. Also known as a 'bison', the buffalo was an important food source for the Indian tribes and its hide was also used in the construction of tepees and to make clothing. The buffalo was also sometimes revered as a totem animal, i.e. venerated as a direct ancestor of the tribesmen, and its skull used in ceremonial fashion.

Bull of Apis Sacred bull, thought to be the son of Hathor.

Bulu Sacrificial rite.

Bundles, sacred These bundles contained various venerated objects of the tribe, believed to have supernatural powers. Custody or ownership of the bundle was never lightly entered upon, but involved the learning of endless songs and ritual dances.

Bushel Unit of measurement, usually used for agricultural products or food.

Bushi Warrior.

Byrny Coat of mail.

Cacique King or prince.

Cailleach Bheur A witch with a blue face who represents winter. When she is reborn each autumn, snow falls. She is mother of the god of youth (Angus mac Og).

Calchas The seer of Mycenae who accompanied the Greek fleet to Troy. It was his prophecy which stated that Troy would never be taken without the aid of Achilles.

Calpulli Village house, or group or clan of families.

Calumet Ceremonial pipe used by the north American Indians.

Calypso A nymph who lived on the island of Ogygia.

Camaxtli Tlascalan god of war and the chase, similar to Huitzilopochtli.

Camelot King Arthur's castle and centre of his realm.

Caoineag A banshee.

Caravanserai Traveller's inn, traditionally found in Asia or North Africa.

Cat A black cat has great mythological significance, is often the bearer of bad luck, a symbol of black magic, and the familiar of a witch. Cats were also the totem for many tribes.

Cath Sith A fairy cat who was believed to be a witch transformed.

Cazi Magical person or influence.

Ceasg A Scottish mermaid with the body of a maiden and the tail of a salmon.

Ceilidh Party.

Cerberus The three-headed dog who guarded the entrance to the Underworld.

Chalchiuhtlicue Goddess of water and the sick or newborn, and wife of Tlaloc. She is often symbolized as a small frog.

Channa Guatama's charioteer.

Chaos A state from which the universe was created – caused by fire and ice meeting.

Charon The ferryman of the dead who carries souls across the River Styx to Hades.

Charybdis *See* Scylla and Charybdis.

Chicomecohuatl Chief goddess of maize and one of a group of deities called Centeotl, who care for all aspects of agriculture.

Chicomoztoc Legendary mountain and place of origin of the Aztecs. The name means 'seven caves'.

Chinawezi Primordial serpent.

Chinvat Bridge Bridge of the Gatherer, which the souls of the righteous cross to reach Mount Alborz or the world of the dead. Unworthy beings who try to cross Chinvat Bridge fall or are dragged into a place of eternal punishment.

Chitambaram Sacred city of Shiva's dance.

Chrysaor Son of Poseidon and Medusa, born from the severed neck of Medusa when Perseus beheaded her.

Chryseis Daughter of Chryses who was taken by Agamemnon in the battle of Troy.

Chullasubhadda Wife of Buddha-elect (Sumedha).

Chunda A good smith who entertains Buddha.

Churl Mean or unkind person.

Circe An enchantress and the daughter of Helius. She lived on the island of Aeaea with the power to change men to beasts.

Citlalpol The Mexican name for Venus, or the Great Star, and one of the only stars they worshipped. Also known as Tlauizcalpantecutli, or Lord of the Dawn.

Cleobis and Biton Two men of Argos who dragged the wagon carrying their mother, priestess of Hera, from Argos to the sanctuary.

Clio Muse of history and prophecy.

Clytemnestra Daughter of Tyndareus, sister of Helen, who married Agamemnon but deserted him when he sacrificed Iphigenia, their daughter, at the beginning of the Trojan War.

Coatepetl Mythical mountain, known as the 'serpent mountain'.

Coatl Serpent.

Coatlicue Earth mother and celestial goddess, she gave birth to Huitzilopochtli and his sister, Coyolxauhqui, and the moon and stars.

Codex Ancient book, often a list with pages folded into a zigzag pattern.

Confucius (Kong Fuzi) Regarded as China's greatest sage and ethical teacher, Confucius (551–479 BC) was not especially revered during his lifetime and had a small following of some three thousand people. After the Burning of the Books in 213 BC, interest in his philosophies became widespread. Confucius believed that mankind was essentially good, but argued for a highly structured society, presided over by a strong central government which would set the highest moral standards. The individual's sense of duty and obligation, he argued, would play a vital role in maintaining a well-run state.

Coyolxauhqui Goddess of the moon and sister to Huitzilopochtli, she was decapitated by her brother after trying to kill their mother.

Crodhmara Fairy cattle.

Crow Usually associated with battle and death, but many mythological figures take this form.

Cu Sith A great fairy dog, usually green and oversized.

Cutty Girl.

Cyclopes One-eyed giants who were imprisoned in Tartarus by Uranus and Cronus, but released by Zeus, for whom they made thunderbolts. Also a tribe of pastoralists who live without laws, and on, whenever possible, human flesh.

Daedalus Descendant of the Athenian King Erechtheus and son of Eupalamus. He killed his nephew and apprentice. Famed for constructing the labyrinth to house the Minotaur, in which he was later imprisoned. He constructed wings for himself and his son to make their escape.

Dagda One of the principal gods of the Tuatha De Danann, the father and chief, the Celtic equivalent of Zeus. He was the god reputed to have led the People of Dana in their successful conquest of the Fir Bolg.

Dagon God of fish and fertility; he is sometimes described as a sea-monster or chthonic god.

Daikoku God of wealth and one of the gods of luck.

Daimyō Powerful lord or magnate.

Daksha The chief Prajapati.

Dana Also known as Danu, a goddess worshipped from antiquity by the Celts and considered to be the ancestor of the Tuatha De Danann.

Danae Daughter of Acrisius, King of Argos. Acrisius trapped her in a cave when he was warned that his grandson would be the cause of his ultimate death. Zeus came to her and Perseus was born.

Danaids The fifty daughters of Danaus of Argos, by ten mothers.

Daoine Sidhe The people of the Hollow Hills, or Otherworld.

Dardanus Son of Zeus and Electra, daughter of Atlas.

Dasharatha A Manu amongst men, King of Koshala, father of Santa.

Deianeira Daughter of Oeneus, who married Heracles after he won her in a battle with the River Achelous.

Demeter Goddess of agriculture and nutrition, whose name means earth mother. She is the mother of Persephone.

Demophoon Son of King Celeus of Eleusis, who was nursed by Demeter and then dropped in the fire when she tried to make him immortal.

Dervish Member of a religious order, often Sufi, known for their wild dancing and whirling.

Desire The god of love.

Deva A god other than the supreme God.

Devadatta Buddha's cousin, plots evil against Buddha.

Dhrishtadyumna Twin brother of Draupadi, slays Drona.

Dibarra God of plague. Also a demonic character or evil spirit.

Dik-dik Dwarf antelope native to eastern and southern Africa.

Dilipa Son of Anshumat, father of Bhagiratha.

Dionysus The god of wine, vegetation and the life force, and of ecstasy. He was considered to be outside the Greek pantheon, and generally thought to have begun life as a mortal.

Dioscuri Castor and Polydeuces, the twin sons of Zeus and Leda, who are important deities.

Divan Privy council.

Divots Turfs.

Dog The dog is a symbol of humanity, and usually has a role helping the hero of the myth or legend. Fionn's Bran and Grey Dog are two examples of wild beasts transformed to become invaluable servants.

Dōshin Government official.

Dossal Ornamental altar cloth.

Doughty Persistent and brave person.

Dragon Important animal in Japanese culture, symbolizing power, wealth, luck and success.

Draupadi Daughter of Drupada.

Draupnir Odin's famous ring, fashioned by Brokki.

Drona A Brahma, son of the great sage Bharadwaja.

Druid An ancient order of Celtic priests held in high esteem who flourished in the pre-Christian era. The word 'druid' is derived from an ancient Celtic one meaning 'very knowledgeable'. These individuals were believed to have mystical powers and in ancient Irish literature possess the ability to conjure up magical charms, to create tempests, to curse and debilitate their enemies and to perform as soothsayers to the royal courts.

Drupada King of the Panchalas.

Dryads Nymphs of the trees.

Dun A stronghold or royal abode surrounded by an earthen wall.

Durga Goddess, wife of Shiva.

Durk Knife.

Duryodhana One of Drona's pupils.

Dvalin Dwarf visited by Loki; also the name for the stag on Yggdrasill.

Dwarfs Fairies and black elves are called dwarfs.

Dwarkanath The Lord of Dwaraka; Krishna.

Dyumatsena King of the Shalwas and father of Satyavan.

Ea God of water, light and wisdom, and one of the creator deities. He brought arts and civilization to humankind. Also known as Oannes and Nudimmud.

Eabani Hero originally created by Aruru to defeat Gilgamesh, the two became friends and destroyed Khumbaba together. He personifies the natural world.

Each Uisge The mythical water-horse which haunts lochs and appears in various forms.

Ebisu One of the gods of luck. He is also the god of labour and fishermen.

Echo A nymph who was punished by Hera for her endless stories told to distract Hera from Zeus's infidelity.

Ector King Arthur's foster father, who raised Arthur to protect him.

Edda Collection of prose and poetic myths and stories from the Norsemen.

Eight Immortals Three of these are reputed to be historical: Han Chung-li, born in Shaanxi, who rose to become a Marshal of the Empire in 21 BC. Chang Kuo-Lao, who lived in the seventh to eighth century AD, and Lü Tung-pin, who was born in AD 755.

Einheriear Odin's guests at Valhalla.

Eisa Loki' daughter.

Ekalavya Son of the king of the Nishadas.

Electra Daughter of Agamemnon and Clytemnestra.

Eleusis A town in which the cult of Demeter is centred.

Elf Sigmund is buried by an elf; there are light and dark elves (the latter called dwarfs).

Elokos (Central African) Imps of dwarf-demons who eat human flesh.

Elpenor The youngest of Odysseus's crew who fell from the roof of Circe's house on Aeaea and visited with Odysseus at Hades.

Elysium The home of the blessed dead.

Emain Macha The capital of ancient Ulster.

Emma Dai-o King of hell and judge of the dead.

En-lil God of the lower world, storms and mist, who held sway over the ghostly animistic spirits, which at his bidding might pose as the friends or enemies of men. Also known as Bel.

Eos Goddess of the dawn and sister of the sun and moon.

Erichthonius A child born of the semen spilled when Hephaestus tried to rape Athene on the Acropolis.

Eridu The home of Ea and one of the two major cities of Babylonian civilization.

Erirogho Magical mixture made from the ashes of the dead.

Eros God of Love, the son of Aphrodite.

Erpa Hereditary chief.

Erysichthon A Thessalian who cut down a grove sacred to Demeter, who punished him with eternal hunger.

Eshu (Yoruba) God of mischief. He also tests people's characters and controls law enforcement.

Eteocles Son of Oedipus.

Eumaeus Swineherd of Odysseus's family at Ithaca.

Euphemus A son of Poseidon who could walk on water. He sailed with the Argonauts.

Europa Daughter of King Agenor of Tyre, who was taken by Zeus to Crete.

Eurydice A Thracian nymph married to Orpheus.

Excalibur The magical sword given to Arthur by the Lady of the Lake. In some versions of the myths, Excalibur is also the sword that the young Arthur pulls from the stone to become king.

Fabulist Person who composes or tells fables.

Fafnir Shape-changer who kills his father and becomes a dragon to guard the family jewels. Slain by Sigurd.

Fairy The word is derived from 'Fays' which means Fates. They are immortal, with the gift of prophecy and of music, and their role changes according to the origin of the myth. They were often considered to be little people, with enormous propensity for mischief, but they are central to many myths and legends, with important powers.

Faro (Mali, Guinea) God of the sky.

Fates In Greek mythology, daughters of Zeus and Themis, who spin the thread of a mortal's life and cut it when his time is due. Called Norns in Viking mythology.

Fenris A wild wolf, who is the son of Loki. He roams the earth after Ragnarok.

Ferhad Sculptor who fell in love with Shireen, the wife of Khosru, and undertook a seemingly impossible task to clear a passage through the mountain of Beysitoun and join the rivers in return for winning Shireen's hand.

Fialar Red cock of Valhalla.

Fianna/Fenians The word 'fianna' was used in early times to describe young warrior-hunters. These youths evolved under the leadership of Finn Mac Cumaill as a highly skilled band of military men who took up service with various kings throughout Ireland.

Filheim Land of mist, at the end of one of Yggdrasill's roots.

Fingal Another name for Fionn Mac Chumail, used after MacPherson's Ossian in the eighteenth century.

Fionn Mac Chumail Irish and Scottish warrior, with great powers of fairness and wisdom. He is known not for physical strength but for knowledge, sense of justice, generosity and canny instinct. He had two hounds, which were later discovered to be his nephews transformed. He became head of the Fianna, or Féinn, fighting the enemies of Ireland and Scotland. He was the father of Oisin (also called Ossian, or other derivatives), and father or grandfather of Osgar.

Fir Bolg One of the ancient, pre-Gaelic peoples of Ireland who were reputed to have worshipped the god Bulga, meaning god of lighting. They are thought to have colonized Ireland around 1970 BC, after the death of Nemed and to have reigned for a short period of thirty-seven years before their defeat by the Tuatha De Danann.

Fir Chlis Nimble men or merry dancers, who are the souls of fallen angels.

Folkvang Freyia's palace.

Fomorians A race of monstrous beings, popularly conceived as sea-pirates with some supernatural characteristics who opposed the earliest settlers in Ireland, including the Nemedians and the Tuatha De Danann.

Frey Comes to Asgard with Freyia as a hostage following the war between the Aesir and the Vanir.

Freyia Comes to Asgard with Frey as a hostage following the war between the Aesir and the Vanir. Goddess of beauty and love.

Frigga Odin's wife and mother of gods; she is goddess of the earth.

Fuath Evil spirits which lived in or near the water.

Fulla Frigga's maidservant.

Furies Creatures born from the blood of Cronus, guarding the greatest sinners of the Underworld. Their power lay in their ability to drive mortals mad. Snakes writhed in their hair and around their waists.

Furoshiki Cloths used to wrap things.

Gae Bolg Cuchulainn alone learned the use of this weapon from the woman-warrior, Scathach and with it he slew his own son Connla and his closest friend, Ferdia. Gae Bolg translates as 'harpoon-like javelin' and the deadly weapon was reported to have been created by Bulga, the god of lighting.

Gaea Goddess of Earth, born from Chaos, and the mother of Uranus and Pontus. Also spelled as Gaia.

Gage Object of value presented to a challenger to symbolize good faith.

Galahad Knight of the Round Table, who took up the search for the Holy Grail. Son of Lancelot, Galahad is considered the purest and most perfect knight.

Galatea Daughter of Nereus and Doris, a sea-nymph loved by Polyphemus, the Cyclops.

Gandhari Mother of Duryodhana.

Gandharvas Demi-gods and musicians.

Gandjharva Musical ministrants of the upper air.

Ganesha Elephant-headed god of scribes and son of Shiva.

Ganges Sacred river personified by the goddess Ganga, wife of Shiva and daughter of the mount Himalaya.

Gareth of Orkney King Arthur's nephew and knight of the Round Table.

Garm Hel's hound.

Garuda King of the birds and mount Vishnu, the divine bird, attendant of Narayana.

Gautama Son of Suddhodana and also known as Siddhartha.

Gawain Nephew of King Arthur and knight of the Round Table, he is best known for his adventure with the Green Knight, who challenges one of Arthur's knights to cut off his head, but only if he agrees to be beheaded in turn in a year and a day, if the Green Knight survives. Gawain beheads the Green Knight, who simply replaces his head. At the appointed time, they meet, and the Green Knight swings his axe but merely nicks Gawain's skin instead of beheading him.

Geisha Performance artist or entertainer, usually female.

Geri Odin's wolf.

Giallar Bridge in Filheim.

Giallarhorn Heimdall's trumpet – the final call signifies Ragnarok.

Giants In Greek mythology, a race of beings born from Gaea, grown from the blood that dropped from the castrated Uranus. Usually represent evil in Viking mythology.

Gilgamesh King of Erech known as a half-human, half-god hero similar to the Greek Heracles, and often listed with the gods. He is the personification of the sun and is protected by the god Shamash, who in some texts is described as his father. He is also portrayed as an evil tyrant at times.

Gladheim Where the twelve deities of Asgard hold their thrones. Also called Gladsheim.

Golden Fleece Fleece of the ram sent by Poseidon to substitute for Phrixus when his father was going to sacrifice him. The Argonauts went in search of the fleece.

Goodman Man of the house.

Goodwife Woman of the house.

Gopis Lovers of the young Krishna and milkmaids.

Gorgon One of the three sisters, including Medusa, whose frightening looks could turn mortals to stone.

Graces Daughters of Aphrodite by Zeus.

Gramercy Expression of surprise or strong feeling.

Great Head The Iroquois Indians believed in the existence of a curious being known as Great Head, a creature with an enormous head poised on slender legs.

Great Spirit The name given to the Creator of all life, as well as the term used to describe the omnipotent force of the Creator existing in every living thing.

Great-Flank One of Ravana's monsters.

Green Knight A knight dressed all in green and with green hair and skin who challenged one of Arthur's knights to strike him a blow with an axe and that, if he survived, he would return to behead the knight in a year and a day. He turned out to be Lord

Bertilak and was under an enchantment cast by Morgan le Fay to test Arthur's knights.

Gruagach A kind of brownie, usually dressed in red or green as opposed to the traditional brown. He has great power to enchant the hapless, or to help mortals who are worthy (usually heroes). He often appears to challenge a boy-hero, during his period of education.

Gudea High priest of Lagash, known to be a patron of the arts and a writer himself.

Guebre Religion founded by Zoroaster, the Persian prophet.

Gugumatz Creator god who, with Huracan, formed the sky, earth and everything on it.

Guha King of Nishadha.

Guidewife Woman.

Guinevere Wife of King Arthur; she is often portrayed as a virtuous lady and wife, but is perhaps best known for having a love affair with Lancelot, one of Arthur's friends and knights of the Round Table. Her name is also spelled Guenever.

Gulistan *Rose Garden*, written by the poet Sa'di

Gungnir Odin's spear, made of Yggdrasill wood, and the tip fashioned by Dvalin.

Gylfi A wandering king to whom the Eddas are narrated.

Haab Mayan solar calendar that consisted of eighteen twenty-day months.

Hades One of the three sons of Cronus; brother of Poseidon and Zeus. Hades is King of the Underworld, which is also known as the House of Hades.

Haere-mai Maori phrase meaning 'come here, welcome.'

Haere-mai-ra, me o tatou mate Maori phrase meaning 'come here, that I may sorrow with you.'

Haere-ra Maori phrase meaning 'goodbye, go, farewell.'

Haji Muslim pilgrim who has been to Mecca.

Hakama Traditional Japanese clothing, worn on the bottom half of the body.

Hanuman General of the monkey people.

Harakiri Suicide, usually by cutting or stabbing the abdomen. Also known as seppuku.

Hari-Hara Shiva and Vishnu as one god.

Harmonia Daughter of Ares and Aphrodite, wife of Cadmus.

Hatamoto High-ranking samurai.

Hathor Great cosmic mother and patroness of lovers. She is portrayed as a cow.

Hati The wolf who pursues the sun and moon.

Hatshepsut Second female pharaoh.

Hauberk Armour to protect the neck and shoulders, sometimes a full-length coat of mail.

Hector Eldest son of King Priam who defended Troy from the Greeks. He was killed by Achilles.

Hecuba The second wife of Priam, King of Troy. She was turned into a dog after Troy was lost.

Heimdall White god who guards the Bifrost bridge.

Hel Goddess of death and Loki's daughter.

Helen Daughter of Leda and Tyndareus, King of Sparta, and the most beautiful woman in the world. She was responsible for starting the Trojan War.

Heliopolis City in modern-day Cairo, known as the City of the Sun and the central place of worship of Ra. Also known as Anu.

Helius The sun, son of Hyperion and Theia.

Henwife Witch.

Hephaestus or **Hephaistos** The Smith of Heaven.

Hera A Mycenaean palace goddess, married to Zeus.

Heracles An important Greek hero, the son of Zeus and Alcmena. His name means 'Glory of Hera'. He performed twelve labours for King Eurystheus, and later became a god.

Hermes The conductor of souls of the dead to Hades, and god of trickery and of trade. He acts as messenger to the gods.

Hermod Son of Frigga and Odin who travelled to see Hel in order to reclaim Balder for Asgard.

Hero and Leander Hero was a priestess of Aphrodite, loved by Leander, a young man of Abydos. He drowned trying to see her.

Hestia Goddess of the hearth, daughter of Cronus and Rhea.

Hieroglyphs Type of writing that combines symbols and pictures, usually cut into tombs or rocks, or written on papyrus.

Himalaya Great mountain and range, father of Parvati.

Hiordis Wife of Sigmund and mother of Sigurd.

Hoderi A fisher and son of Okuninushi.

Hodur Balder's blind twin; known as the personification of darkness.

Hoenir Also called Vili; produced the first humans with Odin and Loki, and was one of the triad responsible for the creation of the world.

Hōichi the Earless A *biwa hōshi*, a blind storyteller who played the biwa or lute. Also a priest.

Homayi Phoenix.

Hoori A hunter and son of Okuninushi.

Horus God of the sky and kinship, son of Isis and Osiris. He captained the boat that carried Ra across the sky. He is depicted with the head of a falcon.

Hotei One of the gods of luck. He also personifies humour and contentment.

Houlet Owl.

Houri Beautiful virgin from paradise.

Hrim-faxi Steed of the night.

Hubris Presumptuous behaviour which causes the wrath of the gods to be brought on to mortals.

Hueytozoztli Festival dedicated to Tlaloc and, at times, Chicomecohuatl or other deities. Also the fourth month of the Aztec calendar.

Hugin Odin's raven.

Huitzilopochtli God of war and the sun, also connected with the summer and crops; one of the principal Aztec deities. He was born a full-grown adult to save his mother, Coatlicue, from the jealousy of his sister, Coyolxauhqui, who tried to kill Coatlicue. The Mars of the Aztec gods. In some origin stories he is one of four offspring of Ometeotl and Omecihuatl.

Hurley A traditional Irish game played with sticks and balls, quite similar to hockey.

Hurons A tribe of Iroquois stock, originally one people with the Iroquois.

Huveane (Pedi, Venda) Creator of humankind, who made a baby from clay into which he breathed life. He is known as the High God or Great God. He is also known as a trickster god.

Hymir Giant who fishes with Thor and is drowned by him.

Iambe Daughter of Pan and Echo, servant to King Celeus of Eleusis and Metaeira.

Icarus Son of Daedalus, who plunged to his death after escaping from the labyrinth.

Ichneumon Mongoose.

Idunn Guardian of the youth-giving apples.

Ifa (Yoruba) God of wisdom and divination. Also the term for a Yoruban religion.

Ife (Yoruba) The place Obatala first arrived on Earth and took for his home.

Igigi Great spirits or gods of Heaven and the sky.

Igraine Wife of the duke of Tintagel, enemy of Uther Pendragon, who marries Uther when her first husband dies. She is King Arthur's mother.

Ile (Yoruba) Goddess of the earth.

Imhetep High priest and wise sage. He is sometimes thought to be the son of Ptah.

Imam Person who leads prayers in a mosque.

In The male principle who, joined with Yo, the female side, brought about creation and the first gods. In and Yo correspond to the Chinese Yang and Yin.

Inari God of rice, fertility, agriculture and, later, the fox god. Inari has both good and evil attributes but is often presented as an evil trickster.

Indra The King of Heaven.

Indrajit Son of Ravana.

Indrasen Daughter of Nala and Damayanti.

Indrasena Son of Nala and Damayanti.

Inundation Annual flooding of the River Nile.

Iphigenia The eldest daughter of Agamemnon and Clytemnestra who was sacrificed to appease Artemis and obtain a fair wind for Troy.

Iris Messenger of the gods who took the form of a rainbow.

Iseult Princess of Ireland and niece of the Morholt. She falls in love with Tristan after consuming a love potion but is forced to marry King Mark of Cornwall.

Ishtar Goddess of love, beauty, justice and war, especially in Ninevah, and earth mother who symbolizes fertility. Married to Tammuz, she is similar to the Greek goddess Aphrodite. Ishtar is sometimes known as Innana or Irnina.

Isis Goddess of the Nile and the moon, sister-wife of Osiris. She and her son, Horus, are sometimes thought of in a similar way to Mary and Jesus. She was one of the most worshipped female Egyptian deities and was instrumental in returning Osiris to life after he was killed by his brother, Set.

Istakbál Deputation of warriors.

Izanagi Deity and brother-husband to Izanami, who together created the Japanese islands from the Floating Bridge of Heaven. Their offspring populated Japan.

Izanami Deity and sister-wife of Izanagi, creator of Japan. Their children include Amaterasu, Tsuki-yomi and Susanoo.

Jade It was believed that jade emerged from the mountains as a liquid which then solidified after ten thousand years to become a precious hard stone, green in colour. If the correct herbs were added to it, it could return to its liquid state and when swallowed increase the individual's chances of immortality.

Jambavan A noble monkey.

Jason Son of Aeson, King of Iolcus and leader of the voyage of the Argonauts.

Jatayu King of all the eagle-tribes.

Jesseraunt Flexible coat of armour or mail.

Jimmo Legendary first emperor of Japan. He is thought to be descended from Hoori, while other tales claim him to be descended from Amaterasu through her grandson, Ninigi.

Jizo God of little children and the god who calms the troubled sea.

Jord Daughter of Nott; wife of Odin.

Jormungander The world serpent; son of Loki. Legends tell that when his tail is removed from his mouth, Ragnarok has arrived.

Jorō Geisha who also worked as a prostitute.

Jotunheim Home of the giants.

Ju Ju tree Deciduous tree that produces edible fruit.

Jurasindhu A rakshasa, father-in-law of Kans.

Jyeshtha Goddess of bad luck.

Ka Life power or soul. Also known as ba.

Kai-káús Son of Kai-kobád. He led an army to invade Mázinderán, home of the demon-sorcerers, after being persuaded by a demon. Known for his ambitious schemes, he later tried to reach Heaven by trapping eagles to fly him there on his throne.

Kaikeyi Mother of Bharata, one of Dasharatha's three wives.

Kai-khosrau Son of Saiawúsh, who killed Afrásiyáb in revenge for the death of his father.

Kai-kobád Descendant of Feridún, he was selected by Zál to lead an army against Afrásiyáb. Their powerful army, led by Zál and Rustem, drove back Afrásiyáb's army, who then agreed to peace.

Kali The Black, wife of Shiva.

Kalindi Daughter of the sun, wife of Krishna.

Kaliya A poisonous hydra that lived in the jamna.

Kalki Incarnation of Vishnu yet to come.

Kalnagini Serpent who kills Lakshmindara.

Kal-Purush The Time-man, Bengali name for Orion.

Kaluda A disciple of Buddha.

Kalunga-ngombe (Mbundu) Death, also depicted as the king of the netherworld.

Kama God of desire.

Kamadeva Desire, the god of love.

377

Kami Spirits, deities or forces of nature.

Kamund Lasso.

Kans King of Mathura, son of Ugrasena and Pavandrekha.

Kanva Father of Shakuntala.

Kappa River goblin with the body of a tortoise and the head of an ape. Kappa love to challenge human beings to single combat.

Karakia Invocation, ceremony, prayer.

Karna Pupil of Drona.

Kasbu A period of twenty-four hours.

Kashyapa One of Dasharatha's counsellors.

Kauravas or Kurus Sons of Dhritarashtra, pupils of Drona.

Kaushalya Mother of Rama, one of Dasharatha's three wives.

Kay Son of Ector and adopted brother to King Arthur, he becomes one of Arthur's knights of the Round Table.

Keb God of the earth and father of Osiris and Isis, married to Nut. Keb is identified with Kronos, the Greek god of time.

Kehua Spirit, ghost.

Kelpie Another word for each uisge, the water-horse.

Ken Know.

Keres Black-winged demons or daughters of the night.

Keshini Wife of Sagara.

Khalif Leader.

Khara Younger brother of Ravana.

Khepera God who represents the rising sun. He is portrayed as a scarab. Also known as Nebertcher.

Kher-heb Priest and magician who officiated over rituals and ceremonies.

Khnemu God of the source of the Nile and one of the original Egyptian deities. He is thought to be the creator of children and of other gods. He is portrayed as a ram.

Khosru King and husband to Shireen, daughter of Maurice, the Greek Emperor. He was murdered by his own son, who wanted his kingdom and his wife.

Khumbaba Monster and guardian of the goddess Irnina, a form of the goddess Ishtar. Khumbaba is likened to the Greek gorgon.

Kia-ora Welcome, good luck. A greeting.

Kiboko Hippopotamus.

Kikinu Soul.

Kimbanda (Mbundu) Doctor.

Kimono Traditional Japanese clothing, similar to a robe.

King Arthur Legendary king of Britain who plucked the magical sword from the stone, marking him as the heir of Uther Pendragon and 'true king' of Britain. He and his knights of the Round Table defended Britain from the Saxons and had many adventures, including searching for the Holy Grail. Finally wounded in battle, he left Britain for the mythical Avalon, vowing to one day return to reclaim his kingdom.

Kingu Tiawath's husband, a god and warrior who she promised would rule Heaven once he helped her defeat the 'gods of light'. He was killed by Merodach who used his blood to make clay, from which he formed the first humans. In some tales, Kingu is Tiawath's son as well as her consort.

Kinnaras Human birds with musical instruments under their wings.

Kinyamkela (Zaramo) Ghost of a child.

Kis Solar deity, usually depicted as an eagle.

Kishar Earth mother and sister-wife to Anshar.

Kitamba (Mbundu) Chief who made his whole village go into mourning when his head-wife, Queen Muhongo, died. He also pledged that no one should speak or eat until she was returned to him.

Knowe Knoll or hillock.

Kojiki One of two myth-histories of Japan, along with the *Nihon Shoki*.

Ko-no-Hana Goddess of Mount Fuji, princess and wife of Ninigi.

Kore 'Maiden', another name for Persephone.

Kraal Traditional rural African village, usually consisting of huts surrounded by a fence or wall. Also an animal enclosure.

Krishna The Dark one, worshipped as an incarnation of Vishnu.

Kui-see Edible root.

Kumara Son of Shiva and Paravati, slays demon Taraka.

Kumbha-karna Ravana's brother.

Kunti Mother of the Pandavas.

Kura Red. The sacred colour of the Maori.

Kusha or Kusi One of Sita's two sons.

Kvasir Clever warrior and colleague of Odin. He was responsible for finally outwitting Loki.

Kwannon Goddess of mercy.

Labyrinth A prison built at Knossos for the Minotaur by Daedalus.

Lady of the Lake Enchantress who presents Arthur with Excalibur.

Laertes King of Ithaca and father of Odysseus.

Laestrygonians Savage giants encountered by Odysseus on his travels.

Laili In love with Majnun but unable to marry him, she was given to the prince, Ibn Salam, to marry. When he died, she escaped and found Majnun, but they could not be legally married. The couple died of grief and were buried together. Also known as Laila.

Lakshmana Brother of Rama and his companion in exile.

Lakshmi Consort of Vishnu and a goddess of beauty and good fortune.

Lakshmindara Son of Chand resurrected by Manasa Devi.

Lancelot Knight of the Round Table. Lancelot was raised by the Lady of the Lake. While he went on many quests, he is perhaps best known for his affair with Guinevere, King Arthur's wife.

Land of Light One of the names for the realm of the fairies. If a piece of metal welded by human hands is put in the doorway to their land, the door cannot close. The door to this realm is only open at night, and usually at a full moon.

Lang syne The days of old.

Lao Tzu (Laozi) The ancient Taoist philosopher thought to have been born in 571 BC a contemporary of Confucius with whom, it is said, he discussed the tenets of Tao. Lao Tzu was an advocate of simple rural existence and looked to the Yellow Emperor and Shun as models of efficient government. His philosophies were recorded in the Tao Te Ching. Legends surrounding his birth suggest that he emerged from the left-hand side of his mother's body, with white hair and a long white beard, after a confinement lasting eighty years.

Laocoon A Trojan wiseman who predicted that the wooden horse contained Greek soldiers.

Laomedon The King of Troy who hired Apollo and Poseidon to build the impregnable walls of Troy.

Lava Son of Sita.

Leda Daughter of the King of Aetolia, who married Tyndareus. Helen and Clytemnestra were her daughters.

Legba (Dahomey) Youngest offspring of Mawu-Lisa. He was given the gift of all languages. It was through him that humans could converse with the gods.

Leman Lover.

Lethe One of the four rivers of the Underworld, also called the River of Forgetfulness.

Lif The female survivor of Ragnarok.

Lifthrasir The male survivor of Ragnarok.

Lil Demon.

Lofty mountain Home of Ahura-Mazda.

Logi Utgard-loki's cook.

Loki God of fire and mischief-maker of Asgard; he eventually brings about Ragnarok.

Lotus-Eaters A race of people who live a dazed, drugged existence, the result of eating the lotus flower.

Ma'at State of order meaning truth, order or justice. Personified by the goddess Ma'at, who was Thoth's consort.

Macha There are thought to be several different Machas who appear in quite a number of ancient Irish stories. For the purposes of this book, however, the Macha referred to is the wife of Crunnchu. The story unfolds that after her husband had boasted of her great athletic ability to the King, she was subsequently forced to run against his horses in spite of the fact that she was heavily pregnant. Macha died giving birth to her twin babies and with her dying breath she cursed Ulster for nine generations, proclaiming that it would suffer the weakness of a woman in childbirth in times of great stress. This curse had its most disastrous effect when Medb of Connacht invaded Ulster with her great army.

Machi-bugyō Senior official or magistrate, usually samurai.

Macuilxochitl God of art, dance and games, and the patron of luck in gaming. His name means 'source of flowers' or 'prince of flowers'. Also known as Xochipilli, meaning 'five-flower'.

Madake Weapon used for whipping, made of bamboo.

Maduma Taro tuber.

Mag Muirthemne Cuchulainn's inheritance. A plain extending from River Boyne to the mountain range of Cualgne, close to Emain Macha in Ulster.

Magni Thor's son.

Mahaparshwa One of Ravana's generals.

Maharaksha Son of Khara, slain at Lanka.

Mahasubhadda Wife of Buddha-select (Sumedha).

Majnun Son of a chief, who fell in love with Laili and followed her tribe through the desert, becoming mad with love until they were briefly reunited before dying.

Makaras Mythical fish-reptiles of the sea.

Mana Power, authority, prestige, influence, sanctity, luck.

Manasa Devi Goddess of snakes, daughter of Shiva by a mortal woman.

Manasha Goddess of snakes.

Mandavya Daughter of Kushadhwaja.

Man-Devourer One of Ravana's monsters.

Mandodari Wife of Ravana.

Mani The moon.

Manitto Broad term used to describe the supernatural or a potent spirit among the Algonquins, the Iroquois and the Sioux.

Man-Slayer One of Ravana's counsellors.

Manthara Kaikeyi's evil nurse, who plots Rama's ruin.

Mantle Cloak or shawl.

Manu Lawgiver.

Manu Mythical mountain on which the sun sets.

Mara The evil one, tempts Gautama.

Markandeya One of Dasharatha's counsellors.

Mashu Mountain of the Sunset, which lies between Earth and the underworld. Guarded by scorpion-men.

Matali Sakra's charioteer.

Mawu-Lisa (Dahomey) Twin offspring of Nana Baluka. Mawu (female) and Lisa (male) are often joined to form one being. Their own offspring populated the world.

Mbai (Igbo) Person of great intelligence, also known as Ekake (Ibani), which means 'tortoise'.

Medea Witch and priestess of Hecate, daughter of Aeetes and sister of Circe. She helped Jason in his quest for the Golden Fleece.

Medusa One of the three Gorgons whose head had the power to turn onlookers to stone.

Melpomene One of the muses, and mother of the Sirens.

Menaka One of the most beautiful dancers in Heaven.

Menat Amulet, usually worn for protection.

Mendicant Beggar.

Menelaus King of Sparta, brother of Agamemnon. Married Helen and called war against Troy when she eloped with Paris.

Menthu Lord of Thebes and god of war. He is portrayed as a hawk or falcon.

Mere-pounamu A native weapon made of a rare green stone.

Merlin Wizard and advisor to King Arthur. He is thought to be the son of a human female and an incubus (male demon). He brought about Arthur's birth and ascension to king, then acted as his mentor.

Merodach God who battled Tiawath and defeated her by cutting out her heart and dividing her corpse into two pieces. He used these pieces to divide the upper and lower waters once controlled by Tiawath, making a dwelling for the gods of light. He also created humankind. Also known as Marduk.

Metaneira Wife of Celeus, King of Eleusis, who hired Demeter in disguise as her nurse.

Metztli Goddess of the moon, her name means 'lady of the night'. Also known as Yohualtictl.

Michabo Also known as Manobozho, or the Great Hare, the principal deity of the Algonquins, maker and preserver of the earth, sun and moon.

Mictlan God of the dead and ruler of the underworld. He was married to Mictecaciuatl and is often represented as a bat. He is also the Aztec lord of Hades. Also known as Mictlantecutli. Mictlan is also the name for the underworld.

Midgard Dwelling place of humans (Earth).

Midsummer A time when fairies dance and claim human victims.

Mihrab Father of Rúdábeh and descendant of Zohák, the serpent-king.

Milesians A group of iron-age invaders led by the sons of Mil, who arrived in Ireland from Spain around 500 BC and overcame the Tuatha De Danann.

Mimir God of the ocean. His head guards a well; reincarnated after Ragnarok.

Minos King of Crete, son of Zeus and Europa. He was considered to have been the ruler of a sea empire.

Minotaur A creature born of the union between Pasiphae and a Cretan Bull.

Minúchihr King who lives to be one hundred and twenty years old. Father of Nauder.

Miolnir Thor's hammer.

Mithra God of the sun and light in Iran, protector of truth and guardian of pastures and cattle. Also known as Mitra in Hindu mythology and Mithras in Roman mythology.

Mixcoatl God of the chase or the hunt. Sometimes depicted as the god of air and thunder, he introduced fire to humankind. His name means 'cloud serpent'.

Mnoatia Forest spirits.

Moccasins One-piece shoes made of soft leather, especially deerskin.

Modi Thor's son.

Moly A magical plant given to Odysseus by Hermes as protection against Circe's powers.

Montezuma Great emperor who consolidated the Aztec Empire.

Mordred Bastard son of King Arthur and Morgawse, Queen of Orkney, who, unknown to Arthur, was his half-sister. Mordred becomes one of King Arthur's knights of the Round Table before betraying and fatally wounding Arthur, causing him to leave Britain for Avalon.

Morgan le Fay Enchantress and half-sister to King Arthur, Morgan was an apprentice of Merlin's. She is generally depicted as benevolent, yet did pit herself against Arthur and his knights on occasion. She escorts Arthur on his final journey to Avalon. Also known as Morgain le Fay.

Morholt, the Knight sent to Cornwall to force King Mark to pay tribute to Ireland. He is killed by Tristan.

Morongoe the brave (Lesotho) Man who was turned into a snake by evil spirits because Tau was jealous that he had married the beautiful Mokete, the chief's daughter. Morongoe was returned to human form after his son, Tsietse, returned him to their family.

Mosima (Bapedi) The underworld or abyss.

Mount Fuji Highest mountain in Japan, on the island of Honshū.

Mount Kunlun This mountain features in many Chinese legends as the home of the great emperors on Earth. It is written in the *Shanghaijing* (*The Classic of Mountains and Seas*) that this towering structure measured no less than 3300 miles in circumference and 4000 miles in height. It acted both as a central pillar to support the heavens, and as a gateway between Heaven and Earth.

Moving Finger Expression for taking responsibility for one's life and actions, which cannot be undone.

Moytura Translated as the 'Plain of Weeping', Mag Tured, or Moytura, was where the Tuatha De Danann fought two of their most significant battles.

Mua An old-time Polynesian god.

Muezzin Person who performs the Muslim call to prayer.

Mugalana A disciple of Buddha.

Muilearteach The Cailleach Bheur of the water, who appears as a witch or a sea-serpent. On land she grew larger and stronger by fire.

Mul-lil God of Nippur, who took the form of a gazelle.

Muloyi Sorcerer, also called mulaki, murozi, ndozi or ndoki.

Mummu Son of Tiawath and Apsu. He formed a trinity with them to battle the gods. Also known as Moumis. In some tales, Mummu is also Merodach, who eventually destroyed Tiawath.

Munin Odin's raven.

Murile (Chaga) Man who dug up a taro tuber that resembled his baby brother, which turned into a living boy. His mother killed the baby when she saw Murile was starving himself to feed it.

Muses Goddesses of poetry and song, daughters of Zeus and Mnemosyne.

Muskrat North American beaver-like, amphibious rodent.

Muspell Home of fire, and the fire-giants.

Mwidzilo Taboo which, if broken, can cause death.

Nabu God of writing and wisdom. Also known as Nebo. Thought to be the son of Merodach.

Nahua Ancient Mexicans.

Nakula Pandava twin skilled in horsemanship.

Nala One of the monkey host, son of Vishvakarma.

Nana Baluka (Dahomey) Mother of all creation. She gave birth to an androgynous being with two faces. The female face was Mawu, who controlled the night and lands to the west. The male face was Lisa and he controlled the day and the east.

Nanahuatl Also known as Nanauatzin. Presided over skin diseases and known as Leprous, which in Nahua meant 'divine'.

Nandi Shiva's bull.

Nanna Balder's wife.

Nannar God of the moon and patron of the city of Ur.

Naram-Sin Son or ancestor of Sargon and king of the Four Zones or Quarters of Babylon.

Narcissus Son of the River Cephisus. He fell in love with himself and died as a result.

Narve Son of Loki.

Nataraja Manifestation of Shiva, Lord of the Dance.

Natron Preservative used in embalming, mined from the Natron Valley in Egypt.

Nauder Son of Minúchihr, who became king on his death and was tyrannical and hated until Sám begged him to follow in the footsteps of his ancestors.

Nausicaa Daughter of Alcinous, King of Phaeacia, who fell in love with Odysseus.

Nebuchadnezzar Famous king of Babylon. Also known as Nebuchadrezzar.

Necromancy Communicating with the dead.

Nectar Drink of the gods.

Neith Goddess of hunting, fate and war. Neith is sometimes known as the creator of the universe.

Nemesis Goddess of retribution and daughter of night.

Neoptolemus Son of Achilles and Deidameia, he came to Troy at the end of the war to wear his father's armour. He sacrificed Polyxena at the tomb of Achilles.

Nephthys Goddess of the air, night and the dead. Sister of Isis and sister-wife to Seth, she is also the mother of Anubis.

Nereids Sea-nymphs who are the daughters of Nereus and Doris. Thetis, mother of Achilles, was a Nereid.

Nergal God of death and patron god of Cuthah, which was often known as a burial place. He is also known as the god of fire. Married to Aralu, the goddess of the underworld.

Nestor Wise King of Pylus, who led the ships to Troy with Agamemnon and Menelaus.

Neta Daughter of Shiva, friend of Manasa.

Ngaka (Lesotho) Witch doctor.

Night Daughter of Norvi.

Nikumbha One of Ravana's generals.

Nila One of the monkey host, son of Agni.

Nin-Girsu God of fertility and war, patron god of Girsu. Also known as Shul-gur.

Ninigi Grandson of Amaterasu, Ninigi came to Earth bringing rice and order to found the Imperial family. He is known as the August Grandchild.

Niord God of the sea; marries Skadi.

Nippur The home of En-lil and one of the two major cities of Babylonian civilization.

Nirig God of war and storms, and son of Bel. Also known as Enu-Restu.

Nirvana Transcendent state and the final goal of Buddhism.

Noatun Niord's home.

Noisy-Throat One of Ravana's counsellors.

Norns The fates and protectors of Yggdrasill. Many believe them to be the same as the Valkyries.

Norvi Father of the night.

Nott Goddess of night.

Nsasak bird Small bird who became chief of all small birds after winning a competition to go without food for seven days. The Nsasak bird beat the Odudu bird by sneaking out of his home to feed.

Nü Wa The Goddess Nü Wa, who in some versions of the Creation myths is the sole creator of mankind, and in other tales is associated with the God Fu Xi, also a great benefactor of the human race. Some accounts represent Fu Xi as the brother of Nü Wa, but others describe the pair as lovers who lie together to create the very first human beings. Fu Xi is also considered to be the first of the Chinese emperors of mythical times who reigned from 2953 to 2838 BC.

Nuada The first king of the Tuatha De Danann in Ireland, who lost an arm in the first battle of Moytura against the Fomorians. He became known as 'Nuada of the Silver Hand' when Diancecht, the great physician of the Tuatha De Danann, replaced his hand with a silver one after the battle.

Nunda (Swahili, East Africa) Slayer that took the form of a cat and grew so big that it consumed everyone in the town except the sultan's wife, who locked herself away. Her son, Mohammed, killed Nunda and cut open its leg, setting free everyone Nunda had eaten.

Nut Goddess of the sky, stars and astronomy. Sister-wife of Keb and mother of Osiris, Isis, Set and Nephthys.

Nyame (Ashanti) God of the sky, who sees and knows everything.

Nymphs Minor female deities associated with particular parts of the land and sea.

Obatala (Yoruba) Creator of humankind. He climbed down a golden chain from the sky to the earth, then a watery abyss, and formed land and humankind. When Olorun heard of his success, he created the sun for Obatala and his creations.

Oberon Fairy king.

Odin Allfather and king of all gods, he is known for travelling the nine worlds in disguise and recognized only by his single eye; dies at Ragnarok.

Odur Freyia's husband.

Odysseus Greek hero, son of Laertes and Anticleia, who was renowned for his cunning, the master behind the victory at Troy, and known for his long voyage home.

Oedipus Son of Leius, King of Thebes and Jocasta. Became King of Thebes and married his mother.

Ogdoad Group of eight deities who were formed into four male-female couples who joined to create the gods and the world.

Ogham One of the earliest known forms of Irish writing, originally used to inscribe upright pillar stones.

Oiran Courtesan.

Oisin Also called Ossian (particularly by James Macpherson who wrote a set of Gaelic Romances about this character, supposedly garnered from oral tradition). Ossian was the son of Fionn and Sadbh, and had various brothers, according to different legends. He was a man of great wisdom, became immortal for many centuries, but in the end he became mad.

Ojibwe Another name for the Chippewa, a tribe of Algonquin stock.

Okuninushi Deity and descendant of Susanoo, who married Suseri-hime, Susanoo's daughter, without his consent.

Susanoo tried to kill him many times but did not succeed and eventually forgave Okuninushi. He is sometimes thought to be the son or grandson of Susanoo.

Olokun (Yoruba) Most powerful goddess who ruled the seas and marshes. When Obatala created Earth in her domain, other gods began to divide it up between them. Angered at their presumption, she caused a great flood to destroy the land.

Olorun (Yoruba) Supreme god and ruler of the sky. He sees and controls everything, but others, such as Obatala, carry out the work for him. Also known as Olodumare.

Olympia Zeus's home in Elis.

Olympus The highest mountain in Greece and the ancient home of the gods.

Omecihuatl Female half of the first being, combined with Ometeotl. Together they are the lords of duality or lords of the two sexes. Also known as Ometecutli and Omeciuatl or Tonacatecutli and Tonacaciuatl. Their offspring were Xipe Totec, Huitzilopochtli, Quetzalcoatl and Tezcatlipoca.

Ometeotl Male half of the first being, combined with Omecihuatl.

Ometochtli Collective name for the pulque-gods or drink-gods. These gods were often associated with rabbits as they were thought to be senseless creatures.

Onygate Anyway.

Opening the Mouth Ceremony in which mummies or statues were prayed over and anointed with incense before their mouths were opened, allowing them to eat and drink in the afterlife.

Oracle The response of a god or priest to a request for advice – also a prophecy; the place where such advice was sought; the person or thing from whom such advice was sought.

Orestes Son of Agamemnon and Clytemnestra who escaped following Agamemnon's murder to King Strophius. He later returned to Argos to murder his mother and avenge the death of his father.

Orpheus Thracian singer and poet, son of Oeagrus and a Muse. Married Eurydice and when she died tried to retrieve her from the Underworld.

Orunmila (Yoruba) Eldest son of Olorun, he helped Obatala create land and humanity, which he then rescued after Olokun flooded the lands. He has the power to see the future.

Osiris God of fertility, the afterlife and death. Thought to be the first of the pharaohs. He was murdered by his brother, Set, after which he was conjured back to life by Isis, Anubis and others before becoming lord of the afterlife. Married to Isis, who was also his sister.

Otherworld The world of deities and spirits, also known as the Land of Promise, or the Land of Eternal Youth, a place of everlasting life where all earthly dreams come to be fulfilled.

Owuo (Krachi, West Africa) Giant who personifies death. He causes a person to die every time he blinks his eye.

Palamedes Hero of Nauplia, believed to have created part of the ancient Greek alphabet. He tricked Odysseus into joining the fleet setting out for Troy by placing the infant Telemachus in the path of his plough.

Palermo Stone Stone carved with hieroglyphs, which came from the Royal Annals of ancient Egypt and contains a list of the kings of Egypt from the first to the early fifth dynasties.

Palfrey Docile and light horse, often used by women.

Palladium Wooden image of Athene, created by her as a monument to her friend Pallas who she accidentally killed. While in Troy it protected the city from invaders.

Pallas Athene's best friend, whom she killed.

Pan God of Arcadia, half-goat and half-man. Son of Hermes. He is connected with fertility, masturbation and sexual drive. He is also associated with music, particularly his pipes, and with laughter.

Pan Gu Some ancient writers suggest that this God is the offspring of the opposing forces of nature, the yin and the yang. The yin (female) is associated with the cold and darkness of the earth, while the yang (male) is associated with the sun and the warmth of the heavens. 'Pan' means 'shell of an egg' and 'Gu' means 'to secure' or 'to achieve'. Pan Gu came into existence so that he might create order from chaos.

Pandareus Cretan King killed by the gods for stealing the shrine of Zeus.

Pandavas Alternative name for sons of Pandu, pupils of Drona.

Pandora The first woman, created by the gods, to punish man for Prometheus's theft of fire. Her dowry was a box full of powerful evil.

Papyrus Paper-like material made from the pith of the papyrus plant, first manufactured in Egypt. Used as a type of paper as well as for making mats, rope and sandals.

Paramahamsa The supreme swan.

Parashurama Human incarnation of Vishnu, 'Rama with an axe'.

Paris Handsome son of Priam and Hecuba of Troy, who was left for dead on Mount Ida but raised by shepherds. Was reclaimed by his family, then brought them shame and caused the Trojan War by eloping with Helen.

Parsa Holy man. Also known as a zahid.

Parvati Consort of Shiva and daughter of Himalaya.

Passion Wife of desire.

Pavanarekha Wife of Ugrasena, mother of Kans.

Pegasus The winged horse born from the severed neck of Medusa.

Peleus Father of Achilles. He married Antigone, caused her death, and then became King of Phthia. Saved from death himself by Jason and the Argonauts. Married Thetis, a sea nymph.

Penelope The long-suffering but equally clever wife of Odysseus who managed to keep at bay suitors who longed for Ithaca while Odysseus was at the Trojan War and on his ten-year voyage home.

Pentangle Pentagram or five-pointed star.

Pentecost Christian festival held on the seventh Sunday after Easter. It celebrates the holy spirit descending on the disciples after Jesus's ascension.

Percivale Knight of the Round Table and original seeker of the Holy Grail.

Persephone Daughter of Zeus and Demeter who was raped by Hades and forced to live in the Underworld as his queen for three months of every year.

Perseus Son of Danae, who was made pregnant by Zeus. He fought the Gorgons and brought home the head of Medusa. He eventually founded the city of Mycenae and married Andromeda.

Pesh Kef Spooned blade used in the Opening the Mouth ceremony.

Phaeacia The Kingdom of Alcinous on which Odysseus landed after a shipwreck which claimed the last of his men as he left Calypso's island.

Pharaoh King or ruler of Egypt.

Philoctetes Malian hero, son of Poeas, received Heracles's bow and arrows as a gift when he lit the great hero's pyre on Mount Oeta. He was involved in the last part of the Trojan War, killing Paris.

Philtre Magic potion, usually a love potion.

Pibroch Bagpipe music.

Pintura Native manuscript or painting.

Pipiltin Noble class of the Aztecs.

Pismire Ant.

Piu-piu Short mat made from flax leaves and neatly decorated.

Po Gloom, darkness, the lower world.

Polyphemus A Cyclops, but a son of Poseidon. He fell in love with Galatea, but she spurned him. He was blinded by Odysseus.

Polyxena Daughter of Priam and Hecuba of Troy. She was sacrificed on the grave of Achilles by Neoptolemus.

Popol Vuh Sacred 'book of counsel' of the Quiché or K'iche' Maya people.

Poseidon God of the sea, and of sweet waters. Also the god of earthquakes. His is brother to Zeus and Hades, who divided the earth between them.

Pradyumna Son of Krishna and Rukmini.

Prahasta (Long-Hand) One of Ravana's generals.

Prajapati Creator of the universe, father of the gods, demons and all creatures, later known as Brahma.

Priam King of Troy, married to Hecuba, who bore him Hector, Paris, Helenus, Cassandra, Polyxena, Deiphobus and Troilus. He was murdered by Neoptolemus.

Pritha Mother of Karna and of the Pandavas.

Prithivi Consort of Dyaus and goddess of the earth.

Proetus King of Argos, son of Abas.

Prometheus A Titan, son of Iapetus and Themus. He was champion of mortal men, which he created from clay. He stole fire from the gods and was universally hated by them.

Proteus The old man of the sea who watched Poseidon's seals.

Psyche A beautiful nymph who was the secret wife of Eros, against the wishes of his mother Aphrodite, who sent Psyche to perform many tasks in hope of causing her death. She eventually married Eros and was allowed to become partly immortal.

Ptah Creator god and deity of Memphis who was married to Sekhmet. Ptah built the boats to carry the souls of the dead to the afterlife.

Puddock Frog.

Pulque Alcoholic drink made from fermented agave.

Purusha The cosmic man, he was sacrificed and his dismembered body became all the parts of the cosmos, including the four classes of society.

Purvey To provide or supply.

Pushkara Nala's brother.

Pushpaka Rama's chariot.

Putana A rakshasi.

Pygmalion A sculptor who was so lonely he carved a statue of a beautiful woman, and eventually fell in love with it. Aphrodite brought the image to life.

Quauhtli Eagle.

Quetzalcoatl Deity and god of wind. He is represented as a feathered or plumed serpent and is usually a wise and benevolent god. Offspring of Ometeotl and Omecihuatl, he is also known as Kukulkan.

Ra God of the sun, ruling male deity of Egypt whose name means 'sole creator'.

Radha The principal mistress of Krishna.

Ragnarok The end of the world.

Rahula Son of Siddhartha and Yashodhara.

Raiden God of thunder. He traditionally has a fierce and demonic appearance.

Rakshasas Demons and devils.

Ram of Mendes Sacred symbol of fatherhood and fertility.

Rama or Ramachandra A prince and hero of the Ramayana, worshipped as an incarnation of Vishnu.

Ra-Molo (Lesotho) Father of fire, a chief who ruled by fear. When trying to kill his brother, Tau the lion, he was turned into a monster with the head of a sheep and the body of a snake.

Rangatira Chief, warrior, gentleman.

Regin A blacksmith who educated Sigurd.

Reinga The spirit land, the home of the dead.

Reservations Tracts of land allocated to the native American people by the United States Government with the purpose of bringing the many separate tribes under state control.

Rewati Daughter of Raja, marries Balarama.

Rhadha Wife of Adiratha, a gopi of Brindaban and lover of Krishna.

Rhea Mother of the Olympian gods. Cronus ate each of her children, but she concealed Zeus and gave Cronus a swaddled rock in his place.

Rill Small stream.

Rishis Sacrificial priests associated with the devas in Swarga.

Rituparna King of Ayodhya.

Rohini The wife of Vasudeva, mother of Balarama and Subhadra, and carer of the young Krishna. Another Rohini is a goddess and consort of Chandra.

Rōnin Samurai whose master had died or fallen out of favour.

Rubáiyát Collection of poems written by Omar Khayyám.

Rúdábeh Wife of Zál and mother of Rustem.

Rudra Lord of Beasts and disease, later evolved into Shiva.

Rukma Rukmini's eldest brother.

Rustem Son of Zál and Rúdábeh, he was a brave and mighty warrior who undertook seven labours to travel to Mázinderán to rescue Kai-káús. Once there, he defeated the White Demon and rescued Kai-káús. He rode the fabled stallion Rakhsh and is also known as Rustam.

Ryō Traditional gold currency.

Sabdh Mother of Ossian, or Oisin.

Sabitu Goddess of the sea.

Sagara King of Ayodhya.

Sahadeva Pandava twin skilled in swordsmanship.

Sahib diwan Lord high treasurer or chief royal executive.

Saiawúsh Son of Kai-káús, who was put through trial by fire when Sudaveh, Kai-káús's wife, told him that Saiawúsh had taken advantage of her. His innocence was proven when the fire did not harm him. He was eventually killed by Afrásiyáb.

Saithe Blessed.

Sajara (Mali) God of rainbows. He takes the form of a multi-coloured serpent.

Sake Japanese rice wine.

Sakuni Cousin of Duryodhana.

Salam Greeting or salutation.

Saláman Son of the Shah of Yunan, who fell in love with Absál, his nurse. She died after they had a brief love affair and he returned to his father.

Salmali tree Cotton tree.

Salmon A symbol of great wisdom, around which many Scottish legends revolve.

Sám Mighty warrior who fought and won many battles. Father of Zál and grandfather to Rustem.

Sambu Son of Krishna.

Sampati Elder brother of Jatayu.

Samurai Noblemen who were part of the military in medieval Japan.

Sanehat Member of the royal bodyguard.

Sangu (Mozambique) Goddess who protects pregnant women, depicted as a hippopotamus.

Santa Daughter of Dasharatha.

Sarapis Composite deity of Apis and Osiris, sometimes known as Serapis. Thought to be created to unify Greek and Egyptian citizens under the Greek pharaoh Ptolemy.

Sarasvati The tongue of Rama.

Sarcophagus Stone coffin.

Sargon of Akkad Raised by Akki, a husbandman, after being hidden at birth. Sargon became King of Assyria and a great hero. He founded the first library in Babylon. Similar to King Arthur or Perseus.

Sarsar Harsh, whistling wind.

Sasabonsam (Ashanti) Forest ogre.

Sati Daughter of Daksha and Prasuti, first wife of Shiva.

Satrughna One of Dasharatha's four sons.

Satyavan Truth speaker, husband of Savitri.

Satyavati A fisher-maid, wife of Bhishma's father, Shamtanu.

Satyrs Elemental spirits which took great pleasure in chasing nymphs. They had horns, a hairy body and cloven hooves.

Saumanasa A mighty elephant.

Scamander River running across the Trojan plain, and father of Teucer.

Scarab Dung beetle, often used as a symbol of the immortal human soul and regeneration.

Scylla and Charybdis Scylla was a monster who lived on a rock of the same name in the Straits of Messina, devouring sailors.

Charybdis was a whirlpool in the Straits which was supposedly inhabited by the hateful daughter of Poseidon.

Seal Often believed that seals were fallen angels. Many families are descended from seals, some of which had webbed hands or feet. Some seals were the children of sea-kings who had become enchanted (selkies).

Seelie-Court The court of the Fairies, who travelled around their realm. They were usually fair to humans, doling out punishment that was morally sound, but they were quick to avenge insults to fairies.

Segu (Swahili, East Africa) Guide who informs humans where honey can be found.

Sekhmet Solar deity who led the pharaohs in war. She is goddess of healing and was sent by Ra to destroy humanity when people turned against the sun god. She is portrayed with the head of a lion.

Selene Moon-goddess, daughter of Hyperion and Theia. She was seduced by Pan, but loved Endymion.

Selkie Seals with the capacity to become humans, leaving their seal-skins to take human form.

Seneschal Steward of a royal or noble household.

Sensei Teacher.

Seriyut A disciple of Buddha.

Sessrymnir Freyia's home.

Set God of chaos and evil, brother of Osiris, who killed him by tricking him into getting into a chest, which he then threw in the Nile, before cutting Osiris's body into fourteen separate pieces. Also known as Seth.

Sgeulachd Stories.

Shah Nameh *The Book of Kings* written by Ferdowski, one of the world's longest epic poems, which describes the mythology and history of the Persian Empire.

Shaikh Respected religious man.

Shaivas or Shaivites Worshippers of Shiva.

Shakti Power or wife of a god and Shiva's consort as his feminine aspect.

Shaman Also known as the 'Medicine Men' of Indian tribes, it was the shaman's role to cultivate communication with the spirit world. They were endowed with knowledge of all healing herbs, and learned to diagnose and cure disease. They could foretell the future, find lost property and had power over animals, plants and stones.

Shamash God of the sun and protector of Gilgamesh, the great Babylonian hero. Known as the son of Sin, the moon god, he is also portrayed as a judge of good and evil.

Shamtanu Father of Bhishma.

Shankara A great magician, friend of Chand Sadagar.

Shashti The Sixth, goddess who protects children and women in childbirth.

Shesh A serpent that takes human birth through Devaki.

Shi-en Fairy dwelling.

Shinto Indigenous religion of Japan, from the pre-sixth century to the present day.

Shireen Married to Khosru. Her beauty meant that she was desired by many, including Khosru's own son by his previous marriage. She killed herself rather than give in to her stepson.

Shitala The Cool One and goddess of smallpox.

Shiva One of the two great gods of post-Vedic Hinduism with Vishnu.

Shogun Military ruler or overlord.

Shoji Sliding door, usually a lattice screen of paper.

Shu God of the air and half of the first divine couple created by Atem. Brother and husband to Tefnut, father to Keb and Nut.

Shubistán Household.

Shudra One of the four fundamental colours (caste).

Siddhas Musical ministrants of the upper air.

Sif Thor's wife; known for her beautiful hair.

Sigi Son of Odin.

Sigmund Warrior able to pull the sword from Branstock in the Volsung's hall.

Signy Volsung's daughter.

Sigurd Son of Sigmund, and bearer of his sword. Slays Fafnir the dragon.

Sigyn Loki's faithful wife.

Símúrgh Griffin, an animal with the body of a lion and the head and wings of an eagle. Known to hold great wisdom. Also called a symurgh.

Sin God of the moon, worshipped primarily in Ur.

Sindri Dwarf who worked with Brokki to fashion gifts for the gods; commissioned by Loki.

Sirens Sea nymphs who are half-bird, half-woman, whose song lures hapless sailors to their death.

Sisyphus King of Ephrya and a trickster who outwitted Autolycus. He was one of the greatest sinners in Hades.

Sita Daughter of the earth, adopted by Janaka, wife of Rama.

Skadi Goddess of winter and the wife of Niord for a short time.

Skanda Six-headed son of Shiva and a warrior god.

Skrymir Giant who battled against Thor.

Sleipnir Odin's steed.

Sluagh The host of the dead, seen fighting in the sky and heard by mortals.

Smote Struck with a heavy blow.

Sohráb Son of Rustem and Tahmineh, Sohráb was slain in battle by his own father, who killed him by mistake.

Sol The sun-maiden.

Soma A god and a drug, the elixir of life.

Somerled Lord of the Isles, and legendary ancestor of the Clan MacDonald.

Squaw North American Indian married woman.

Squint-Eye One of Ramana's monsters.

Squire Shield- or armour-bearer of a knight.

Srutakirti Daughter of Kushadhwaja.

Stone Giants A malignant race of stone beings whom the Iroquois believed invaded Indian territory, threatening the Confederation of the Five Nations. These fierce and hostile creatures lived off human flesh and were intent on exterminating the human race.

Stoorworm A great water monster which frequented lochs. When it thrust its great body from the sea, it could engulf islands and whole ships. Its appearance prophesied devastation.

Styx River in Arcadia and one of the four rivers in the Underworld. Charon ferried dead souls across it into Hades, and Achilles was dipped into it to make him immortal.

Subrahmanian Son of Shiva, a mountain deity.

Sugriva The chief of the five great monkeys in the Ramayana.

Sukanya The wife of Chyavana.

Suman Son of Asamanja.

Sumantra A noble Brahman.

Sumati Wife of Sagara.

Sumedha A righteous Brahman who dwelt in the city of Amara.

Sumitra One of Dasharatha's three wives, mother of Lakshmana and Satrughna.

Suniti Mother of Dhruva.

Suparshwa One of Ravana's counsellors.

Supranakha A rakshasi, sister of Ravana.

Surabhi The wish-bestowing cow.

Surcoat Loose robe, traditionally worn over armour.

Surtr Fire-giant who eventually destroys the world at Ragnarok.

Surya God of the sun.

Susanoo God of the storm. He is depicted as a contradictory character with both good and bad characteristics. He was banished from Heaven after trying to kill his sister, Amaterasu.

Sushena A monkey chief.

Svasud Father of summer.

Swarga An Olympian paradise, where all wishes and desires are gratified.

Sweating A ritual customarily associated with spiritual purification and prayer practised by most tribes throughout North America prior to sacred ceremonies or vision quests. Steam was produced within a 'sweat lodge', a low, dome-shaped hut, by sprinkling water on heated stones.

Syrinx An Arcadian nymph who was the object of Pan's love.

Tablet of Destinies Cuneiform clay tablet on which the fates were written. Tiawath had given this to Kingu, but it was taken by Merodach when he defeated them. The storm god Zu later stole it for himself.

Taiaha A weapon made of wood.

Tailtiu One of the most famous royal residences of ancient Ireland.

Tall One of Ravana's counsellors.

Tammuz Solar deity of Eridu who, with Gishzida, guards the gates of Heaven. Protector of Anu.

Tamsil Example or guidance.

Tangi Funeral, dirge. Assembly to cry over the dead.

Taniwha Sea monster, water spirit.

Tantalus Son of Zeus who told the secrets of the gods to mortals and stole their nectar and ambrosia. He was condemned to eternal torture in Hades, where he was tempted by food and water but allowed to partake of neither.

Taoism Taoism (or Daoism) came into being at roughly the same time as Confucianism, although its tenets were radically different and were largely founded on the philosophies of Lao Tzu (Laozi). While Confucius argued for a system of state discipline, Taoism strongly favoured self-discipline and looked upon nature as the architect of essential laws. A newer form of Taoism evolved after the Burning of the Books, placing great emphasis on spirit worship and pacification of the gods.

Tapu Sacred, supernatural possession of power. Involves spiritual rules and restrictions.

Tara Also known as Temair, the Hill of Tara was the popular seat of the ancient High-Kings of Ireland from the earliest times to the sixth century. Located in Co. Meath, it was also the place where great noblemen and chieftains congregated during wartime, or for significant events.

Tara Sugriva's wife.

Tartarus Dark region, below Hades.

Tau (Lesotho) Brother to Ra-Molo, depicted as a lion.

Taua War party.

Tefnut Goddess of water and rain. Married to Shu, who was also her brother. She, like Sekhmet, is portrayed with the head of a lion. Also known as Tefenet.

Telegonus Son of Odysseus and Circe. He was allegedly responsible for his father's death.

Telemachus Son of Odysseus and Penelope who was aided by Athene in helping his mother to keep away the suitors in Odysseus's absence.

Temu The evening form of Ra, the Sun God.

Tengu Goblin or gnome, often depicted as bird-like. A powerful fighter with weapons.

Tenochtitlán Capital city of the Aztecs, founded around AD 1350 and the site of the 'Great Temple'. Now Mexico City.

Teo-Amoxtli Divine book.

Teocalli Great temple built in Tenochtitlán, which is now Mexico City.

Teotleco Festival of the Coming of the Gods; also the twelfth month of the Aztec calendar.

Tepee A conical-shaped dwelling constructed of buffalo hide stretched over lodge-poles. Mostly used by native American tribes living on the plains.

Tepeyollotl God of caves, desert places and earthquakes, whose name means 'heart of the mountain'. He is depicted as a jaguar, often leaping at the sun. Also known as Tepeolotlec.

Tepitoton Household gods.

Tereus King of Daulis who married Procne, daughter of Pandion King of Athens. He fell in love with Philomela, raped her and cut out her tongue.

Tezcatlipoca Supreme deity and Lord of the Smoking Mirror. He was also patron of royalty and warriors. Invented human sacrifice to the gods. Offspring of Ometeotl and Omecihuatl, he is known as the Jupiter of the Aztec gods.

Thalia Muse of pastoral poetry and comedy.

Theia Goddess of many names, and mother of the sun.

Theseus Son of King Aegeus of Athens. A cycle of legends has been woven around his travels and life.

Thetis Chief of the Nereids loved by both Zeus and Poseidon. They married her to a mortal, Peleus, and their child was Achilles. She tried to make him immortal by dipping him in the River Styx.

Thialfi Thor's servant, taken when his peasant father unwittingly harms Thor's goat.

Thiassi Giant and father of Skadi, he tricked Loki into bringing Idunn to him. Thrymheim is his kingdom.

Thomas the Rhymer Also called 'True Thomas', he was Thomas of Ercledoune, who lived in the thirteenth century. He met with the Queen of Elfland, and visited her country, was given clothes and a tongue that could tell no lie. He was also given the gift of prophecy, and many of his predictions were proven true.

Thor God of thunder and of war (with Tyr). Known for his huge size, and red hair and beard. Carries the hammer Miolnir. Slays Jormungander at Ragnarok.

Thoth God of the moon. Invented the arts and sciences and regulated the seasons. He is portrayed with the head of an ibis or a baboon.

Three-Heads One of Ravana's monsters.

Thrud Thor's daughter.

Thrudheim Thor's realm. Also called Thrudvang.

Thunder-Tooth Leader of the rakshasas at the siege of Lanka.

Tiawath Primeval dark ocean or abyss, Tiawath is also a monster and evil deity of the deep. She took the form of a dragon or sea serpent and battled the gods of light for supremacy over all living beings. She was eventually defeated by Merodach, who used her body to create Heaven and Earth.

Tiglath-Pileser I King of Assyria, who made it a leading power for centuries.

Tiki First man created, a figure carved of wood, or other representation of man.

Tirawa The name given to the Great Creator (*see* Great Spirit) by the Pawnee tribe who believed that four direct paths led from his house in the sky to the four semi-cardinal points: north-east, north-west, south-east and south-west.

Tiresias A Theban who was given the gift of prophecy by Zeus. He was blinded for seeing Athene bathing. He continued to use his prophetic talents after his death, advising Odysseus.

Tisamenus Son of Orestes, who inherited the Kingdom of Argos and Sparta.

Titania Queen of the fairies.

Tlaloc God of rain and fertility, so important to the people, because he ensured a good harvest, that the Aztec heaven or paradise was named Tlalocan in his honour.

Tlazolteotl Goddess of ordure, filth and vice. Also known as the earth-goddess or Tlaelquani, meaning 'filth-eater'. She acted as a confessor of sins or wrongdoings.

Tohu-mate Omen of death.

Tohunga A priest; a possessor of supernatural powers.

Toltec Civilization that preceded the Aztecs.

Tomahawk Hatchet with a stone or iron head used in war or hunting.

Tonalamatl Record of the Aztec calendar, which was recorded in books made from bark paper.

Tonalpohualli Aztec calendar composed of twenty thirteen-day weeks called trecenas.

Totec Solar deity known as Our Great Chief.

Totemism System of belief in which people share a relationship with a spirit animal or natural being with whom they interact. Examples include Ea, who is represented by a fish.

Toxilmolpilia The binding up of the years.

Tristan Nephew of King Mark of Cornwall, who travels to Ireland to bring Iseult back to marry his uncle. On the way, he and Iseult consume a love potion and fall madly in love before their story ends tragically.

Triton A sea-god, and son of Poseidon and Amphitrite. He led the Argonauts to the sea from Lake Tritonis.

Trojan War War waged by the Greeks against Troy, in order to reclaim Menelaus's wife Helen, who had eloped with the Trojan prince Paris. Many important heroes took part, and form the basis of many legends and myths.

Truage Tribute or pledge of peace or truth, usually made on payment of a tax.

Tsuki-yomi God of the moon, brother of Amaterasu and Susanoo.

Tuat The other world or land of the dead.

Tupuna Ancestor.

Tvashtar Craftsman of the gods.

Tyndareus King of Sparta, perhaps the son of Perseus's daughter Grogphone. Expelled from Sparta but restored by Heracles. Married Leda and fathered Helen and Clytemnestra, among others.

Tyr Son of Frigga and the god of war (with Thor). Eventually kills Garm at Ragnarok.

Tzompantli Pyramid of Skulls.

Uayeb The five unlucky days of the Mayan calendar, which were believed to be when demons from the underworld could reach Earth. People would often avoid leaving their houses on uayeb days.

Ubaaner Magician, whose name meant 'splitter of stones', who created a wax crocodile that came to life to swallow up the man who was trying to seduce his wife.

Uisneach A hill formation between Mullingar and Athlone said to mark the centre of Ireland.

uKqili (Zulu) Creator god.

Uller God of winter, whom Skadi eventually marries.

Unseelie Court An unholy court comprising a kind of fairies, antagonistic to humans. They took the form of a kind of Sluagh, and shot humans and animals with elf-shots.

Urd One of the Norns.

Urien King of Gore, husband of Morgan le Fey and father to Yvain.

Urmila Second daughter of Janaka.

Usha Wife of Aniruddha, daughter of Vanasur.

Ushas Goddess of the dawn.

Utgard-loki King of the giants. Tricked Thor.

Uther Pendragon King of England in sub-Roman Britain; father of King Arthur.

Utixo (Hottentot) Creator god.

Ut-Napishtim Ancestor of Gilgamesh, whom Gilgamesh sought out to discover how to prevent death. Similar to Noah in that he was sent a vision warning him of a great deluge. He built an ark in seven days, filling it with his family, possessions and all kinds of animals.

Uz Deity symbolized by a goat.

Vach Goddess of speech.

Vajrahanu One of Ravana's generals.

Vala Another name for Norns.

Valfreya Another name for Freyia.

Valhalla Odin's hall for the celebrated dead warriors chosen by the Valkyries.

Vali The cruel brother of Sugriva, dethroned by Rama.

Valkyries Odin's attendants, led by Freyia. Chose dead warriors to live at Valhalla. Also spelled as Valkyrs.

Vamadeva One of Dasharatha's priests.

Vanaheim Home of the Vanir.

Vanir Race of gods in conflict with the Aesir; they are gods of the sea and wind.

Varuna Ancient god of the sky and cosmos, later, god of the waters.

Vasishtha One of Dasharatha's priests.

Vassal Person under the protection of a feudal lord.

Vasudev Descendant of Yadu, husband of Rohini and Devaki, father of Krishna.

Vasudeva A name of Narayana or Vishnu.

Vavasor Vassal or tenant of a baron or lord who himself has vassals.

Vedic Mantras, hymns.

Vernandi One of the Norns.

Vichitravirya Bhishma's half-brother.

Vidar Slays Fenris.

Vidura Friend of the Pandavas.

Vigrid The plain where the final battle is held.

Vijaya Karna's bow.

Vikramaditya A king identified with Chandragupta II.

Vintail Moveable front of a helmet.

Virabhadra A demon that sprang from Shiva's lock of hair.

Viradha A fierce rakshasa, seizes Sita, slain by Rama.

Virupaksha The elephant who bears the whole world.

Vishnu The Preserver, Vedic sun-god and one of the two great gods of post-Vedic Hinduism.

Vision Quest A sacred ceremony undergone by native Americans to establish communication with the spirit set to direct them in life. The quest lasted up to four days and nights and was preceded by a period of solitary fasting and prayer.

Vivasvat The sun.

Vizier High-ranking official or adviser. Also known as vizir or vazir.

Volsung Family of great warriors about whom a great saga was spun.

Vrishadarbha King of Benares.

Vrishasena Son of Karna, slain by Arjuna.

Vyasa Chief of the royal chaplains.

Wairua Spirit, soul.

Wanjiru (Kikuyu) Maiden who was sacrificed by her village to appease the gods and make it rain after years of drought.

Weighing of the heart Procedure carried out after death to assess whether the deceased was free from sin. If the deceased's heart weighed less than the feather of Ma'at, they would join Osiris in the Fields of Peace.

Whare Hut made of fern stems tied together with flax and vines, and roofed in with raupo (reeds).

White Demon Protector of Mázinderán. He prevented Kai-káús and his army from invading.

Wolverine Large mammal of the musteline family with dark, very thick, water-resistant fur, inhabiting the forests of North America and Eurasia.

Wroth Angry.

Wyrd One of the Norns.

Xanthus & Balius Horses of Achilles, immortal offspring of Zephyrus the west wind. A gift to Achilles's father Peleus.

Xipe Totec High priest and son of Ometeotl and Omecihuatl. Also known as the god of the seasons.

Xiupohualli Solar year, composed of eighteen twenty-day months.

Yadu A prince of the Lunar dynasty.

Yakshas Same as rakshasas.

Yakunin Government official.

Yama God of Death, king of the dead and son of the sun.

Yamato Take Legendary warrior and prince. Also known as Yamato Takeru.

Yashiki Residence or estate, usually of a daimyō.

Yasoda Wife of Nand.

Yemaya (Yoruba) Wife of Obatala.

Yemoja (Yoruba) Goddess of water and protector of women.

Yggdrasill The World Ash, holding up the Nine Worlds. Does not fall at Ragnarok.

Ymir Giant created from fire and ice; his body created the world.

Yo The female principle who, joined with In, the male side, brought about creation and the first gods. In and Yo correspond to the Chinese Yang and Yin.

Yomi The underworld.

Yudhishthira The eldest of the Pandavas, a great soldier.

Yuki-Onna The Snow-Bride or Lady of the Snow, who represents death.

Yvain Son of Morgan le Fay and knight of the Round Table, who goes on chivalric quests with a lion he rescued from a dragon.

Zahid Holy man.

Zál Son of Sám, who was born with pure white hair. Sám abandoned Zál, who was raised by the Símúrgh, or griffins. Zal became a great warrior, second only to his son, Rustem. Also known as Ním-rúz and Dustán.

Zephyr Gentle breeze.

Zeus King of gods, god of sky, weather, thunder, lightning, home, hearth and hospitality. He plays an important role as the voice of justice, arbitrator between man and gods, and among them. Married to Hera, but lover of dozens of others.

Zohák Serpent-king and figure of evil. Father of Mihrab.

Zu God of the storm, who took the form of a huge bird. Similar to the Persian símúrgh.

Zukin Head covering.